Performing Identities on the Stages of Quebec

Francophone Cultures and Literatures

Michael G. Paulson and Tamara Alvarez-Detrell
General Editors

Vol. 15

PETER LANG
New York • Washington, D.C./Baltimore • Boston
Bern • Frankfurt am Main • Berlin • Vienna • Paris

Jill Mac Dougall

Performing Identities on the Stages of Quebec

PETER LANG
New York • Washington, D.C./Baltimore • Boston
Bern • Frankfurt am Main • Berlin • Vienna • Paris

Library of Congress Cataloging-in-Publication Data
Mac Dougall, Jill R.
Performing identities on the stages of Quebec / Jill Mac Dougall.
  p. cm. — (Francophone cultures and literatures; vol. 15)
  Includes bibliographical references (p.   ) and index.
  1. Theater—Québec (Province)—History—20th century. 2. Theater—
Political aspects—Québec (Province). 3. John the Baptist's Day—Québec
  (Province). 4. Street theater—Québec—Québec. 5. Plaques
  tectoniques/Tectonic plates. 6. Nationalism—Québec (Province).
  I. Title. II. Series.
  PN2305.Q4M23   792'.09714'09045—dc20   95-22893
                  ISBN 0-8204-3004-8
                  ISSN 1077-0186

Die Deutsche Bibliothek-CIP-Einheitsaufnahme

Mac Dougall, Jill:
Performing identities on the stages of Quebec / Jill Mac Dougall.
–New York; Washington, D.C./Baltimore; Boston; Bern;
Frankfurt am Main; Berlin; Vienna; Paris: Lang.
(Francophone cultures and literatures; Vol. 15)
  ISBN 0-8204-3004-8

Cover design by Nona Reuter.
Cover photo: Jacques Lavallée.

The paper in this book meets the guidelines for permanence and durability
of the Committee on Production Guidelines for Book Longevity
of the Council of Library Resources.

© 1997 Peter Lang Publishing, Inc., New York

All rights reserved.
Reprint or reproduction, even partially, in all forms such as microfilm,
xerography, microfiche, microcard, and offset strictly prohibited.

Printed in the United States of America.

A mes enfants

David, Alicia, Jonathan

Contents

Preface	ix
Introduction: Ceci est à l'extérieur... but this is INSIDE	1
I. Performing the Dream State: La Saint Jean/National Holiday	9
1. Pagans, Priests, Politicians, and Poets	13
2. At the Gates of the Country	43
II. Of Commodities and Kin: *Salut Vielle Branche!* A Street Comedy in Old Quebec	71
3. Overtures	75
4. Archetypes and Ideologies for Sale	97
III. Tectonic Plates: *Plaques tectoniques* A Bicontinental Work in Progress	135
5. Journeys	139
6. Geopoetics/Geopolitics	165
Epilogue: Neverendum	201
Bibliography	215
Index	227

Preface

My interest in the symbiosis of Québécois theatre and identity politics stems from three rather ambiguous relationships: my link to theatre as a practitioner and a scholar; my connection to Quebec, which I consider as home although I was neither born there nor presently live there; and my perception of national identity itself. Considering myself as crossed by hybrid and fluctuating identities which have little to do with my passport, I find the notion of a singular collective identity both seductive and repulsive, and in any case, highly elusive.

This is a reflection on the nature of collective identity seen from the flip-flop angle of a North American linguistic minority which has to date obstinately refused to die, to assimilate, or to become an independent nation-state. The theatrical metaphor, "stages of Quebec," refers to three public arenas where collective identity is played out: the national stage where the street becomes the showcase of the state; the local stage where ethnicity based in language, popular history, and family roots is forged and frequently inverted; the global stage where local and national identities emerge, cross, collide, and atomize in a multiplicity of gazes. Above all, this work is a reflection on performance as a privileged and fleeting moment of collective identity rituals.

Based in the ephemeral of performance, this work spans fifteen years. I began this research well before conceiving of it as "a work" when I moved to Montreal in 1981, returning to North America after over twenty years absence during which I had lived in primarily francophone milieus in Europe and Africa working as an actor, director, theatre researcher and translator in France, Zaire, and the Ivory Coast. I lived in Montreal for four years before moving to New York, then Philadelphia.

I arrived in Quebec during the quiet aftermath of the first Referendum in which the OUI to independence was defeated by a near 20% margin of the vote. I was intermittently preparing this manuscript for publication through 1996, the year following a second independence Referendum, which by a hair-line vote maintained Quebec's provincial status within the Canadian Federation. Unwitting bookends, these events frame this study on identity politics and performance rituals in fin-de-siècle Quebec.

Subjectively, I remain attached to a community who welcomed me and with whom I maintain strong professional and personal ties. Ideologically, I adhere to minority national claims for autonomy and recognition, but recoil from chauvinistic nationalism, both of which are prevalent in Quebec's sovereignty movement. Methodologically, I have alternately approached this material from the intimate angle of an active, participating subject—a translator/ethnographer—and the more detached view point of a social history or literary analyst. My own curiosity as to what might constitute collective identity and its symbolic power remains the underlying motor of this study.

Far from a seamless narrative, this work continually moves back and forth between my position as observer and the data, between micropictures of personal communications and performances and macropictures of history and the socio-political context. My intent is not to present a univocal Québécois persona, but to travel through historical strata of identity tropes and the multiple voices resonating on contemporary Québécois stages.

I would like to acknowledge all the witting and unwitting fellow travelers of this journey, beginning with the participants of the live performances which constitute the three core studies of this book. I would especially like to thank those who have provided personal interviews, documents, and valuable insights: Jacques Drolet, Maureen Martineau, Nicole-Eva Morin, and Pauline Voisard from the Théâtre Parminou; Marie Brassard, Richard Fréchette, Marie Gignac, and Robert Lepage from the Théâtre Repère. For visuals of the three events, I thank the photographers Jacques Lavallée, Pierre Dessureault, Claudel Huot and Johnnie Eisen. Thanks to Ron Hill (Penn State Delaware County) for his technical assistance. My appreciation also goes to Jonathan Franco and Fabienne Papin who assisted in the last phase of the research.

For their lively interest, their perception of Québécois identity politics, and their generosity over the years, I owe thanks to many other friends from Quebec including Gilles Bibeau and Ellen Corin, Abla Farhoud, Raymond Bégin and Nicole Bonenfant. I also wish to thank the Theatre Department at the Université du Québec à Montréal and the Performance Studies Department at New York University for the context they initially provided toward formulating this project.

I am indebted to a number of critical readers for their incisive comments and interest in the outcome of this work: Barbara Kirshenblatt-Gimblett, Richard Schechner, and Ngugi wa Thiong'o (Performance Studies, New York University); Michael Taussig (Anthropology, Columbia University); Sherry Simon (French Studies, Concordia University in Montreal).

Finally, I can not measure my thanks to my husband, Stanley Yoder for his patient support, critical insights, and technical assistance in producing this book.

INTRODUCTION

Ceci est à l'extérieur...
But this is INSIDE!

Photo: A.M. Guérineau, courtesy *Nuit blanche*.

> The boundary is Janus-faced and the problem of outside/inside must always itself be a process of hybridity, incorporating new 'people' in relation to the body politic, generating sites of meaning and inevitably, in the political process, producing unmanned sites of political antagonism and unpredictable forces for political representation.
>
> Homi K. Bhaba (1990:4)

Inside/Extérieur

Since numerous paradoxical lines travel through Québécois identity poetics and politics—and, inevitably, through my research on the subject—I thought it appropriate to open with a display of what the literary critic Jean Larose calls "l'ironie, une exquise spécialité québécoise" [irony, an exquisite Québécois specialty] (1989:176). The photo montage on the previous page appeared in a special issue of *Nuit blanche, l'actualité du livre* entitled "Maudite langue!" [cursed language]. The two photographs evoke two juxtaposed performances in February 1989. One is the annual tourist attraction, the Quebec City Winter Carnival signalled by the grinning snowman *le Bonhomme de neige* posted over the entry to the fortified city of *Vieux Québec*. The other—of disrupting political tones—is indicated by the two banners, one above the gate to the historic city reading: "Ceci est à l'extérieur," and the second inside its walls declaring: "But this is INSIDE!"

Curious endogenous reversal, the sign on the outside is in French, but peering through the rampart walls toward the historical heart of Quebec touted as the "birthplace of French America," the viewer can spy the sign in English declaring this is actually the INSIDE. Unless one *is* on the "inside," that is familiar with the political context and the language issue in Quebec, the signs are enigmatic. They relate to the specific circumstances of a crisis provoked by what many Québécois experienced as yet another threat to the survival of the *fait français* in North America.

In 1988 the Canadian Supreme Court passed judgement on the constitutionality of Bill 101, which the Parti Québécois provincial government had instigated in 1977. The Court upheld the premise of French as the sole *official* language of the province and the clauses pertaining to citizens' rights to be educated in their own language, and agreed to limit immigrant access to English schooling within the province, but declared that the *loi d'affichage* was unconstitutional. This law had prohibited signs posted on public establishments in Quebec to be in any language other than French. Those who had designed the law were obviously less concerned with any Italian, Greek, Hebrew, or Arabic signs which might dot the streets, than with eliminating English signs and affirming the *visage français* [French face] of Quebec. The Canadian Supreme Court decision and the subsequent waffling of the Parti Libéral government under the direction of Robert Bourassa, desperately seeking a compromise, produced the 1989 *Loi 178*. This allowed signs inside commercial establishments to be in any language, while maintaining that signs posted on the outside had to be in French.[1]

Bill 178 satisfied neither the francophone nor the anglophone nor the allophone[2] populations of Quebec. The anglo-minority considered the legislation cheating with the dominant law of the land. The French-speaking majority in Quebec considered the bill a foolish concession to a power which had no business tampering with what were by the 1980s assumed as franco-linguistic rights, and which was backed by a constitution Quebec had never ratified. The debate reignited the war of signs, ludicrous to many speaking from "l'extérieur."[3] Demonstrators—from both the older generation, who had fought for national linguistic rights, and the younger generation, who had until then never considered language as other than a given—took to the streets brandishing signs which proclaimed "Québec, je t'aime en français."

The poetic and the ironic permeate the political in a country whose national differentiating marker is primarily linguistic specificity. The French-Québécois idiom is historically a point of contention; fear of disappearing into the great anglo-majority has long driven nationalist aspirations. Despite the will to include all linguistic communities and the claims to territorial autonomy which drive contemporary nationalist rhetoric, the mercurial verb is the glue of the nation and leitmotif of its official polity. The "Extérieur/INSIDE!" inversion relates to an immediate context, the problem of the *maudite langue* and the compromise on language laws, and to the pervasive fear of territorial or—worse yet—mental occupation by the dominant anglo-other.

But the signs are also a playful commentary on the quirky nature of contemporary Québécois identity politics and on national identity itself in the postmodern moment. Linguistic minority in the Americas, but a majority within its own borders and certainly the most influential "minority" community in the Canadian Federation, the Québécois have made a capital of their history and language. Although short-changed by history—the infamous *Conquête* by the English in the 18th-century and the withdrawal of the French regency—and never emerging as a nation-state along the lines of the Spanish, Portuguese, and English colonies, French Canada has tenaciously held to the idea of *la nation* through historical claims as *peuple fondateur*. Repeatedly voicing national specificity, but repeatedly refusing official sovereignty, a *petit peuple* of six million which increasingly depends on immigration to reinforce its population and its image as a modern, inclusive state, Quebec is a paradox of the postcolonial era. A state whose sovereignty hinges on narrow referendum margins, a territory whose territoriality is challenged by indigenous peoples, an economy which can not escape dependency on multinational capital, Quebec is a nation which is and is not.

Contemporary Québécois identity thrives on the ambivalent, slipping back and forth across imaginary borders between subjects, languages, and spaces. It is in this ironic gap, where the anxiety over collective identity meets its critical counterpart and where the longing for wholeness clashes with the postmodern explosion of identity tropes that I wish to situate this interpretation of performing identities on the stages of contemporary Quebec. Since my stance is that of a translator—mediating between the oral and written media, between socio-political contexts, and between languages—I am, ipso facto, balancing on the see-saw between 'l'intérieur/inside' and 'outside/l'extérieur.'

Genesis of this research

When I undertook this research in 1988, my intention was to describe the shifts in national identity representations which took place in Québécois theatre during the "post-Référendum" years, the decade following the 1980 defeat of the OUI to independence. I wanted to show how Québécois theatre had deconstructed essentialist identity from the inside while challenging postmodern clichés of constructed identity, of the end of history and meaning which belied very evident emotive connections to a collective self alive in the world outside of academia.

Two elements sparked my initial project: viewing the 1988 premiere of *Plaques tectoniques/Tectonic Plates*, a bicontinental, four-year work in progress by the Théâtre Repère of Quebec City and reading Richard Handler's[4] 1988 publication on Québécois cultural politics in the 1970s. The theatrical venture, seeking to reach beyond the confines of a culturally closed time/space, and the anthropological interpretation of an already waning cultural polity, which—whatever the author's intention—metonymically constituted a picture of Quebec to the outsider, were the initial intellectual irritants driving this research.

Encompassing productions I had witnessed in the 1980s, my original plan described the changes in the dominant theatrical trends during the decade. Between 1981 and 1989 Québécois theatre projected dramatic shifts in representing the national self. From the 1981 *Before the War, at l'Anse à Gilles*[5]—an example of the theatre of ethnographic realism which flourished in the latter 1970s—through the confined bio-narratives and the postmodern desert settings which marked productions of the latter 1980s, including the 1989 premiere version of *Tectonic Plates*, my outline traced a rather tidy chronological narrative of the decomposition of a cohesive national subject as represented in Québécois theatre.

My analysis might have remained circumscribed by the literal stage of theatrical representation if events in the political arena at the turn of the decade had not reoriented this research toward the national problem. It appeared absurd to speak of the demise of nationalism in the midst of the Québécois nationalist renaissance which occurred in the early 1990s. My decision to attack directly at the heart of the nationalist problem through the 1990 *Saint Jean/fête nationale* shifted the meaning of stage to the public space and the virtual stages of Quebec history, while casting a new light on performing the problem of minority identity on the ever-emerging national stage.

Three Stages

My intention is to demonstrate the simultaneously conflicting discourses and subject positioning of a cultural space named *Québec* which I will describe through three performance clusters on three stages. The rationale behind the selection of the three case studies hinges on the spatial metaphor of *contemporary stages:* the national, the local, and the international. The first is the 1990 national celebration in Montreal; the second is a parodic portrayal of Québécois family roots performed in the tourist mecca of Old Quebec City; the third is an intercultural venture performed in Quebec and Canada, in Scotland and England. The ambitions, the backers, the target audiences, and the signifying spaces radically differentiate the performances. Yet all three—their underlying themes and their enunciating conditions—touch on Québécois linguistic politics, on the representation of history, and the problem of a culturally specific subject.

The first part of this study, **Performing the Dream State**, centers on the historical and symbolic universe of *la Saint Jean* and how the 1990 Montreal performance of *la nation* plays ironically with history and the dream of an ideal state, specifically Québécois, but capable of incorporating diverse ethnic subjects. Unfolding in a cosmopolitan Montreal, yet reliant on shopworn symbols of an insular French-Canadian/Catholic nationalism to produce its irony, the 1990 Saint Jean can only be comprehended with knowledge of archaic forms of *nationalisme*. Through ideologically diversified accounts of Saint-Jean performances over three centuries, the first chapter treats the history of the holiday in its shifts from Church to State ritual. Chapter 2 interprets the 1990 event in relation to the apparent defeat of the national project following the 1980 Referendum through its rebirth following the 1990 collapse of the Meech Lake agreement, and explores the dream state: the utopia of performance and the utopia of an independent, culturally diversified yet harmonious *Québec*.

The Parminou's *Salut vieille branche!*, a 1989 summer tourist production in Old Quebec City, is the second case study. This parody of Québécois genealogy plays with the idea of a monolithic Québécois subject defined through history and blood ties. Chapter 3 introduces the twenty-year-old activist company and the context of the performance. Chapter 4 is a play-by-play reconstruction and analysis of the performance. **Commodities and Kin** treats the internal contradictions of an inside joke, which simultaneously problematizes any sort of national essence by exposing it as a reified commodity, yet promotes "national" kinship through self-deprecation.

The third case study, Théâtre Repère's four-year work in progress, *Plaques tectoniques/Tectonic Plates*, is the most complex. Its themes and realization process split open the question of Québécois identity, while remaining rooted in the problem of minority national identity and the individual artist. Chapter 5 touches on the genesis of the company and of the internationally-recognized director Robert Lepage, while providing an overview of the production's thematic and material evolution. Chapter 6 focuses on the intriguing contradictions inherent in the geopoetic/geopolitical metaphor of the title. **Tectonic Plates** describes an excursion into intercultural performance which, ironically, leads back to the individual subject and Québécois cultural politics. Representative of the avenues Québécois spectacle has forged on the international theatre scene and of the artist's necessity to speak from a particular site, *Plaques/Plates* simultaneously defies cultural boundaries and draws back into the cocoon of the individual self. The strictly theoretical Tower of Babel, the dismissal of history and of trans-cultural class divisions, and the return to the narcissistic and pathologically divided self describe a trajectory leading back to the collective identity problematic.

The **Neverendum** epilogue rexamines Québécois identity poetics and politics and the role Québécois artists play in the light of the October 1995

Referendum. By treating such divergent perspectives I hope to elucidate the relationship between nationalism and national identity, but to avoid collapsing them. Each performance speaks of ideological networks crisscrossed by the national project, yet none legitimizes a uniform national subject. Ultimately, it is the problematic nature of national identity itself—in the postcolonial world of the floundering but ever powerful nation-state—which continually asserts itself in Quebec's search for identity and, with all its ironies, is incorporated into the collective subject.

Note on Translations

Unless otherwise indicated in the text, I am the translator of all written and oral materials drawn from the French which appear thorughout this book.

Notes

1. For a more detailed discussion of the struggle for French language rights in Canada, see Coulombe (1995).

2. Allophone, which means literally "other sounds," is the term used in Canada for all non-anglophone or non-francophone speech.

3. In *Oh Canada! Oh Quebec!* Mordecai Richler gleefully describes some of the more burlesque episodes in the war of signs and speaks of a language police sniffing out any refusal to comply to Bill 101. Although many critics in Quebec dismissed the author as "quelqu'un de l'extérieur," the book created quite a stir in Québécois literary and political circles. Richler embodies the ambivalence of the insider/outsider in that he was born and bred in Montreal, but has always maintained a distance from the francophone, mainstream culture of Quebec. Yet he passes for an expert in Québécois cultural politics in the anglophone world and has become a dissident hero, resisting cultural uniformity, in the current multicultural world of Québécois immigrant writers.

4. Handler's *Nationalism and the Politics of Culture in Quebec* (1988) is a probing analysis of collective identity constructs as seen through the *official* cultural policy during the Parti Québécois era. A good deal of the negative reaction from Québécois intellectuals stemmed from the work's sole concern with institutional policy which hardly represented all of Quebec. "Québec isn't just some tomato cooperative or the provincial government," said Gilles Bibeau, himself a prominent anthropologist and an opponent of insular nationalism. "Why didn't he look at theatre or literature?" (personal interview 1989). Bibeau's indignation points out the limits of an ethnography seeking to capture a people and the old anthropological bind of power relationships: the "big brother"—in this case American—anthropologist passing as author/authority over a small community.

5. This play by the locally celebrated playwright Marie Laberge portrays life in a small fishing village on the eve of World War II. However unconvential the heroine of the drama, performed in a Montreal institutional venue with expensive trappings and rose-colored gels, the production reflected nostalgia for a bygone era of innocence and identification with an idealized folk.

I

PERFORMING THE DREAM STATE

La Saint Jean/National Holiday

Photo: Jacques Lavallée, Studio Image en Tête.

C'est parfois vérité
Et c'est parfois mensonge
Mais la plupart du temps
C'est le bonheur qui dit
Comme il faudrait de temps
Pour saisir le bonheur
A travers la misère
Emmaillée au plaisir
Tant d'en rêver tout haut
Que d'en parler à l'aise

        Gilles Vigneault
        Les gens de mon pays

        Sometimes it's true
        And sometimes it's false
        [lies or illusions]
        But most of the time
        Good times decide
        How much we need time
        To capture good fortune
        Through all of the misery
        Enmeshed in the pleasure
        Dreaming out loud
        Or speaking at leisure

> Notre pays, c'est nos illusions. Nous avons les deux pieds dedans. Notre pays c'est notre rêve.
>
> Félix Leclerc
> (Bertin 1987:307)

The *Saint Jean* or Quebec national holiday is a nexus of historical, political, and symbolic threads which is best approached through the words of the two most celebrated national *chansonniers* [singers/poets] who played important roles in forging 20th-century Québécois identity and in promoting the dream of sovereignty. Félix Leclerc and Gilles Vigneault are producers and products of contemporary Québécois myths. Their material is the stuff dreams are made of and their instrument is the word. In a country whose national status remains problematic and which is so dependent on language to justify its existence, it is not surprising that symbolics and the imaginary are capital resources. As Leclerc says "our two feet are planted in illusions... our country is our dreams."

Heir to Leclerc's popularity, Gilles Vigneault's star rose during the mid-1960s and swelled with the growing Québécois independence movement. His *Gens du pays*, launched during the 1975 *fête sauvage* [alternative or wild celebration] which heralded the 1976 victory of the separatist Parti Québécois, rapidly became the unofficial "national anthem" of the yet to be official nation-state. Vigneault's songs speak of the "common folk" of days gone by, assimilated by the magic of poetry into the contemporary *gens d'aujourd'hui à fabriquer demain* [those who will build/be built tomorrow].

"Parfois vérité, parfois mensonge," Vigneault's quote applies to the construction of any historical narrative as well as to this oxymoronic nation—which is and is not a state—and to an imagined national subject, a *gens du pays* around which poets and historians spin their tales. Studying the complex evolution of the Saint Jean and Québécois nationalism, I have found myself caught in a web of *mensonges*, of illusions and partial truths. When I first decided to attack the history of the celebration, I naively thought the material would provide a convenient frame to my entire study of performing Québécois identities. Peering into accounts of *Saint Jean* over three centuries led me instead into a messy history of competing hegemonies and the xenophobic nationalist discourse which flourished in the first part of this century. I could not treat the 1990 event as an isolated performance since the *fête nationale* is located in multiple and often contradictory histories of Nouvelle-France, of French Canada, and of a thirty-year-old Quebec. Working through fragments of performances gleaned over three centuries, I argue that the event has always been a site of contested control between powers seeking to capture the grass-roots imagination.

The Dream State—self-consciously attributed to the 1990 celebration of the nation evident in its titling by the Comité de fête as *Un pays à faire rêver*—is an appropriate mode for performing the ever-emergent and liminal state of *Québec*. Minority at large, majority *chez nous,* yet resisting sovereign-nation status, Quebec is a latter-20th century puzzle. The country of Vigneault's *gens du pays* is as much an imaginary space as it is a politically or geographically bound entity. This dream territory where *vérité* and *mensonge* meet is the country long coveted by poets, as well as by priests and politicians seeking to incorporate the pagans, those who are yet to be captured by what Michael Taussig (1996) calls "the magic of the state."

Chapter One
Pagans, Priests, Politicians, and Poets

June 1990: Under the Sign of a Controlled Dream

The preparations for the 1990 *Saint Jean* or Quebec national holiday took place in a politically charged atmosphere. Falling in an era of renewed nationalist sentiment and on the day after the collapse of the Meech Lake agreements—which would have sanctioned Quebec's status as a distinct society within the Canadian confederation—the festivities promised an excitement not seen since the Saint Jean celebrations of the 1970s which had heralded the Parti Québécois rise to power. Current events on the national Canadian stage and publicity for the staged national Québécois holiday vied for space in the Montreal press. Articles announcing the festivities or citing the history of the Saint Jean meshed with political news and polemics surrounding the rebirth of *indépendantiste* sentiment.

Bearing the precautionary title of "Un défilé à l'enseigne d'un rêve contrôlé" [A parade under the sign of a controlled dream] an article previewing the event scheduled the next day appeared in the widely distributed Montreal newspaper *La Presse* on June 23. The journalist Jean-Pierre Bonhomme quotes an interview with Richard Blackburn[1], the *maître d'oeuvre* of the 1990 parade who sums up the spectacle created by eight *concepteurs visuels* and some two-thousand participants as follows.

> Ce sera un long bas-relief ambulant et chacune de ses parties sera "porteuse d'un sens": celui, précisement, de cette convergence d'énergie que le Québec a accumulée depuis une trentaine d'années. Pour tout dire, il équivaudra, comme au théâtre, à une petite thérapie de groupe, à un rêve éveillé, à un contact avec l'intime qui animera la conscience. (*La Presse* 23 June 1990)

> It will be a long, mobile bas-relief and each of its parts will be a "vehicle of meaning": precisely, that of the converging energies which Quebec has accumulated in the past thirty years. In other words, it will be, as in the theatre, the equivalent of a short group therapy, a wakened dream, an intimate contact which will arouse consciousness.

The dream, theoretically under the control of its artistic producers, must speak directly to the Québécois imaginary. It is a *rêve éveillé*, not a "daydream" but a "wakened dream," historically contextualized in "the energies which Quebec has accumulated in the past thirty years." The dream is alive in a political context marked by a renaissance of the Québécois independence project and an historical context of recent memory. The thirty years refer to the period since the *Révolution tranquille* [Quiet Revolution], the symbolic originary point of the modern nation of Quebec.

On a political level the need to control the dream may refer to the events of the latter sixties, when Québécois nationalism erupted on the public stage during the Saint Jean fête, provoking the twenty-year official interdiction of the parade. Or it may refer to the immediate context, the virtual historical moment which would transform the dream of independence into a political reality. Blackburn speaks of *un contact avec l'intime qui animera la conscience*. The meanings behind the French word *conscience* [conscience, awareness, or consciousness] denotes two domains: the ideological world and the emerging world of the psyche. Here the psyche is figured as collective and engaged in the somewhat oxymoronic activity of a wakened dream.

Both the symbolic and the political are brought into play in the announcing of the parade. The private space of the psyche or the inner stage, is here projected onto the public stage and the collectivity participating in the performance. But the dream is controlled and directed like a group therapy or a *mise en scène*. The collective nature of the dream and its undetermined control raises questions as to who is the subject of the dream. Who is dreaming and who is being dreamt? And why is the stated dream, already contained and directed, placed under the protective umbrella of the sign?

Ultimately, it is not only the indeterminate space of the imaginary that the director of the parade wistfully seeks to control, but the unpredictable nature of the coming public performance. The article and detailed listings of how the parade would unfold (including "surprise" events) recalls the painstaking plans of former festivity organizers who attempted to map out the Saint Jean eighty-six years before.

In 1904 the organizers of the Société Saint-Jean-Baptiste (SSJB), the French-Canadian nationalist society founded in 1834, proposed the following formula which I have translated from SSJB archives as recorded by its official historian, Robert Rumilly (1975:193).

1. Saint Jean bonfire on the eve of the fête
2. Three processions parading in their districts, meeting at Notre Dame Cathedral

3. A general procession every five years
4. A mass at Notre Dame, appropriate sermon
5. Banquet at noon, with one or two speeches
6. *Fête champêtre* [picnic] at Parc de la Fontaine in the afternoon, followed by patriotic speeches
7. Concert and fireworks in the evening

Whether in 1990 or in 1904, even the best-laid plans remain hypothetical and subject to disruption once the performance hits the streets. The Saint Jean is a fête, and it is the indeterminate nature of the fête which compromises efforts to "control the dream." The history of the *fête de Saint Jean* is a history of attempts to control the fête which runs parallel to the history of political control within Quebec, alias French Canada, alias Bas-Canada or Lower Canada, alias Nouvelle-France, alias *Canada*.

What's In a Name?

During the thirty years that are cited in the article announcing the parade (*cette convergence d'énergie que le Québec a accumulé depuis trente ans*) the name *Québec* had come to signify in national rhetoric a new people claiming a new state justified by origins, social history, linguistic and cultural specificity, as well as automnous material progress. Most pertinent in establishing Quebec as distinct from "French Canada" was the emphasis on the territorial grounding of *le peuple*.

Before the 1960s, "Québec" designated the city of Quebec or the province of Quebec. The two "founding peoples" referred to each other as "the French" and "*les Anglais.*" The displacement of French Canada —stigmatized as the nomenclature of a subordinated people—in favor of *Québec* signified a symbolic emancipation. But like the other lexemes which have designated the territory extending north and south of the lower Saint Lawrence, the word Quebec is a locus of contested identities and power relationships.

Changes in the name of the region and in its pronunciation indicate historical articulations and fluctuations in hegemonic positions. The name *Canada* derives from the Iroquois *Kanata* designating "village" or—ironic, considering the ensuing French and English invasions—"where I live" (Assiniwi 1973:26). This nomenclature would come to designate the territory the official discoverer of Nouvelle-France, Jacques Cartier, claimed in the name of François I by planting a cross in the soil of Gaspé in 1534. In a second voyage Cartier explored the Hochelaga River [Saint Lawrence] and the sites which would become Quebec City [Stadacone] and Montreal [Hochelaga].

A thorn in the side of Québécois nationalists seeking to justify national legitimacy through language and colonial history, Canada is a name usurped from the native peoples upon whom the French colonists were initially dependent for their very survival. As for the town Samuel Champlain founded as a fort and fur trading post seventy-four years after Cartier's initial voyage, *Québec* is borrowed from the Micmac *gepeg* meaning "strait" or "difficult passage" (Assiniwi 1973:113; Weinmann 1987:14).

Through the 1763 Treaty of Paris, following the defeat of the French forces, Nouvelle-France—including the territory known as Canada—passed from the French to the British crown. The 1791 Constitutional Act divided the land bordering the Saint Lawrence river into two British provinces with distinct governing assemblies: Upper Canada (Ontario) and Lower Canada (Quebec). Following a revolt in Lower Canada, the 1840 Union Act declared the two Canadas one—theoretically anglophone—dominion. The name Canada would be henceforth articulated in a predominantly English accent. And Quebec, with the adoption of the British North American Act in 1867 and the incorporation of New Brunswick and Nova Scotia would become a province among four in the Canadian Confederation.

Scattered through forced or voluntary emigration, the French Canadians were faced with their irrevocable minority position and a dubious claim to equal power in the Confederation. What would drive the national project through the 19th and 20th centuries was the symbolic motor of history—resumed in the current Québécois motto "Je me souviens"—and semiotics: the French language, the shifting sign, the name.

Twentieth-century Québécois nationalists have often bristled at the fact that, although *Canada* was "notre découverte,"[2] the English had co-opted the country's name along with other symbols of French-Canadian origin, such as the maple leaf,[3] and even *O, Canada*, the current Canadian national anthem, composed by a 19th-century *Patriote*. For the *Canadiens-français* the English appropriation of Canada and their subsequent hyphenated status symbolized annexation, colonization, and minoritization. By the mid-20th century, "French Canadian" rang with a number of derogatory connotations: a folklorized nation, a cultural remnant of a materially obsolete world; a nation of penitents under the control of the local Catholic church which extolled the virtues of sacrifice in this world in order to reach a higher status in the world beyond; an exploited people whose own government under

Duplessis lured Wall Street investors with the promise of abundant resources and "cheap and docile labor" (Young & Dickinson 1988:256).

What's in a name? In any minority embedded in a nation-state, the power to impose its name represents major political stakes. This is doubly true in Quebec where national specificity is defined primarily through the French language and where the affirmation of the name Quebec also signifies a geographically-bound entity with an established political status. French Canada evokes a sub-people; Quebec evokes a bounded geo-political entity with the right to self-determination.

Québec as a national designation is a recently accepted convention. The *fête nationale québécoise* is even more recent. Despite its association with the nationalist cause since the mid-1800s, June 24 did not become the official national holiday until 1977, a year after the victory of the Parti Québécois. Proclaiming the Saint Jean as the *fête de tous les Québécois*, René Lévesque, leader of the provincial government and the separatist party, confirmed the secularization of the holiday.

The long process of separating civil from clerical power had accelerated during the Quiet Revolution in the 1960s. The Church's loss of political control over the province was already a social fact, evident in the desertion of the churches and the steadily declining birth rate. The traditional French-Canadian and Catholic family of fifteen-some children had already begun to disappear with the industrialization of the province in the early 1900s. Severance from the Church was radically declared in the street eight years before Lévesque's pronouncement, when during the 1969 Saint Jean parade, dissidents screaming "Down with Saint Jean-Baptisme," decapitated the effigy of the patron saint, symbol of French-Canadian submission.[4]

Despite the secularization of the holiday and the shattering of the myth, popular parlance retains the name of the saint. Contemporary Québécois refer more frequently to the *fête Saint Jean* than the *fête nationale*. Cutting off history that is embedded in language is more difficult than cutting off a papier-maché head or declaring official holidays. Yet this half-affectionate, half-ironic naming of the holiday has little to do with religious affiliation. The summer fête is celebrated for the sake of the fête, recalling that the mutation from the religious to the political was not the first slippage of the June 24 holiday which originated as a solstice celebration. The *Saint-Jean* national holiday has its origins in at least three eras: the 17th-century French regency, the 19th-century birth of French-Canadian nationalism, the 20th-century emergence of Québécois nationalism. Yet, because it is a fête, it is never totally contained in ideological or historical parameters.

The Astounding Fireworks of Nouvelle-France

Well before the New World came into existence, the Catholic Church had already absorbed the pre-Christian solstice rites of northern Europe. The June fête was in the words of an early 20th-century Canadian priest "one of those naive customs that the Church preserved... and turned toward the glory of God."[5] The folklorist Arnold Van Gennep (1949) describes the eve of Saint-Jean-Baptiste day in French villages as a celebration of the longest days of the year and of the first fruits of the season, of light and fertility. One of the central features of the "pagan" festival is the lighting of a bonfire which couples would jump if they wished to marry that year.

Rechannelling the fire and the light into a Christian narrative, the Church represented Saint John the Baptist as the figure of light announcing the advent of Christ. Drawing on the popular fête and the power of the Church, the French Crown appropriated the symbols and the fire itself to magnify its own glory, to create "the magic of the state." Derivative symbolics and competing hegemonies mark the history of Saint Jean in Nouvelle-France.

That the Saint Jean crossed the Atlantic with Normand settlers[6] and became such a popular fête in French America may have corresponded as much to the summer solstice celebration as its coincidence with the Catholic calendar. It is not surprising—in a country with such long and trying winters—that the French immigrants would have marked the coming of summer, with or without the sanction of the Church. Nor is it surprising that the clerical and military authorities sent by the King of France to convert the Indians and organize the French settlers would seek to control the festivities and to turn the *paganus*[7] into an obedient collective.

French Jesuit archives from the 17th century describe the missionaries grappling with harsh material conditions and a recalcitrant population. Lost martyrs and victorious conversions—of Huguenots as well as "Savages" —pepper the latter 1600s records. The *Relations des Jésuites* also document the celebration of Catholic holidays organized by clerics, *seigneurs* [nobles of the colony], and French military officers. In a period when the French crown meshed with the cross of the Holy Roman Church, the dividing lines of power were hardly clear cut. The complicity of the regency's ecclesiastic and civil authorities and the wish to capture the energy of the popular fête are evident in Father Le Jeune's witnessing of the 1636 Saint Joseph[8] celebration at the fort of Quebec. Translated in Reuben Thwaites seventy-two volume (1896–1901) compiling of 17th and 18th century *Jesuit Relations and Allied Documents*, Le Jeune's first-person account speaks of spectacular pyrotechnics.

A sophisticated display of fireworks followed the hoisting of the flag and the firing of the cannon. The saint's name appeared in letters of fire and fourteen rockets were launched "to the astonishment of the French and still more of the Savages" (Thwaites 1898, 11:67). A miniature castle was also set ablaze with pinwheels surrounding a cross of flames and rockets spewing from its towers. It is the Governor who lit the display, making it clear to the *Sauvages*, continues the priest, "that the French were more powerful than Demons, that they commanded the fire" (Thwaites 1898, 11:71).

Jesuit records continually refer to the complicity of cross, crown, and cannon in Nouvelle France. A 1646 display on Saint Jean eve includes the militia firing five cannon balls and two or three rounds of muskets after Governor Montmagny, flanked by two priests singing *Ut quent laxis*, lit the bonfire (Thwaites 1898, 28:207). June entries from 1666 *Relations* describe Iroquois attacks in the Montreal settlement, gifts offered by Hurons for the new church in Quebec town, and a Saint Jean bonfire which was attended by dignitaries of the colony, including Marquis de Tracy and Quartermaster General Jean Talon, and which was "celebrated with every possible magnificence":

> Monseigneur the Bishop, robed in pontifical vestments, was there with all the clergy and our fathers in surplices... He presented the torch, made of white wax, to Monsieur de Tracy, who handed it back to him, and insisted upon his being the first to light the fire. (Thwaites 1899, 50:189–90)

These accounts testify to the friendly tussle of *l'Eglise et la Couronne* in attempting to capture the imaginary of the pagans. Since Jesuit records are our primary sources, who might be in charge of these early fêtes and of the "faithful flock" is highly debatable. Neither the *habitants* who continued to celebrate the coming of summer on both banks of the Saint Lawrence nor the *sauvages* have left written accounts of the amazing pyrotechnical displays in Nouvelle-France.

The Saint Jean would not become the site of local national aspirations until over two centuries later. After the *Conquête*—the retreat of the French forces and the ceding of the territory to the crown of England in 1763—many of the clergy, the *seigneurs*, the soldiers, the woodsmen and the farmers remained on the land that became Lower Canada. We can assume that they continued to celebrate the summer solstice and that priests and nobles repeated the ritual tug-of-war to light the Saint Jean fires. The ambiguity as to who might control the fête—clerical, civil or populist forces—appears even more evident in the official founding event of the

Québécois national holiday: an 1834 garden party in Montreal, then capital city of Bas-Canada, territory of the British Crown.

The Radical Saint Jean of Lower Canada

The first patriotic Saint Jean opened with a toast, "Au Peuple, source primitive de toute autorité légitime," at an *al fresco* banquet on June 23, 1834. Over sixty men gathered in John Picoté de Belestre-McDonnell's garden, rue Saint Antoine, on Saint John eve. The participants included the instigator of the banquet, Ludger Duvernay, editor of the radical *La Minerve* newspaper and founding father of the future Société Saint-Jean-Baptiste, militant organ of latter-19th and early-20th century French-Canadian nationalism; the host, John McDonnell, a Montreal lawyer, member of the City Council and a supporter of democratic reform in Lower Canada; the mayor of Montreal, Jacques Viger, who presided over the ceremony; and other members of the Montreal bourgeoisie who supported a reform movement sweeping through the two Canadas. This Saint Jean celebration was of a decidedly political nature, as a sampling of some of the twenty-five toasts recorded in Rumilly's *Histoire de la Société Saint-Jean-Baptiste de Montréal*[9] indicate.

> To the People, original source of all legitimate authority
> To the Assembly of Lower Canada, faithful organ of the Canadian People
> To the honorable Louis-Joseph Papineau, Speaker of the Assembly, zealous defender of the People's Rights
> To Elzéar Bédard... force behind the 92 Resolutions on the state of the Province, and to the 56 members who formed the glorious majority of the vote
> To O'Connell and our Irish compatriots
> To Mackenzie and Bidwell, and all the other Reformists in Upper Canada
> To Daniel Tracey and the victims of May 21
> To the government of the United States
> To General Lafayette... (Rumilly 1975:19)

The guest list and the toasts signal that this June 1834 banquet—since read as the founding event of French-Canadian nationalism—might just as well have heralded an independent Canadian republic. This holding of Great Britain was divided into Upper Canada (over 157,000 inhabitants, primarily anglophone) and Lower Canada (over 479,000 inhabitants, primarily francophone). Despite the dominant number of the francophone population, the rhetoric of the *Patriotes* gathered in McDonnell's garden speaks less of reclaiming French power in the Americas than of uniting against British imperialism. The ninety-two resolutions passed by Papineau's Canadian party and the "glorious majority" of the Assembly are a list of grievances directed toward London. Cloaked in the mantle of "we the people, *source primitive de toute autorité légitime*," this group of bourgeois patriots were demanding more financial and legislative autonomy. The heroes toasted were those of the American Revolution (Lafayette and the government of the United States), of 19th-century reformists from Upper and Lower Canada with decidedly anglo names (O'Connell, Mackenzie, Bidwell) as well as the patrician lawyer Louis Papineau—who would gladly obtain home rule yet maintain his seignorial privileges—and the martyrs of a skirmish with British soldiers during the 1832 election campaign. The common enemy of these Canadian patriots of Scottish, Irish, and French descent was British imperial rule.

One of the guests at the 1834 garden party, a student named Georges-Etienne Cartier, sang a song he had composed, a hymn to *Canada*. According to Robert Rumilly, *O Canada! mon pays, mes amours*—the melody of which would become the Canadian national anthem—was launched at the 1834 event (Rumilly 1975:20). However, this diachronic complicity of Canadian nationalisms should not cloud the fact that signs of ethnic polarity were also apparent in this first *fête nationale*. Mayor Viger offered another song, a few couplets from an anonymous French Revolution hymn citing Saint Jean as protector of those seeking to overthrow the tyranny of *une race enemie*.

> They struck down tyranny
> We also will destroy it.
> Since fate has designated an enemy race
> Watch over us Saint John, guide us to victory.[10]

In the circumscribed world of these bourgeois patriots legitimizing their claims in the name of *le Peuple*, the identity of this "enemy race" is highly ambivalent.

However troubled the ideological underpinnings of the 1834 Saint Jean banquet, the will to dress the Christian saint in the guise of a revolutionary figure appears clearly. The celebrants reserved two toasts to the clergy. One hailed liberal priests of the province "fortunately for the country, numerous." The other was more of an ironically cloaked threat directed toward the Catholic hierarchy: "May they be united, and serve as example to their flock. They will be supported and respected by joining in the cause with the Assembly and the people" (Rumilly 1975:20).

The Patriots toasting the Saint Jean drew, wittingly or unconsciously, on a dual symbolism. The radical side of John the Baptist—biblical challenger of civil authority engaged in a movement that cost him his head—meshes with a populist French-Canadian Jean-Baptiste. That the "Jean-Baptistes" involved in the uprisings which followed four years later might also lose their heads, could not have entered the minds of these reformists.

After London's refusal to recognize the ninety-two resolutions of the Lower-Canadian Assembly, rebels began arming while British military rule tightened. In the winter of 1837 fighting broke out in the townships along the Richelieu River provoking more repressive measures from the Crown. Patriot farms were burned and the legislative assembly dissolved. In 1838 a splinter group led by the radical Robert Nelson declared the independent republic of Lower Canada. Nelson's February border mission failed as did a November uprising directed by an underground military lodge.

The rebels were poorly organized and ill-equipped. They had little material support from the Lower-Canadian politicians who had so heartily toasted *le Peuple*, and certainly not from the Church which urged the population to remain calm. Those who had dared to take up arms in the townships north and east of Montreal were excommunicated, exiled, or executed. Without financial backing or central organization and with slim popular following, the insurrection was quickly mastered by the British army. The inflammatory rhetoric of the politicians and poets of the 1834 celebration was not enough to sustain the revolution. The instigator of political reform in Lower Canada, Louis-Joseph Papineau, and the instigator of the first national holiday, Ludger Duvernay had already fled the country.

Over a thousand citizens were arrested. Twelve insurgents were summarily tried and hung by the British crown, their patriotic heads dangling in unwitting emulation of the decapitated Saint John the Baptist. Others were sent to penal colonies in Australia.

The Submissive Saint Jean of French Canada

As Heinz Weinmann (1987) argues in his study of the genealogy of Québécois history, it was not the mid-18th-century English victory over the French forces on the Plains of Abraham but the mid-19th-century squelching of the *révolte des Patriotes* which signalled the veritable *Conquête de Canada*. The events of 1837–38 testify to a popular movement bereft of leaders and successfully nipped in the bud. Understandably, it is not the aborted revolution, but the 1834 garden party with its feisty speeches, which became the marker of the Québécois national holiday.

In the years which followed the first "patriotic holiday" the figure of Saint Jean would be subject to another displacement: after a short-lived radical career, the saint returned to the haven of the Church. Shifting to the role of protector of the established order with the consolidation of the Catholic Church and the British Crown, Saint Jean became a symbol of submission. At the same time, fueled by the live memory of the *hivers rouges* [red winters] of 1837–38 and the Crown's response to the rebellion, a specifically ethnic and insular French-Canadian nationalism began to flourish.

Any ambivalence as to the causes of the revolt in Lower Canada was dispelled by the envoy from London, Lord Durham. The Governor of all British North America distinguished clearly the causes of dissent in Lower and Upper Canada, or what he referred to in the reserved and geographically distant language of Victorian England as "the troubles in Canada." Racial and not ideological causes were at the heart of the Lower Canadian rebellion and these could be resolved by assimilating the francophone population —which the Durham report dismisses as a people without literature or culture—into the anglophone population of Canada. London dictated the 1840 Union Act which combined Upper and Lower Canada into one—and as if by magic wand—*English* dominion. Instead of joining the two Canadas in the bosom of the Empire, the Union Act would widen the wedge between the English and French speaking populations and create further resentment on the part of French-Canadians.

The 1837–38 Patriot rebellion put a temporary halt to any quasi-revolutionary holiday. When the Saint Jean resurfaced after the 1840 Union Act, its symbolic essence had again mutated. The telos of the Société Saint-Jean-Baptiste, which was officially founded in 1843 and legally recognized in 1849, appeared dramatically different from its 1834 origins: the association established itself as a *société de bienfaisance* [charity]. Bearing the motto "Rendre le peuple meilleur" [Make the people better], the SSJB allied with both the Protestant and Catholic churches to declare battle against poverty and intemperance.

Having returned from exile in Vermont, the instigator of the 1834 banquet, Ludger Duvernay participated in the founding of the SSJB and the Saint Jean festivities of 1843 which consisted of a mass at the Notre Dame cathedral followed by a procession to the Saint Jacques cathedral. The procession, which would evolve into the national *défilé* [parade] years later, was rooted in Catholic ritual, but was tinged with secular remnants of patriotic identity. As described in the official history of the SSJB (Rumilly 1975:52) the banner of the local *Société de Tempérance* led the parade which included a band playing *Vive la Canadienne* and the new banner of the SSJB[11] depicting Saint Jean on one side and a French-Canadian farmer on the other. All of the SSJB *sociétaires*, marching four abreast, wore the maple leaf on their lapels. The dinner, which might have recalled the 1834 founding banquet, was canceled. The newly founded Société Saint-Jean-Baptiste established its charitable vocation by donating the funds gathered for the banquet to a town near Montreal which had been devastated by a fire. The traditional bread blessed by the clerical authority would have to suffice. The tone of this manifestation is a far cry from the inflammatory discourse of the 1834 banquet. True, there could hardly be toasts in the wake of revolutionary passions turned to moderation and temperance.

Submission to the rule of the Church and the British Crown would continue to dominate the Saint Jean festivities organized by the SSJB throughout the second half of the 19th century. This symbolic alliance was apparent in the opening of the 1850 parade with the British flag followed by the Catholic school banners, in the 1868 crowd's "hurrahs for the Pope and the Queen" (Rumilly 1975:94). Compliance to the Crown would include the English-language signs over the shops which bordered the public stage of the event.

The trope of French-Canadian docile obedience—the negative pole of Québécois identity—draws on the image of *le petit Saint Jean* which took hold in the latter 19th-century parades. In 1866, apparently inspired by an Italian custom, a Montreal tailor named Chalifoux introduced a live child dressed in a sheep skin and accompanied by a live lamb to represent the Saint in the June 24 procession (Rumilly 1975:87). The role of the Church and the reduction of the national subject to a child and his innocent lamb[12] would provoke outrage among 20th-century nationalists from Olivar Asselin,[13] who derided the "mouton national" as early as 1904, to the rebels of the latter 1960s.

Read *a postiori* the appearance of the child and the lamb coincided significantly with the 1887 creation of the Canadian Confederation, which would seal the minority status of the Franco-Canadian population. The *petit Saint Jean* embodied a mythical French-Canadian subject, a child abandoned in the wilderness by the *mère patrie*. The lamb was an even more damning symbol of a dutiful flock of sheep. Neither would seem to belong in a demonstration of national self-importance. Yet in the representational economy of any minority nationalism, rejection and oppression in themselves constitute symbolic capital.

Loyal, mais Français

The 1867 British North American Act declared the territories of Quebec, Ontario, Nova Scotia, and New Brunswick[14] one Canadian Confederation, reducing Quebec to a province among four whose population constituted only some 33 percent of Canada. Although granting equal status to the French language and assuring provincial parliaments, the Confederation also undercut any numerically-based legitimacy of French-Canadian claims to equal power. Moreover, French-Canadians were continuing to emigrate, seeking jobs and opportunity in western Canada and the United States. That not all of the newly defined citizens of Quebec province were happy with their minority status appeared evident in the reaction of the SSJB which strove to reunite the French-Canadians dispersed across North America.

In 1874 the SSJB organized a mammoth Saint Jean demonstration in Montreal. Some 18,000 emigrants converged on Montreal for the June 24 celebration. To greet the returning sons and daughters of the nation, merchants displayed signs reading "Loyal, mais Français" (Rumilly 1975:103). With such dramatic shifts in national definition over a short three decades since the Patriot rebellion, loyalty to what sovereign power remains ambiguous. However, ties to the language and to French-Canadian traditional institutions appeared reinforced.

The festivities began with a mass at the Notre Dame Cathedral. Congregating outside the Cathedral, the SSJB lieutenants opened the parade, followed by the Swiss guard [soldiers of the Pope], then representatives of the legal and medical professions, then clergymen and political authorities. The latter included Wilfred Laurier who, thanks to the massive vote of French-Canadians, would become the first Canadian Prime Minister from Quebec in 1896. Then came the floats furnished by artisan corporations: the stone cutters, the tanners and cobblers, the painters and blacksmiths, the plumbers and tinsmiths, the bricklayers, carpenters and roofers, the butchers. A banquet for some 12,000 at the Hôtel de Ville followed. At this event the president of the SSJB read a blessing of the *fête nationale canadienne*, which Pope Pius IX had telegraphed.

The religious framing of the 1874 event merged with its political telos and the new-fangled device of the telegraph. This was a homecoming for French-Canadians, grouped under the symbolic umbrellas of *la foi et la langue*. To the formation of the Canadian Confederation, French-Canadians responded with a *Convention générale des Canadiens français*. Four hundred French-American delegates held a convention after the celebration. The delegates spoke of a dream to reunite *tous les Canadiens* and, impossibly, reclaim entitlement to the land. They also spoke of a troubling reality: the case of Louis Riel.

Riel was a French-Canadian-Indian métis who had formed a resistance group to protest Manitoba's entry as the fifth province of the Confederation in 1870. At the time of the 1874 Saint Jean fête, Riel was living as an outlaw in Vermont, a veritable turnstile for *exilés*. He sent a message proclaiming the solidarity of the Métis branch of the French-Canadian tree. In 1885 Riel handed himself over to authorities of the Crown and was hung as a traitor. Although the Church had officially condemned the rebellion in Manitoba, it did not hesitate to claim Louis Riel as the last French-Canadian martyr. There was no Saint Jean parade the summer following the execution.

With the addition of Manitoba, British Columbia, and Prince Edward Island, Quebec was by the end of the 19th century a province among seven, its population approximately one fourth of the Confederation.[15] As claims to shared Canadian hegemony receded into history, French-Canadian nationalism surged ahead. The latter part of the 1800s saw the birth of a nationalist party and the materialization of numerous symbolic markings dedicated to the martyrs of aborted revolts. In the year of Riel's execution, Honoré Mercier created the Parti National. Mercier was a politician and a fervent supporter of the Société Saint-Jean-Baptiste, which continued to preside over the annual celebration and the construction of monuments. The SSJB instigated the erection of templates and obelisks in honor of the 1838 victims. In 1893 the association inaugurated the Monument National, a building which would house political meetings, performances, and dinners for local dignitaries.

Despite the success of French-Canadian politicians such as Wilfred Laurier in taking advantage of the federal system, resentment over sub-national status in Quebec was festering. In the wake of maturing industrial capitalism the province was economically impoverished. With little political or economic clout in the big picture, *nationalistes* sought to make of Quebec a symbolic fortress. The symbolic is the privileged arena of any nation; symbolic value increases when the nation is not a state. The never-more-to-be glories of an idealized past and a xenophobic distrust of all that is not "native and fine" (Whisnant 1983) characterized the official Saint Jean manifestations of the early 20th century.

Une race glorieuse

The 1924 Saint Jean parade in Montreal responded to criticisms which French-Canadian patriots had levelled at the event since the early 1900s. Answering a survey the SSJB conducted for the 1904 festivities, one critic deplored the frivolous commercial side of the national procession which "should be other than a circus... It is not the time nor the place to exhibit furs, grocery stores, or cigar ads" (Rumilly 1975:190). In 1911 the nationalist historian Henri Bourassa congratulated the organizers for having eliminated the "national sheep" [*mouton national*] from the para-religious procession and for being more aggressively nationalistic.

Although the infamous sheep would reappear through the years and survive multiple attacks, although clerical authority was far from diminishing, and although small commercial interests would inevitably drive the parade, the 1924 procession marked a shift in the nature of the event. The SSJB organized a parade under the theme *Ce que l'Amérique doit à la race française* [What America Owes the French Race], which for the first time staged *l'histoire nationale*. On June 24, 1924 twenty-four lavish floats representing periods in the history of the French province rode through Montreal. Heroes of the French colonial era dominated these *chars allégoriques*. Under the theme of "What America Owes to the French Race," the floats confirmed the notion that *français* indeed defined a race and that this race, irrevocably a minority in the Americas, could prove its worth through its glorious past.

Char allégorique appears an appropriate vehicle for a nation whose hold on political reality appeared lost in mythologized history. The 1924 Saint Jean consecrated French-Canadian historical figures while locking them into an accomplished past. That this compromised the political future of the nation appears evident in the prayer written by Victor Morin which consecrated the 1924 Saint Jean.

> O Saint John the Baptist, fearless vindicator of morals and rights, predecessor of the Messiah, patron of French-Canadians, illuminate our spirit in the search for justice and safeguard our life by maintaining our institutions, our language, and our faith. Help us preserve the traditions of our forefathers in all their purity so that we might accomplish the Lord's plan on this American land and thus merit eternal happiness in the celestial fatherland.[16]

La patrie lay in the world beyond immediate political reality, either in an Elysian after-life or in a glorious past.

The parade following the mass was a procession of twenty-four floats illustrating, in chronological order, events and characters in the history of French America. Among the tableaux figured Cartier's 1534 discovery voyage, Champlain's founding of Quebec City in 1608, Louis Hébert's founding family,[17] the arrival of the Jesuit missionaries in 1625, the 1640 foundation of Ville Marie [Montreal], Marguerite Bourgeoys establishing convent schools in 1653, Dollard des Ormeaux "mastering the Iroquois" in 1660, La Vérendrye expanding the borders of *Canada* in 1743, portraits of Papineau and Lafontaine between 1832 and 1842, and Duvernay's founding the SSJB in 1834.

Here History begins with Cartier's *découverte* in 1534 and ends with Duvernay's founding gesture of the French-Canadian nation in 1834, exactly three centuries later. The SSJB historian describes the spectators' reaction to the performance as "the astonishment of a people who had never thought themselves so glorious" (Rumilly 1975:313). This recalls the "astounded natives" of the first Saint Jean fireworks in Nouvelle-France, but here the "natives" appear to be fascinated by their own magnified image.

Around five in the afternoon, the procession reached the Jeanne-Mance Park at the base of the Mont Royal, the mountain which stands at the center of the city. The band struck up "O Canada" and the crowd joined in the singing of this curiously ambivalent national anthem. On the summit of the Mont Royal, Mgr. Deschamps blessed the template of what would become the immense metallic cross consecrated during the 1934 centennial of the SSJB and the hallmark of Montreal. At the top of the mountain a choir sang in Latin, while at the foot of the mountain, the mayor, members of the SSJB, and an anonymous crowd responded to the sacred verses. The festivities ended with "une soirée de folklore" at the Monument National and the presentation of *Bene merenti de Patria* medals to Laurent-Olivier David, who as former SSJB president had overseen the construction and dedication of the edifice, and to Marie Gérin-Lajoie, who was a prominent patron of charitable organizations.

The 1924 Saint Jean presents a symbiosis of *l'Eglise, la Nation, la Race*. In the words of the nationalist historian Canon Lionel Groulx, speaking at the Congrès National which followed, "nous pourrions croire que l'idéal de l'Etat se confond avec l'idéal de la race" [the ideal of the State fuses with the ideal of the race] and proclaims the "moral government of the race" (Rumilly 1975:315). By a circular contract the race embodies moral authority, which in turn legitimates the race.

Although the 1924 Saint Jean described a turning point in the parade as a depiction of French-Canadian history rather than a religious procession, the event reconfirmed the status quo of Catholic orthodoxy, improbable bedfellow of the primarily Anglo-Protestant Canadian government. The 1924 celebration reinforced a mythological past and created a screen to the political present.

In the 1930s as the troubling events in Europe reached North American shores, the symbolic power of the French-Canadian Church and the glorious past of *Canada* would accrue, while the Church's capacity to deal with social-economic reality in Quebec diminished. The Church could not protect its flock from industrialization and urbanization, which accelerated through the mid-20th century, nor from the Depression and the Second World War.

A Great Darkness

As the United States and Canada reluctantly came to recognize the Nazi threat and the need to mobilize for war, the province of Quebec elected a prime minister on his promise to keep the people out of the strife in Europe. Maurice Duplessis and his Union Nationale party rose to power in a period marked by the effects of the Depression, a traditional mistrust of involvement in what were deemed "the wars of Great Britain," and intense xenophobic nationalism. The twenty-year rule of the Union Nationale —interrupted by a brief four years of the Parti Libéral—has since become known as a period of obscurantism, corruption, and exploitation: a "Great Darkness" which delayed Quebec's entry into the modern world. This revised symbolism could not be predicted when the Union Nationale came into office bearing the protective slogan of *la Foi, la Famille, la Langue*.

In light of the fact that French Canadians considered themselves victims of British imperialism and that a faction of the population had recently conducted an *Achat chez nous* [Buy from our people] campaign designed to oust "foreign" merchants who were predominantly Jews[18]—those ubiquitous pagan Others—one could hardly expect the population to mobilize for the *maudits Anglais* or the *maudits Juifs*. Although provincial priests condemned Nazism, the official rhetoric of the French-Canadian church threw Jews, Free Masons, French Populists, Spanish resistance fighters, and Bolsheviks or Communists into the same reprehensible bag. They were deemed "pagans of modern times."

In Rumilly's 1975 history of the SSJB, curious discrepancies between a fraternal 'Latin' essence and Latin insurgents emerge. The historian describes the Spanish *résistants* who came to Quebec seeking support as unwelcome heathens, whereas the supporters of Mussolini deserved a hearty welcome as members of the great Latin family. The *Front Populaire* appears as a group of barbarians sweeping over France, whereas Maréchal Pétain would be acclaimed as a savior of French values. The author's bias permeates his eye-witness description of the 1939 Saint Jean parade.

The 1939 parade coincided with a five-year hiatus of the Union Nationale occupied by the Parti Libéral. That the Liberal Party of Quebec—which favored collaboration with the Federal government, economic autonomy for Quebec, and changes as "drastic" as women's suffrage—did occupy the seat of government in those turbulent years is an indication that Québécois political loyalties were far from monolithic. The allegiance of the SSJB and its official historian, Robert Rumilly, is less ambivalent.

The theme of the 1939 celebration was "French-Canada has remained faithful." The festivities opened on Saint Jean eve with a banquet for local dignitaries at the Windsor Hotel. The key speaker was the national historian, Abbé Groulx. A bonfire at the Lafontaine Park followed the dinner. Recalling the 1666 collaboration of ecclesiastic and civil authority, Mgr. Maurault blessed the fires lit by M. le Maire Houde. Rumilly was among the crowd gathered around the popular mayor.

As was customary, a mass opened the celebration on June 24. The afternoon procession on the rue Sherbrooke took place under a threatening sky, but the weather held. Rumilly describes the event with the excitement of a child.

> Here comes the parade! Here they are! Policemen in colonial helmets, white-gloved firemen, aldermen in top hats... And the Ukrainian delegation in national costume. And the floats! Vaquelin battling the waves... the missionaries in a pagoda. And the bands... and the Swiss guard! Young men proud to be dressed in a spruce uniform... stripes sparkling on their cuffs... How slender they are, how French, and how young... (Rumilly 1975:482)

The author's tone grows somber at the thought that one of these young men might wear the repulsive khaki uniform and be shipped off to fight on foreign soil, as he himself had been in 1918, and that one might be burned alive in a tank. Rumilly goes on to stipulate the root of the evil threatening the innocent sons of *la nation*: "some Jewish tenderer will have sold the uniform, hideous as a bag, in which these children will rot someplace" (Rumilly 1975:482).

While the war raged on in Europe, the French-Canadian province appeared to withdraw into an historical mythos. The 1942 Saint Jean coincided with the tricentennial celebration of the 1642 establishment of Ville Marie, alias Montreal. Locking out English financiers and Irish delegations, the SSJB reserved the celebration to *Canadiens*. "The celebration irritates the English loyalists of Montreal," claims Rumilly, "French-Canadians persist in this aberrational love of Canada while London is bombarded" (Rumilly 1975:505). Hitler's ambitions never extended to the Americas, insists the author, and any such pretension was just a ploy to enlist the province's support of the war.

The theme of the 1943 parade was "Hommage à la mère canadienne." Still within the four year reign of the Parti Libéral, this event simultaneously marked feminine suffrage and a harking back to traditional values. Under the direction of Adélard Godbout, the Parti Libéral government had pushed through three major reforms: obligatory education for children between six and fourteen; the transformation of Montreal Power into Hydro-Québec; and the vote for *Canadiennes-françaises*.

The 1940 granting of universal suffrage might have played a role in the selecting of *la mère canadienne* as the theme of the 1943 parade. This is not to say that French-Canadian women were clamoring for a part in the Saint Jean pageantry, but that the patriarchal SSJB might have been anxious to keep women in their maternal role and out of politics. Testifying to the 1943 context still shadowed by the war in Europe and the call to arms, Rumilly offers a more immediate explanation of the parade's theme, claiming this "Homage to the French-Canadian Mother" related directly to keeping the sons of Quebec out of the war. Rumilly links the choice of the theme to an incident which occurred in November 1942. Armand Sabourin, a French-Canadian military chaplain serving in the British army, declared in the local press that the English-Canadian mother was far more spartan in sending her sons off to war than was the French-Canadian mother, who held her sons by the apron strings and remained unwilling to deliver them to the holocaust. Immediately following this, the SSJB Congress opted for the 1943 theme, intended to "wash the French-Canadian mother free from the gratuitous insult one of her denatured sons had pronounced" (Rumilly 1975:523).

Whatever the reasons behind the thematic choice, the *mère canadienne* depicted in the 1943 *chars allégoriques* was decidedly traditional. She was in her place at home, cooking bread, tending to the hearth and the health of her family. This event indicates the remarkable glow of traditional values in a world surrounded by the darkness of the war outside and *la grande noirceur* within the province.

Artists Building and Disrupting the Nation

In 1947 artists appeared in the designing of the national parade. The director of the SSJB, Roger Varin, commissioned students from the Montreal Ecole de Beaux Arts to design and build the floats of the 1947 parade, titled *La patrie, c'est ça!* This avant-garde experiment proved a fiasco. The Montreal public, accustomed to historical personae portrayed by live actors, appeared mystified by the abstract representations of the parish, the city, or the province in the floats designed by the apprentice plastic artists. The spectators "expected to see the traditional schoolhouse, the old cemetery, the weaver at her loom... No applause rose when a great Saint Jean-Baptiste in cardboard appeared on the last float, instead of the adorable child with his lamb" (Rumilly 1975:557).

The SSJB historian goes on to say that the traditional parts of the celebration—the bonfire, the mass, the banquet which gathered some 800 *convives* around Mayor Houde and Edouard Monpetit, founder of the University of Montreal—were more successful. The mayor gave a speech which solicited the participation of a greater number of the five million French-Americans in the SSJB who by contributing just two cents per person could further the cause.

But few of the contributors seemed motivated by the 1947 parade. Couched in a retrospective irony, "La Patrie, c'est ça!" was a flop. The problematic relationship between national symbols and their performative production, between artists and financing agents, and the inherent dependency on a fluctuating popular acquiescence appears dramatically in this episode.

In 1948 two diametrically opposed symbolic events followed the dubious 1947 alliance of artists and nationalists. The first was the official consecration of the fleurdelisé as the national Québécois flag. The second was a declaration of internationalist artists, which would later be interpreted as the precursory sign of the Quiet Revolution and the overthrow of backward traditionalism.

In January 1948 the Prime Minister of Quebec, Maurice Duplessis, officialized the fleurdelisé which would become the emblem of contemporary Quebec. The pale blue flag, marked by a white cross and the four lily-shaped crests of the defunct French monarchy, flew over the Québécois parliament building in place of the Union Jack when the decree was pronounced. In the summer of the same year, a group of Québécois surrealist artists published a work entitled *le Refus global*. The painter Paul-Emile Borduas introduced "The Global Refusal," a manifesto denouncing the control of the Church, the State, and the Rationalist Order, seen as the causes of fascism and the Great War. The *Refus* was an invitation to overthrow authority and to "make way for magic... for objective mystery... for love... for what is truly needed" (Cook 1969:281).

This proclamation of 20th-century pagans advocating civil and religious disobedience and challenging the traditionalist rhetoric of *la nation* has since been interpreted as the initial spark of the latter-1960's revolution and the founding event of contemporary Quebec. The scholar James de Gaspé Bonar stated during a 1985 symposium at the Canada Arts Council that Borduas and his co-signers "created the myth of the birth of the Québécois people... Awakened to surrealism, psychoanalysis, and Marxism... a number of artists could no longer accept the great ideological conservatism of the elite... These artists can be considered as the inventors of the new Québécois mindscape..." (Wallace 1990:153). The official displacement of conservative nationalism would not occur for a dozen years after the publication. And the creation of a new "Québécois mindscape," as well as the artist as *maître d'oeuvre* of the nation, would not be forthcoming until the 1970s.

History Begins Here: A Quiet Revolution

In 1960, after sixteen years of Duplessis government, the Parti Libéral under Jean Lesage would return to power. Paul Sauvé, who took over the position of provincial Prime Minister after Duplessis' passing and governed for a brief one hundred days before his own untimely death, would be remembered for one word in his inaugural speech: "Désormais..." [Henceforth] which announced the opening of a new era. The thirty years which would follow constitute the history of the modern Québécois nation, to which Blackburn, the 1990 director of the Saint Jean parade, referred as "thirty years of accumulated energy." The year 1960 separates an archaic *Canada* from an emergent Québécois nation.

As the contemporary historical critic Jocelyn Létourneau points out, *la révolution tranquille* is an arbitrary nomenclature, as is *la grande noirceur*. The recording and interpretation of History is obviously a construction, periods are arbitrary, and names are summational. Yet these hold incredible symbolic weight in defining collective identity. And the social history of the three decades deemed "modern Quebec" does indicate major transformations in the way the society functioned and perceived of itself.

Many of the reforms undertaken during the 1939–44 PLQ government came to fruition in the 1960s. Democratic access to public schooling shifted education from the hands of the clergy to the state and the newly created

Ministère de l'éducation. Development of the province's natural resources—in particular the hydro-electric power of the north—promised prosperity. As Minister of Natural Resources, René Lévesque, future leader of the Parti Québécois, was instrumental in this move to free the province from the "Power Companies." Lévesque promoted the nationalization of energy resources with the slogan *Maîtres chez nous* [masters at home], a slogan which undoubtedly heralded the future victory of the separatist party over a decade later.

During the 1960s the PLQ would splinter into three competing factions: radical and "soft-core" separatists, *souverainists* such as Lévesque—who might never have pushed toward a Québécois independence referendum had he not been under popular pressure—who formed the Parti Québécois in 1968; federalists pursuing power through the central government, riding on the coat tails of Pierre-Elliot Trudeau, who became Prime Minister of Canada the same year; more patient politicians such as Robert Bourassa, who would slide in and out of power in Quebec for the next thirty years.

As the Quiet Revolution swept over the province, how was the SSJB, the symbolic guardian of arriere-guard French-Canadian nationalism, reacting? With the emergence of the Quiet Revolution the conservative brand of nationalism—entrenched in the great Catholic family and a glorious past—went out of style. Two Saint Jean parade themes framing the events of the 1960s indicate a shift in the SSJB's orientation. In 1962 the title was "Epanouissement du Canada Français" [Florishing of French Canada]. Here it is no longer a question of waiting for the celestial *patrie* or basking in the glorious legacy of an accomplished past, but in the fulfillment of the present community. In 1968 the title was "Québec et sa vocation internationale." Bolstered by General de Gaulle's declaration of "Vive le Québec libre!" in July 1967, the 1968 parade title represents a dramatic shift in the conception of Quebec as a possible nation among nations.

A Head Falls, A Party Rises

Yet "Quebec and its international vocation" was a premature term in a period when Quebec's national status remained far from clear. For more extreme and impatient elements of the population the *révolution tranquille* was proving a bit too quiet. Proletarian factions of the proverbial *peuple* were seething after years of exploitation. Inspired by national liberation movements in Africa—particularly Algeria—a group of insurgents formed the Front de Libération du Québec (FLQ). Viewing the Québécois as a colonized proletaria, as the *nègre blanc de l'Amérique*, the FLQ had begun striking at the anglo-dominated bourgeoisie, at local and federal government figures, and at symbols of the Crown in 1963. The robberies of a bank and a dynamite arsenal, the bombs set outside the Royal Army military casernes and in mail boxes of the wealthy and predominantly English-speaking Westmount neighborhood of Montreal were the acts of a small minority. However, their impact was widespread.

In 1968—over a century after the aborted Patriot rebellion—a popular revolt erupted on the Québécois national stage. In the streets of Montreal, theatricalized by the Saint Jean event. the parade degenerated into a riot. Pierre Elliott Trudeau—"native son," leader of the Canadian Liberal Party and soon to be Prime Minister—sat in the official tribune with local dignitaries. Separatists bombarded the tribune with tomatoes, eggs, and bottles. Policemen on horseback chased spectators into Lafontaine Park. Numerous demonstrators were arrested, including the leaders of the Rassemblement pour l'Indépendance Nationale, an officially recognized party which would later join forces with the more moderate Parti Québécois formed that same year by a Liberal Party splinter group.

Violence again overtook the 1969 parade. In front of the luxurious Ritz Carlton Hotel, demonstrators swarmed over the float bearing Saint-Jean-Baptiste. The vehicle was overturned, decapitating the effigy. Severing the head of the patron saint, long held as a symbol of subservience, signified the shattering of a mythic shell and the ultimate break with an archaic French and Catholic nationalism. Yet this explosion, however co-opted in future nationalist discourse, did not indicate national cohesion nor lead to Québécois independence. These disruptions and the last terrorist acts of the FLQ—the kidnapping of the British commercial attaché, James Cross, and the kidnapping and assassination of Pierre Laporte, Minister of Labor and Immigration—succeeded in frightening the majority of the Québécois population more than stimulating national liberation sentiments.

As in the 1800s, the rebellion was quickly mastered by the forces of the Crown. The 1968–69 riots provoked a ban on the June 24 parade. The 1970 October Crisis, culminating in Laporte's death and Trudeau's declaring the War Measures Act, meant the dispatching of Royal Canadian troops and tanks to control a largely peaceful population who woke up one October morning to find themselves occupied.

The Parti Québécois would profit from this climate of terror and bewilderment. Assuming the ambivalent role of speaker for national independence and safeguard against nationalistic passions, René Lévesque would ride to power in 1976 on an incredible wave of popular energy. Appropriately, those who created this dynamic were in good part poets, musicians, and actors. The celebration of the national holiday is an indication of how performers seized and fueled the symbolic power of the nation in the mid-1970s.

After the riots, the decapitation of the patron saint, and the banning of the parade at the close of the 1960s, the official Saint Jean came to a halt, although popular *fêtes de quartier* [neighborhood parties] continued. In 1975 the Saint Jean resurrected in the form of a gigantic *fête sauvage* [impromptu celebration] on the top of Mount Royal. This event heralded and prepared the 1976 Parti Québécois victory. The agents behind the "pagan" nation's celebratory rites *sur la montagne*—which gathered together an audience of some one hundred thousand people—were a feminist politician and popular poets and musicians. Since the year was 1975, *Année Internationale de la Femme*, it was fitting that feminist figures take over from the dying patriarchal SSJB. It was also fitting that popular *chansonniers*—from the older Félix Leclerc to the young turks such as Gilles Vigneault—play a primary role in this *fête sauvage*. Vigneault's "Gens du pays" would henceforth take on the quality of a national anthem. These fêtes were populist identity rituals which fused the folk imagery and ideals of a socially progressive state which would protect the emerging nation as one family.

A year and a half after the *fête sur la montagne,* the nation celebrated the victory of the Parti Québécois voted in on November 15, 1976. The PQ was immediately active in remaking the government in a culturally specific Québécois image and in pushing through language legislation which would assure the survival of the *fait français* in North America. Rebellious nationalist fervor and national paranoia subsided as the population let the government take control.

In the year following the 1976 election, Lévesque declared June 24 the Québécois national holiday This was to be a secular manifestation, a continuation of the *fêtes sauvages* and *fêtes de quartier*.[19] The PQ government allotted funding to numerous municipalities and neighborhood communities who built mini-parades with bicycles instead of floats and mini-spectacles with local talent. Picnics, *breuveries*, and dancing in the streets were favored in lieu of pompous demonstrations of national self-importance or quasi-religious processions. The Société Saint-Jean-Baptiste did not receive any governmental support to celebrate the Saint Jean. For obvious reasons the new and yet-to-be-automnous state of Quebec needed to maintain its separation from a conservative Catholic past, to keep alive its populist image as heroes of the fête, and to reassure the Canadian and the Québécois population that the turbulent events manifested in the October Crisis were indeed history.

Saint Jean mass at the Saint Joseph Oratory in Montreal, 1980.
Photo: Jacques Lavallée, Studio Image en Tête.

38 Performing the Dream State

Fête sauvage in Old Quebec, 1978. Photo: Jacques Lavallée, Studio Image en Tête.

Notes

1. Lest names deceive, Blackburn is a long-established family name in francophone Quebec. Richard Blackburn is a well-known Québécois theatre director. Since the 1990 parade, he has produced other mass spectacles, including the 350th celebration of the founding of Montreal.

2. Anglo-Canadian nationalists retort that Jacques Cartier, this latter-day explorer of the New World, can hardly be considered the discoverer of Canada. John Cabot had already claimed the unmapped territory for the British crown when he reached the Newfoundland coast in 1497. Weinmann points out the ironies in this contemporary of Columbus—also born in Genoa, as Giovanni Caboto—landing in what would become Canada on June 24 or Saint Jean day (Weinmann 1987:68).

3. According to the *Guide éthnographique des fêtes de la Saint-Jean* published by the Confédération des Loisirs du Québec (1976), the maple leaf was adopted as national emblem by the Montreal chapter of the SSJB in 1836.

4. "Let us kill Saint John the Baptist! Let us burn the papier-maché traditions with which they have tried to build a myth around our slavery" (Vallières 1971: 20). "A bas le Saint-Jean-Baptisme" was a popular rallying cry of young radicals in the 1960s who viewed the saint as a symbol of submission, an archaic remnant of the Church's stronghold on the province. Marxist and nationalist, these rebels identified with liberation front movements in Africa and the Black Power movement in the United States. This association with slavery and liberation movements is evident in Pierre Vallières' *Les nègres blancs d'Amérique* [*White Niggers of America*] written from the Manhattan House of Detention for Men where he was held after demonstrating for *Québec libre* in front of the United Nations.

5. "...une de ces coutumes naïves que l'Eglise a conservées... et tournées à la gloire de Dieu" (From a 1923 pamphlet, *Saint Jean-Baptiste* by Father Alexandre Dugré, Montreal: Oeuvre des tracts).

6. The first commoners to travel from Old France were hardly "settlers" in that New France was principally a *comptoir d'exploitation* for the lucrative fur trade. The trappers and *voyageurs* were single males, frequently indentured, and totally dependent on native populations for their livelihood, indeed their survival. They were reputed to be as difficult for the French regency to keep in check as the Indians themselves. The *habitant* settling of families and farms on the banks of the Saint Lawrence—a systematic policy of land colonization

with New French peasantry working on the *seigneuries* [territories granted by the Crown to small nobles]—began in the 1620s.

7. Derived from the Latin *paganus* translated as "villager" or "rustic" in the 1993 New Shorter Oxford Dictionary, in medieval English *pagans* denoted both infidels and civilians, that is those who were not the soldiers of Christ. Throughout this chapter, I use the word pagan in its widest sense to refer to populations whose beliefs, customs, ideas, actions dissonate with hegemonic order or are not expressed through the dominant discourse.

8. Celebrated in March, Saint Joseph Day refers to the first patron saint of New France. The popular preference for Jean-Baptiste—both as a holiday and a boy's name so prevalent in the 19th century that it came to signify the French Canadian everyman—was recognized by the Church of Rome much later when Pope Pius X declared John the Baptist the patron saint of French-Canadians in 1908 (See "Pourquoi Saint-Jean Baptiste a-t-il été choisi patron des Canadians français?" by Gérard Turcotte, *L'information nationale* July-August 1981).

9. In my descriptions of the festivities organized by the Société Saint-Jean-Baptiste in the latter 19th and early 20th centuries, I frequently refer to texts drawn from the SSJB archives as cited by its official historian, Robert Rumilly. The Rumilly history and the pamphlets or other documents provided by the SSJB have proved useful in a reference capacity and in my gleaning a sense of the French-Canadian nationalism which drove the Duplessis era through the 1950s. Although many contemporary Québécois nationalists identify with the Patriot movement, very few would endorse the archaic and xenophobic nationalism often expressed by the SSJB.

10. "Ils ont frappé la tyrannie, Nous saurons l'abattre comme eux, Si le sort désigne une race ennemie, Veille sur nous, Saint Jean, fais-nous victorieux" (Rumilly 1975:20).

11. The flag of the *Patriote* rebellion—and the Canadian republic proclaimed by Robert Nelson—was a plain green, white, and red banner. Ostensibly dissociating from the revolt in Lower Canada, the SSJB multiplied symbols of a peaceful folk bound to nature and the church. The *Patriote* tricolor still appears on the Québécois national holiday.

12. According to the *Guide éthnographique des fêtes de la Saint-Jean* published by the Confédération des Loisirs du Québec in 1976 and distributed by the SSJB, children frequently appeared in the Saint Jean processions of the latter 1800s. The "little Saint John" was accompanied by other children representing historical figures such as Cartier, Champlain, or a Huron Indian. The

anonymous authors of the brochure interpret the child Saint Jean and his lamb as the metaphor of a young people.

13. The journalist Olivar Asselin (1874–1937) was a founder of the Ligue Nationalist whose ideologist was Henri Bourassa, politician, grandson of Louis-Joseph Papineau, and founder of the Montreal *Le Devoir* newspaper in 1910. The League advocated for economic reform in Quebec and against British imperialism during the Boer war in South Africa. First a virulent critic of what he viewed as the provincial, Catholic, passive nature of the SSJB, Asselin later became the society's president.

14. New Brunswick or *l'Acadie* vibrates in French-Canadian history and Longfellow's "Evangeline" as the land from which the Acadians were chased in the 1750s south toward Nova Scotia and New England, some proceeding to Louisiana where they became Cajuns.

15. Alberta and Saskatchewan joined the Confederation in 1905. Newfoundland became the tenth province in 1949, thus forming with the Yukon/Northwest territories the geopolitical unit known as Canada.

16. "O saint Jean-Baptiste, intrépide vengeur de la morale et du droit, précurseur du Messie, patron des Canadians français, éclairez nos esprits dans la recherche de la justice et assurez notre survivance par le maintien de nos institutions, de notre langue et de notre foi. Faites que nous conservions dans toute leur pureté les traditions de nos pères, afin d'accomplir les desseins de Dieu sur cette terre d'Amérique et de mériter le bonheur de la patrie céleste" (Rumilly 1975:312).

17. Settling in 1617, Louis Hébert, his wife Marie Rollet, and their three children are said to be the original *habitants* or French-Canadian settlers. In 1620 one of Hébert's daughters gave birth to the first child to survive in New France.

18. In *Jews & French Quebeckers, Two Hundred Years of Shared History*, Langlais and Rome explore the roots of anti-semitism in Quebec which played a role in the *Achat chez nous* campaign. Promoted by the SSJB, Montreal newspapers, and Catholic nationalistes, and endorsed by both Duplessis and the PLQ leader Godbout, the campaign urged Québécois to buy from their own people and to boycott Jewish businesses (Langlais & Rome 1991:96–100).

19. For descriptions of the Saint Jean in the early years of the PLQ government, see *Lachés lousses* (Chicoine et al. 1982).

Chapter Two
At the Gates of the Country

After the Party

Following the 1976 victory of the Parti Québécois, francophone Quebec seemed to be in the midst of one great national independence party. The PQ's promotion of the Québécois language and culture coupled with the prospect of sovereignty created an effervescence. The virtual nature of independence and the indeterminacy of the outcome contributed to the excitement of the latter seventies. However, the party could not go on perpetually nor could the Lévesque government forever stall submitting to vote the question of national sovereignty which had driven its electoral program.

At last held on May 20, 1980, the national Referendum put a definite damper on the national party. By a 20 percent margin of the vote, the Québécois said NON to national sovereignty. Considering the funds available to the federal anti-referendum campaign directed by Prime Minister Trudeau, and considering its scare tactics, which sent a good portion of the non-francophone populations fleeing with their money, and considering the precautionary and confusing terms in which the Referendum question was couched, it is surprising that even 40 percent responded by OUI. The 1980 Referendum was but a timid sounding of opinion vis-à-vis Québécois separation from the Canadian federation.

In fact, the issue addressed was not even separation, but the Québécois government's proceeding to negotiate with Ottawa toward a sovereignty with association status. Put to plebescite, this "having your cake and eating it too" did not fare well. Radical separatists—even though voting OUI—deplored the wishy-washy terms of the question. The non-francophone citizens were, as expected, predominately opposed to a separate Quebec. What appeared singularly depressing to the *indépendantistes* was that the majority of French-speaking Québécois had rejected sovereignty.

This defeat put a temporary damper on the national party, but not an end to nationalist passions or the Parti Québécois. Rarely have defeated political leaders been so acclaimed as when René Lévesque stepped out to announce the victory of the NON. The crowd wept and cheered. In the following elections Lévesque and the PQ would retain their popularity, remaining in power as impotent guardians of an apparently deflated nationalist dream for four more years.

Even more sobering than the defeat of the Referendum was the repatriation of the Canadian constitution in 1982, in spite of Quebec's veto. Refusing its own autonomy and the federal constitution,[1] Quebec was technically a no-man's state. The overriding of Quebec's veto, the supreme court's 1984 decision that the French-language Bill 101 was unconstitutional, and the defeat of the PQ in the 1986 provincial elections seemed to confine the dream of a sovereign Quebec to a symbolic closet through the end of the decade.

The Post-national Saint Jean

In the 1980s, although I recall numerous debates among friends and in the media about the lost dream of an independent and progressive Quebec—discussions frequently marked by a profound nostalgia or a bitter resignation—I never connected the Saint Jean to anything like a national holiday. Following the NON to independence, the (post)national fête seemed to flounder in search of an ideal. In the wake of the deflated dream, the Saint Jean eve neighborhood parties and June 24 picnics continued while organized festivities were held safely in check by corporate sponsors who packaged the event in "bigger is better" wrappings. The Saint Jean was stripped of political or symbolic significance.

In his analysis of the years following the Referendum—a period he dubs *la petite noirceur* [little darkness] as a parodic salute to the Duplessis era—the Québécois cultural critic, Jean Larose, cynically describes a 1981 attempt to resurrect the parade. Following on the defeat of the OUI and under the promise to keep politics out of the event, the 1981 celebration appears to Larose as a return to the "bon vieux nationalisme canadien-français" (Larose 1986:31). But it's worse, he claims, in that the effigy of the patron saint standing in front of the Saint Joseph Oratory is now ten feet high and is represented as an adult: "...this means that the 'grande noirceur' has perhaps survived the ordeal of modernity" (p. 31). The author goes on to cite the program of the parade, which invites the people "to become, once again, what we have always dreamt of being" (p. 41) and which boasts of the technological feats behind the construction of *chars allégoriques* [floats] which figure characters from Vigneault's *Gens du pays*[2]. The eighteen-foot high child, the thousands of feet of aluminum foil used, the giant photographs of past parades rising from the floats aggrandizes the icons yet drains them of significance. A passé image of the nation appears in postmodern representational contours.

Evacuating the political and riding under the logos of commercial sponsors, the 1980 festivities in Montreal streets and parks employed mass-spectacle techniques, tons of machinery and pyrotechnical megawatts, and projection devices which magnified popular Québécois artists. The beer companies which sponsored these events were so ubiquitous that the bottle appeared to have become the national emblem. It was not Quebec, but the state of Labatt or Molson or whatever brewery happened to hold the franchise of the fête.

Although there was flag waving and the ritual fireworks, these events did not seem to be the expression of national pride. Throughout the 1980s the threat of nationalist upheaval appeared buried in the past, contained in the mythological labyrinth of a history cut short of fulfillment.

1990: A Reason to Celebrate

Yet, at the close of the decade, three major political events rekindled the national dream in Quebec. The 1990 Saint Jean took place against a political backdrop marked by the resurgence of the language problem, NAFTA negotiations, and the collapse of the Meech Lake agreements concerning Quebec's status in the Canadian Confederation.

First, 1989 demonstrations in Quebec City, Montreal, and Ottawa erupted in reaction to a compromise the PLQ was negotiating on the language issue. In the fall and winter of 1989, popular forces—including adolescents who had grown up in the post-referendum era and who raised their voices much to the surprise of their elders—mobilized around the three-century issue of French-language survival in the Americas.

Second, much to the consternation of Canadian nationalists, Québécois politicians and financiers were promoting the North American Free Trade Agreement. The NAFTA debate was very heated in Canada and in Quebec. Many separatists saw free trade as opening economic doors to Québécois autonomy. Others saw it as a selling out to American capitalism and the ultimate end to the dream of a socially progressive sovereign Quebec state.

Third, negotiations for Québécois acceptance of the federal constitution, which would at last bring all the peoples of the Canadian mosaic under one cohesive law, were floundering at Meech Lake. In the 1987 talks Quebec had imposed five conditions which included its being recognized as a "distinct society" within the Confederation. Agreed upon by the ten provincial and the federal Prime Ministers, the Meech Lake Accord was to be ratified by the provincial legislatures by June 23, 1990. As the deadline approached, it became increasingly clear that the agreement would be nullified. The Newfoundland and Manitoba delegates were adamantly opposed. The crisis came to a head when Newfoundland withdrew from the agreement and Lucien Bouchard, a minister of the federal government and future Prime Minister of Quebec, resigned in protest to the modifications designed to make the agreement more acceptable to the other provinces. In Manitoba hostility toward Quebec's privileged status crystallized around the rights of the original conquered and minoritized peoples of North America: the Amerindian First Nations. Elijah Harper, a Native Canadian activist and member of the Manitoba legislature, had become known for his use of symbols such as an eagle feather and his stubborn resistance to any agreement concluded without the First Nations.

The image of a Canadian mosaic—which the federal government had so long touted to encompass the traditionally dissident province of Quebec, the Native Canadian communities, the immigrant communities who represented a substantial demographic proportion of the country, and the Canadian provinces themselves which split into economically privileged and underprivileged regions—became unglued, collapsing like a house of cards with the disintegration of the Meech Lake agreement.

In Quebec the collapse polarized *indépendantiste* sentiments which had been dormant. Polls showed a majority of the population favored separation. The first *fête nationale* of the new decade and the first official manifestation since the 1969 banning of the parade was prepared in an aura of expectation reminiscent of the mid-1970s. The context, however, was quite different. Marked by a divergence of political ideologies and an increasing awareness of the divisive nature of nationalism, occurring during the government of the PLQ—which has traditionally promoted individual rights, economic expansion, and federalism—the nationalism of 1990 Quebec differed from the Parti Québécois era where national subjectivity was founded on what was seen as the fulfillment of an historical legacy. The national subject that reinvented itself during the 1960s was again permutating and dividing.

Nowhere is this schizogenesis more evident than in Montreal, the urban stage of the 1990 Saint Jean fête at the center of this study. Montreal is one of the most cosmopolitan and intercultural cities of the Americas. The second most populated francophone city in the world, touted as a link between Europe and America, Montreal is also an entry port to a number of Canadian immigrants, passing through before stabilizing in other regions or electing home in Quebec. The city represents the paradoxical situation of

Quebec defining itself as a distinct society, but dependent on immigration to increase its population and symbolic capital. Montreal is a cosmopolitan center which exemplifies the eclectic quality of a globally spinning minority population and its need to extend beyond narrow nationalist mythologies to gain support for the sovereignty cause.

Montreal is a most appropriate space for a post-modern national ritual, striving for coherence among variegated elements and steeped in ambiguities since the nation celebrated is not officially a state. The year 1990 is a most appropriate time, because the promise of a nation-state was once again on the horizon. Its very liminality was a reason for Québécois to feel like celebrating, to rediscover *le goût de fêter*. In keeping with the liminal flavor of the virtual nation, the official theme of the 1990 national holiday was *Un pays à faire rêver* evoking an ideal dream country hovering on the threshold of reality. The title of the mass spectacle scheduled the evening of June 24 in Montreal was *Aux portes du pays* [At the Gates of the Country].

Saint Jean Eve in Montreal

The headline of the June 23 Montreal French and English newspapers announced MEECH EST MORT (*La Presse*) or MEECH IS DEAD (*The Gazette*). The Québécois Prime Minister Robert Bourassa declared "English Canada must clearly understand that whatever is said, whatever is done, Quebec is today and forever a distinct society, capable of ensuring its own development and destiny" (*The Gazette* 23 June 1990).

The day of the closure to the aborted Meech Lake agreement which fell on Saint Jean eve, I was in Montreal, ostensibly to continue my research but mainly to visit with my family and friends. I was staying with my friend Abla Farhoud, a Lebanese-Québécois playwright who lives in a cooperative on Hutchison Street. She invited me to a Saint Jean Eve supper organized in the courtyard of the coop. Here, Abla suggested with wry humor, I might find ethnographic data for my research on performing Québécois identity.

The *Coop de la rue Hutchison* lives in three two-story apartment buildings, rehabilitated with government funding and managed by the collective. On an economic scale, the members of the Hutchison Street Coop range between those on welfare or temporarily unemployed and those earning a comfortable living. Rents are designed on a sliding scale, with the collective assuming the financial responsibility of filling in the gaps in the up-and-down incomes of the ensemble of the residents. Although all of the adult members of the Hutchison coop have lived in Montreal for at least twenty years, not all were born in the city. On an ethnic scale, as designed by some nationalist Québécois census bureau, about half might fall in the category of "Québécois, pure laine, de race française" [dyed in the wool Quebeckers of the French race]. But these categories would be absurd to the Montrealers gathered here, who include a *Libano-Québécoise*, a *Belgo-Québécoise*, and an anglophone *Jamaïco-Québécoise*.

The meal was a couscous ordered from a North African restaurant and served with wine fabricated by the "Belgo-Québécoise" and aged in the cellars of the Coop. Dinner conversation centered on the Meech Lake talks and what might follow. Although the guests expressed excitement over the sheer indeterminacy of the moment, there was also a great deal of cynicism expressed toward political figures. All raked both Brian Mulroney, Prime Minister of Canada, and Robert Bourassa, Prime Minister of Quebec, over sardonic coals. Lamenting the void of leadership, most viewed politicians with a jaundiced eye either as *des incapables* [incompetent] or as vultures waiting to pick up the scraps. Yet, somewhere between the couscous and the dessert, someone remembered that Bourassa was to address the Québécois people on television that evening. The group persuaded one person to run upstairs and turn on his VCR recorder. Although none wanted to break up the party to go listen, the group entertained the idea that—who knows—this might indeed be an historical moment worthy of documentation.

Talk shifted to definitions of nationhood. One of the party exclaimed: "Do you know where Meech Lake is? It's in Quebec." And another responded that if we were going to talk about territory as a founding principle of the nation, we'd have to deal with the native populations first, that to speak of the French and the English communities as the two "founding peoples" of Canada was unspeakably arrogant in the face of the Indian nations.[3] Another expressed the idea that if First Nation rights were to be upheld within Quebec, Quebec itself had to be recognized as a state.

There was a prevailing resentment over the refusal to acknowledge the simple fact of Quebec's "distinct society" status within the Confederation. Although none considered English-Canada as a monolithic enemy Other, several of the party felt that Canadians in general did not understand *la réalité Québécoise* and were often ignorant of both the language and the history of Quebec. Particularly galling was the notion that Québécois might be simply another immigrant minority within the great "Canadian mosaic." The group viewed multiculturalism,[4] a word frequently appearing in federal discourse, with great mistrust. Multiculturalism was perceived as simply a reenforcement of anglo-domination, another ploy to erase the *fait français* from the Americas. The problem of the linguistic rights of minorities within Quebec—allophone or anglophone North Americans—could not be resolved until the threat of disappearance lifted, until *indépendance*. The conversation at this Saint Jean Eve supper can be resumed as an uncomfortable acknowledgement of the bipolar minority/majority position of Quebec: negotiating nationhood in the face of the anglo-hegemony of the continent, while doubting national legitimacy in the face of immigrant and First Nation claims.

While this conversation unfolded, the VCR was recording Bourassa's speech which appeared in next day's news. His talk centered on Quebec's constitutional future which the Prime Minister declared he would negotiate only with the Ottawa government, not the provinces. In the June 24 media, politicians made declarations which leaned in the direction of federal consolidation or Québécois separation. The Liberal Party leader—and future Prime Minister of Canada—Jean Chrétien urged the Québécois to remain calm, while Jacques Parizeau, leader of the PQ, called for new elections. Appearing that afternoon on television, Canadian Prime Minister Brian Mulroney proclaimed "It's a sad day for Canada" and wished the Québécois a happy holiday. Front pages and prime time were also devoted to the holiday itself, to histories of the Saint Jean and descriptions of the official festivities.

Although the Saint Jean fell conveniently on a Sunday, the official events were postponed because of the threat of rain. It did not rain that morning and a few thousand would-be spectators gathered outside of the Société Saint-Jean-Baptiste headquarters to protest the cancellation of the event. Others organized impromptu parades or proceeded with their plans. Interestingly, these included members of the Montreal Chinese community who celebrated with a Lion Dance procession. The popular fête was not about to be canceled because of the weather. Despite showers on the night of June 24, neighborhoods held street parties—*fêtes sauvages* reminiscent of the 1970s which to many represent the "real Saint Jean"—where groups danced in the rain to local bands or took shelter in cafés to toast the holiday.

Attending the Parade with "Outsiders"

The next morning was clear, a pristine blue and a sunlit stage for the national parade to roll down rue Sherbrooke, crossing the city from west to east, cheered on by thousands of spectators lining the avenue. Over 200,000 people participated in what was dubbed in next day's Montreal press "A manifestation of national solidarity never before seen" (*Le Devoir* 26 June 1990).

Despite this, I had found no Québécois friends with whom to attend the parade. Most of these were artists and most were also partisans of Québécois independence, yet they were apparently not interested in this staged demonstration of nationalist fervor. They were busy elsewhere or they might watch on television—which was broadcasting the entire eight-some hours of the event—or they were actually performing in the parade. One actor friend sourly informed me he would be playing a chimney sweep. I wound up going to the Québécois national celebration with two out-of-town friends I had met in Philadelphia and an *anglo-québécoise*. My friends Marcie, an American, and Jerry, a Zairian, introduced me to their hostess, Emily.

Although I had lived in Montreal for over four years, the afternoon I spent with Emily was the first prolonged contact I had ever had with an English-speaking Montrealer. The image I held of the city's anglophone population corresponded to that projected by the more vocal anti-Québécois groups such as the Alliance for the Preservation of English in Canada. Self-righteously proclaiming their minority status in Quebec, while fully enjoying the privileges of their majority status in North America, these groups are notorious for trampling Québécois flags and claiming fraternity with militant English-language-rights groups in Florida and California.

Anglo-fanatics are a group Emily would have nothing to do with. Native of an Ontario Mennonite rural community, Emily came to Quebec as a student in the 1970s. She had lived in Montreal for over fifteen years, shared in the excitement of the dream of independence, voted OUI in the *souveraineté-association* Referendum, and remained an ardent fan of Gilles Vigneault and other Québécois *chansonniers* who had fueled the nationalist movement. If Emily was not totally bilingual, her six-year old daughter who attended a francophone school was. While recognizing the necessity to speak French in a francophone community, Emily expressed anger at her daughter's being chided by playmates for speaking English with other anglophone children or her mother. Emily typifies the ambivalent insider/outsider, attached to Québécois culture, but recoiling from an excessive Québécois nationalism which would obliterate her difference or that of other immigrant minorities. Unlike Eastern European, African, Asian, or Caribbean immigrants to Quebec, Emily also represents the overwhelmingly dominant White-Anglo-Protestant majority in North America.

As we walked to the rue Sherbrooke, Emily made wry remarks about not wearing red, lest this be taken as a sign of Canadian federal allegiance. Along the way she bought a small fleurdelisé as a protective shield. As our improbable little group sought a strategic position on the crowded street, a flag-bearing Emily was approached by a reporter with a tape recorder.

Apparently taking her for a francophone but then distinguishing her accent, the interviewer quickly switched from French to English to ask whether Emily thought the parade might degenerate into violence as it had in the late sixties and what the collapse of the Meech Lake talks signified. Emily replied that the circumstances were different, that the atmosphere was auspicious, not to open revolt but perhaps to change. She was fairly sure there would be no violence, that the parade was "under control," but she could not predict the future of Québécois independence. During the interview, helicopters continually circled overhead.

Preliminary Signs: Helicopters, Flags and T-shirts

Before the parade began, signs framed the performance space. Small planes inscribed "Bonne fête Québec" in white puffs across the blue sky. Helicopters—the watchful eye of both the television cameras and the crowd control police—circled above. All of the Montreal police force had been mobilized to assure a peaceful event and the media were ubiquitous.

Flags constituted a floating border along the rue Sherbrooke stage. Windows and balconies lining the avenue were decorated with balloons and Québécois flags. Among the many spectators standing on either side of the street carrying the blue and white fleurdelisé, a few waved the green, white and red banner of the 19th-century Patriot movement. In an effort to theatricalize the street under the sign of a "unified nation," organizers had requested that spectators not wear any partisan political buttons or institutional uniforms, but that they dress in the blue and white colors of the Québécois flag. Some had complied, but more evident costuming were the faces painted with fleurs-de-lis and the T-shirts bearing slogans and cartoons which self-consciously signalled the renewed *indépendantiste* sentiment.

These T-shirts sold by vendors weaving through the crowd had become a flash-success cottage industry that June. Selling for from $5.00 to $15.00, they were imprinted with slogans such as *Enfin OUI René*. "At last YES René" playfully recalled the 1980 Referendum organized under René Lévesque. Vendors circulated during the entire parade, selling artifacts relating to the political context. Trinkets such as small vials of "Meech Lake Water," a red and blue liquid that remained separate however much the vial was shaken, sold for two Canadian dollars.

In these precursory signs of the parade, the event appeared more in the mode of playful parody than driven by nationalist passions or the anarchic fury which had disrupted the 1968 and 1969 parades. As Emily had indicated in her interview, the climate a decade and a half later was certainly different. Despite the reopening of the national dream, there seemed to be little need for all the precautionary measures surrounding the parade. True to the hopes of Richard Blackburn, director of the mega-spectacle, the event would unfold under the self-reflexive "sign of a controlled dream" (*La Presse* 23 June 1990).

Floating Allegories

Designed by performance and graphic arts professionals, the floats were lavish tableaux deployed over the full breadth of the avenue. The *Comité de la fête nationale* and other Québécois government agencies, unions and commercial corporations financed the spectacle, the total cost of which was estimated at 700,000 Canadian dollars (*Le Devoir* 26 June). The parade consisted of ten thematic units which broke down into some forty sequences, directed by nine designers and animated by over 2,000 performers. Each of the floats and the accompanying cortege comprised a progressive tableau stretching over two kilometers. The distance to be covered from the point of origin to the final destination at the *Stade Olympique* was approximately five kilometers. Sandwiched between the thematic floats were limousines bearing municipal and provincial government officials as well as back-stage producers of the fête.

The entire parade, from the head of the procession leaving the avenue du Parc and rue Sherbrooke intersection to the last float's reaching the stadium at Sherbrooke and Pie XII, would last some five hours. Although no single spectator could possibly view the entire performance, television cameras promised full coverage of the event. The ten themes of this "controlled dream" had been announced in the June 23 press under the following titles:

- *Le Mouton de Troie* [The Trojan Sheep]
- *Place aux femmes* [Make Way for Women]
- *Ecole au coeur du changement* [School, Heart of Change]
- *On s'affaire* [We are Busy/We are in Business]
- *La distance apprivoisée* [Domesticated Distance]
- *Nourrir le Québec* [Feeding Quebec]
- *Une force en mouvement* [A Force in Movement]
- *Les Arts au Québec* [The Arts in Quebec]
- *Les Couleurs de l'énergie* [The Colors of Energy]
- *Ouverture du Québec sur le monde* [Quebec Open to the World]

Although the parade was a material and structured representation, it was obviously other than this check list of *chars allégoriques* or the preordained number of performers and kilometers of theatricalized space. It was a series of floating allegories, symbolic clusters that could be interpreted according to each spectator's point of view. It was also a fête with its disorderly implications and defiance to structure.

In my reading I am as "dream analyst" seizing fragments of the performance which relate both to the celebration of progress—"thirty years of accumulated energy" borne by the magic of spectacle—and the reverse side of the modern nationalist narrative, the ironic which wafted through the event. The parade took place in the allegorical mode pushing toward the parodic. As a figurative treatment of *Saint Jean* history, the first tableau would frame the event as not only a look at the changes in the construction of a national subject, but as a metacommentary on the parade itself.

Le Mouton de Troie or the Problematic National Subject

It was not a military band which opened the parade but a troupe of mimes, acrobats, and cyclists. Juggling balls, blowing whistles, executing somersaults, or careening down the street on bicycles, monocycles, and tandems, these performers recalled the small alternative parades organized after the banning of the official parade. However, instead of substituting for the *chars allégoriques*, these cyclists and acrobats prepared the way for a monumental float of sophisticated symbolism.

The *Mouton de Troie*—an enormous and rather menacing skeleton of a sheep whose black metallic head flashed in the sunlight—invaded the street. The body of the animal was a gigantic carcass, a 28-foot-high frame on which perched twenty-four children dressed as *petits Jean-Baptistes*. Either settled on the animal's ribs or spilling out onto the pageant wagon, these boys and girls were between the ages of five and fifteen. Other youngsters holding thongs connected to the vehicle walked in front of, beside, or behind the float, apparently leading, accompanying or driving the Trojan Sheep. Some wore black T-shirts marked with the circled Y peace sign. Others wore imitation zebra and leopard skins.

Contingents of Montreal schools, the children also represented the multiracial face of the city. Many were what Québécois and Canadian governmental texts label "visible minorities." As the kids passed by with their gigantic animal in tow, they waved and mugged to the spectators lining the rue Sherbrooke, who—some of them probably proud parents—cheered on the cortege.

Iconically, the *Mouton de Troie* is a multi-layered allegory rich in poetic dissonance. The animal parodies the lamb of submission and the *ouailles* or obedient Catholic flock, the metaphor which has so strongly marked Québécois political lore. This lamb is not the innocent white lamb which first appeared, accompanied by the equally innocent child Jean-Baptiste, in the mid-19th-century processions. The sheep has grown to monstrous proportions, and it is not white but black. The *mouton noir* offers the reverse image of the "national" character: marginal, dissident, and obstinately refusing to follow the flock.[5] To top it all, the sheep, indicates the title, is actually a Trojan horse in disguise and full of surprise invaders.

Out of its entrails pour dozens of live children. If the sheep carcass represents an eviscerated myth, the children who take over the street represent the immediate reality of the parade, as well as discrepancies between historical inscriptions of *le petit Saint Jean* and the majority of the population. The children who occupy the symbolic creature and the street are not the cherubic, white, and solitary boy child of former times, but of both genders and a multiplicity of ages and ethnic origins which contrast sharply with traditional representations.

An interview (*La Presse* 24 June 1990) with the last traditional little *Jean-Baptiste* who rode in the 1963 parade Saint Jean highlights these contrasts. Michel Boisvert recalls his experience as a six-year-old portraying the boy saint in the 1963 Montreal parade. His memories include the blue and white float, the shepherd's staff topped with a cross, and the scratchy wool tunic he was forced to wear. Boisvert recalls being told to sit still and not to scramble for the money which appreciative spectators threw onto the float. The article features a picture of the thirty-three-year old truck driver holding a Québécois flag and his two-year old daughter in his arms. The curly blond and fair-skinned girl resembles her father, who was—he admits with a grain of pride and cynicism—*un petit Saint Jean typique*. Although the pictorial representation of the "typical little Saint John" had never corresponded to a French-Canadian genotype (nor to the Mediterranean patron saint for that matter), traditional iconography has systematically portrayed the national subject as a curly blond child.

The performers in the *Mouton de Troie* tableau are far from either the idealized *petit Saint Jean* or the negative projection of the obedient child. The youngsters are visibly not *Québécois pure laine* or "dyed in the (white) wool Québécois." They are a hybrid ensemble which shatters any notion of a monolithic national subject. And they do not seem to be obeying, but rather taking control of the street. They are not wearing the harsh wool tunic of penitents, but T-shirts proclaiming the born in the 1960s international peace movement and "wild animal skins." What emerges from the *Mouton de Troie* is a variegated tribe of *petits sauvages*.

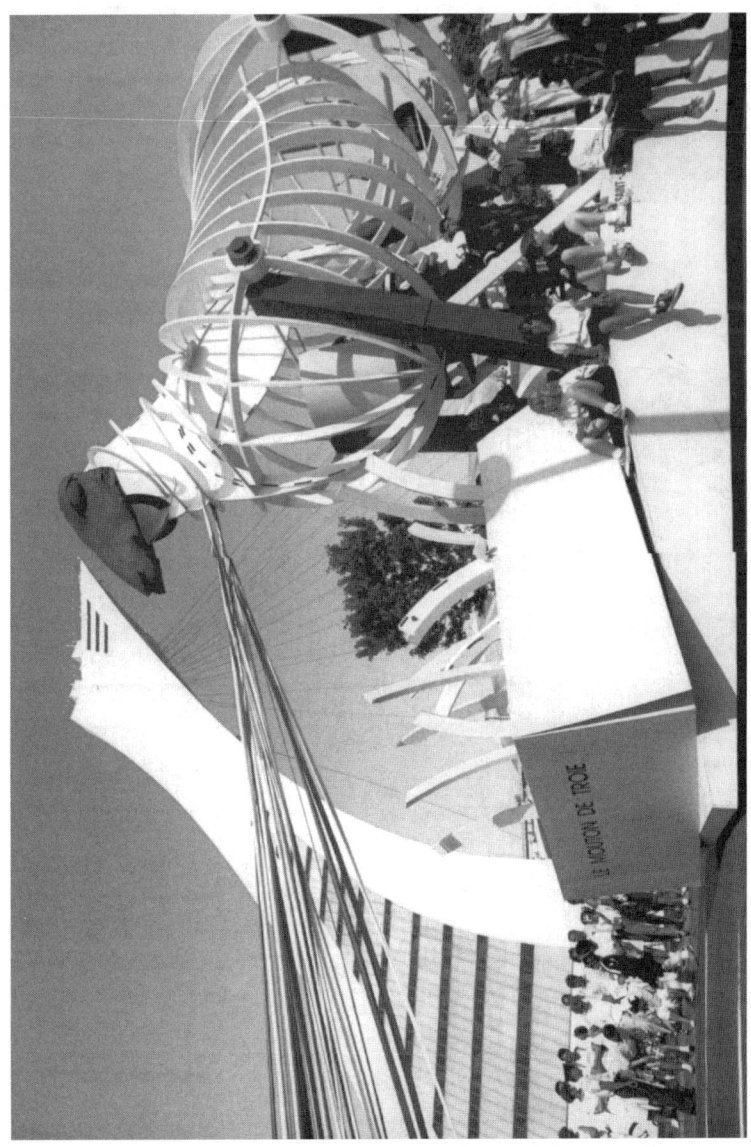

"The Trojan Sheep" reaching the Olympic Stadium. Photo: Jacques Lavallée, Studio Image en Tête.

56 *Performing the Dream State*

Des petits Saint Jeans sauvages. Photo: Jacques Lavallée, Studio Image en Tête.

The national subject is splintered and adulterated, a black sheep filled with multicolored children. The allegory of "The Trojan Sheep" is highly ambiguous. On one level, it is a subversive gift because the innocent lamb has been eviscerated to reveal an army of Québécois reinforcements. On another level, the very diversity of the icon and its ironic nature is another type of Trojan gift. The cortege disturbs essentialist notions of Québécois identity and throws *le peuple* into a postmodern limbo. Summations of the who, what, where, when of Québécois history are undermined by the projection of diversity and the self-referential frame of this peculiar national identity ritual.

This poetically playful representation of the national subject as a joyous fusion of multiple identities testifies to the inclusive quality of current québécois nationalism, the shift from *un petit peuple* to a modern nation welcome to all who accept its quirky history. This dream of an ethnically diverse but harmonious state introduces the dominant theme of the parade: the great modern dream of progress and prosperity for all.

A Celebration of Modernity

Although they are self-contained tableaux, grouped together the majority of the *chars allégoriques* describe a narrative of "thirty years of accumulated energies," a performance of the social, material and technological progress of Quebec since its official leap into modernity in 1960.

An eloquent example is the second float, entitled *Place aux femmes* [Make Way for Women]. The multi-referential title touches on various elements displayed in the passing cortege. *Place aux femmes* is a remnant of "women in their place," i.e. confined to hearth and home contrasted with occupation of the public space by Québécois women in the past thirty years. The expression could be construed either as imperative, an order to "Make way for women," or an accomplished fact of possession, "The space belongs to women." Both interpretations were pertinent to the unfolding spectacle which described the historical narrative of the *Québécoises*, from the granting of the vote to the seizing of political and economic power.

This progressive tableau opened with the figuration of an early 20th-century political campaign band wagon with an immense *urne électorale* [ballot box]. The float was pulled by men garbed as priests in robes and politicians in top hats. More top-hatted figures, as well as women in flowered garden party hats, stood at the head of the band wagon and saluted the crowd. The principal float was followed by a series of mini-floats, cartoon houses on wheels which were pulled by other men dressed as priests.

Women in 1940's bourgeois costume wearing little veiled hats, below the knees dresses, and small heeled shoes marched defiantly beside and behind the houses, whose doors were all flung open to reveal they had escaped domestic confines.

This cluster was followed by a group of marching women dressed in mechanic's overalls which announced the arrival of a huge red construction machine designed for excavating enormous cavities. A woman sat in the pilot's cabin, driving the monstrous machine which shot out shovels on tentacular mobile arms extending the width of the avenue. This strange mechanical ballet was directed by a dozen some women sitting on the machine, women dressed in overalls and coiffed with bandannas, women sitting in the driver's seat.

The *Place aux femmes* tableau closed with the passing of male-chauffeured, white and pastel convertibles. Here well-known *femmes politiques*—many dressed in garden party hats—sat waving at the crowd. In this progressive narrative, history begins with the vote and ends with accession to political power. A tidy line between the granting of the vote and the rise to governmental authority is drawn, as if all women driving sophisticated machines or riding in convertibles were included in the great national progressive dream.

The political underpinnings of this narrative of feminist liberation are not surprising since 1990 marks the fiftieth anniversary of women's right to vote in the province of Quebec. In 1940, twenty-two years after acquiring federal voting privileges, *les Québécoises* were granted the provincial vote. This fell in the four-year hiatus of the conservative Duplessis regime, period in which the Liberal Party of Quebec was in power, as it is again during the 1990 Saint Jean. Some of the women in the convertibles represent the twenty-three delegates to the Québécois *Assemblé nationale*, six of whom are members of the Cabinet. Out of 125 delegates this might not appear a proportional representation of half the population, but considering that over the forty years which followed the granting of the vote, only seven women had ever been elected to government office, the present composition of the Assembly appears as an accomplishment and a promise of further progress.

This narrative of women's liberation thus originates with an octroi, the vote granted by politicians and priests pulling the band wagon, and ends with a seat in the government and in the chauffeured convertibles. In the middle are two other significant clusters: women deserting their homes and women driving machines. The first of these relates to the explosion of the myth of the French-Canadian matriarchy. The second relates to an egalitarian and technological dream.

"Make Way for Women." Photo: Jacques Lavallée, Studio Image en Tête.

The priests pulling the deserted houses and the women marching defiantly in the public space evoke an historical articulation, a period when women ceased producing the great French-Canadian Catholic family. In a dramatic demographic turnover, the birth rate plummeted and the average Québécois woman would move from the position of one of the highest producers of children in the world to among the lowest.[6] Birth control and a major shift in how women were defining their roles inevitably challenged the concept of a French-Canadian "race" or nation of blood brothers. Both *la foi* and *la race* of the nationalist trope of the Duplessis era were to disintegrate with this demographic transformation, leaving only *la langue* as identifying pole.

The founding fathers of this "matriarchy," who are represented by the priests, the institution of the church and not the biological fathers who are traditionally absent from the foyer, are under the illusion of pulling an institution. But the houses are already empty. The matriarch has left home. She has deserted the foyer to appear in the driver's seat of a mechanical wonder. The physical passage of women driving a mammoth machine figures the symbolic passage into modernity.

Assimilated into the narrative of ascension to political power, this sequence also represents the egalitarian ideals that have marked Québécois nationalist rhetoric in the latter twentieth century. As Dominique Clift has pointed out in a penetrating analysis of the history of Québécois nationalism (Clift 1982), both the periods of inward-turned, obscurantist nationalism of the Duplessis era and the independence-oriented nationalism of the Parti Québécois era have incorporated egalitarian ideals into their rhetoric. That there did exist an economic and educated elite, a professional class within the francophone nation, did not detract from the principle that the French-Canadians formed a nation of down-trodden peers. Curiously, the Liberal Party which has traditionally favored the notion of individual fulfillment rather than that of the nation, and that has promoted laissez-faire economics rather than the providing welfare state, has frequently been implemental in the nationalist dream. In the transition from the feudal nationalism of the Duplessis era to the rise of the folk-state during the Parti Québécois government to the 1990 emphasis on "the best deal" for an economically viable independent Quebec, the Liberal Party has been the architect of nationalism.

The single ideological force that runs through these diverse forms of nationalism and liberal economics is the egalitarian principle of all are created equal. And it is this principle which runs through the entire representation: women can escape their confinement and subordination to become political agents; immigrants can achieve a position in the nation; the nation as a whole is marching forward.

Of all the tableaux, *Place aux femmes* comprised the most literal reference to social history and the most linear construction of the parade. Yet the majority of the forthcoming floats reflected the dominant theme of Quebec's advance from the *Révolution tranquille* to its *Ouverture sur le monde*, title of the last float. A narrative of progress and a modernist dream of equality and social harmony underlay the master narrative of the parade.

L'école au centre du changement featured children pushing giant blocks inscribed, on one side, with historical data concerning the reform of education since the Duplessis era. The large letters on the other side of the blocks assembled to form the slogan: *Québec, je t'aime en français*. The tableau indicates the crucial role the democratization of education played in the Quiet Revolution and how vital French-language education is in expanding and consolidating the franco-minority nation. As in the *Mouton de Troie* tableau, many of the children were members of "visible minorities."

The *On s'affaire* [We are Busy/We are in Business] cortege featured giant computers and men and women in business suits who scurried busily down the rue Sherbrooke, brandishing attaché cases and waving hastily to the crowd. Access to the corporate world for French-Canadians, even those living in the commercial center of Montreal, is of relatively recent history. The Québécois "affairistes" or entrepreneurs—terms of admiration or contempt according to the ideology of the interlocutor—became a major force of development as the dominant English-Canadian business class began pulling its marbles out of the game during the panic surrounding the 1980 referendum. With the PLQ's ascension to power and the Free Trade agreement with the United States, the Québécois business class rose to a dominant position in the latter 1980s. The *On s'affaire* tableau ironically reinforces the possibility of national economic viability while reducing the symbolic capital of the national subject: the Québécois, underdog and poet, condescending to the will of the almighty dollar. The *affairistes* all wore the uniform of Wall Street.

Other tableaux cited Quebec's capturing of resources and the economy. "Feeding Quebec," sponsored by a consortium of local supermarkets, featured tractors pulling wagons of live sheep, cows, and pigs, followed by a float with a giant cornucopia of papier-maché vegetables. "A Force in Movement," sponsored by local unions featured a Montreal *métro* car and an 18th-century frigate riding an ocean comprised of hundreds of blue and white signs waving in synchrony. "The Colors of Energy" represented Manic 5, the quasi-legendary dam built on the Manicougan River in the late 1960s, popular symbol of Quebec's economic growth and the nationalization of hydro-electric resources.

"Quebec Opening to the World," the last float of the parade, featured a giant globe twirling on its axis and surrounded by people in national costumes carrying the flags of many nations. The official pageant, which had opened with a picture of internal diversity, closed with a tableau of global diversity. Projecting Mother Earth as a harmonious community of nations in which Quebec could take its place, this float punctuated the last line to the parade's narrative of progress.

Yet it would be reductive to describe the parade solely as a modernist dream. Although the representation successfully eradicated the pain of history to portray a positive picture of the nation, disturbing elements shot through the performance. One was the darker side of modernity as seen through two sequences of the procession—a silent salute to the homeless and a float focused on ecological devastation—which were not mentioned in the announcements of the parade or the reports of the following day. The other disruptive element was the fête itself, which continually threatened to flow over the boundaries of the "controlled dream."

Fêtes and troubles-fête

Discordant notes interrupted this performance of an American dream *à la québécoise*. One such note was the fête which broke out in spurts, unsettling the boundaries between the spectacle and the audience. The other were *troubles-fête* [party poopers], sour notes that sounded in this celebration of modernity.

The festive note was appropriately sounded by the performance artists who had prepared the celebration. First announced as *Arts au Québec*, this title shifted to *Loges du parterre* [Ringside seats]. The tableau might have been a reminder of the important role artists have played in the politics and representation of *la Nation*, but it proved more an indication that this was a gigantic street party. This float dedicated to the arts in Quebec consisted primarily of musicians and dancers who blurred the boundaries of "high and low art," classical ballet and Quebec folk dances. Limousines carrying personalities, local artists, directors, and even critics followed. The spectacle was not confined to the float; dancers stationed on the balconies overlooking the rue Sherbrooke periodically danced to whatever the music of the passing cortege.

Another tableau entitled "Mastering Distance" featured Brazilian and other Afro-Caribbean music which is highly popular in Montreal. People in the street began to move to the music while on the balconies young ballerinas in white tutus rubbed bodies in the *lambada*. People ran along side the float or jumped onto the band wagon to dance with the performers. For a brief moment the fête threatened to lap over the representational boundaries of the "controlled dream."

Contrasting to the joyous anarchy of the fête were two sobering tableaux: an elaborate float entitled *l'Arbre désenchanté* [The Disenchanted Tree] and a stark cortege prepared by the Montreal chapter of the *Armée de Salut* [Salvation Army]. A negative travesty of the "The Enchanted Tree" fairy tale, the *Arbre désenchanté* float depicted soot-covered chimneys and skeletal trees from whose branches hung the debris of civilization. Reverse side of the modernist dream, the tableau portrayed an ecological nightmare. An even more dissonant note to the narrative of progress rang in the Salvation Army's procession. This was not a float but a silent cortege of men and women marching beside a park bench pulled on castor wheels. The bench, a freshly-painted green, bore a small sign in French reading: "The money for this float has been donated to the homeless." In the midst of all the mega-structures extolling material accomplishments and social harmony, the empty bench signalled the existence of those absent from the great feast, the increasing number of *sans abris* in Montreal. Anonymous except for their title as "homeless," these street people did not appear to be part of *la Nation* invited to take possession of the national stage at the end of the parade.

Marching to the "Gates of the Country"

The media had invited the spectators to join in the march behind the banner following the last float. The banner proclaiming QUEBEC EN MARCHE extended the breadth of rue Sherbrooke. Wearing the colors of the flag or not, eagerly waving flags or hesitating to step into the street, flocks of people lining the side walks joined the tail end of the parade. The procession swelled as it moved toward the stadium, where a *salut au drapeau* would close the afternoon event.

My friends and I looked at each other and shrugged "why not?" before joining the crowd occupying the rue Sherbrooke. Marching is hardly the word for the disorderly group which thronged through the street. Most people were singing Vigneault's (un)official national anthem, which captured nationalist aspirations in the latter 1970s. A curious hymn to the nation that—instead of speaking of military might such as the "bombs bursting in air" of the U.S. anthem or of racial superiority such as "qu'un

"Québec en marche." Photo: Jacques Lavallée, Studio Image en Tête.

sang impur abreuve nos sillons" of the French anthem—speaks of love. *Gens du pays, c'est à votre tour de vous laisser parler d'amour* [People of the country, it's your turn to hear about love] is a popular melody appropriate for any celebratory occasion in Quebec, from a child's birthday party to the national holiday.

With a good deal of self-consciousness and gusto, Emily and I joined in the song. Since Jerry and Marcie were totally mystified, I suggested the three of us try the South African liberation hymn. We gave it a try, but it was impossible to sing in total dissonance with the surrounding mass. In any case, we had problems remembering the lyrics. As we walked down rue Sherbrooke, I heard a woman exclaim "Mais c'est Lucien Bouchard." The enormously popular Québécois political figure who would become Prime Minister of the province five years later was mingling with the crowd.

Since neither the Olympic stadium nor the subway could contain all 200,000 of the fêtards, the media had directed participants to choose between assembling at the *stade olympique* in down-town Montreal or proceeding to the evening festivities on Sainte-Hélène island, at the outskirts of the city. My friends and I opted for the evening show and moved toward the subway. Although the crowd-control police had assured safe passage, Emily remained very nervous. She continued to wave her little Québécois flag and arranged to meet back at her place in case we lost each other.

We arrived safely on the island and "Aux portes du pays," as the evening event was titled. The guards at the gates of this country, bounded by a metal fence and the waters of the Saint Lawrence, verified that no one brought in arms or their own alcohol, since *la bière Labatt* held the franchise for the evening event. Later that evening, as the terrain filled up, the security guards were forced to refuse would-be spectators access "aux portes du pays."

Our group moved to the graveled space which stretched from the stage and camera platforms to the beer and hot-dog vending tents. We staked out our small territory and sat on our bags or sweaters. An immense screen, which would project a larger-than-life image of the performers, dominated the performance arena. A sea of Québécois flags waved across the space, blocking out even the massive screen. Cries of *Assis* or "Sit down" (so we can see) vied with cries of *Debout* or "Stand up" (the legendary cry of Québécois separatists). The media estimated over 100,000 spectators were present for the evening event.

The spectacle per se opened with a speech by Jean Duceppes, the aging theatrical director and *vieux nationaliste* who had long militated for Québécois independence and played a major role in organizing the 1990 *fête nationale*, who had instructed the population to wear the blue and white colors of the fleurdelisé and rode next to Montreal's mayor in the first limousine of the parade. On the brink of realizing a national dream and in what would be his last public appearance, Duceppes tottered to the microphone to announce the opening of the show and to wish the audience *Bienvenue aux portes du pays*. "Quebec is our only country," he declared to the clamor of the crowd.

This welcoming message would be repeated by all of the popular singers featured in the program—which included Gilles Vigneault himself, composer of *Gens du pays*, a poet, a fiddler, and an expert dancer of the jig—and younger *chansonniers* such as Michel Rivard and Paul Piché, as well as Diane Dufresne, the brassy and versatile Québécois international star, and an emerging singer, Laurence Jalbert.

After Duceppes' introduction, Michel Rivard greeted the public with a *Bienvenue chez vous* [Welcome to your home] which brought cheering audience members to their feet wildly waving flags, accompanied by more cries to "sit down" echoed by "stand up." Continuing once the clamor died, Rivard played with the defunct Meech Lake agreement and the improbable notion of Canadian unity by inviting the audience to tell the time across the continent: "In British Columbia it's six o'clock; in Ontario it's nine o'clock; in Newfoundland it's nine thirty... et ici, c'est bien trop tard" [and here it is much too late]. Newfoundland's peculiar half-hour time zone and its prime minister's refusal to even submit to vote the Meech Lake agreement were fodder for the singer's joke. In any case, Rivard claimed, in Quebec independence is overdue. Then the *chansonnier* welcomed non-francophone tourists and immigrants, *anglophones et allophones* to an idyllic nation. *Québec, pays de rêve*, a utopia *sans racisme, sans sexisme, et sans violence*.

Full of references to a dream nation of harmony and joy, the spectacle also vibrated with political reality. "Non, non, non, je changerai pas de ton. Oui, oui, oui, je prendrai le nom du pays," chanted the performers. The crowd shouted back "On veut un pays." Diane Dufresne launched a song declaring "I am from a Quebec with new wings" while a giant white bird fluttered its wings above.

The 1990 Saint Jean on the Ile Sainte-Hélène ended in different manners. The popular media stars, lined along the front of the stage and projected onto the giant screen, joined hands to sing *Gens du pays* with the audience. Disparate groups gradually moved from the "Gates of the country" to the gates of the subway. Some lingered on Sainte Hélène Island to see the closing *feu de joie*, the Saint Jean bonfire organized by the SSJB, which recalled the pagan fires of solstice lore, but which were primarily designed to keep too many citizens from clogging the exits and the subway trains.

I said goodbye to Emily, Jerry, and Marcie at a subway intersection and returned to rue Hutchison. My friend Abla was curled up on her sofa watching television, where the last sparks of the bonfire were broadcast live. "Alors... C'était beau?" she asked with a yawn. In the quiet room with the fête reduced to a few dying embers on a small screen, the gigantic street party I had just witnessed seemed unreal.

Further Dream Interpretations

The 1990 *fête nationale* was front page news in all the Montreal papers the following day. For the francophone press, the event was seen as a manifestation of Québécois national pride and solidarity never before seen. The enthusiasm of the crowds marching to the stadium and the chanting of "On veut un pays" [We want a country] was interpreted as a declaration of independence, a street referendum with a resounding OUI. A well-known actor stated: "In the soul of the Québécois, sovereignty is already a fact" (*La Presse* 26 June 1990).

Many articles mentioned the calm and maturity the participants had shown. A credit to the organizers, but also to the improvised logistics of the over 200,000 fêtards occupying the public space, the event did appear a "controlled dream." The press interpreted this as the sign of a dignified and adult nation ready to assume its own destiny. Even the traditional rebel projection of the Québécois character was absorbed affectionately into the national event. When the fleudelisé—wrapped by high winds around its pole—refused to unfurl during the salute to the flag at the stadium, Nicole Boudreau, director of the Comité des fêtes, declared "You see, our flag is as rebellious as we are" (*Le Devoir* 26 June 1990).

Other accounts capitalized on how immigrant communities had participated in Saint Jean festivities. The mayor of Montreal, Jean Doré, remarked that this event brought together not only *Québécois de souche*, but Québécois of all origins (*La Presse* 26 June 1990). Nothing in the media coverage suggested any problems which might disturb the image of a joyous, mature, diverse but united nation. The Salvation Army's silent march for the homeless and the ecologically-oriented "Disenchanted Tree" float which had caught my attention were not even cited as part of the parade. Except for the brief mention of a group of skinheads who had appeared bearing Canadian flags before being disbanded, there were no discordant notes. No one was to rain on this parade and nothing was to tarnish the dream, not even an ironic comment on how grounding the nation in the dream and the collective euphoria of the fête was in itself problematic.

A retrospective analysis of the performance framed as *Un pays à faire rêver*, or in the intriguing terms of the parade's director, as a "controlled dream... a group therapy" (*La Presse* 23 June 1990) opens ontological questions as to the nature of the national subject and nationalism itself. Who is the subject dreaming and who is being dreamt? Does the subject have a national Québécois character? Or is this an American dream articulated in French? And why is the parade, an overtly theatrical representation, depicted as a "group therapy"? Is someone sick? Does the nation need healing?

As a theatrical representation the 1990 Saint Jean effectively portrays a new view of the national subject. For the first time the Montreal parade depicts not the glorified figures from French Canadian past nor *gens du pays* folk heroes, but a culturally diverse and economically grounded, globally-oriented people. Even those who are excluded from this dream of harmony and progress can meld into the representation without fissures appearing in the collective subject. In the ephemeral moment of the performance the subject emerges with an unnatural wholeness. In the utopia—the out of time/space—of the fête, the nation appears as a singular entity.

Paradoxically this politically charged ritual glosses over political dissonance.[7] The 1990 Saint Jean is steeped in utopian ideals: material progress, the meshing of multiple cultures, the peaceful realization of statehood which appears just within reach. These ideals appear in many national holidays, but specific signs mark this nation as Québécois. It is a peculiar patriotic event which rides under a banner of lilies and opens with bicycles rather than military bands. And what is this odd national anthem sung throughout the celebration and which speaks not of victory but of desire? "People of the country, it is our turn to hear about love" makes little sense to citizens of more powerful, established nations founded on military might, star-gazing at their conquests like the United States or crushing the enemy Other like the French. What the poet invites the "people of the country" to contemplate is the heart of desire itself.

Although I am not assuming that all Québécois are poets, a status that would probably be hotly denied by the business class, I am pointing to a poetic motor which has continually driven Québécois nationalism, a unique propensity to reify *l'imaginaire québécois* as if it were a national resource. Examples of the collective imaginary referred to as an organ of the national body or as a national bank abound. Pierre Bourgault, ardent nationalist and leftist intellectual who participated in the 1970s independence movement, speaks of the Québécois as *un peuple à l'imaginaire mutilé* [a people whose imaginary has been mutilated] (Bourgault 1989:119). Heinz Weinmann, literary scholar and immigrant to Quebec, has based two major works on his reading of the Québécois imaginary (Weinmann 1987, 1990). The metteur-en-scène, Richard Blackburn, speaks of the parade he is preparing as a manifestation of a specifically Québécois imaginary that is *folle et débridée* [crazy, unbridled] (*La Presse* 23 June 1990). In these tropes the imaginary is figured as an individual limb, as a national psyche, and as a wild force similar to natural energy.

It is the very power of the imaginary that is at stake in these definitions of national identity. What is being confronted in the urban ritual of the 1990 Montreal Saint Jean fête is less the dream of nationhood than the power of the dream. The ability to draw energy from the symbolic—which national rites of more powerful nations such as the United States do naively—this Québécois rite does self-consciously. Projected into the imaginary, both the subject and the nation appear in their self-referential theatricality and their intrinsic ambiguity.

The minority Québécois nation might emerge as a utopic state under the sign of progress and harmony, if this in itself were not a dream state, if the *gens du pays* were really a cohesive whole, if the motor driving the dream were more than desire itself. If, however, the state of Québec were to become a political reality, the nation would lose what might be its most precious commodity: the dream itself.

Notes

1. The Canadian Constitution voted by the British parliament in 1867 could not be modified by the federal government as long as it remained in London. The document Queen Elizabeth handed over to Ottawa has not to this day been ratified by Quebec. Any argument concerning Quebec's linguistic policy or even its right to secede is *ipso facto* subject to cancellation by a constitution whose legitimacy has not been recognized in Quebec.

2. Adulated in popular song and the quasi-national anthem, "gens du pays" are evoked recurrently in Vigneault's poems. The "people of the country" cited in this rendition include "people of paper, of wood, of print; of the sea and the wind, of fishing; of dance and song; of nature, of sports, of pride... *gens d'aujourd'hui à fabriquer demain.*" Larose (1987:36) deconstructs these tropes as a regressive fascination with an idealized self.

3. For obvious reasons Native Canadians have been generally hostile to the Québécois national project. The Québécois have big symbolic and territorial stakes in gaining the support of "Native Québécois" who comprise about 1% of the province's population. Seeing parallels between their histories, Québécois have been sympathetic to First Nation nationalism. This popular sympathy for the cause was, however, severely put to test at the end of the 1990 summer during a confrontation between a group of Mohawk activists and the town of Oka in Quebec near the Ontario and New York border.

4. Translated by Jean Papineau as *Le Marché aux illusions: La méprise du multiculturalisme*, Neil Bissoondath's *Selling Illusions* (1994) is a critique of the paternalist nature of state multiculturalism which encourages the production of folklore but stamps out any minority pretense to political power. The success of the translation is an indication of how pertinent Bissoondath's deconstruction of multiculturalism appeared to Québécois intellectuals.

5. Describing the parade in the June 26 *Le Devoir* in an article entitled "Les concepteurs ont proposé une vision novatrice du défilé," Paul Cauchon remarks that the *mouton noir* is "a wink at the past, symbol of a Quebec that is stronger and stronger, or image of a 'black sheep' who does what he pleases." The reporter applauds the innovative aspect of the parade yet complains about the abstract quality of some tableaux, in particular *Place aux femmes* which followed *Mouton de Troie*. To anyone such as my out-of-town friends unfamiliar with the history of the parade, the *Mouton de Troie* was inordinately abstract and quite bewildering, whereas *Place aux femmes* connected to a more universal women's rights struggle.

6. The demographer Lyse Frenette points out that although Québécois fertility rates began to decline toward the end of the 19th century, the province's rates remained the highest in the western world through the late 1950s (Henripin & Martin 1991:67).

7. I do not mean to dismiss the political implications of this manifestation and what the 1990 event predicted for the future of the Québécois independence movement which, as the 1995 Referendum would prove, was strengthened. What I do wish to convey is that a cohesive national identity englobing all voices exists only in the imaginary or in the fleeting moment of the performance.

II

OF COMMODITIES AND KIN

Salut vieille branche!
A Street Comedy in Old Quebec

The Professor (Nicole Eva Morin). Photo: Pierre Dessureault.

Vous êtes au bazar, celui du Québec de cette fin de siècle... C'est une "vente de garage" de notre imaginaire, de nos vieilles peurs et de nos espoirs...

Le Québec est devenu un bazar. Tout s'y vend, tout peut s'y acheter.

Daniel Latouche
Le Bazar

[You are in the bazaar of fin-de-siècle Quebec. It's a "garage sale" of our imaginary, of our old fears and hopes...

Quebec has become a bazaar. You can sell anything here; you can buy anything here.]

PROFESSEUR: Justement, j'ai une couple de lignées à vendre, ça remonte à 1663. J'vends pas cher...
[I just happen to have a few lineages for sale, dating back to 1663. And cheap.]

TRASH: Ma lignée ne m'intéresse pas. Par contre, si t'as une ligne à vendre...
[I ain't interested in my lineage. But if you're selling a line (of dope)...]

Théâtre Parminou
Salut vieille branche!

National identity is a symbolic nexus grounded in the slippery terrain of the imaginary. In *Imagined Communities* Benedict Anderson (1991) has amply demonstrated that the cohesion of any nation which came into being between the 18th and 20th centuries is based on imaginary constructs. In Quebec—as in other minority nations embedded in modern states—reliance on the imagination becomes even more acute. The minority nation, which exists principally along the disputed border between the imaginary and political reality, depends heavily on the cultural production which keeps alive images of a collective identity rooted in history and genealogy.

But what happens when history and genealogy are exposed as national myths instead of founding truths? When the past, the family, and the imaginary itself—the "natural resources" supporting the national dream—are viewed as a museum of passé images? They become, as the political scientist and essayist Daniel Latouche (1990:25) points out, "an attic filled with *vieilleries*, with old stuff." Reified history—remnants of the founding families of Nouvelle-France and the 18th-century *Conquête* thrown in with myths born thirty years ago at the birth of modern *Québec*—are subject to being bartered off in the great garage sale of "our imaginary, of our old fears and hopes..."

> It's amazing how much outdated stuff we've managed to accumulate in only thirty years. So much memorabilia that one wonders if there will be room in our attic for the new myths which are already showing signs of age and need to be protected from the elements: Québécois entrepreneurship, the international opening, the search for excellence, the technological turn (Latouche 1990:25).

Latouche is drawing his metaphor from the 1980s and the promise of economic expansion: NAFTA, free trade, global markets, technological expertise, and an economically viable Quebec. But the symbolic market the commentator speaks of is an internal one: the Québécois garage sale is still a neighborhood affair. Who would perceive the sentimental value behind the objects—used as they might be—if not the Québécois? Too old to be functional, too ordinary and too new for rare antiques, yet too priceless to trash, the images must be recycled within the community. Or sold to the newcomer, the immigrant trying to get a foot-hold into this curious community.

Latouche's imaginary bazaar has all the paradoxical earmarks of an inside joke. The book's target audience is the *nouveau Québécois*, the contemporary immigrant to Quebec, who is being initiated into the national community through a self-deprecating burlesque: the nation is but a collection of worn symbols, but we cannot bear to throw them away. The underpinnings of the imaginary bazaar are two-fold. First, the Québécois symbolic and historic nexus is self-consciously represented as a local commodity. Second, the recognition of this commodification is only possible because we—*nous, les Québécois*—share cultural assumptions and can laugh at ourselves. If you can enjoy the joke as an affectionate poke at the nation, you may become part of *la famille*.

The "national garage sale" of Québécois identity myths anchored in founding families and history constitute the driving motor of *Salut vieille branche!*, a 1989 Parminou street comedy performed in Old Quebec City. The title of the production initially denotes some of the contradictory elements driving the performance. "Vieille branche" or "old branch" refers to the family tree rooted in botanical metaphors and ages gone by. Appropriately, the word *salut* translates both as an archaic greeting [hail] or a contemporary greeting [hi]. Thus, when juxtaposed to the sacred family tree, "Salut vieille branche" connotes respect for and an almost flippant familiarity with the ancestors.

The production implies a nostalgia for historic kinship which is repeatedly undermined by the self-conscious reification of roots and the parodic underpinnings of the production. Here both history and the collective subject become problematic. Can genealogy be the diachronical network of a collective Québécois subject if history and kinship are products of the present, commodities to be sold in the contemporary Québécois bazaar? The complex intertwining of historical, symbolic and political roots in this parodic performance reveals why parody itself is such an appropriate vehicle of fin-de-siècle Québécois identity.

Chapter Three
Overtures

The Théâtre Parminou

Salut vieille branche! was the 1989 contribution to a series of street-theatre comedies based on Québécois history that the Parminou Theatre had begun producing in 1980. Most of the six creators[1] of this production had been working with the Parminou since its founding in the early 1970s. All had been involved periodically in the annual historical productions performed for summer visitors on the Place Royale of Old Quebec City. Since their inception these historical productions have been financed by the *Direction du patrimoine* of the Québécois Ministère des affaires culturelles [MAC].

The MAC is one of the principal sponsors of the company, whose income has depended mainly on government subsidies—provincial and federal[2]—and social organizations such as unions or cooperatives. Except for periodic *spectacles maison* [house productions] created for the general public—a sort of luxury forum which allows the actors to explore issues outside of contractual demands—the company does not rely on box office receipts for its survival.

Founded in 1973 as the *Coopérative des travailleuses et travailleurs en théâtre des Bois-Francs*, the Théâtre Parminou is structured both financially and artistically as a cooperative. On a rotational basis, all permanent members of the company have held financial, promotional, artistic, and general housekeeping responsibilities. A theatre company which has sought to maintain a communal mode of operation for over two decades, the Parminou scrupulously selects contracts which correspond to their ideological orientation and commitment to produce theatre for *les gens ordinaires*.

In a document produced in 1991 to commemorate the company's eighteenth birthday, Maureen Martineau—one of the cooperative's first members and one of the four actors in *Salut* wrote: "Without locking itself into a closed doctrine, the Parminou Theatre is a collective which continues to favor the search for a popular and accessible theatre which is both innovative and relevant."[3]

This search for a Québécois populist theatre has not been a purely formalistic concern but an active effort to establish a grass-roots foundation. One of the meanings of Parminou is "among us." Rejecting both classicist high art and the artistic ghettos of the metropolitan avant garde, the company has sought to reach a public outside of habitual theatre goers. In the early 1970s the Parminou established its base in Victoriaville. This town is situated in Bois Francs, a region midway between the cultural capitals of Montreal and Quebec City.

Yet Victoriaville—which hosts an international new music festival—is hardly a cultural hinterland, nor is the Parminou really a grassroots theatre. The troupe is composed of professionally trained actors emerging from such corporatist institutions as the Ecole Nationale de Théâtre of Montreal and the Conservatoire du Québec. Its productions tour throughout Quebec and Canada and have traveled to Europe and Africa.

The company has defined itself as *nationale* and *militante*. It is "national" because it represents Québécois activist theatre in international festivals and because the language of its productions is resolutely and self-consciously Québécois. Punctuated by puns and tongue-in-cheek references to local history and politics, the language of the Parminou productions targets principally an "inside" audience. Yet the company can hardly be seen as a purely Québécois product. The actors' historical mentors include *commedia*, *théâtre de la foire,* and the Berliner Ensemble, as well as Québécois theatres of the 1960s such as Le Grand Cirque Ordinaire or Théâtre Euh!.[4] And, as in the case of *Salut vieille branche!*, Parminou creations continue to explore American "pop culture" genres such as stand-up comedians and video clips. The Parminou members see themselves inscribed in a global history of *théâtre populaire.*

This is at any rate how Maureen Martineau's historical appraisal of the Parminou presents the company in 1991. Written "in a period when 'political theatre' rides alone" [dans une période où "le théâtre politique" fait cavalier seul], the document describes the evolution of the Parminou troupe as part of a global historical movement, but also part of the particular history of Quebec with its three-century-old cultural past and its thirty-year-old political past.

The company is a contemporary oddity, a lone rider, because it is a "political theatre," a term Martineau sets in problematizing quotation marks. Because of its stance as a specifically Québécois and socially-oriented theatre, the company has often been viewed by Québécois cutting-edge artists as an anachronism. Collective creations, theatre cooperative ensembles, social criticism, and an anchoring in local popular culture went out of vogue some time ago. By the 1980s "activist theatre" seemed a remnant of another era. Yet the company owes its survival—and its continued financing—to their baseline principles, as well as to a certain flexibility which belies a dogmatic reputation.

The company has continually evolved over the years. Changes are evident in the marketing of the company, whose self-presentation has moved from a "homemade" style to slick, electronically-produced brochures and videos. The Parminou collective has shifted from selling itself as folk culture to marketing itself as a professionally-crafted product. In the summer of 1989 the company was relocating to a brand new cultural center financed by the provincial government and the municipality of Victoriaville.

Significant ideological changes have also taken place, particularly in the company's attitude toward Québécois nationalism. At its inception the Parminou collective declared itself *indépendantiste et socialiste*. Ten years later the word "indépendantiste" was dropped. The Parminou was part of the younger faction of the nationalist wave which brought the Parti Québécois into power in 1976. The company continued to be part of the Québécois government cultural reconstruction project throughout the early eighties. The Parminou still enjoys a privileged relationship with the MAC and other agencies of the provincial government.

However, since the company began to work with immigrant and native peoples in Quebec and to explore the international stage, the nature of the dyed-in-the-wool Québécois subject has come under great scrutiny. Recognizing other minority national rights has fragmented the notion of a Québécois every-person. An increased awareness of the privileged position of the *peuple québécois* has considerably nuanced the treatment of the historical Québécois subject.

When the Parminou theatrical collective began, and the mainstay actors were in their early twenties, the fusion of a Québécois liberation movement and leftist ideals appeared natural. By the end of the 1980s—as *Québec* approached its thirtieth birthday and the original Parminou members were either well into their thirties or entering their forties—ideologies were no longer clear-cut. The Québécois national project blurred with the increased awareness of other minority demands, and the Parminou had multiplied its militant causes by incorporating overarching geopolitical concerns into its ideological agenda. Commenting on this expansion, Martineau states that a Marxist analysis was no longer sufficient to grasp social reality and required the complement of "une vision féministe, ecologiste, pacifiste, etc..." This check list of global movements is an indication of how complex the cause had become. Things appeared simpler a decade earlier when I first saw the Parminou perform in the summer following the 1980 Referendum.

1980: "Your story's not bad"

My initial contact with the Parminou coincided with my first trip to Quebec in June 1980. After living in France, Zaire, and Ivory Coast for over twenty years, I was returning to North America via Quebec. I had friendly connections with several people from the university and theatre milieus and I needed a francophone environment for my children who were nearing high school age. In choosing to migrate to Quebec I was exercising the rights of a privileged immigrant who selects a home country.

I had heard of the Parminou through an African friend, a theatre colleague from the Ivory Coast, where I had been working for two years. He had spoken with great enthusiasm about the company's activist approach and also about how he identified with Quebec's struggle as a colonized and minoritized nation. He told me: "Ils sont comme nous, ces gens là." [These people are just like us.] I was determined to become one of "us" in Quebec.

I went to Quebec as a visitor who was also a prospective immigrant. I approached Quebec with the double-edged excitement of a tourist about to discover "home." In June 1980, after two rather sterile days in Montreal, I traveled to Quebec City. I stepped off the bus directly onto the Château de Frontenac boardwalk, which dominates a wide passage of the Saint Lawrence River and extends to the (in)famous Plains of Abraham. I asked a pedestrian how to get to the Place Royale—the only address I had for the Parminou—and was directed to the funicular elevator. The cablecar carried me down the cliff to the oldest section of the city. I disembarked and went to the central square where I found the company rehearsing for their afternoon performance.

The first Parminou production I would witness was also the first of the company's historical series on the Place Royale of Old Quebec City. The piece was called *Ton histoire est une des pas pires*, a title which plays off the inherent double-entendre of *histoire* as "history" or "story." The montage of short narratives from French-Canadian lore included the legendary Madeleine de Verchère, who at the age of fourteen saved her parents' farm from an Iroquois attack; Quebec City during the 1850 fire; and witchcraft in New France. The production centered on popular Québécois heroes rather than the "great figures of History." The style was light farce. Traditional music announced the performance and punctuated the tableaux.

The staging used the architecture of the Place Royale, still under reconstruction and not yet the internationally consecrated tourist site it would become a few years later.[5] The surrounding graystone houses and their scaffolding, the archeological excavations, the narrow alley leading up from the Saint Lawrence, and the makeshift platforms set up for the show constituted the décor. The day was warm and clear, the sort of weather which always appears miraculous in this corner of the northern hemisphere. The sky constituting the roof of this theatre was a remarkable blue. The performance itself was highly energetic; both actors and spectators seemed fully engaged.

I, the spectator discovering Quebec, felt swept into a magical moment. I was totally charmed by the space, the music, the stories, and the excitement the production generated. Since a summer music festival was taking place at the same time, traditional Québécois and Acadian music filled the streets of the 17th-century town until late into the 20th-century night.

My first naive impressions were of a people anchored in tradition and evolving within a space of convivial festivity. These impressions—governed by the rush of discovery and the desire to take it all in at once—were not an entirely personal projection. A festive atmosphere invariably reigns over the Old Quebec City summer celebrations. This was, however, far from a total picture of Québécois political reality.

In the summer of 1980, Quebec was still riding on the momentum of the national construction project and the Parti Québécois mandate. But the country was also emerging from the May Referendum on national sovereignty which had proved more divisive than unifying. The independence project stood defeated by over 19% of the ballots cast; the vote of the francophone population was split into two factions.

Not everyone was celebrating that June, as a conversation I had with an acquaintance a few days after the festival made clear. Charles, my interlocutor, was a journalist of Radio Québec. He asked a question which clashed with my initial impressions of a joyous people: "Qu'est-ce qui vous amène ici dans cette période de dépression nationale?" [What brings you here in this period of national depression?] The tone was cynical, somewhat accusatory, and genuinely curious.

I was at a loss for an answer. I understood Charles was referring to the defeat of the Referendum, although I was hardly in a position to have noticed any signs of despondency. His choice of words intrigued me. What exactly was a national depression? How did the depressed state of a collective psyche manifest itself? Moreover, how could it be so well hidden to my tourist gaze? What I had witnessed on the Place Royale was a celebration of collective identity, not the funeral for its demise.

What now appears remarkable is how few references were made to the "defeated" national cause during that summer (or the ensuing four years I spent in Montreal for that matter). It was as if the passions mobilized before the vote had carried through the 1980 summer months despite the seeming collapse of the political cause. Charles' admonition that it was somehow inappropriate to tour the country or party in *Vieux Québec* at such a time left me perplexed. I was not only perceiving Quebec with the exotic thrill of the "tourist coming home," but I was suddenly aware of how odd the picture of general joviality was in the light of recent events. What was to have been a major articulation of Québécois history had just collapsed without leaving an apparent trace.[6] Certainly there had been no sign of "national depression" in *Ton histoire est une des pas pires*.

Throughout the 1980s the Parminou would continue to perform history on the Place Royale. As a frequent witness to their annual summer performances, I would follow the evolution of the activist company's shifting perspective on historical ideals which were such a major component of Québécois identity building. The 1989 production of *Salut vieille branche!* would indicate a hyper-reflexivity and a deep-rooted malaise with the very concept of a monolothic national subject. Ironically, the montage which would turn both the historical master narrative and the Québécois subject on their heads centers on a theme which lends itself more than any other to essentialist notions. The topic which generated the piece is the genealogy of the founding families of Quebec.

1989: The Pervasive Fear of Disappearing

For the nationalist cause, 1989 was a liminal period. Debate over the ratification of the Meech Lake agreement and over the North Atlantic Free Trade Agreement—which Quebec heavily favored and Ottawa resisted—droned on and permeated the complex tissue of Québécois nationalism.

The economic future of Quebec was at the forefront of nationalist concerns. In April, Hydro-Québec signed a seventeen-billion dollar contract with the state of New York, the biggest contract the power company—which Lévesque had reclaimed in the name of *maîtres chez nous* a few decades earlier—had ever obtained. In May, a Cree delegate from the Bay James region, bastion of Hydro-Québec, presented a petition to the Canadian High Court to block the expansion of the project.

In 1989 the cultural, as well as the economic, status of Quebec was at stake. Protesting the Bourassa government's renegotiation of French-language rights, some 60,000 demonstrators gathered in Montreal. Many were teenagers who had never considered the *fait français* as other than a given of their daily existence. After years of remaining dormant in the wings, Québécois separatist sentiments were reappearing on the national stage.

This neo-nationalism was carried by the economically-directed thinking of a younger generation of PLQ politicians, who would emerge as one of the major forces in the early 1990s, and the rebellious passions of a still-younger generation. Yet in this picture of *renaissance nationaliste* old symbolic references lingered on. The most persistent trope was that of disappearing,[7] with its corresponding affirmation of—or clutching at—genetic and historical roots. This thread was interwoven in the Parminou's 1989 parodic production.

The theme of founding families was set forth by the Patrimoine or "National Heritage" division of the MAC in an open call for proposals to which the company responded. All of the Parminou productions on the Place Royale had been sponsored by the Patrimoine division, which is responsible for the renovation, management, and animation of historic sites, as well as the maintenance of historical and Québécois family archives dating from the 17th-century to the present.

The connection between the Patrimoine and genealogy is self-evident. In a state which is not a state, national legitimacy lies in a collective past. If the myth of the "French race" dissolved after the Duplessis era, the concern for historical roots remains strong in fin-de-siècle Quebec. Besides financing and managing historical sites and monuments, the Patrimoine division oversees the genealogical archives of Quebec. Any citizen may trace his or her family lineage, free of charge. The Patrimoine supports kinship associations such as the *Société des Tremblay* to which any person bearing the highly common name of Tremblay may belong.

Interest in family trees and kinship lines is obviously not a Québécois peculiarity. What is unusual is the intimate connection of genealogy to the state. The government is the official guardian of the family tree, as if this were a national treasure like a building or an artifact. The defunct construct of Quebec as "just one big family" has paradoxically augmented research into genealogical origins. The tendency to reify kinship ties or to transform family history into a national monument is acute when the nation is itself unofficial. The pervasive fear of dying as a culture translates into the enshrining of family roots.

The creators of *Salut vieille branche!* were quick to deny any interest in the glorification of national ancestry. In an informal interview Jacques Drolet, one of the four actors of the production, described the onset of the theatrical creation as follows: "Okay, we got the contract. Then we started improvising around the family tree, around roots. Nobody in the group was really interested in their family's origins so we started working on the basics, on sexual reproduction."[8] This ambiguous position marks *Salut vieille branche!* which is a parodic salute to the ancestors, as well as a self-mocking admission of the production's commercial nature. In 1989 economic power appeared the primary justification of national autonomy. Yet symbolic remnants of the French-American family lost in the wilderness and in danger of disappearing remained strong.

The recurrent fear of disappearing is an integral part of the Québécois political imaginary. The fear is both a quasi-legendary component of Québécois identity—Latouche's great national bazaar or "our old fears and hopes"—and a motor driving the national identity search. That this syndrome could remain alive despite three decades of self-affirmation was brought home to me in a conversation I had with two friends before the performance.

A Micropicture: "Est-ce qu'une culture peut mourir?"

An hour before the performance, Nicole, Raymond, and I were seated in a café on one of the streets adjacent to the Place Royale. We had formerly collaborated in hosting the Parminou's *Ton histoire est une des pas pires* in a 1981 Ivory Coast tour. Since then we had attended other Parminou performances on the Place Royale together. We were thus renewing something of a tradition in this meeting.

Raymond, a Québécois diplomat, had served as cultural attaché in the Ivory Coast and as director of protocol in the Quebec capital. Nicole was currently the public relations director of Vidéo Femmes, an international, feminist film association. Politically both are progressive liberals and members of the Parti Québécois. And I, after the initial personal conversation concerning our families and activities, was to assume the role of cultural expert. I realized this when Raymond—after a brief preamble on how I had been involved in producing theatre in various countries and was now involved in performance studies at New York University—asked the following question: "Est-ce qu'une culture peut mourir?" [Can a culture die?]

I was as stymied by this question as I had been by the "national depression" question nine years earlier. My silence was simply more embarrassing, because I was being taken for an expert rather than a naive tourist. Instead of seeking an answer, I again became more intent on examining the terms of the question. What is a culture, can it die, is it like a human individual with a predictable life-span or like a plant with cyclic rebirth? If Raymond—who was, as cultural ambassador, constantly implicated in the representation of Québécois culture—was asking the question, it is because there are gnawing doubts concerning the past and future of Québécois culture, but also concerning the ontology of culture itself.

Placing culture within biological metaphors indicates that it is a mortal entity.[9] Framing this as a question indicates the idea might be absurd. And yet there is the old fear that the people will disappear, that the strain will dry up and die. "Can a culture die?" I managed a retarded "No, I don't think so," although my mind was then filling, not with this francophone minority strategically asserting its difference in an anglo-dominated world, but with lost peoples and lost languages, with disappeared species. Raymond rushed on enthusiastically, citing the demonstrations led by young Québécois contesting the Bourassa government's attempts to compromise on linguistic policy. He indicated that although hope was at a low ebb during the decade following the referendum, it was now rising. "Il y a de l'espoir maintenant."

Hope for what? A viable society? Survival as a people? The dream of independence? Consecration as a state? He went on to say that his ministry organized visits for tourists in Québecois families, so that foreigners could see "comment on fonctionne" [what makes us tick]. Hope for the future of Quebec thus lies in the continuing struggle for the *fait français* in North America, but also in the staging of family life for the foreign tourist.

This was an auspicious opening to *Salut vieille branche!* which was, as we spoke, announced by a parade on the Place Royale. Ultimately it was the contradictions underlying the Patrimoine policy of genealogical preservation and those underlying Raymond's discourse (spoken against the grain of my bewildered silence) which emerge in the Parminou production of *Salut vieille branche!*. This production is about ancestral roots and kinship ties, but it is also about the staging and commodification of these connections to the past.

Embedded Theatres

The café where I met with my friends is on a side street which runs up to the Place Royale. The Parc la Cetière, where platforms have been set up for the afternoon performance of *Salut vieille branche!*, stands adjacent to the Place Royale, cornerstone of the contemporary tourist mecca of *Vieux Québec*. Founded in the early 17th-century, Old Quebec stands within fortifying walls which separate the old from the new city, dominated by the 20th-century sky-scrapers of the provincial government.

A 1989 brochure published by the MAC and distributed in the tourist information centers, describes the Place Royale as the "birthplace of French America... one of the oldest sites of North America." Here, states the pamphlet, "visitors can admire three centuries of history as they stroll down its narrow, colorful streets." Situated on the first level of Cape Diamant, the cliff which rises from the banks of the Saint Lawrence, the Place Royale designates a central square and the arteries leading up from the river to the old city.

Established in 1608 by Samuel de Champlain as a fur trading post in the name of the king of France, the area was the first commercial center of Nouvelle-France. Despite its official inauguration as "Place Royale" with the unveiling of the neo-classical bust of Louis XIV, the square retained its generic name of *place du marché* well into the 20th century. After numerous displacements during the renovation project, the statue of the Roi Soleil once again defines the epicenter of the square.

A certain attachment to the defunct French regime dominated the massive restoration project undertaken by the provincial government in the late 1960s. Tastefully restored as a French-colonial town, the space today bears little trace of the intervening centuries during which the Place Royale remained a commercial area for merchants and dockers, as well as the dwellings of French-Canadian and Irish-immigrant families at the bottom of the social ladder. The brochure provided by the MAC indicates that "Toward 1860, the decline started to set in... by 1950 it had become a poor district, constantly threatened by fire and decay." This decay was one of the original justifications in appropriating the space for cultural conservation and transforming the area into a tourist history museum.

The rehabilitation project was a bone of contention among architects, historians, and the agents of the MAC. The official guardians of culture argued that the Place Royale should be reconstituted in a coherent and original form. The architects argued there was no reason to favor 17th-century architecture and destroy other period buildings. The social historians argued that the expropriation of inhabited buildings and the obliteration of the years between the French Regency and contemporary Quebec represented the antithesis of history. Ultimately the "coherent and original" option prevailed in the reconstruction of the Place Royale.

Today it is easier to imagine history-textbook natives and colonists trading goods on the square or swashbuckling Louis XIV soldiers parading through the narrow streets than to imagine the street kids, merchants, and local café clients who occupied the neighborhood some fifty years ago. The 1989 square resembled a fresh-off-the-press school manual: clean, tastefully illustrated, and coherent. It is a 20th-century rendition of a French-colonial site, replete with cardboard figures and biographies of the original inhabitants such as the Wine Merchant, the Baker, the Settler, who have been reconstituted through historical research. These ossified signs of history stand next to the French restaurants and American ice-cream parlors, the crafts shops, and souvenir stands of the contemporary tourist mecca. Since colonial architecture has been carefully reconstructed and all traces of social history have been virtually obliterated from the scene, it is not "three centuries of history" the visitor can admire "while strolling through the narrow, colorful streets," but the collapsing of three centuries into its present mise-en-scène as a tourist site. This staging is complete with "interpretation centers" and "animation" projects such as the Parminou's *Salut vieille branche!* which are designed to bring history to life.

The exterior shell theatre of *Salut* is thus the Place Royale, "birthplace of French America" and contemporary tourist attraction. The Parminou competes for an audience among the throngs of summer visitors who fill the streets of the historic site and continue to spill forth from the funicular elevator or down the steep steps of the *escalier casse-cou* [breakneck stairs] leading from the Château de Frontenac boardwalk. The streets and central square of the Place are a theatre of multiple spectacles. Some have been scheduled through official channels; others have sprouted up like wildflowers. Local mimes and jugglers or Peruvian musicians draw audiences at the foot of the *escalier casse-cou* and on the central square. The Place Royale is a market of spectacles. In costume and beating the drum, the four actors of *Salut* file through the streets of the Place Royale. A hallmark of the Parminou historical performances, the parade announces the show is about to begin. The audience has, for the most part, already assembled at the Parc la Cetière.

This site and the spectators who have already gathered for the afternoon performance—some thirty adults clustered under an awning which shields them from the summer sun, plus some fifty others and numerous children who spill out onto the sun-exposed grassy area—constitutes a second theatre. This embedded theatre is defined by a few chairs under an awning, a platform, and a painted backdrop depicting woods and a house with two cut-out windows. The architecture of la Cetière lends itself to a proscenium arrangement. It is bounded on two sides by a natural stone rampart and a restored building. The other two sides open to streets which lead from the Place up the side of the cliff to the Château Frontenac.

The stage stands against the gray-stone wall of an historic building. Both the painted backdrop and a makeshift curtain strung on a wire, which runs from the platform to the left wing, evoke a self-conscious theatricality. The side curtain is a pale blue studded with white graphics, suggesting waves and fleur-de-lis. Iconically, the curtain will indicate the Québécois flag and the Atlantic Ocean passage between France and the Nouveau Monde. Theatrically, the curtain will function as a device to hide props or entrances and as a self-referential sign.

The architecture of la Cetière, the stage, and the naive curtains ironically describe the configuration of a proscenium theatre. The intimacy of the space in the middle of the tourist mecca, the platform set against what the tourist brochure describes as "a very old dwelling" and the frequent use of draperies to self-consciously reveal or hide the presence of the actors create a theatrical arena whose essential characteristic is its own theatricality. Whether for pragmatic, ideological, or aesthetic reasons, the creation of a *théâtre à l'italienne* has the effect of underlining the citational nature of the performance. Set in a theatre embedded in a theatrically historicized space, this production speaks first of its own framework and of history as a mise-en-scène designed for summer tourists. That these tourists might also be natives is evident from the conversation of the audience and in the opening segments of the production. An opening patter and an opening song introduce the issues behind this self-conscious representation of national ancestry.

Opening Patter: Roots, a Thorny Matter

No future, no past[10]
As the parade comes to a close, an actress enters the theatre. Dressed in a white laboratory coat, coiffed with a wig—a bald crown surrounded by shocks of gray hair—and masked by gigantic, coke-bottle glasses and a clown nose, the actress is immediately encoded as the stereotypical Professor. The Professor deliberately closes the blue side curtain leading to the wings and thus signals the opening of the play.

The Professor is carrying a massive volume, a mock antiquated book which is titled *Salut vieille branche!*. With a doddering yet determined step, the Professor moves forward to address the audience.

PROFESSOR: *(in a trembling but authoritative voice)* Our ancestors! Who today knows our ancestors? The first families who planted the trunk of our great genealogical tree, who put down roots and bore fruits. We are all blossoms on the great founding tree.

(In a more confidential tone) I just happen to have a few lineages for sale, dating

back to 1663. And cheap. I have some Gagnons here (*tapping the book*). Any Gagnons around? What about Morins? Any Morins here? *(Pointing to someone in the audience who has stood up to leave)* Hey, you there, young fellow... Yes, you, the young punk who's trying to hide behind his neighbor...

The "young punk" detaches hinself from the audience. He is an actor in his late thirties who is coiffed in a black bandanna and wearing a camouflage vest. Inscribed across his back are two words in English: NO FUTURE. He looks around him and then toward the Professor with a "Who me?" gesture. He moves reluctantly to the frontal-stage area while muttering "Moi, pourquoi toujours moi?" [Why always me?] accompanied by numerous *'Sti... Ca'... Ta'*. These *sacres* or specifically French-Canadian curses are barely articulated, but provoke an immediate laugh of recognition in the audience.

The Professor continues the sales pitch, expounding on the value of knowing one's genealogy. "Aren't you interested in learning about your ancestors?" questions the Professor. The Punk responds with a thrust of the middle finger. "But you have to know where you come from to know where you're going!" exclaims the Professor. The Punk says nothing, but displays first the NO FUTURE on his back, and then opens his vest to reveal another inscription on the two sides of the lining: NO... PAST.

"But I am the living proof of the past," splutters the Professor. "I have spent over forty years in libraries and archives, pouring over historical documents."

"Listen," replies the other character, "I ain't interested in no lineage or folk. But if you're selling a line of coke..."

Both look furtively to either side. Then the Professor beckons to the Punk and they move toward the privacy of the wings.

This opening sequence invites a "How many errors can you find in the picture?" game or rather "How many frames are there to the picture?" The buffoon Professor is proffering ancestral roots to a class composed of summer visitors on the Place Royale, a theatre for tourists, which houses the smaller theatre of the production. But the Professor is not only a clown lecturing to the crowd, extolling the ancestors in a literally flowery language. He is also a salesman. Spotting a prospective client, his tone slips into that of a street vendor.

The product he is selling is a branch of the Québécois ancestral tree, an entitlement to collective history. The Professor persona represents the past buried in historical documents, the "forty years spent in libraries and archives." The character is embarking on a mock-history lesson cast in historical assumptions learned on Québécois school benches. But the classroom of this cartoon Einstein is also the theatre. The pupils are the spectators whom the actress addresses directly and from whom she invites the "young punk" to step forward.

There is an inherently disturbing side to the Professor's character. Wearing a clown mask, the "Professor" is an actress in disguise. Shifting from the estimed repository of knowledge to the salesman, hawking a line of historical goods, (s)he is not trustworthy. The Professor is at once the disinterested historian and the vendor who sells family lineages like candy bars or post cards on the Place Royale. To further complicate the parodic *mise-en-abyme*, the actress behind the mask is also Québécois. She is of the Gagnon, Tremblay, or Morin[11] family line and she is performing for those who also might bear the name Gagnon, Tremblay, or Morin.

The theatre is the classroom of a strange history lesson which undermines its own authority. The Professor's lesson casts back to the creation of the performance when the actors poured over historical data on the founding families and churned the raw material into a street comedy. And the Professor's sales pitch relates not only to the financing institution of the production—to the Patrimoine division of the MAC—but also to the actor as conscious mediator, as a salesperson of kinship and Québécois identity.

What is being sold on the tourist marketplace of Old Quebec City are patrimonial names, blood-ties, kith and kin, family history, all dressed in botanical metaphors. The Professor's discourse—up for sale in the summer bazaar of Old Quebec City—is a burlesque rendering of the genealogical tree. The roots and branches, stems and blossoms leading back to the founding trunk of the nation are offered to the tourists. Although the Professor is selling this inestimable product for a minimal fee, the "client" singled out in the audience is not interested.

He wears the uniform of a contrasting stereotypical category: the drop-out from school and society, the "young punk." His name—as it appears in the working script—is *Trash*. This name and the NO PAST/NO FUTURE slogans he brandishes on his body smack of nihilism. Not surprisingly, these words are in English and play upon the pervasive fear of disappearing as a distinct linguistic community in an anglo-dominated America. Contrary to the Québécois national motto *Je me souviens* [I remember], Trash would rather forget and lose himself in a timeless world of drugs. He is not interested in lines connecting to Québécois family history but in other lines: not in folk but in coke.

Trash announces himself in English through signs which are stamped on his clothes or through gestures such as a thrust of the finger (scripted literally as "fuck you" in the stage directions). But Trash does not speak in English. He barely speaks at all except to spit out negative utterances. His idiom which runs parallel to the Professor's flowery language is the *sacre*. The recurrent *'Sti... Ca'... Ta'...* of Trash's speech are half-articulated renditions of indigenous swearing, the voicing of the sacred and the damned, which here simultaneously reflect a refusal of the bill of goods being sold and an affirmation of Québécois linguistic specificity. The minimal indications of Catholic cult objects—"sti" for *hostie* [the host], "ca" for *calice* [chalice], "ta" for *tabarnacle* [tabernacle]—throw back to traditional, popular heresy in a country whose history is enmeshed in Catholic symbolism.[12] Although these words hardly retain blasphemous power today, they frequently pepper Québécois street speech, along with "fock" and "la marde."

Paradoxically, although Trash denies any interest in his cultural roots, the persona represents a linguistic specificity which makes him immediately recognizable to the audience. The character is simultaneously a mark of cultural difference and its dismissal. He is inscribed as Québécois, but one who is barely articulate, and who apparently has no use for collective history.

If the Professor's packaging for sale of Québécois genealogy is disturbing, Trash's nihilistic denial of any bonds to the past is equally so. The two characters present historical roots as a problem and announce the ideological tension underlying *Salut vieille branche!*. A continual denouncing of essentialist identity and of the commodification of history runs parallel to the assumption of cultural bonds and the need to preserve them.

Overt Disguises and Problematic Pronouns

Chanson du début [Opening Song]

Two actors playing a flute and a drum enter from the street to the audience's left and march up on the platform singing. They are dressed in pale blue overalls and '50s-style black canvas sneakers. During the first verse of the song they are joined by the other two actors who have shed their "Professor" and "Punk" attributes to reveal identical overalls and sneakers. These constitute a working uniform, an actor's disguise over which they will slip other disguises as the performance unfolds.

Nous voilà réunis	Here we are gathered
Pour un grand événement	For a great event
Vous vous êtes déguisés	You've disguised
En touristes d'été	As summer tourists
Avec votre crème à glace	With your ice cream cones
Et pis vos cerfs-volants	And your kites

[vos cerveaux lents]	[your slow brains]
Vos caméras ciné	With your cameras and
Vos bermudas charmants.	Charming bermuda shorts.

The instruments and the melody of the song are reminiscent of 17th-century music, but the text is decidedly contemporary. With its references to summer tourists bearing cameras and bermudas, the song is a commentary on the immediate context of the performance. For this "great event" the actors of the *Coopérative des travailleurs et travailleuses en théâtre des Bois-Francs* are disguised in generic working garb. In this self-mocking farce even the spectators are disguised. They are told they are already in the costume of vacationers, replete with cameras, ice cream cones and summer toys. Their "kites"—or "slow brains" as the homonym translates—indicate that this is not a time for serious thinking but for fun, for vacating the mind. Yet what is asked of the audience projected into the multiple framings of this "great event" is rather taxing.

Mais pendant ce temps-là	But in the meantime
Nous on s'est renseignés	We've looked into
A savoir d'où l'on vient	Just where we come from
Pour savoir où l'on va.	To learn where we're going.

Repeating the Professor's injunction—"You need to know where you come from to know where you're going"—the actors are also performing the Professor's role. They too have poured over historical documents concerning Québécois genealogy in order to produce this spectacle. The theatre is indeed a classroom, but a topsy-turvy one where the "truth" of the lessons is constantly undermined by the self-conscious role-playing of both actors and spectators.

Faudrait pas se choquer	Don't get upset
Si vous vous reconnaissez	If you recognize yourself
Car croyez-le ou non	Because believe it or not
Nous sommes tous parents.	We're all related.
Nous sommes tous descendants	We're all descendants
Des premières familles	Of the founding families
Tremblay, Morin, Fleury	Tremblay, Morin, Fleury
Prirent souche au pays.	Put down roots here.

The song goes on to warn the audience that they shouldn't be shocked or angry if they recognize themselves because "we are all related," blood descendants of the first families, the Tremblay, Morin, and Fleury who established roots in the country. In shifting from the second person plural (you the audience) to the first person plural (we the descendants) the song envelopes the spectators and the performers in a collective *nous*.

There is little doubt that *Salut* addresses a primarily Québécois audience. Not only the specific references to the few hundred founding families of Nouvelle-France, but also the language used in the production are culturally bound. The popular idiom and numerous double-entendres predefine an audience of insiders. In fact the space is filled with francophone Québécois willing to assist in the curious self-mocking identity ritual which is unfolding, willing to play the role of the Québécois and the tourist.

But the "we" predicated in this verse is problematic for several related reasons. First, assuming the oxymoronic role of both the tourist and the native, the spectator becomes a tourist in his or her own culture. And the guides leading the tour are but actors. Second, this "nous" will be a portrait of the Québécois mediated through parody. As the next verse —reestablishing the performer/spectator division—states, the spectator and the spectators' ancestors will be made the object of ridicule. Third, the last segment of the song stipulates that "we" turn out to be not an homogenous ethnic unit at all but a hybrid.

Faudrait pas se choquer	Don't get upset
Si vous vous reconnaissez	If you recognize yourself
Car on va rire de vous	For we'll make fun of you
Et de votre parenté.	And of your kin.
Pour faire des enfants forts	To have strong children
On a voulu se croiser	We decided to mix
Avec les autochtones	With natives
L'Irelande et le Niger.	With Ireland and Niger.

After locating the subject in a "you and your kin," the verse retreats back to a nebulous *on* inclined to breed with "natives, Ireland and Niger." Keeping in mind that on the performative level oral rhythmic demands are as imperative as symbolic demands, there remains a host of contradictions. The use of the impersonal pronoun *on* (which is generally translated as the passive voice in English) to express desire—*on a voulu* or "it was wished"—indicates that the subject is everyone and no one. Omnipresent yet absent, this subject occupies no stable position.

The words gloss the contemporary Québécois as a genealogical and temporal cross-breed. The anonymous founders of Nouvelle-France mingled with the equally anonymous *autochtones*, with "natives" who are significantly scripted with a generic lower-case letter. Then the founding ancestor, a nebulous *on*, mixed with Ireland and Niger, two modern nation states, as their capitalization indicates.

The three peoples described in this segment indicate different periods and different factors in the shaping of Québécois demographics. Less a willful agent—desiring to produce strong off-spring as the song indicates—than a victim of circumstances, many of the Frenchmen seeking fortune in the Nouveau Monde did marry Amerindian women because of the initial scarcity of female compatriots. "Cross-breeding" with the Irish corresponded to a later period: the 19th-century wave of Irish immigrants, who did not share the language of the francophone community but who shared the Catholic religion and a political-economic status in relation to the crown of England. The insertion of Niger—which metonymically refers to Africa—is a more recent addition to the genetic pool of Quebec.[13]

By grouping Native Amerindians, Irish immigrants, and Africans under the umbrella of Québécois identity, the opening song opens up a postmodern can of worms. Any notion of an homogenous "racially pure" subject is dismissed as primordial nonsense. And yet the concept of "founding families" and collective roots is a presupposition of this text. After debunking Québécois roots as merely flowery tropes up-for-sale, the opening song reestablishes the notion of a founding collectivity which encompasses the audience. We are all linked by blood ties; we are all of one family, although we have mingled with others. The roots of the family tree reach out to include other immigrants to the New World, travelers from three centuries, as well as the rooted natives of French-Canadian prehistory.

The Irish and African strains cited in the closing line of the opening song will not reappear in the rest of the production. The *autochtone* will recur frequently, indicating that any American identity is shadowed by the nagging presence of the original other. The path to Québécois identity is strewn with unresolved problems. What to do with the immigrant who is now more than ever a demographic capital? What to do with the native whose presence constantly undermines "our" claims to the land? And who is this hybrid "we" anyway?

The role the spectator is asked to play—in spite of his or her slow brain and vacationer's disguise—is hard work. Invited to assume the problematic mantle of a tourist in one's own culture, to assist in the parodic deconstruction of one's cultural identity, and to join in the mocking of one's own kin is a heavy task for a summer stroller on the Place Royale. The opening patter and song attempt to englobe the audience in a performative complicity. *Nous, les acteurs* are making fun of *vous et votre parenté*. But we are in fact all kinfolk in the present moment of an "inside joke." The spectators have been warned that they and their ancestors will be made the brunt of mockery. Yet, "we"—actors and spectators—are after all in the same boat, however murky the genetic pool or the cultural waters might be.

Notes

1. All the creators of *Salut vieille branche!* have been agents in shaping the history of the Parminou and the company's historical series on the Place Royale. The four actors who impersonate over forty characters in *Salut* are Réjean Bédard, Jacques Drolet, Maureen Martineau, and Nicole-Eva Morin. Michel Cormier and Hélène Desperrier directed the play.

2. As of 1995, the Parminou company no longer receives subsidies from the Canada Arts Council.

3. "Sans se référer à une doctrine fermée, le Théâtre Parminou est un collectif qui continue à privilégier la recherche d'un théâtre populaire et accessible, à la fois novateur et pertinent" (Maureen Martineau's "Le Théâtre Parminou, 18 ans d'art et d'engagment," unpublished document provided by the Parminou).

4. Ensemble companies such as Le Grand Cirque Ordinaire and Théâtre Euh! flourished during the early 1970s. At the same time playwrights such as Jean-Claude Germain and Michel Tremblay were challenging the dramatic conventions of traditional theatre and creating a new idiom of "born in Quebec" theatre.

5. UNESCO declared the Place Royale and Vieux Québec *joyau du patrimoine mondial* or "world heritage site" in 1985.

6. A body of literature analysing the defeat of the separatist movement appeared after a long hiatus. Indeed, many of the political analyses which proliferated years later speak of national shock as well as national depression. Partisans of independence were stunned by the negative outcome of the referendum and the "business goes on as usual" attitude following the NON. Analysts speak of a "post-referendum syndrome," glossing the national psyche as an individual psyche, subject to traumatism and schizophrenic disorders. Basically these analyses have sought to understand why *la nation* failed to even broach the question of independence when only minimal obstacles stood in the way. It was not only the anglophone and allophone minorities which had voted against

Québécois independence, but half of the francophones voting.

7. In 1989 a film broadcast on Québécois television caused a considerable stir. *Disparaître* [To Disappear]—produced by Lise Payette, the PQ and feminist militant who had organized the 1975 *fête sur la montagne*—was a politically ambiguous picture of Québécois demographics. *Disparaître* flits from the achievements of Quebec in the last thirty years to the aging of the indigenous "Québécois pure laine" population, from the threat to the *fait français* in North America to the "immigrant problem" in Europe and the United States. The film which pulls on the most sensitive cord of Québécois nationalists—the fear of disappearing as a cultural entity—provoked discomfort among the immigrant Québécois population and outrage among many "pure wool" Québécois, including those who remained committed to the independence project.

8. Personal interview with Jacques Drolet in Montreal, July 1989.

9. Richard Handler's deconstruction of Québécois nationalism was also running through my mind during this conversation. Culture is projected as biologically bound, with a human life span (1988:46–47).

10. The title "No future, no past" figures in the *Salut vieille branche!* working-script. All of the titles and dialogue which I have translated or paraphrased are drawn from the unpublished script, graciously provided by the Parminou.

11. The surname of the actress portraying the Professor is, in fact, Morin.

12. For further ruminations on the religious, psychological and historical implications of the Québécois *sacre* see Weinmann (1987:444).

13. Although Africans were part of the Canadian cultural landscape well before the 20th-century (See Winks 1971; Williams 1989), they did not enter into Québécois identity politics until the recent immigration of Haitians and West Africans.

The theatre: Parc la Cetière. Photo: Pierre Dessureault

The Couple (Jacques Drolet and Maureen Martineau). Photo: Pierre Dessureault.

Chapter Four
Archetypes and Ideologies for Sale

Of Dubious Origins

Accouplement #1 [Coupling #1]
The last phrases of the opening song are immediately followed by the appearance of two actors behind the painted backdrop. Like patrons of a boardwalk photographer, two heads pop up in the window frames of the "house in the woods." The woman is wearing candy-pink plastic curlers. The man is wearing a shaggy gray wig and clenching a pipe between his teeth.

WOMAN: Salut, vieille branche. [Hi, old branch.]
MAN: Salut, vieille souche. [Hi, old trunk.]
WOMAN: You know something?
MAN: Try me.
WOMAN: Well, there's something's been bothering me.
MAN: What's that?
WOMAN: I've been wondering about our ancestors. Did you ever stop to think how they got their family names?
MAN: Well, that there...
WOMAN: Just take Desfossés for example.
MAN: You don't think they did it (*gesturing with his pipe and forefingers*) in the *fossé* [gutter], do you?
WOMAN: Now I didn't say that, did I? But what about those that are named Desruisseaux?
MAN: They did it in *ruisseaux* [brooks]?
WOMAN: Desmarais?
MAN: Not in the *marais* [swamps]
WOMAN: Or Deslile? (Deslile which could mean "of the islands" is also a popular brand of yogurt in Quebec.)
MAN: Please, not in our yogurt... that's disgusting.
WOMAN: And what about Ruelles?
MAN: In back alleys? Spare me, I'm so ashamed.
WOMAN: You know, our history there...
  She jerks her head upward to a sign which appears behind the forest backdrop: C'EST FOU RAIDE! [It's just plain screwy!]
MAN: Like you, I was going to say our history there is... but then...
  Another banner waves above the backdrop: MAIS C'EST VRAI! [But it's true!]

The gallery of Québécois stereotypes is expanding. After the "Professor, repository of knowledge," and the "Punk, depository of trash," appears the Couple. She wears curlers; he chomps on a pipe. She provokes conversation with questions; he answers with futile exclamations. The two windows side-by-side indicate the complicitous duality of the "Couple," defined by gender roles and caught in an intimate family portrait. Their attributes—particularly the pink plastic curlers—signal that they are contemporary, North American "common folk." They are Québécois because of their idiom and their topic of conversation: French-Canadian family names, *nos ancêtres, notre histoire là*.

"Our history there..." which is "just plain screwy" is also caught in an intimate family portrait, in the backstage of history. Here reduced to the common denominator of male/female copulation, family names leave little room for romantic aggrandizing of the ancestors, not if surnames etymologically reflect siring off-spring in the gutter, in brooks, in swamps, in back alleys, or in yogurt containers.

Sites of haphazard or improbable fornication, Desruisseaux or Deslisle are not the surnames most frequently mentioned in Québécois genealogical archives, or in the 1989 telephone book of Quebec City for that matter. By citing names that are undeniably Québécois, but which are not as frequent as Tremblay or Morin or any of the legendary founding families such as Dion, Cloutier, or Hébert,[1] the creators of *Salut vieille branche!* appear to dismiss any monolithic foundational trunk. By reducing names to the site of conception, the play attacks the basic metaphor of patrimony: the name of the father. By citing the "unmentionable" act through suggestive gestures, the Couple turns venerable family names into the fodder of grotesque puns.

The dominant tropes which run through the production, rhythmically punctuating the performance, are built around male/female coupling. Stripped down to the barest essential, undressed of its flowery metaphors, the genealogical theme is exposed as chance sexual encounters occurring in inappropriate sites.

Historical Travesties

L'éclipse du Roi Soleil [Eclipse of the Sun King]
As the two heads of the Couple disappear behind the backdrop, a voice is heard singing "Allez, croisez, multipliez-vous." An actress enters on the ground level and moves across the grass in a burlesque rendition of the minuet. Coiffed in a Louis XIV wig, masked in a phallic *commedia* nose, and wrapped in a gold brocade and red velveteen cape—which seems to have been retrieved from the dusty wardrobe of some bankrupt theatre company—(s)he is a buffoon

representation of the decadent reign of the Sun King. Twirling to a minuet, trilling out biblical injunctions, a theatrical Louis XIV invites the population to "Go forth, breed and multiple" for the glory of their king.

> The French Empire must shine over the world
> Since her king is a sun.
> Go forth, breed and multiply,
> Daughters of the king and soldiers,
> And fend without me. [Démerdez vous sans moi.]
> Go forth, breed and multiple,
> Bask in my glorious rays before my eclipse.

Repeating the last line in a operatic closure, Louis prepares a grandiose exit. As the actress turns to leave with a dramatic swirl of the cape, the Sun King trips on his regal robes and falls headfirst onto the ground. And the figure of a brief but potentially glorious French regime in the Americas comes to an abrupt halt.

It is ironic that this burlesque king, who demands the reproduction of the French colonial species while announcing his imminent withdrawal, appears on the Place Royale. A neo-classical bust of Louis XIV stands at the epicenter of the reconstructed square. The Sun King continues to throw his perpetually dying rays over what has since become a small tourist kingdom.

As a founding patron of Nouvelle-France—the king who attempted to secure the settlement by encouraging families in the principally male population—*le Grand Louis* does merit a slot in this ancestral bazaar. In the mid-17th century, young women—*filles du roi* or orphans under the charge of the crown—were dispatched to the colony under the obligation to marry as quickly as possible. However, the expansion of the French people on the banks of the Saint Lawrence coincided with the declining rays of a regime. Before Louis XIV's death, French power in North America was already compromised by the bartering off of Acadia, Newfoundland, and the Hudson Bay area. Fifty years later, another, less illustrious, Louis would cede Nouvelle-France to England.

The Parminou rendition of the Sun King is an actress in theatrical robes and a sausage nose, who lasts barely the time of a minuet before falling headfirst onto the ground. This parodic Louis has an acid edge: The "founding father" is also impotent. Despite his divine right and his biblical injunctions, despite his dispensing subjects to distant colonies to propagate, he is not a provider. The buffoon Sun King projects the trope of abandonment, the failing *pater familias* who sires and then leaves his offspring to fend for themselves: *Démerdez-vous sans moi*.

The "fend without me" imperative is a pervasive remnant of the pioneer mythology of the New World. But in French Canada this does not translate into the empowering national myth of self-reliance as it has in the United States. The sons of democracy living in the wilds of the New World could hardly overthrow a royal father who disappeared at their birth, a sun whose rays dissipate before the glorious new day. As such, the bumbling king projects less the glory of French colonial power or its revolutionary overthrow by up-start children, than the pure disappearance of the male parent.[2]

La fille laide [The ugly girl]
A burst of shrill laughter heralds the next persona. Stepping over the body of the fallen Sun King, a burly male actor dressed in a frilly nylon rendition of a 17th-century collar and bonnet, and masked with a whiskered pig's snout, invades the theatrical space. As the vanishing king crawls toward the wings, the actor in Miss Piggy/*fille du roi* drag lurches toward the audience. Amidst hefty sighs and strident giggles, (s)he announces:

"I will soon be twenty-five, on November 25 of 1663. That's very soon. None will have me. I might end up at the convent. It seems that virtue is indeed my most enduring quality."

The *fille laide* exits, laughing hysterically at her joke. Behind the blue curtain, the laughter turns to violent sobs.

Following on the heels of the "founding father," the maternal ancestor enters. This she which is obviously a he, this evident 20th-century construction of a 17th-century *fille de roi* and old maid at the age of twenty five, is the sign of parody itself. A running gag in *Salut vieille branche!*, this character will reappear frequently throughout the performance, accosting spectators verbally or even physically. The character's repeated outbursts and assaults on the public, which provoke both laughter and discomfort, are similar to the more aggressive techniques of nightclub female impersonators who sit on men's laps and snip off their ties.

The *fille laide* is a multileveled travesty. (S)he represents both the 17th-century potential spinster, about to be condemned to lifelong celibacy, and a daughter of the king, ripe and ready to colonize the Nouveau Monde all by herself, since no man in France will have her for a wife. But the evident masking of the actor—a stylistic hybrid of Miss Piggy, a drag queen dressed in the garb of a French regency ingenue, and the macho burlesque of a

Archetypes and Ideologies for Sale

The Ugly Girl (Réjean Bédard). Photo: Pierre Dessureault.

sex-starved woman—disrupt the historical references. The persona cannot be located in a particular period, genre, or gender.

Like the Sun King, the Ugly Girl uses overt cross-dressing to underline the parodic frame of the performance. Both travesties rely on a play between Québécois historical assumptions and the citational quality of the mask. Working through gender reversals and self-conscious mimicry, the actors repeatedly flip the historical coin over to reveal its parodic underside. Characterization operates through outrageous stereotypes revealed as pure surface. The masks are theatrical implosions which subvert not only historical myths but the burlesque nature of the production.

Nothing can truly be taken seriously in this farce, not even farce itself. Because the representational frame is repeatedly underscored, even the parodic intention becomes suspect. It is perhaps not "you and your kin" who are being made the subject of mockery, but the performance itself. The actors are constantly reminding the audience that no image and no word of *Salut vieille branche!* can be taken seriously. Processed through the parodic machine, nothing—including parody itself—stands quite straight.

Spectator Poulain Plays his Role

Accouplement #2
The husband and wife appear again at their respective windows. They repeat their initial greetings of "Salut vieille branche, salut vieille souche." Then the wife states she is still worried about how the ancestors got their names.

WOMAN: Just how did they come to be called Poulain [colt] for example?
MAN: You don't really think they did it (*gesture of fingers signifying fornication*) with a ... (*uttering a derogatory whinny*).
WOMAN: And what about Leboeuf [beef]?
MAN: Not with a b...!
WOMAN: Or Cauchon [pig]!
MAN: Please, not with a... (*Snorting like a pig.*) But there's worse, you know.
WOMAN: (*Leaning forward with great curiosity*) Worse?
MAN: There's Lelièvre [rabbit]. (*She giggles with delight.*) And Létourneau [starling or idiomatically "birdbrain"].
WOMAN: And what about Papillon [butterfly]? Now frankly that's just plain sick.
MAN: Shameful.

The Couple disappears below the window frames as the Professor reappears.

Requesting more information, the ever-inquisitive and sales-conscious Professor moves into the audience asking "Are there any Poulain here, any Létourneau present?"

One spectator stands and says "My name is Poulain." "Now where do you suppose that came from?" asks the Professor. "Ça vient du fait que mes ancêtres étaient à cheval sur les principes." [That's because my ancestors rode firmly on their principles.]

Despite the fact that the opening song of *Salut vieille branche!* included the audience in a collective *nous* (disguised as actors and tourists for the event) and that the opening patter requested audience participation ("Any Morin here? Any Tremblay?"), the spectator cannot be written into the script. What Poulain does in agreeing to enter into the family-name word game is remind us of the indeterminant present, the ultimate time zone of this "historical" production.

Inviting audience participation and setting up recurrent patterns, the piece works through the live medium and substitutes rhythmic punctuation for dramatic structure. There is no rise-climax-fall nor chronological narrative to the production, which is just a series of recurrent themes and of *lazzi à la québécoise*. By *Accouplement #2* and the Professor's second intervention—sequence in which Spectator Poulain agrees to play his role—the structure and style of *Salut vieille branche!* are established.

Video clips and stand-up comedy are the models for this production. The first cuts time into the microsegments of television MTV, commercials, or news flashes. Most of the segments of *Salut vieille branche!* are under three minutes and most are interchangeable. The second popular genre implies a "living on the edge" rapport with the spectator, who may be called on at any moment to participate in the performance game. The Professor invites the spectator to come forth and share his or her history with the group. While the actor can always hide behind the mask, the spectator has little idea of what is to follow.

The complicity of the audience was an underlying—yet unsigned—clause of the initial contract the actors put forth in the opening song of *Salut*. By publicly joining in the game, spectator Poulain confirms this complicity. By accepting the mask he also becomes part of the Québécois ancestral gallery as viewed by the Couple peering through their windows out over the stage and the audience. The spectators thus become actors reflected in the distortional mirror of the farce.

Treasured Tropes of Misery

Le Professeur et le scorbut [The Professor and scurvy]
Commenting on Poulain's remark about his ancestors' principles, the Professor continues: "Strong principles and a strong stomach, no doubt. Because according to my extensive research, I can certify that many did not make it to the New World. The trip lasted anywhere from three weeks to three months, depending on the wind and the map. This was time enough to come down with numerous diseases, especially scurvy, characterized by a high fever, bloody gums, falling teeth..."

A masked figure wearing a tricorn hat appears at the blue curtain. The mask, which covers the actor's entire face, has dark circles under the eyes and the mouth of a classical tragedy mask. A red stringy material oozes from the downcast lips. Strapped to his waist is a cardboard boat which the actor rocks with each slow step. He moans: "I joined the Carignan regiment as a soldier, not a sailor. Crossing the Atlantic is no Sunday outing on Lac Saint-Jean, let me tell you... If you want to try it, you'd better wait until they invent vitamin C."

"Indeed," continues the Professor. "And many suffered from yet another disease: homesickness. In those days, one out of three immigrants returned to France."

Hearing this the voyager halts and then does an about face, returning to port and sighing "Ah, my country, back to my beloved country."

The Professor calls after him. "Wait a minute. Don't leave yet. It was only an historical observation. The Compagnie des Cents Associés needs you to populate Nouvelle-France." The scorbutic mask has disappeared. "Bah," says the Professor, "he wouldn't have produced strong children anyway."

In the Professor's biomedical history lesson, demographic data and symbolic clusters overlap. The enumerated symptoms of scurvy and the statistics on the first immigrants lend factual support to the popular mythology of colonial misery and the escape back to Europe.[3] With one out of three ancestors disappearing before even founding a family, it is no wonder that French hegemony never took secure hold in North America. The dominant symbolic line crossing the Professor's history lesson is "no one wanted to be here in the first place."

In *Le Bazar* Daniel Latouche has set up a mock history lesson which demonstrates how fragments of history retained from contemporary Québécois classrooms emphasize the misery and incompetence of the first settlers. This history jumps from the 1534 Cartier expedition when "The French, late in comparison with the English and the Spanish, finally discovered what was left to discover, thinking it was China incidentally" to the 1600s when "The French, competent as ever, just couldn't get settled. They caught scurvy, their teeth fell out, and then they went back to France" (Latouche 1989:53). The scurvy-ridden and recalcitrant colonist is a popular figure in the Québécois gallery of historical prototypes.

The Professor's presentation is not quite as ludicrous, but the anachronisms show the actors/characters are juggling with historical data. Subtle evidence of chronological discrepancies appear in the Professor's lesson. The mask states he has joined the Carignan-Salières regiment, which held the dubious honor of driving the Iroquois from the territory around 1667. The Professor begs the mask to stay and help the Compagnie des Cents Associés colonize, but this organization of French traders, founded in 1627, was dissolved in 1663. The interplay between the 20th-century Professor and the 17th-century soldier, the flagrant anachronisms of outings on Lac Saint-Jean and vitamin C indicate that the production's objective is less historical accuracy than the display of historical myths, redeemed from the symbolic attic and recycled for the local, contemporary bazaar.

Trash et le sud [Trash and the south]
As the Professor exits, Trash enters from the opposite side. Kicking his feet against the ground as he moves to the platform, beating his head against the podium, and vitiating the ancestors with his characteristic half-articulated *'Ca... 'Sti... 'Ta...* curses, Trash asks: "Why, why did they have to land here? These ancestors must have been pretty stupid. I mean, nobody lived in America then."

He pulls out a switch blade and continues his litany. "... They could have gone to Mexico or Florida, 'sti... But no, they had to come here, to the coldest frigging place in America...'ca..."

He plays with the knife, sliding it over his forearm. Sweeping his gaze over the audience, Trash declares "Good thing they're dead already, these ancestors, or I'd take care of them." He exits, still spitting out half-articulated *sacres*.

Trash is the opposite of the erudite scholar. If the Professor passes as "the living proof of history"—albeit not always accurate—Trash represents the denial of history. Despite his perpetuation of history through the Québécois *sacres*, Trash pretends to stand outside of history. He wears the sign of NO PAST and he does not have the slightest notion of the originary conflicts in the settling of the Americas. He has been following the Professor's lesson enough to accept the notion of ancestors, but Trash is a contemporary subject. He is frustrated that his ancestors are not his immediate parents so that he might settle their score for having landed in the "coldest frigging place in America." Supposing that these temporally distant relatives were free agents with 20th-century hindsight, he castigates them for not having made a more sensible choice and pushed farther south. His references to warmer regions are not grounded in French-colonial history—in Lousiana, the Antilles, or the South Pacific—but in tourist culture. Québécois who can afford to escape the long northern winters flock to contemporary North American vacation colonies: to Florida, Mexico, or Puerto Rico.

Trash at once annihilates and perpetuates history. In the first instance he erases any notion of struggling for the land. "Nobody lived in America then," he presumes, thus a clean slate before the arrival of the French. The Spanish conquest never occurred, and certainly there were no native populations living in the virgin territory. In the second instance Trash's projection of an eternal winter land—and the moronic ancestor who might have chosen this as home—leads directly back to popular Québécois tropes. This harsh climate, this god-forsaken land could only be the choice of a bumbling ancestor, a prototypical born loser. 'Ca... 'Sti... 'Ta...

If the Professor is the problematic embodiment of historical scholarship and Trash is the embodiment of historical denial, both perpetuate commonly treasured tropes of misery. Performed on a splendid summer day before an audience that appears in good health, the piece automatically relegates historical misery to a symbolic museum. The following sequence contrasts the grim retrospectives of the Professor and Trash by representing ancestors who face a bright future in the Nouveau Monde.

Nouvelle-France Immigrants

A moi [Mine]

Faut-il cumuler tant de misère	What toll of misery
Pour nous porter sur cette mer?	Bore us to this sea?
Portés par l'attrait de la terre	Borne by promised land
Ecoutez cette prière, mon Dieu.	Lord, hear our prayer.

This song, reminiscent of a 17th-century ballad, accompanies the arrival of the "ancestors." The mast of a clipper propping up a flag—not the fleur-de-lis of the 17th-century French crown, but the contemporary French red, white and blue *tricolore*—appears above the blue curtain. Four bobbing heads, rolling to the waves of the Atlantic, follow. One wears a wide-brimmed straw hat, one a purple *mousquetaire* hat with an ostrich feather, one a small brown tricorn, and the last a beaver hat.

Archetypes and Ideologies for Sale 107

New World Immigrants (Jacques Drolet, Nicole Eva Morin, Maureen Martineau, Réjean Bédard). Photo: Pierre Dessureault.

As if landing, the straw-hat character jumps onto the stage and climbs up on a soapbox platform to proclaim: "Fini la France et la misère, à moi l'espace, à moi la terre" [Enough of France and hardship, space for me, land for me]. At the end of his speech, the *habitant* kicks up his heels, jumps from the crate, and disappears behind the forest backdrop.

Each of the travelers in turn steps up on the soapbox to state their motives for traveling to the New World. Each speech is punctuated by a resolute *à moi* [for me].

The adventuring nobleman, represented by an actress in a royal purple, plumed *mousquetaire* hat, says he has come for land titles and honors.

An actress coiffed in a drab tricorn and wearing a barrel marked *TONNELIER* [cooper] follows. He is a craftsman who has invested in commerce. "For me the *place du marché*," he declares, casting back to the alias of the Place Royale.

The beaver-hatted persona replaces the merchant on the soapbox. "Enough of bad luck," he announces. "For me hunting and beaver skins."

The four initial travelers have landed, but the parade of prototypical ancestors continues.

An actress, wearing a nun's habit over her blue overalls and sneakers, jumps up to announce she is tired of a life of renunciation, "For me the challenge of education."

Another actress, in blue-overall workdress but coiffed in a frilly *fille du roi* bonnet takes over the soapbox. She chirps she's had enough of living as a *pauvre fille*, "For me, at last, dowry and family."

The last character enters reluctantly as the *fille du roi* jumps off the soap box. An actor wearing a cowboy bandanna wound in pirate style around his head, thus resembling Trash, and peering myopically through thick-lensed glasses, thus resembling the Professor, the persona is a composite. Timidly waving the French tricolor flag, the sign which heralded the travelers' entrance from across the tawdry, blue-Atlantic curtain, the character moves to the soapbox.

He pipes out in a brave yet croaking voice, "Enough of... For me..." He looks around for supporters before mounting the soapbox, but he is alone. He takes a deep breath and then bleats out another try for self-affirmation: "Fini... A moi..."

He shrugs and then addresses the audience directly: "Well, I guess there's nothing left for me here." In a final salute of false bravado, he moves across the platform, still waving the mast-head flag while repeating *à moi* in an uncertain voice. His pace quickens until he escapes behind the forest backdrop.

Framed by the introductory song which describes the misery of the common traveler to the Nouveau Monde and the exit of a "lost soul" left holding the French banner, this sequence is a parade of the more prominent Québécois prototypes. By shifting hats the four actors evoke seven ancestors who appear and disappear, as if moving through a turnstile: 1) A farmer looking for richer soil, a future *habitant* or settler; 2) A court noble in search of land and honor; 3) A craftsman who wishes to become a merchant; 4) An adventurer who wishes to get rich by becoming a trapper or *coureur des bois*; 5) A nun who would throw off convent shackles to become a teacher; 6) A *fille du roi* who would acquire a dowry and erase being an orphan by becoming a mother; 7) A lost soul who has no idea why he has come.

Paradoxically, the first six ancestors, who fall into the generic categories of traditional Nouvelle-France professions, are presented under the banner of individualism. *A moi* is the title of the sequence and the rhythmic device which ties the speeches together. These are the prototypes of contemporary Québécois history lessons. That the characters might be individuals with vested interests and personal motivations creates a rift in the stereotype. The characters are drawn from a textbook, yet they have demands of a highly individualistic nature. The quotation marks propping up the anonymous ancestor are challenged by the possibility of an individual *moi* driving the 17th-century immigrant.

What of the last character, who pitifully waves the flag, who croaks out incomplete phrases in the voice of a male adolescent, who cannot articulate just what is *fini* and what is *à moi*? Described in the working script simply as *un jeune* [a young guy], wearing a bandanna that recalls Trash and coke-bottle glasses that recall the Professor, just what period, age, and social category the lost soul belongs to is uncertain. This *homme qui cherche,* who will appear periodically throughout the performance, has no teleological rationale, no reason to have come to New France, no vocation to direct him. He appears to search for an anchor across the diachronic and synchronic seas. He has forgotten or never found his purpose. He is left holding an historically absurd flag, a banner in search of a nation. He is neither here nor there, neither now nor then.

Juxtaposed with the historical prototypes—the Trapper, the Settler, the King's Daughter, the Missionary, the Merchant—the anonymous *jeune* seems to be without an identity. All the roles have been taken. Or have they? Perhaps his role is precisely that of the *Perdu*, the subject lost in the

Americas. As a lost soul in search of an identity he merits a prime position in the Québécois ancestral gallery.

The Native Tree

L'Arbre autochtone (Passé)
Coiffed by a massive wig of black hair and a feathered headband and wearing a bark mask, a figure enters and petrifies with arms outstretched like tree branches. "It is in this valley that my tribe took root," announces the mask. "It is in on the banks of this river that I grew, under this sun that I flourished."

Dancing a sort of jig and singing a French-Canadian ditty, two actors enter. They are wearing stocking caps and *ceinture fléchée* [woven chevron sashes] which encode them as *Anciens Canadiens*.

Youkayo, youkayo,	
A la pêche à la rivière	Fishing in the river
Youkayo, youkayo,	
Vous ne m'attendez pas.	You're not expecting me.

Still singing the song of carefree fishermen who will "capture the fish unawares," the two *Canayens* begin to saw at the trunk of the Native Tree. The mask topples into their arms and the woodsmen carry the frozen figure off stage.

This sequence introduces the problematic figure of the *autochtone*. Evocation of the Amerindian, the Native Tree is also an indication of the prophylactic quotation marks framing this representation. Symbolic cluster which fuses nature and pre-colonial inhabitants into one, the mask is a hypostasis of the aboriginal Other. Playing off the global botanic metaphors of *Salut*, the mask also suggests that a Native Tree exists prior to and outside of the Québécois genealogical complex.

Of all the masks which parade through *Salut,* the Native Tree is the only one which stands outside of the irreverential self-mocking frame. This mask is the sign of representation itself. It is the indication of an absence. It speaks in French and in a disembodied voice. It remains impassive as the woodsmen chop it down and cart it off. Sign of the absent Other and the ravaged land, the Tree is not party to the inside joke between *nous, les Canayens.*

That the woodsmen are indeed elements of the Québécois historical fun house is obvious. What could be more *typiquement canadien* than a lumberjack, taming the wilds of North America? But the iconography of the *Canayens*, the stocking caps and the chevron belts, refer less to Nouvelle-

France than a more recent period in Québécois history. *L'époque de la ceinture fléchée* denotes the national construction period when folk crafts were appropriated as the traditional backbone of the Québécois nation. In the working script the *Canayens* are singing "une chanson folklorique quétaine" [a kitch folk song]. For the Parminou—who has throughout its historical series strongly identified with Québécois folk tradition—citing a folksong for its *quétaine* quality demonstrates an ironic reflexivity. Even the use of the term "Canayen" is a self-deprecating reference to the French Canadian.

Because it is such a blatant representation of an absent subject, the Native Tree reinforces the parody of *nous et notre parenté* [us, our kith and kin]. The Tree stands impassively in the agitation of the historical archetypes jostling for positions in the Nouveau Monde. Among the *coureurs des bois, habitants*, and *filles du roi*, among the Catholic missionaries, the craftsmen and merchants, and among the "lost in the Americas" immigrants, the *autochtone* is the opposite side of the mirror, uninterested in the projections which flit across the surface and continue to people the Québécois bazaar.

Libidinal Exploration of the Nouveau Monde

La Fille laide #2
A squeal heralds the second appearance of the Ugly Girl. The frilly bonnet and pig snout emerge above the blue Quebec flag/Atlantic ocean curtain. Gasping and giggling she announces:

"You know, I have heard that there are six men for every woman in Nouvelle-France. Well, I'm perfectly willing to take on all six."

Miming a rapid backstroke, she swims across the Atlantic toward the stage, in the direction of the Americas.

Missionaires
Singing phrases of the *Jubilate Deo*, an actor steps onto the platform. He is wearing the wide-brimmed black hat, white plastron, and prominent cross of a 17th-century priest. His face is covered with a white mask bearing an enormous phallic nose. He steps forward on the platform, his arms stretched out as if to address a crowd of disciples.

He announces he has received the formidable task of establishing parishes among the French settlers, as well as evangelizing the "savages who run naked through the woods." He is wondering if he will be able to control the "tempestuous ardor of the female beauties and their taste for the exotic" because "to them, clothed as I am, I will certainly appear exotic."

Perhaps, the priest continues, he should avoid this fatal attraction and diabolical temptation by removing his clothes and running naked through the woods himself.

A second missionary dressed in a white skullcap and cape and masked by the ubiquitous *commedia* sausage nose enters. Surprised in his reverie, the first missionary makes a hasty sign of the cross and then exits with a perfunctory bow to his Jesuit brother.

A 17th-century Missionary (Réjean Bédard). Photo: Pierre Dessureault.

With his arms stretched in a cross, the second missionary addresses the audience. "Evangelize the savage who runs naked through the woods, this is my calling. And what a noble mission it is. I am certain of great success with the Hurons, because I myself happen to be a *gai... luron"* [a "gay blade" or a "gay Huron"].

He guffaws at his joke. Then he cocks his head and hypertrophied nose in an expectant pause. He waits for a laugh from the audience which is not forthcoming. "Don't you get it? ... *gai luron/gai Huron*... no?" A few snickers from the spectators acknowledge the pun. The second missionary dismisses the audience with a jerk of the hand and then, resuming a devout posture and the liturgical song which opened the tableau, backs away and exits through the panels of the forest backdrop.

Le Coureur des soeurs Bois [Running the Woods Sisters]
The head of a beaver followed by the brim of an enormous beaver hat emerges from behind the panels. The actor wearing the hat is crawling across the stage and sniffing the ground. He stands, revealing a tail which hangs to his heels, and sniffs the air. He looks at the audience. It is the Lost Soul, who with a shrug of his shoulders as if to say "no game available," begins speaking in a *Midi* [southern France] accent.

"Hein, engagez-vous qu'ils disaient." "Sign up, they said. You'll find forests full of game, rivers and lakes full of fish, they said. What they didn't say is that women are rare in this country."

He cocks his head toward a burst of laughter coming from his left. Two women coiffed in colonial bonnets appear to be rowing in his direction. "Hey, did you see the *colon?"* asks the first woman. "He certainly looks like a *colon*," says the other. "Did you catch the *habitant*?" says the first. "Sure looks like a *habitant*," laughs the second. "And did you catch the tail?" asks the first woman. Both collapse with laughter. "I think we should get a closer look." Having reached the platform, they climb up as if disembarking.

Confronting the beaver-tailed New World savage, the two *filles du roi* introduce themselves politely. "I'm Jérémienne Bois [Woods]," says the first. "And I'm Eloise Bois, her sister," says the second. "Et moi je suis un coureur des bois" [And I'm a runner of the woods], declares the man twirling his enormous tail between his legs.

The Woods sisters let out a shriek and begin running in place, as if to escape the man. Also running in place with his tongue and his tail wagging, the Trapper pursues the women in a cartoon chase. He doubles the speed and passes them. The women look at each other and then escape through the panels.

Realizing he is left alone, the Trapper drops the tail, and turns toward the audience with a helpless shrug. "Comment je vais me brancher en Nouvelle-France sans une femme?" [How can I connect in Nouvelle-France without a woman?] With the defeated attitude of the Lost Soul, the man retreats behind the backdrop, dragging his tail behind him.

The Marriage Business

Mariage d'affaire
As if he had been observing the scene below, the Professor appears in one frame of the Couple's windows and announces: "In those days, daughters of the king and soldiers would meet at Madame Bourdon's. This is where marriages were arranged."

Two figures in military tricorn hats recalling the colonial brigades appear trumpeting "Allons chez Madame Bourdon." Two other figures coiffed in the frilly bonnets of the king's daughters appear trumpeting "We are at Madame Bourdon's." After exchanging greetings with a few perfunctory nods of the head, the two men and the two women begin wooing a potential mate and selling their wares. They are speaking, moving, and competing to a rap-song beat.[4]

The men have but two weeks to find a wife or they will lose their fishing and hunting privileges which are the immediate reason for establishing roots in Nouvelle-France. The women have also come to find opportunity, but if not wed, they might be sent back to France. The men boast of acquisitions such as a stall on the Place Royale or a pot in pewter. The women boast of dowries accorded by King Louis and flaunt their body wares, clapping on their hips and breasts which will bear and nurture forthcoming generations.

The heftier of the two soldiers—the one who has vaunted his pewter pot—picks up the heftier woman saying "I'll take you because you're fat. At least I'm sure you'll last through winter," and exits carrying his bride.

The slighter leftover man and woman shrug their shoulders toward the audience and then move hesitantly toward each other. The match might still be productive they declare in rap rhythm. The couple could "plant roots and bear fruits." *Marché conclu!* [It's a deal!] says the Husband. *Mon doux Jésus!* [Sweet Jesus!] concludes the Wife.

After exploring the libidinal economy of the ancestors, the play tackles the business of marriage. Previous scenes have explored sexual drive and haphazard couplings as the motor of Québécois genealogy. In this scene, ancestry is the fact of a material exchange. The marriage business is, like any other, a negotiation of goods. Fishing rights and dowries, market stalls and flesh, pewter pots and wombs can all be bartered. In any case, everything in the 17th-century was considered the property of the French regency.

Desperate to people the Nouveau Monde and thus capture both the Canadian territory and the capital of errant males in search of furs in the wilderness, Louis XIV sent young and able bodied men and women to reproduce and found a colony. The king's daughters were packed off to the New World with a small dowry and the order to marry. The enlisted soldiers were equally subjects of the crown and obliged to marry within fifteen days or lose all claim to the land and risk being summarily shipped back to Europe.

The Parminou projects the 17th-century model through a modern rap. The song and dance advertise bodies and other products for sale. Here the actors pick up the materialist analysis announced in the Professor's opening sales pitch for family lineages. The biological and cultural reproduction of ancestors is a "marriage business" where bodies, objects, and symbols are self-consciously depicted as commodities.

The anachronistic rap has the effect of simultaneously reactivating and problematizing history. Played in the contemporary mode, historical data escapes textbook truth and becomes a dilemma of the present. The actors constantly remind the audience that we are not in 17th-century New France but in a street theatre on the 20th-century Place Royale.

The Ugly Girl Finds her Mate

La Fille laide #3
"Coo-coo" giggles the Ugly Girl. The pig mask peeks over the blue curtain, and then bursts into the arena. In search of a prospective husband, the character has at last crossed the ocean and arrived in Nouvelle-France, the promised land where males outnumber females six to one. Spying "likely prospects," she moves straight toward the audience and directly accosts male spectators.

"Well, hello there," she coos in a husky voice to a man pushing a baby stroller. "My what nice, strong arms," she exclaims, palpating her victim's shoulder. "Now *you* could produce healthy children..." Noticing the child in the stroller, who is staring in wide-eyed wonder at the mask, and the woman by the man's side who wears a wry grin, the Ugly Girl turns away. "Oh dear, I guess he's already taken."

"Hey there, handsome," she continues, pouncing on another spectator, a younger man who stands with a friend. As if suddenly noticing her prospective catch is also accompanied, the Ugly Girl falters. "No, he's too good looking. I'd have to watch him all the time."

"Oh, but this one is perfect," she exclaims heading toward a solitary spectator in the crowd. "Young, muscular, and in his prime. And ugly enough for me." The burly actor lumbers toward his prey. "You're a perfect catch." She falls on her knees before the spectator, who after a brief hesitation agrees to play the game.

"Be mine," sighs the mask in a husky voice. "You should know, I have hidden charms. And they're all yours to discover. I'm offering my dowry and my faithfulness. Not a bad deal, wouldn't you say?"

"And there just happens to be a church around the corner." The Ugly Girl swoops the man up in her arms and runs off toward the Notre Dame church on the opposite side of the Place Royale.

The Professor and the Lost Soul Discover the Indians

Un homme qui cherche [A man searching]
The "lost in the Americas" persona who first appeared carrying the flag of the Nouvelle-France immigrants and then wearing the beaver hat of the *coureur des soeurs Bois* appears. He is still searching for a wife, crawling over the terrain composed by the wooden platform, sniffing the ground for tracks.

Discouraged, he stands and addresses the spectators. "Found a family, they said... Have children, they said... They must have forgotten how it's done... Or I just don't have the knack... I always thought it took a man and a woman..." Still searching, he wanders off and exits through the forest backdrop.

Le Professeur et les Iroquois
Lugging a voluminous atlas, the Professor enters. As he speaks, he is taking notes and reflecting on History.

"If Louis XIV had sent more men and women to Nouvelle-France, we would undoubtedly be basking in the sun somewhere in Louisiana at this very moment." The Professor adopts sun-bathing poses. "Or on the banks of the Great Lakes. Or maybe in the Ohio valley. These were all territories we occupied at that time..."

A Carignan soldier stumbles on stage. An arrow is stuck through his head. Yelping and wailing, he crosses the stage. He pauses on his way out to ask the audience: "Would anybody here happen to have an aspirin?"

The Professor gapes at the passing figure and then corrects the history lesson: "Sorry, territory occupied by the Iroquois." He clears his throat apologetically. "Uh, just a slight historical error," he says as he exits.

Un homme qui cherche
The "man searching" reappears. He is wearing a gleeful smile as he steps forward to address the audience.

"You could hardly run after skirts in these parts so I just kept running the woods. There I finally found her. And is she beautiful! She smells wonderful, she has adorable little tits and long hair. She whispers sweet nothings to me, words like 'Kotkanada, Guinibomaga, Kinawedigiak'. Em-hmm but that's nice... There's just one problem: when we sleep together, she tickles me with her feathers."

From behind the forest backdrop, a hand holding a feather reaches out to touch the actor's cheek. Shivering with delight, he turns toward the titillating feather. With a glance over his shoulder, he addresses a final word to the audience: "Excuse me, but I have to run. I have a family to found."

In the Professor's corrected history lesson and in the end to the Lost Soul's quest, the Indian is once again the absent Other. In the Native Tree sequence the bark mask figured the absence of the *autochtone*. Here other devices indicate that this is a theatrical Indian spoken through actors. The gadget-shop arrow stuck through the head of the Carignan soldier and the tickling feather manipulated by a detached hand are as much signs of absence as popular projections of the Indian. The Indian words which have seduced the *coureur des bois* are not an articulated discourse, but "sweet nothings" which the trapper does not understand.

What do these discoveries of the Indian suggest in relation to the Québécois characters? The Professor, still clutching his ponderous history of the ancestors and clinging to the myth of a lost French empire, encounters another history. The *coureur des bois* encounters another culture, or at least what we suspect to be another culture. Disappearing into the "woods" of the theatrical backdrop, he "goes native." He is off to found a family which might not be recorded in any French-Canadian parish registry. Or he is off to form another branch of the national family tree, the Métis. We can only speculate as to how the Lost Soul finally finds his way.

Further Couplings

Accouplement #3
The Couple appear at the windows in time to observe the erstwhile ancestor disappear into the forest. After a pause they begin their dialogue.

WOMAN: *Vieille branche*, something's still bothering me.
MAN: What's that, *vieille souche*?

WOMAN: I wonder how our ancestors chose their names.
MAN: Well, that there...
WOMAN: How come they got names like Rochettes [stones]?
MAN: You don't think they were using gadgets, do you?
(Together shaking their heads "no" and nodding "yes.")
WOMAN: Like in the sex shops?
MAN: Mm-hmm.
WOMAN: Now did I say that? ... But what about Rouleaux [curlers]?
MAN: Please, not with curling irons!
WOMAN: And Houde [a Québécois surname and the franco-phonetic transcription of "hood"]?
MAN: Spare me, not on the top of their cars!
WOMAN: Certainly not. But what about Desharnais [harnesses]? Now talk about sado-macho...
MAN: I am so ashamed.

Both hide their heads, simultaneously sinking below the window frames.

L'ordonnance [Edict]
An actor wearing a 17th-century tricorn and wig marches on stage. He is carrying a thick scroll which marks him as a town crier. He opens the scroll, which spills onto the stage in disorderly fashion, and shouts out the following.

"As of 2 May 1706, it is forbidden to keep pigs in the houses of Quebec."

A woman wearing a colonial bonnet pops up at the window. "Very well," she says, "I guess I'll just have to put my husband out of the house."

This totally gratuitous shtick à la québécoise provokes a burst of laughter in the audience.

Accouplement #4
Like jack-in-the-box figures, the head of the 17th-century matron is replaced by the 20th-century woman in curlers. Her husband appears simultaneously and, for the first time, opens the dialogue.

MAN: Listen up here, old trunk. You can't deny some of our ancestors were virtuous people. Take names like Labonté [goodness] or Lésperance [hope], or Lafoi [faith], or Lacharité [charity].
WOMAN: True enough. But what about the Faucher [*fauché* = dead broke], the Raté [failure], the Haché [chopped up], the Potvin [graft]?
MAN: Uh, well there... It's a damn shame.

After this short-lived attempt to find redeeming value in the ancestors' names, the Husband slides out of sight. He is followed by the Wife who, after a double-chinned and eyebrow-raised pan to the audience, also disappears.

Ancestral Encounters

L'agriculteur d'hier et d'aujourd'hui [The farmer of yesterday and today]
Two men step on the stage. They are dressed in the ubiquitous overalls and sneakers, the "actor-at-work" costume. One wears the straw hat of a *habitant* [settler or farmer]. The other wears a green visor cap stamped with a brand of commercial dairy products. They are accompanied by their "cows" which they push forward as they speak simultaneously.

FARMER OF YESTERDAY: Claudine, move over here so I can get hold of your teat. That's it, right over the bucket.
FARMER OF TODAY: Step up there, Clauding, Claudong, get in line all of you, move along so we can milk you. We haven't got all day, you know; there are over a hundred of you. That's it, get your udder into the nozzle.

The "cows" are identical masks bearing the short-horned muzzle and the black and white spotted coat of a Holstein. They clomp on stage with their "hooves" clothed in sneakers. Throughout the following dialogue the "cows" repeatedly stomp their feet, punctuating the stutterings of the 17th and 20th-century Gagnon farmers who suddenly notice each other.

"Wa-wha-what are you doin' on mh-mmh-my land?" question the two men simultaneously. "Wa-wha-whatt'ya mean your land?" stutter out the two men. "This is my land because I'm a ga-gah-Gagnon." The contemporary farmer declares he is the direct descendant of Mathurin Gagnon who cleared the land in 1662.

"Bu-bu-but I am Mathurin Gagnon" declares the *habitant*. "And yu-yuh-you must be my *descendant*." "Then yu-yuh-you must be my *remontant* [ascendant or 'pick-me-up' drink]," declares the contemporary dairy farmer.

After a—quite literally—slapstick routine where each Gagnon slaps the other on the back or on the jaw to help him enunciate, the farmers move off stage to have a little drink together.

The "cows" are left alone to ruminate on the times. The 17th-century animal moos, "We used to give our maximum in the old days." The 20th-century animal responds with a high pitched moo and a flippant kick of her hind hoof. "Today we only give them 2%, so there."

Exuent the cows.

The Stuttering Gagnons (Réjean Bédard, Jacques Drolet). Photo: Pierre Dessurreault.

Archetypes and Ideologies for Sale 121

Le bateau et le pouceux [The boat and the hitch-hiker]
Standing on the grassy plot that runs parallel to the stage, an actor wearing a yellow hard hat is holding out his thumb as if to hail passing cars. At the blue curtain another actor wearing a tricorn hat appears to be rowing toward the stage.

"Where are you going?" shouts the ocean voyager. "I'm on my way to Bay James," answers the hitch-hiker. With a fraternal wave, the rower continues. "I'm on my way to the New World... No land in France."

"No work in the city," replies the hard-hat. "I'll make some money at the dam then go home." "Me too," answers the 17th-century migrant, "I'll put some money aside and then go back home, back to France, the most beautiful country in the world."

"I guess we're in the same boat, hein?" says the construction worker. The rower suddenly doubles his speed and comes to a screeching halt in front of the hitch-hiker. "Welcome aboard," says the 17th-century traveler. "Hey, you're not afraid of adventure," replies the hard-hat as he climbs into the vehicle.

L'Arbre autochtone (Présent)
As the fellow travelers speed away, the Native Tree enters and takes his position, planted at center stage.

"It is in this reserve that my tribe took root. It is on the banks of this bay that I grew, under this sun that I flourished."

And, as in the previous Native Tree tableau, two *Canayens* descend on the tree, singing and dancing to the tune of "Youkayo, youkayo, youkayo sur la rivière." But this time they are wearing yellow hard hats marked HYDRO-QUEBEC and they are attacking the Tree with a chain saw.

The Native Tree falls into the arms of the Hydro-Québec workers and is carted off stage.

These sequences suggest historical junctions which have been virtually absent in the previous flash sequences of *Salut vieille branche!*. Here ancestors and descendants meet in the same theatrical time byte. These improbable encounters represent an intersection of temporal parallels. All three of these tableaux suggest the continuity of historical subjects, despite the disruption of technological changes.

In the "Farmer of today and yesterday," the stuttering Gagnons project history as reiteration. Their speech is—quite literally—redundant. Their argument centers on the Gagnon entitlement to the land, which proves to be one and the same. As the two Gagnons join in celebrating their shared claim to the land, their "cows" are left to reflect on the technological gap between the 17th-century and the 20th-century farms.

In the "Boat and the hitch-hiker," a 17th-century migrant worker hooks up with a 20th-century migrant worker. They become fellow travelers in search of work, animated by the promise of riches, new horizons and the eventual return home of the prodigal son. The technological gap is erased when the hitch-hiker jumps aboard the 17th-century immigrant's boat and both speed away to find work in Nouvelle-France or Nouveau Québec.[5]

The coinciding of these two voyages projects the popular image of the French-Canadian as a perpetually exiled and dislocated subject. The first is "temporarily" settling in the New World wilderness; the second is "temporarily" migrating to the icy regions of New Quebec, site of the Bay James hydro-electric project. It is in this setting that the third ancestral encounter takes place.

The "Native Tree (present)" is a reiteration of the "Native Tree (past)" tableau. Except for the terms "reserve" and "bay," the text of the 20th-century *arbre autochtone* is identical to the 17th-century rendition. As for the invaders, only their hats and their instruments have changed. Because of the citational nature of the tableau and the intemporal quality of the Native Tree, this encounter also collapses centuries into a single moment. But this tableau, a parody within a parody, has a critical edge.

Again the Native Tree is a symbolic cluster referring to an ideal symbiosis between the land and the original inhabitants. Nature and Indian culture appear as cyclic revivals. Despite technological disruptions and the upheaval of progress, the Native Tree provides a stable pole. Or does it? The threat to this ideal Other is implicit in the context represented by the two hard-hats.

They are the same diligent workers carrying out their daily duty of cutting down the trees to make way for progress and unwittingly plundering the land, as their *Canayen* forefathers did. But the scope of the "wilderness taming" is much vaster today. The Hydro-Québec complex—which ironically was the cornerstone of the Québécois *maîtres chez nous* economic independence project—provides a substantial portion of the province's revenue. Completion of the Bay James dams would allow Quebec to sell energy to the United States and would virtually assure economic autonomy. But flooding New Quebec to light New York would signify the destruction of the taiga. Severe criticism from international ecologists and the region's

Archetypes and Ideologies for Sale

The Native Tree, circa 1989. Photo: Pierre Dessureault.

Native Canadians—the veritable *autochtones* who stand outside of the theatrical frame—has challenged the completion of the project.

This introduction of contemporary political reality into *Salut* opens a wedge in the general picture of historical continuity. The time in what the Parminou working script indicates as *passages spatio-temporels* is primarily cyclic. Although the actors have exchanged elements of their costumes or words of their texts as the characters slide from the 17th to the 20th century, the initial message of these ancestral encounters has been *plus ça change, plus c'est pareil* [the more things change, the more they stay the same]. Yet the threat implicit in the last Native Tree sequence casts a doubt on the notion of perpetual rebirth.

The End of the Line?

Faire ou ne pas faire... des enfants [To have or not to have... children]
A couple appears in the windows. The man is wearing the *habitant* straw hat. The woman is wearing a woolen cowl. They are thus encoded as Early Canadian peasants. As if seated in rocking chairs, they are moving back and forth in the window frames.

The man pokes his head out and barks "Joachim, Réjean, Claudine..." in a seemingly endless recital of fourteen names, which leaves him hoarse. "Off to bed with you," he ends in a rasping whisper.

"Husband," says the woman as both rock in and out of audience view. "You'd best get to work on a fifteenth rocking chair." "Expecting another, are we? Well, there's always room for one more," says the man as he keels over and disappears. "Indeed there is," says the woman as she keels over in turn and disappears.

The empty window frames are filled with two newspapers. The newspaper veil is lowered to reveal a man wearing a tie and horn-rimmed glasses. "Eve, darling," he chirps to his companion who is still masked by the morning paper, "Do you remember the conversation we had a while ago?"

The newspaper of the second window is lowered to reveal a woman with a bright red-lipstick mouth and a white terry cloth turban. "Which one, dear?" she responds with the eternally cheerful smile of a toothpaste or a laxative commercial.

"Well, you know, the one about eventually some day considering the possibility of planning a family." As her bright smile twists into a grimace of disgust, the husband hastily states, "I know... I know you said it was best to wait until we had our heated swimming pool and our condo. But we have them now, my dearest."

"But darling," says the wife rustling her newspaper, "this is no world for children." "What is a planet without children?" asks the husband. "What are children without a planet?" answers the wife, batting her eyelashes and panning to the audience for approval.

And then, tapping her finger on a classified advertisement, she continues enthusiastically. "Perhaps we could adopt something... like a little chihuahua."

After processing Québécois history through ancestral encounters of the past and the present, this sequence turns to the future and introduces the troubling notion that history might be finite. In an interview[6] Réjean Bédard, one of the *Salut* actors, declared that the principal question driving the creation—and the question the actors wished to provoke in the audience—was "What kind of ancestors will we be?" If the dialogue of the *couple moderne* is any indication of reality, the answer is there won't be any descendants around to remember their Québécois ancestors. In fact there may be no one left at all. "What is a planet without children?" asks the husband. "What are children without a planet?" responds the wife.

The presence of numerous children in the audience undermines this end-of-the-line pronouncement. But the picture of the contemporary Québécoise who refuses to reproduce the species plays off of the old fear of disappearing as a people. Despite the burlesque nature of the performance, the question of *faire ou ne pas faire... des enfants* is dead serious. It relates to the primordial question of *être ou ne pas être... Québécois*.

The juxtaposed tableaux of the *couple ancien* and the *couple moderne* dramatize Québécois demographics over three centuries. If the woman of Nouvelle-France was at first rare, she made up for lost time by producing large families. Generally married by the age of fifteen and bearing ten to fifteen children, the 17th-century mother's fertility rate rapidly doubled, then quintupled the population within one century. Although the numbers declined with industrialization and urban development, the *Canadiennes* retained the highest fertility rates in the west through the mid-1950s. Yet, by the early 1970s fertility rates were declining to below the number necessary for generation renewal (Henripin and Martin:1991).

This decline is here represented by the voluntarily childless couple. The 1989 *couple moderne* is a union of "yuppies" (or rather "quppies" as they are referred to locally in a doubly ironic take on this recent MADE IN AMERICA product). The modern, prototypical Québécois family in this farce consists of a man, a woman, and eventually a dog. In contrasting with the peasant couple, this Adam and Eve are upper class and still rising. Products of the 1980s "me generation," they are focused on self-gratification rather than survival. They have the luxury of choosing if and when to have children. The wife has forgone pregnancy for a swimming pool and a condo. Now she dismisses genealogical continuity as hopeless anyway since the planet is doomed. She proposes instead to adopt a chihuahua, whose foreign name and presentation in the classified section smacks of the commodity child currently sold and bought on an international adoption market.

This satire of modern wedlock has an ambivalent edge. It is obviously a critique of the "quppy" class. At the same time the text placed in the mouth of the modern Eve carries the ecological and feminist concerns of the Parminou. The picture of the pro-choice, environmentally-conscious woman, who wears her principles like the latest fashion clothes lends an ironic twist to the scene. The parody of the quppy sends back a mocking image of the play itself.

If the prototypical fin-de-siècle family is this sterile couple smiling brightly from their television frame and selling ecology like toothpaste or laxatives, then this may be the end of the line in two respects: that of Québécois genealogy and that of the ideological grounding of the play. Enough playing with history; the show is over. But this is a bazaar of the imaginary and symbols have a persistent after life. This is not the end of the line. The "quppy" couple is not the last entry in the historical gallery, simply the latest.

Last Week I Gave Birth to my Ancestors

D'analphabète à l'étudiante [From illiterate to student]
An actress coiffed in a peasant cowl enters. She is holding what is apparently a soup bowl. "V'là la soupe," she shouts, miming the spooning out of porridge to a brood of hungry children. "Here, swallow that. Stop drooling. Don't drop your bread on the floor. Hey there, leave some for your little brother. Don't waste the food," she clucks to the invisible children.

Then she addresses the audience: "In Nouvelle-France we work hard to make ends meet. We may not be many women, but we sure churn out children. Trouble is you can't just hatch these kids. You have to feed them, raise them, educate them. My hope is that one of my fourteen here gets some instruction. But in 1663 it's not easy for us folks. Still I'll see one or two through proper schooling."

The woman turns the "bowl" onto her head and is now coiffed by a mortarboard.

With a dazzling smile and a toss of her tassel, the student presents herself to the audience. "I am a graduate student at *Uu-Cul* [U.Q. or the University of Quebec[7]]. I'm writing my dissertation on the *filles du roi*. Well, don't snicker like that, you in the back row. Only a very few of the king's daughters were prostitutes. I know what I'm talking about because I've done extensive research."

"And I am proud to say that I am the actual descendant of one of those *filles du roi*," continues the student. "I just discovered my origins. I've been in rebirth therapy, and last week I gave birth to my ancestor."

She goes on to say that she had always suspected women were the makers of history. "And when I think that our genealogical trees are founded by men... *ça m' mets en tabar...*" The student spits out a Québécois *sacre*, before taking a deep breath and pulling herself together.

"Sorry, I'm getting carried away. I think I'll go to the floating baths to calm down." She turns to leave with a final swish of her tassel. Instead of exiting, the student freezes in place.

Du noble au millionaire [From noble to millionaire]
An actress—dressed in the jabot and royal purple, plumed hat of *ancien régime* nobility—walks onto the stage. Sweeping the audience with grandiose gestures, the noble states the following.

"I left Paris for these prairies. I have earned many a title and many a deed to this land. Every year a new descendant sprouts forth who will in turn people the country with numerous descendants: audacity, intelligence and pride define our noble lineage."

Reversing the jabot to reveal a black bow tie and a starched white tuxedo plastron, the noble undergoes metamorphosis. Hanging his hat on the waiting arm of the petrified feminist student and flailing a cigar, the French noble shifts to the persona of the Québécois entrepreneur. With the sweeping gestures of his ancestor, the millionaire addresses the audience.

"I bought buildings which I turned into condos. I acquired entire neighborhoods which I turned into my personal domaine. Research has shown my high lineage. I have it all, but..." The millionaire begins to sob. "But I am miserable. I'm cracking up, I'm stressing out. I am the last descendant of this noble family. I am, in a word, sterile. This is the end."

The Noble/Millionaire freezes with his arms outstretched, as if splayed on a cross.

Voyageurs [Travelers]
An actor enters carrying a black bag and wearing a 17th-century powdered wig. He glances furtively to either side before addressing the audience in rapid-fire speech and a Parisian accent.[8] "Salut les mecs! J'arrive de Paris. Je sais tout, j'ai tout vu, j'ai tout entendu." [Hi guys. Just arrived from Paris. I know everything, I've seen everything, heard everything.]

"And I've come to bring culture to you locals. Yes, indeed, I am the greatest *couturier* of France, in other words, of the world."

Looking around him furtively, the future illustrious *couturier* continues speaking to the audience in more confidential tones. "I've had a few problems with the French police, but I'm here in this new country to teach my descendants how to work the needles so they can compete with the world's greatest designers. I can see it all now." He pauses to stretch an imaginary logos across the stage. "My lineage will be famous. Our name will be Saint Laurent, like the great river." He throws off his wig.

Turning his toes inward and guffawing like the village fool, the actor transforms into his 20th-century descendant. With tongue protruding, the character greets the community in a heavy Québécois accent. "Salut tout le monde. I'm back from Nepal where I met my true spiritual father. He taught me everything there is to know in the who-o-le, entire universe. Including acupuncture. I don't know why, but needles seem to attract me. I'm back home because I know you need me... plus I had a few problems with the local police, but this can happen to anybody."

Looking again to either side, the contemporary needle worker slips his black bag onto the arm of the frozen Noble/Millionaire. His motion to make a quick getaway is suspended. Before he can escape, he freezes, caught in the museum with the other statues.

The ancestors of the *Salut vieille branche!* bazaar have evolved through multiple time frames. The production first portrayed history through the distancing eyes of the Professor, rummaging through his ponderous history book, and the reflexive gaze of the Couple, musing over the names of their forefathers and peering out their windows over the stage and audience below. In a second phase ancestral prototypes paraded before the Couple's gaze and then encountered their contemporary descendants. The final phase of the production proposes a theatrical reincarnation exercise. The 17th-century characters transform into their 20th-century counterparts. Temporal transitions occur in the most elementary theatrical space: the body of the actor.

The 20th-century feminist student recovers her illiterate *fille du roi* ancestor's lost history. The 20th-century millionaire acquires property as his ancestor acquired land titles, but the noble lineage comes to a halt here. Unaware of his ancestral origins, the 20th-century acupuncturist has traveled in search of a spiritual father and returns to unwittingly perpetuate the dubious legacy of his 17th-century forefather.

Flipping elements of their costumes to impersonate first the Nouvelle-France cliché and then the parallel Québécois cliché, the performers in these closing tableaux remind the audience that the *I* who "gave birth to my ancestor last week" is indeed an actor. The ancestors are of recent generation; they were born last week during rehearsal or in the past minutes of the performance.

The frenetic flitting along the diachronic axis and the rapid fire appearance/disappearance of the characters establish the contemporary nature of this take on history. It has the video-clip, fast-food rhythm of contemporary reality. And, since *Salut* never allows the participants to forget the theatrical framing, this history shows its seams. It is a self-conscious creation, a product of the present.

The Last Word

Finale

An actor wearing a beaver hat enters and stands next to the petrified figures of the Student, the Millionaire, and the Needle Worker. The last ancestor addresses the audience with great conviction.

"All I want are the woods. That's the real life. I'm not interested in anything except beaver skins. Who cares about founding a family in Nouvelle-France? They won't catch me. Others can go digging for roots while I'm out hunting. That's where my future is."

This brief speech from the *coureur des bois* seems to waken the ossified statues of the national gallery. Each in turn steps forward and proudly speaks out.

NEEDLE WORKER: We the travelers and adventurers are the original stock of the country.

MILLIONAIRE: We the businessmen, the investors and noble entrepreneurs, are the backbone of this country.

STUDENT: If you really look at history, it's us women who founded this country.

The *coureur du bois* reverses his beaver hat to reveal the bark mask of the Native Tree. In a neutral voice he says: "C'est nous la première souche du pays."

"Salut vieille branche!" shout the other actors, as they bow to the Indian mask. Then, removing their disguises, all four bow to the audience with a final, resounding "Salut vieille branche!"

The applause from the audience is incorporated into the salute to the Native Tree. When the applause dies away, one of the actors announces that *Salut* will be performed again in one hour and twice every Saturday and Sunday afternoon through July and August.

Then the spectators drift away toward other attractions on the Place Royale. Some actors engage in discussion with friends or representatives from the Patrimoine. Other Parminou members begin arranging their materials for the next performance.

Salut vieille branche! began with two complicitous warnings addressed to the audience. First, genealogical knowledge is a product like any other which can be bought and sold on the tourist marketplace of the Place Royale. Second, "you and your kin" will be made a mockery. As promised the production is a farcical parading of Québécois stock characters. The show ends with a last word from the only "straight" character, the Native Tree proclaiming, "I am the original stock of the country."

It is ironic that this character, which the actors and the audience honor with a salute and applause as the original *vieille branche,* is the farthest removed from this curious self-mocking ritual. This hypostasis of nature and the aboriginal stands outside of the family joke. Although the Native Tree may be given the last word, the mask retains a stony silence. It speaks, as do all the masks, through the actor. But the Native Tree is unique in its self-referential symbolism. It is not a speaking subject, but the sign of an absent voice. It escapes the jibes directed at *nous*, at Québécois kith and kin, because it is the citation of an absence.

This is especially evident when the actor grapples with physical reality, fumbling to switch from the beaver hat to the Native Tree mask and disrupting any smooth illusionary magic. Here a seriously intended last word from the original branch meets the wall of theatrical representation and implodes. The entire spectacle was "merely parody." It was all "just for laughs," wasn't it?

Of Commodities and Kin

PROFESSEUR: Justement, j'ai une couple de lignées à vendre. Ça remonte à 1663. Je vends pas cher...
TRASH: Ma lignée ne m'intéresse pas...

Just what does the spectator carry away from this self-conscious commodification of Québécois genealogy if not a series of questions. Just how much is Québécois identity worth, what is the value of kinfolk on the contemporary multicultural market? Can history be salvaged and recycled like so many bits of plastic? Can family lineages be bought and sold like junk food on the historic Place Royale? What is the value of family names when reduced to a few soft-porn titles? Are historical roots and blood ties just so much "commodities and kin" nonsense?

Two elements driving the performance determine that, in fact, *Salut* holds a greater value than the tourist product it passes for. First, the casting of Québécois founding roots in a deconstructive and culturally relativist mode represents a healthy critique of nationalist ideology. Second, the very nature of the self-mockery crossing the performance implies the complicity of the community.

Kinship is portrayed as a burlesque artifact, but this product would not exist were it not for collective bonds. The *nous* or *vous et votre parenté* of the opening song are what give *Salut vieille branche!* any meaning whatsoever. The production is a self-mocking rendition of Québécois origins which presupposes a collective self to be mocked. It is an "inside joke" which can only be understood with inside knowledge.

On the one hand, history and ancestry are exposed as products of the present, contemporary fabrications which can be bartered at the local postmodern bazaar. On the other hand, there is both an assumption of and a longing for cultural kinship, ties to the past and the present of a Québécois community. Dismissing ideological grounding or sentimental attachment is the implosive frame of theatrical parody, which subverts any attempt to carry a serious message. The production speaks of history through open theatrics, which not only challenge historically grounded "truths," but undermine the burlesque framing of the production itself.

If the production dismisses historic veracity as a founding principle, it also shatters the parodic machine and leads back to the persistent question of collective identity. It is tempting to assimilate self-mockery itself into the national character. In doing so we become clients of Daniel Latouche's *bazar de l'imaginaire* which teeters on the same slippery, self-mocking terrain as *Salut*. It all supposes a collective self exists to mock or deconstruct. However this collective is not exclusionary, but an interactive exchange. Anyone sharing in the parodic gymnastics is part of the immediate community.

In her illuminating *A Theory of Parody*, Linda Hutcheon (1985:32) states: "The pleasure of parody's irony comes not from humor in particular, but from the degree of engagement of the reader in the intertextual 'bouncing'... between complicity and distance." The capacity to bounce between complicity and distance is perhaps what best determines the ideal spectator of this 1989 street comedy. And parody, with its mobile positioning of subject and referant, appears a most appropriate mode to express the contemporary Québécois identity problem. The production erodes the perimeters of *l'intérieur*, exposing the raw inner-side of the border itself. The performance plays across the dividing line of self as other.

Notes

1. The Dion and the Cloutier are considered founding families of *Canada*. According to Hubert Charbonneau's analysis (Henripin and Martin 1988), the Québécois descend from less than a dozen families, which include the legendary Louis Hébert, first farmer of Nouvelle-France. Thus, according to the nationalist demographer, the *peuple québécois* form an homogenous population.

2. The absent father and the terror of male impotency haunt the political imaginary of Quebec, particularly in relation to its powerful southern neighbor. As Pierre Anctil, a Québécois cultural researcher has pointed out, "Whereas an average U.S. citizens can recall a triumphant, irrepressible expansionist history, we—in the very early stages of our collective life—had learned to accept an awareness of a certain form of impotence" (Duchacek et al. 1988:19).

3. Many Canadian literary critics have pointed to the thematic lines of "homesickness" and "survival" crossing English and French Canadian literature. In her analysis of recurrent Canadian tropes appropriately titled *Survival*, Margaret Atwood points to the longing for a lost homeland and the major feat of the settlers as, not the conquest of, but sheer survival in the New World. "The survivor has no triumph or victory, but the fact of his survival; he has little after his ordeal that he did not have before, except gratitude for having escaped with his life" (Atwood 1972:18).

4. "Rappe à la québécoise" is not a Parminou invention. The Québécois rap emerged during the 1989 protestations of the PLQ's compromise on established linguistic policy. Bisaillon and Gauthier's *French B.* (B. for bastards) "Je me souviens" struck a familiar note in Quebec while capitalizing on the style of another American minority group: African-Americans. Québécois rap is both an ironic citation of a MADE IN AMERICA product and a vehicle of protest.

5. As mentioned in the first section, this mammoth hydro-electric project instigated in the 1960s has been a source of national pride and national revenue. The Baie James dams and turbines constitute an internationally-recognized engineering feat, capable of producing more energy than "six nuclear reactors of the Three-Miles Island type" (Garreau 1982:364). The complex not only amply assures the demands of Quebec but allows the exportation of up to 1,000 megawatts to New York during periods of peak consumption. If Phase II of the project is brought to completion, the exportable energy capacity would double. But the project has drawn protests from both the Cree population of the region and from environmentalists who see the altering of the taiga as "the northern equivalent of the destruction of the tropical rain forest" (New York Times Magazine, 12 January 1992:20).

6. Bédard is quoted by Carmen Montessuil in the 16 July 1989 *Journal de Montréal* "Les vieilles branches de notre histoire." The journalist interprets Bédard's question, "What kind of ancestors will we be?" as the actors projecting themselves into the future in order to see how "the country we leave will be remembered."

7. U.Q. refers to the Université du Québec, the network of campuses throughout Quebec founded in 1968 with the mandate to popularize higher education and to assure its relevance to the socio-cultural context of Quebec.

8. The fast talking and patronizing Parisian con-artist is a stock character in the Parminou repertory. It is interesting to note the contrasts between this "know-it-all" stereotype and his gullible and gauche Québécois counterpart.

III

TECTONIC PLATES

Plaques Tectoniques
A Bicontinental Work in Progress

Jacques (Robert Lepage) and the goddess Skadi (Lorraine Côté).
Photo: Johnnie Eisen, courtesy Rhombus Media Inc.

By the late 1960s earth scientists had come to realize that continental drift and ocean-floor spreading are themselves part of a wider pattern, now known as plate tectonics...

... The zones crucial to life—and death—are the boundaries between plates, where the plates jostle against, and interact with, each other. These are the regions in which molten rock from the deep Earth rises to the surface, or where cold spreading ocean floor plunges back down into the interior, or where continents collide to throw up mountains, or simply where the plates slide past each other on giant faults. These are the violent places of Earth...

Dr. Peter J. Smith, Geologist
(Prélude, National Arts Centre, 1991)

MADELEINE: He put his hand on my throat as if he was going to strangle me. But it was to grasp what he couldn't read from my lips.

> *Antoine, the deaf librarian, brings his hand to the woman's throat and then signs a phrase. "When you speak, words vibrate."*

He put his hand on my stomach, as you do when you want to feel a child moving in the mother's womb. Then he lay down on the ground and he told me that the vibrations coming from the earth were the same he had felt in my body.

Madeleine (Marie Gignac), Antoine (Richard Fréchette)
(Tectonic Plates, Ottawa, July 1991 version)

It would be difficult to determine which of these opening quotes, that of Peter J. Smith, the earth scientist cited in the Ottawa 1991 program of *Tectonic Plates*, or that of Madeleine, the first character to speak, is more poetic. The first is a translation of geological data into a highly dramatic text; the second is the interpretation of geology through a theatrical character who is mediated through the body of the performer, Marie Gignac. The actress/character voices the actions of the mute librarian Antoine, played by Richard Fréchette, who reads the vibrations of her body and those of the earth. Smith's words slip from the physical to the poetic; the actors' movements relocate poetry in the physical. Both depict biological and geophysical reality as a resonant network of signs.

A series of verbal and visual semaphores, where imagery slips between the body and the planet, between variegated cultural topographies and atomized subjects, *Plaques/Plates* was a bicontinental work in progress created over four years and in six cities. The theme of plate tectonics determined not only the binding metaphor of cultural drift, but the process of the mobile production, conceived by Robert Lepage and the Théâtre Repère of Quebec City, constructed in workshops between 1988 and 1991, and performed in Toronto, Quebec City, Montreal, Glasgow, London, and Ottawa. The contexts, the narratives, the actors, the language of the performances fluctuated as they moved back and forth between Europe and North America.

Yet, like the theory of plate tectonics, *Plaques/Plates* suggests there is an original wholeness behind the fractured *mappa mundi*, a design to the continents' perpetual drift, a welding together of the puzzle pieces. Each performance is in itself a theatrical ritual in search of an improbable and ephemeral wholeness and—despite its gaps and permutations—a work in progress whose telos is the completion of a work of art.

This atomization versus binding together is one of the many contradictions driving *Plaques/Plates*, and, consequently, driving this analysis. It is very tempting to wrap up the planet in a cosmic whole resonating through the body and the word. But as soon as we begin to deal with the agents, the political contexts or the nitty-gritty of the material realization, the image grasped again splits into multiple shards. I have repeatedly confronted these contradictions, and have, as often, drifted into the seismic metaphor underlying the work, only to resurface irately demanding a map.

Multiple productions and complex knottings or splicings of narrative lines—those of the fiction and of the work in progress—*Plaques/Plates* defies a play-by-play chronological analysis. The work must necessarily be captured globally through fragments of the production, its contexts and process. At the same time *Plates'* basic metaphor spins off to the level of an imaginary planetary community, it describes a journey originating in and returning to a place called Québec. As much as it purports global multiculturalism, fluid linguistic borders, or what the translator and literary critic, Sherry Simon, critically cites as "l'avènement d'une polyphonie joyeuse et indifférenciée" (Simon 1991:11), *Plaques/Plates* inevitably circles back *chez nous:* to the group of Québécois artists who instigated the production and to the solitary yet divided individual subject. It is in the gaps and the fluctuations that a collective self appears for a fleeting moment.

Chapter Five
Journeys

Mapping a Journey Past

The *Plaques/Plates* adventure began in 1987 when the producer Michael Morris of the London-based Cultural Industries offered Robert Lepage, the young director from Quebec who had enjoyed a considerable reputation in England and in the international theatre festival arena, the opportunity to coproduce a cross-continental work in progress. The coproduction, financed by the European Economic Community, was destined for Glasgow which the EEC had designated as the 1990 "European City of Culture." The production was thus conceived under the dual sign of European political unity and the ties binding the Old and New Worlds. This would determine the dominant theme driving the first production—the flitting back and forth over the Atlantic of historical and contemporary subjects—and its collage structure of movable "plates."

Plaques tectoniques/Tectonic Plates was created in concentrated periods over four years and across two continents. The idea of a continually evolving and multilingual work in movement was integral to the conception. The production would represent cultural drift and it would incorporate actors from three Euro-American linguistic communities: English, French, and Spanish. The theme of the première production—the separations and intersections of Europe and America—was to coincide with the form and process of the work. When the Théâtre Repère created the first version at the 1988 Toronto World Theatre Festival, *Plaques/Plates* was already scheduled for the 1990 Glasgow production and for a Barcelona production in 1992, the year that the Catalan capital would host the International Olympic summer games. That same year Spain was to be the site of the quincentennial celebration of the Columbus expedition to the Americas, the founding voyage and the original Old and New World collision.

Plaques/Plates darted back and forth over the Atlantic in numerous workshops and productions actualized in Great Britain and Canada. It would miss two appointments in its cross-continental schedule: 1) the 1989 Montreal Festival des Amériques when the company failed to perform, announcing a few days before the performance—ultimate theatrical heresy—that the "show must not go on" because it was not ready; 2) the 1992 Barcelona performance which never materialized. If the creations realized in England and Canada reinforce the baseline metaphor of continental drift, the Montreal festival interruption and the Barcelona closure which never occurred, reinforce the concept of seismic tremors and gaps, and of a basically unpredictable universe.

Collaborating with a reputed Canadian designer, Michael Levine, and with a core team of Repère actors, Lepage prepared the first series of *Plates* for the Toronto World Stage Festival in 1988. The performance was in French and English with smatterings of Spanish and Italian: the original cast included a Québécois of Mexican origin and Christopher Columbus was one of the minor characters who appeared in the montage of the five "plates" or separate stories. In the following year Repère presented a radically restructured version of *Plaques* at Implanthéâtre, their home base theatre in Quebec City. Cosponsored by the Festival des Amériques, this version was primarily in French with some English. The cast consisted of six Repère actors, including Robert Lepage, and a French actor, François Pick, who had joined the group during a European tour of another Repère production.

In April 1990 the company presented a slightly modified edition of the Quebec City version in Montreal. With one exception the cast remained the same.[1] By zeroing in on a few characters and their stories, this version confirmed the dramatic line established in the 1989 version. The content and the structure of these *Plaques* had shifted considerably since the first work in Toronto. The site of seismic fragmentation had swerved from the cultural to the individual.

The Glasgow actors who would participate in the final *Plaques/Plates* production attended the Montreal performances. The 1990 Glasgow and London versions were prepared in several phases. In January Lepage and Repère mainstay Marie Gignac conducted a workshop with a group of actors with experience in writing and directing who had been selected by Michael Morris. The people drawn from this workshop traveled to Montreal to see the third edition and to work with the Repère creators. The group then came together for a two-week workshop and subsequent presentation at the Glasgow Tramway theatre, a version which would then travel to the National Theatre in London. Seven Repère actors and five Glasgow Tramway actors comprised the cast of this version and of the summer 1991 Ottawa presentations, sponsored by the Canadian National Arts Centre. Although the cast and some of the plates had changed in the Ottawa edition, the narrative structure and the thematic underpinnings were already well established by the 1990 Montreal production. The Ottawa performances were announced as "French" or "English" but the production used both official languages of Canada. The British actors had made the effort to prepare the predominantly French version. The francophone actors were at ease in both the English and the French versions.

I have presented this flattened description of a complicated voyage, which crossed over symbolic and political landscapes as it moved through time and space, for two reasons. First, it serves as a map to a journey past which I followed, intermittently, for four years. Second, it points to the fact that, although the production shifted according to agents and contexts, the travelers directing this theatrical journey were essentially a group of actor/creators from Quebec City.

The Théâtre Repère or "Landmark Theatre"

The word "repère" denotes a reference point or a landmark. Sign of a sign, the word leads down overlapping semantic avenues: "repérer" means to locate or pinpoint; "repérage" is the activity of cartographers and film makers tracing their way. "Repère" denotes a discovery process. *Repère* is also the name of a theatre company from Quebec City which has made its mark, both locally and internationally.[2] Founded in 1980, it took only seven years for the company and its main director, Robert Lepage, to achieve notoriety across the Canadian and European theatre scene. The acronym REPERE also denotes a cyclic work process: *ressources, partition, évaluation, représentation*, the translation of the Halprin R.S.V.P. method which Jacques Lessard, the founder of the company, brought back from California where he had worked with Anna Halprin.

Repère creations are always works in progress and they always begin with *ressources sensibles* or tactile resources. The object which launched *Plaques/Plates* was a jigsaw-puzzle map of the world which Robert Lepage brought to the rehearsal space in Quebec City at the start of the collective creation. Brightly colored pieces dumped out on the floor, the puzzle represented a fragmentary vision of the world coupled with the challenge to restore the unity of the map. Seen in retrospect, the jigsaw puzzle is a landmark in the four-year theatrical journey. Appropriately the puzzle map refers to the Repère's recurrent theme of travel and the process of the creative experience which boils down to discovering one's way in a symbolic landscape where the singular cartographer is absent, where the map and its landmarks emerge clearly only once the journey is over.

The initial *repère* of *Plaques tectoniques* was a jigsaw puzzle map. A place was later incorporated into the work in progress after its 1988 premiere. While touring in Paris with another show, the actors visited the historic Père Lachaise cemetery where great figures of arts and letters—including persona of the French Romantic era such as Frederick Chopin and Eugène Delacroix—are buried among more contemporary figures such as Edith Piaf and Jim Morrison. The cemetery is an amazing jumble of tombstones and crypts bearing famous names, where tourists and devotees of defunct artists gather daily. The cemetery served as a workshop site before becoming a signifying place in the subsequent versions of *Plaques/Plates*.

A jigsaw puzzle and a cemetery—a game and a space—were landmarks in this production and in the montage which had brought Théâtre Repère to the public sphere. The starting points of *La Trilogie des dragons/The Dragon Trilogy* which had projected Repère onto the international theatre map were also a game, the Chinese mah-jong, and a space, a Quebec City parking lot which covers an extinct Chinatown. As in *Plates*, the site served both as a tactile environment and a signifying place, metaphorically extending to deeper and wider spaces in the theatrical creation. The tar and the gravel of the parking lot covered pieces of china: broken plates and fragments of a China imagined through the eyes of two little girls from Quebec City. This was a China one might imagine reaching by digging through the oil-coated gravel, "down through the center of the earth." The extinct Quebec City Chinatown symbolically connected to other Chinatowns across the Canadian continent. The production would eventually describe a network of intersecting human relations which moved over seven decades (1910 to 1980) and over three cities: Quebec, Toronto, and Vancouver.

Each "dragon" represented a city, a period, and a piece of the work in progress. The company had conceived the *Trilogie des dragons/Dragon Trilogy* as separate productions of one to two hours between 1985 and 1987. In June 1987 Repère presented a six-hour event at the Montreal Festival des Amériques and launched a series of international festival tours. North American and European critics have described the six-hour production as a "Canadian saga." It is with bits and pieces of interconnecting personal histories that the Repère has indeed created theatrical sagas. It is with mundane objects—a plate, a pair of shoes, a chair—that the Repère has evoked microcosms or "the delicious illusion that the entire universe is concentrated on a small stage for a few hours, and that we can hold it in our hand,"[3] as one Montreal critic stated.

The overwhelming positive response to the *Dragons* productions among not only Québécois and Canadian audiences, but in other American and

European theatre venues, is an indication of how this work—predominantly in French and based on the vision of two little girls from *la basse ville*—crossed linguistic and cultural barriers. Understandably, Québécois critics cite the *Trilogie des dragons* as a major articulation in the history of Québécois theatre. It was not simply a question of projecting products from Quebec onto the international stage, but of very specifically Québécois references connecting to an audience beyond Quebec. *Dragons* coalesced the dominant trends of Québécois theatre in the 1970s, a theatre of ethnographic realism enmeshed in the national political project, and that of the 1980s, which exploited the visual in order to reach out to an international audience. The need to break new ground and reach out to an audience beyond Quebec determined the orientation of many theatrical groups during the eighties. If international festivals and tours were primary objectives, the theatre had to exploit the translinguistic means which had already given access to the international stage to musicians, dancers and performance artists.[4] What was exceptional in the Repère work was that it was reaching an international audience through a specifically Québécois idiom.

Robert Lepage: A National Legend

Rooted in local culture and glowing with international success, *Dragons* became *une oeuvre nationale* and earned the director Lepage the reputation of a *nationaliste passe partout*. Michel Tremblay, the playwright who has been mythologized within his own lifetime as the founder of modern Québécois theatre, declared in a 1990 interview that the production "was one of the most exciting theatre events I've ever seen" and that director Lepage, also mythologized in his lifetime, was the contemporary genius of Québécois theatre.[5]

Touted as a Québécois masterpiece, the *Trilogie des dragons* also created great expectations of the barely ten-year-old company and the barely thirty-year-old Robert Lepage, who has maintained a frenetic rhythm of production. During the 1987 Montreal Festival, Lepage was performing his one-man show *Vinci*, which he created in 1986 and which had, during its London tour, sparked the offer to create the cross-continental *Plaques/Plates*. As *Dragons* toured Europe and continued to accumulate prizes, Lepage worked on other productions. In 1987 he was directing *Pour en finir une fois pour toutes avec Carmen*, creating *Polygraphe*[6] with Marie Brassard, and plotting the *Tectonic Plates* production scheduled for the summer 1988 Toronto festival. By 1988, besides preparing the first edition of *Plates*, he was directing *A Midsummer Night's Dream* at a major institutional Montreal venue and acting in Denys Arcand's film, *Jesus de Montréal*. And the list goes on.[7]

By 1990, year of the Glasgow production, Lepage had been nominated artistic director of the French theatre division of the Canadian National Arts Centre in Ottawa. He considered that this role and the access it gave to funds would allow him to promote Québécois experimental theatres and, amazingly, allow him some rest. By 1992 Lepage had completed the final rendition of *Plates*, was carrying out his duties at the CNAC in Ottawa, and had created another one-man show, *Les Aiguilles et l'opium* based on the transatlantic voyages of Miles Davis and Jean Cocteau. He was also directing *A Midsummer Night's Dream* with the Royal Shakespeare Company at the National Theatre in London, ironic consecration for a thirty-five-year-old artist from Quebec.

The British press has proclaimed Lepage a young Peter Brook, a master magician of the international stage. The Québécois press has hailed him as a local prodigy and attacked him as an opportunist who has sold out to internationalism. Not all of Lepage's productions have met with local success. The ambitious *Plaques* production received mixed reviews from the Montreal critics.

It is hard to be a national legend in one's own time, especially in Quebec. Despite its inordinate artistic production, and the cosmopolitan nature of Montreal, Quebec has a very limited theatre-going public. The country is in itself a small population of some six million. Everyone in the arts world knows everyone else. "Le Québec, c'est une grande cuisine," as people say, and echoes reverberate in a big kitchen. Positive reviews can propel an artist to mythic heights; negative criticisms can annihilate an artist. When this happens, it is like being condemned by a member of the family. It is no wonder that Québécois artists seek out international audiences and that local critics are viewed with a paranoic eye.

Lepage has stated that the Montreal critics never forgave him for canceling *Plaques tectoniques* at the June 1989 Montreal Festival, and that this cancellation played into the tepid response the production received in 1990. The accounts I read in June 1989 simply stated that the director was conducting too many projects at once. Friends sent him flowers, which he interpreted as a funerary offering. Lepage was also sensitive to comments from friends and critics provoked by the Ottawa nomination. Although most praised the nomination, some considered this a sell out, a desertion of Quebec in favor of the bastion of Canadian federalism.

The director's terror of the Montreal press has been compensated by continual support from within the immediate family, that is, the Quebec City press and his original Repère co-workers. Lepage attributes much of his personal success to friends who continue to support his work outside of the company, in his mise-en-scène ventures into institutional venues, his one-man shows, his experimentation in film, his international career. Inversely, the Repère actors consider Lepage, the director, as simply a member of the group. Since he has frequently acted in the collective creations, Lepage directs from inside the work. The actors describe the work not as a democratic process—where everyone has an opinion to express and the work becomes a diluted series of compromises—but as a discovery process in which all are engaged.

The Repère Discovery Process

In a 1985 interview (*Jeu 52*:31–8) Jacques Lessard, the founder of Théâtre Repère, declared that the company was less a *théâtre de recherche* [experimental theatre] than a *théâtre de découverte* [theatre of discovery]. This statement is more humble than it might sound. Historically, Lessard's quote predates the explosive success the company enjoyed a few years later. Processually, *discovery* is about recognizing what is already there. This idea consistently runs through the artists' reflections on their collective creations, which are all "written in space," devised through improvisation.

The Repère's method is a bricolage of various techniques and creative processes. Besides the Halprin R.S.V.P. method cited as a starting point of the Repère work, other methods come into play in the elaboration of the collective creations. In France Lepage had worked with Albert Knapp, the Swiss master of improvisation. Both of these "imported" methods served as loose guidelines in developing an improvisational praxis already established among the actors who created the company. Most of the Repère actors had trained at the Conservatoire de Québec. This training focused on the actor as total creator: writer, director, performer. Some of the Repère actors had also participated in the Ligue Nationale d'Improvisation, which turns improvisation into a sport. Improvising before spectators who have been invited to hiss or throw galoshes as if they were at a hockey game, demands quick thinking, technical mastery, a thick skin, and a blind trust in the outcome.

It is perhaps blind faith in the outcome which best describes the overall method of Repère. A zen-like trust in the unfolding of the creation pervades the performers' explanations of their process: One only discovers what is already out there. The discovery process is allowing meaning to emerge from the object or the space, rather than predetermining the message. This is not a dialectic of ideas, but a treasure hunt for associated symbols and forms which bounce off of concrete objects. For Lepage the initial momentum of the *Dragon Trilogy* was a question of "letting the parking lot speak." Arbitrary *repères*, such as the three dragons or the puzzle map initiate the procedure, but the aleatory plays a primordial role.

The group loves to talk about the serendipitous occurrences during the preparation and the performances, how each element of the production resonated with events beyond the theatre. One of the more remarkable coincidences was the appearance of a Chinese junk which sailed by the theatre during the performance of *Dragons* in Montreal's Old Port. The doors of the converted warehouse were open, thus incorporating the view of the Saint Lawrence and the setting sun into the mise-en-scène. At the precise moment one of the protagonists was performing a ritual to symbolically return home to China, the junk crossed the frame. The audience was amazed to learn later that this encounter was totally fortuitous.

That the junk was carrying tourists along the river did not destroy the artistry of the moment for the Repère. Their productions are, after all, about touring in time and space. Their scenography routinely juxtaposes the profane, mass-produced article (such as the yellow styrofoam plates of McDonald's) to "great works of art" such as da Vinci's Mona Lisa. The trick, for the actor and the spectator, is to discover the sometimes ironic connections between apparently disparate elements. When Marie Gignac, who participated in all of the *Dragons* and *Plaques* productions, says "Sometimes we have the impression that what we do is bigger than we are,"[8] she is speaking of a transcendent network of signs waiting to be discovered. This quasi-mystical belief in a theatre resonating with the universe may be politically problematic, but it is undeniably seductive.

Without sharing the faith, the audience can still be seduced. Part of the spectator's pleasure is participating in the collective discovery process. The performance is a profusion of signs and sensual impressions which demand interpretation. It is a game, a treasure hunt for emergent meanings. Waiting to enter the Ottawa Electric Building before seeing the last production of *Plates*, I overheard the woman behind me say: "I've seen this show three times and I'm still discovering things." I have observed the mutations of the production over four years, read reams of literature on the Repère, and probably written as many notes, and I am still discovering things. The great attraction of *Plaques/Plates* lies in the fact that the performance is both a theatrical journey, which invites the spectator to make connections between the landmarks strung along the way, and a theatrical ritual evolving in the immediate act of *seeing*.

Journeys 147

A Traveling Theatrical Ritual

Limen
Tiers of seats rising from the ground to the rafters surround all four sides of the stage. The audience seated against any of the theatre's walls has a full view of the stage and the spectators on the other three sides.

The stage is a shiny black rectangular surface, which is dominated by the illuminated blue pool cut into the center. On one side of the platform there are two grand pianos whose surfaces, like the pool and the black platform, reflect the spot lights. Two tourist souvenirs, a miniature Eiffel Tower and a Statue of Liberty, stand on the piano tops. On the other side of the stage is a messy heap of wooden chairs and two neatly arranged rows where candles have been placed.

The audience falls silent when an actress, clothed in the white gossamer of Swan Lake, enters and begins to light the candles on the chairs.

This overture is from the final production (Ottawa, 1991), but it describes two constants in all the venues and mise-en-scène. However the theatrical sites shifted over four years and however the details—such as the miniature memorabilia on the piano tops—changed, the general configuration of the space and the ubiquitous mirroring pool remained that of a self-conscious theatrical ritual. The second constant is, paradoxically, the overriding theme of a journey through time and space apparent in the selected sites.

All of the buildings which housed *Plaques/Plates* throughout its four-year journey were vestiges of other eras which had been converted into theatres; all had originally served other functions. The Toronto theatre—situated on Harbor Front, which was itself a former Saint Lawrence port-landing converted into a tourist attraction—had been an ice house. The Quebec City Implanthéâtre was, until the 1970s, a synagogue. The Gare Jean-Talon in Montreal was an abandoned railway station. The Glasgow Tramway was also a former railway station which had been converted into a theatre. The Ottawa venue was formerly an electricity plant.

For the Repère creators these recycled buildings lend an archeological poetry to the space itself. Structures that once housed workers, or Jewish worshipers, or commuters reinforce the base metaphor of transformation and displacement. In two instances—the Gare Jean Talon and the Glasgow Tramway—the theatres had literally served as transitional spaces. Symbolically the theatres are landmarks of a journey through time and space, way-stations in a neither-here-nor-there land.

Again restructured according to the imperious demands of *Plaques/Plates*, all the venues shared the same basic configuration of embedded theatres staring at each other or reproducing the gaze in the reflecting pool. All the sites were closed, orthogonal spaces with no cardinal points, no frontal view. All the theatres were panoptical structures where the gaze converged on the arena below, but also bounced off the four walls of the theatre to meet other gazes. All reflected the elementary notion of the *theatron* or "seeing place," where not only the object of the gaze, but the gaze itself was reflected on all sides.

The Polyvalent Pool

The spectators face other spectators or look down at the shiny black surfaces of the stage and the grand pianos, and at the pool which relentlessly mirrors the scenic action and the spectators' gaze. The pool is a polyvalent medium which serves as a self-reflexive device and as a symbolic vehicle. It is a synecdoche for other bodies of water such as the Atlantic Ocean or a Venetian canal. On a mythical or psychic level, the pool represents the invisible space through which the characters cross over to "the other side." Cemeteries, spiritualist parlors, and psychiatric offices abound in the work. In the scene described below—which figured in all except the first version of *Plaques/Plates*—the pool is at once a psychiatrist's office, the troubled inner space of the patient, and a mythical landscape.

A mythic plate
A steel radio tower structure stands at one end of the performance space. Dry-ice vapors float over the pool and rise up to the last tiers of the audience. Electronic bleats and a bagpipe's notes surround the audience.

A woman with long red hair, bare-breasted and wearing a Scottish kilt, climbs to the top of the tower. She is carrying two swords which she clangs together periodically, entering into the musical composition.

A man with long red hair steps into the pool and sits in one of the two chairs placed in opposite corners of the pool. In the other chair a woman in horn-rimmed glasses is tapping a pencil on her note pad. "Jacques," she begins, "just tell me about this dream you had."

The man moves to the center of the pool to confront the Scottish amazon who has dived from the tower. She offers him a sword. The two characters/bodies wage battle, thrashing about in the water, until Jacques loses his sword. The goddess persona moves behind Jacques and with her weapon describes a line up between his legs and through his spinal column. He collapses into the water. Billows of red cloud the incandescent blue pool.

The panting actress portraying the Scottish amazon moves into the chair Jacques occupied at the beginning of the scene. "Well, Jacques," says the unflappable psychiatrist, apparently ignoring the radical metamorphosis of her patient, "I can see we have a lot of work to do."

On one level the pool figures a fusion of the psychic and the mythic. On another it serves as an ironic device which plays with the social institution of psychotherapy. It is the quotidian space which becomes the dream; it is the logic of the real which tips off balance. The psychiatrist and her patient meet in a swimming pool, a rather odd setting for a therapy session. They sit in ordinary chairs and assume the ordinary poses of patient and therapist, but their lower bodies are immersed in water. This out-of-place notion runs through many of the scenes which occur in the pool. Clients gather for an art auction or a concert or a McDonald hamburger in the aquatic milieu. Wading through the water but carrying out their business as usual, they do not seem to notice that the gallery or the concert hall or the fast-food restaurant is flooded.

Ironic device and metaphorical medium in which the actors literally bathe, the pool also serves to underline the theatricality of the event. It mirrors the scenic images and the spectators peering down at the stage. In some instances the pool serves literally as a projection screen.

The Death of Ophelia
The ballerina character, who opened the theatrical ritual by lighting the candles, plunges to her death in a Venetian canal. Here the dancer is set still, immobilized for posterity in an ephemeral image. Her white skirts and long blond hair float over the water, creating a tableau within the frame of the pool. Two actors dressed as gondoliers spread a sheet over her body and the water.

This surface becomes the screen of a Delacroix *Mort d'Ophélie* painting, emanating from a slide-projector. A voice announces the data behind the painting and the Romantic artist. The slide projector clicks to another frame, another *Death of Ophelia* painting. The voice announces this is a work by the avant-garde artist Madeleine, leader of the "Canadian neo-romantic movement."

The audience is in a university classroom, where an art professor is giving a lecture. At the same time we are in the theatre, where actors portraying gondoliers and an art professor are setting up the screen and operating the slide projector lantern which make Ophelia visible. The projection crystallizes the circular relationship between the plasticity, the physicality, and the fiction of the performance. In the first frame the dancer's body is frozen into a work of art and then covered with the sheet of death. This in turn becomes the screen for the slide projection, which is the only light in the theatre and seems to emanate from nowhere... until there is a mechanical click of the projector announcing another frame and a voice cataloging art commodities. Operating the "magic lantern" is an actor.

The projection serves the visual composition and the narrative, but above all, is a metacommentary on art and the theatrical play of images. The magic involved in this theatrical ritual lies not in illusion, but in the continual transformation of images flitting between the immediate physicality of the theatre—with its trappings and the sometimes clumsy manipulation of machines, objects, furniture by the actors—and the space of the imaginary.

Pianos, Chairs and Other Art Objects

Since the Repère creative journeys begin with *ressources sensibles* or tactile resources, and since the Repère's philosophy is to "let the place, let the object speak," the material plays a major role in the production. Every physical element in *Tectonic Plates* is engaged in poetic displacement, recalling the metaphor of travel and continental drift. Objects constantly permutate from the functional to the symbolic, from the literal to the metaphoric. A piano can be a musical instrument or a transient hotel room in Venice. Books can be used to cite texts or to evoke a bookstore in Montreal. Under a blacklight and stacked in piles, their white-striped bindings can represent the New York skyline.

Everyday objects such as chairs or dishes function as poetic machines. A china plate can serve as a musical instrument or represent an archeological find. Set adrift in the pool, styrofoam plates can suggest a McDonald's restaurant, or boats sailing across the Atlantic, or tectonic plates. The pianos, chairs, and paintings of the productions demonstrate how the material functions as a producer of and a metacommentary on the dubious theatrical art.

In the Toronto premiere of *Plates* a royal blue piano was suspended in the air, along with music stands and chairs of a matching blue. An actor dressed in a black velvet frock coat waded into the pool and introduced himself as Frederick Chopin. He sat on a piano bench which was hoisted up to the suspended blue piano. After an apologetic or consumptive cough, he began to play the *Moonlight Sonata*. But he did not literally *play* the piano; rather he played with the idea of Chopin playing the piano. The music actually came from another piano player outside of the spot-lit frame. The piano—of an outrageous blue—was ostensibly decorative. The piano playing is a paralipsis: the audience is told Chopin will play the piano, but of course neither Chopin nor the piano are real.[9]

The blue piano in the air disappeared in the subsequent versions of *Plates*. In its stead two quite ordinary, black pianos stood on stage level. The discrepancy between the character Chopin and the live musician was maintained, but here the piano player sat vis-à-vis the actor miming the music. The 1989 through 1991 versions upheld this initial ironic commentary, but also brought the pianos directly into the action. The instruments became metaphorical and functional pieces which the actors manipulated and, literally, penetrated. In the opening sequence of the Quebec City production the pianist and another actor slowly turned two grand pianos whose curves interlocked as a voice read a geophysical text on continental drift. Slowly turning on their axis and gradually separating, the pianos symbolized continents moving apart. Yet disrupting the metaphor is the pure resistance of matter. It is easier to envision the correspondence between pianos and continents over millennia than it is for actors to push pianos through space. There is an inevitable gaucheness involved when the physical tries to keep up with the imaginary. This struggle is what repeatedly brings the actors and the spectators back into the space of the theatre.

In other "plates" the piano symbolized living spaces and stages. Gutted out, the grand piano represented a cheap Venetian hotel where three characters from the sixties go to inject heroin: Constance, an erstwhile ballerina from Poland, her Scottish lover, and Madeleine, the Québécois art student touring Venice. The trio enters the basement garret by opening the piano lid. Clapping it shut, the three actors huddle on the piano top until Constance makes this the stage of a solo Swan Lake performance. Drawn from her drug-induced stage to the waiting pool below, Constance plunges into the water where she begins to dance before faltering and drowning. Resurfacing like Ophelia from her watery grave, the dancer appears in subsequent sequences as a chalk-faced muse in white gossamer, opening the piano lid during a concert by a world-renowned virtuoso who is playing the *Moonlight Sonata*.

The pianos and all of the material in *Plaques/Plates* circulate within the dense symbolic network of art and its prosaic rendering in the limits of the theatrical space. A most eloquent example are the chairs which figure in the four editions of the production. In the Toronto version the chairs, painted a bright blue and suspended in the theatrical sky, were a playful commentary on the nature of art. Hanging there attractive and useless, the chairs evoked an absent symphony orchestra. The generic chair, a piece of furniture similar to the one the spectator occupied at that very moment but painted a bright blue and hanging from the flies, suddenly appeared exotic. The chairs of the

152 *Tectonic Plates*

The dead ballerina (Céline Bonnier) emerges from the piano during a Chopin concert (François Pick). Photo: Claudel Huot, Communication Visuelle, courtesy Ex Machina.

The virtuoso (François Pick) and the art student (Marie Gignac) meet at an auction in Venice. Photo: Claudel Huot, Communication Visuelle, courtesy Ex Machina.

Quebec City, Montreal and Ottawa performances were scruffy brown wood chairs of a commonplace variety. In the last version of *Plaques/Plates* these chairs became commodifiable relics.

Relics
A London antique dealer has responded to an estate sale in Paris. He and the family's representative appear on stage, using a desk lamp to light their way through an apparent attic of treasures. When the dealer spies a portrait of George Sand, the Parisian says it is out of the question, he could never sell the painting which is a family legacy. Wouldn't the Londoner rather have these chairs, which have also been in the family for generations. Since the buyer is not interested in the chairs, the seller says, "Very well, you can have the painting if those on the other side agree." "On the other side?" queries the art dealer. "Yes, you know," says the estate owner flipping a desk lamp on and off. He instructs the dealer to rub the lamp and to chant a formula in order to communicate with the ancestors; he also tells him he must remove all metallic objects which might hinder the communication. Forking over his rings and his watch, the bewildered art dealer complies. Holding the lamp, he chants meaningless phrases across the pool. He falters, suddenly realizing he is alone, peering into the darkness. Feebly he wonders aloud what has become of his watch.

That the dealer does acquire the painting and the generic chairs only becomes apparent in a subsequent scene, an auction in a Venetian art gallery.

A Venetian fragment
Two travelers meet at an auction organized by the Preservation of Venice Society. The auction takes place in the central pool. In suits, high-heels, and hats the well-meaning bourgeois gingerly enter the flooded room, using the chairs as step stones, and settle in for the art auction. The London dealer offers various articles for sale: a pair of antique Celtic swords, a model of the Bertollini Liberty Statue, a Delacroix portrait of George Sand, plus some "antique chairs." The painting is sold to a Texas oil merchant.

It is sometime in the 1960s. The two travelers are a man, who is a world-renowned European pianist on tour, and a woman, who is a Québécois art history student touring Europe. When the other clients have left the auction room, the pianist approaches the young woman who stands studying the painting of George Sand. The subject who is gazing down is wearing a dark dress and clutching a white handkerchief; her hair falls loosely over her pale shoulders. The art student tells the pianist that this canvas is in fact a fragment of the original. The other half of the painting, circulating somewhere else in the art world, depicts Frederick Chopin. Although the Romantic novelist appears absorbed in solitary thoughts, she is actually listening to the music of a subject outside the frame, an absent Chopin. The painting was split in two "because some art dealer thought he could make more money that way," says Madeleine. "Since then, pieces of Sand and Chopin float around the world."[10]

The chairs and the fractured painting comprise a metacommentary on art as performance or commodity. The *Plaques/Plates* chairs describe familiar objects, palpable reference points to the four-year work in progress. The split painting embodies the paradox of the artist striving for self-expression while tributary to the laws of the art market. The painting of George Sand listening to a forever absent Chopin also indicates one of the defining tropes of the 1989 to 1990 *Plaques/Plates*. Ghosts from the 19th-century European Romantic school, which strove to break away from classical canons in order to express the individual artist, Sand and Chopin emerged periodically through all of the versions. Irrevocably split in two, the Sand portrait and her androgynous persona emerged as a defining element in the 1989 Quebec City version.

Sketch of Sand and Chopin by Delacroix, courtesy of the Louvre Museum, Paris.

Narrative Tectonics: From the Atlantic to the Specific

Ultimately *Plaques/Plates* is a trace of its own evolution. Following the 1988 premiere of *Tectonic Plates* at the Toronto World Festival and the missed appointment of *Plaques tectoniques* at the 1989 Festival des Amériques, Lepage and his Repère coworkers decided they were trying to say too much in one production. At the start of the Quebec City edition Lepage announced he wanted to focus on the neo-romantic artist and he personally wished to play a bi-gendered character. These two themes were drawn from seminal knots in the first version of *Plaques/Plates*.

The original plan behind the theatrical adventure was to create a series of short vignettes in periodic workshops. These vignettes would be like pieces of a puzzle map which, refined through the Repère cyclic method, would then come together in a marathon spectacle of six to twelve hours, similar to the *Dragon Trilogy*, but far more ambitious. Envisioned as interlocking pieces of a jigsaw puzzle, each section could be presented alone or fit into a larger picture. The initial concept of self-standing plates marked the first phase of the work in progress. The 1988 Toronto World Festival version was a series of five independent stories announced by titles projected onto the back wall of the theatre and embedded in the mock Chopin concert which opens the play. The five plates of this first version centered on travel, across the Atlantic Ocean and through Venetian canals.

Plate 1 *The Cruise*
   Passengers of diverse origins meet on an Icelandic cruise. Most of the travelers are pairs, lovers or honeymoon couples. One is single: a young archeologist from Quebec who is recovering from a broken love affair. Couples separate and join together in the Arctic night. The actors use beach mattresses to portray this shuffling. As in a card game, the mattresses show a neutral side and then flip over to reveal a couple or a person alone, flip back to the neutral, and back again to reveal an exchange of bodies. By the end of the sequence, the solitary traveler from Quebec has found a mate, but another traveler sleeps alone.

Plate 2 *Banquets*
   This scene begins with a 15th-century wedding banquet someplace in Italy. During the festivities, the bride goes into labor. The guests pull the tables apart and from the chasm emerges a hand holding an egg, followed by a triumphant Christopher Columbus. This reminder of the proverbial Columbus' egg narrative[11] embedded in the master narrative of the New World discovery announces another banquet across the Atlantic. Commanding the guests to hoist the sails, the explorer takes the helm. The table cloths become sails as the actors push tables and chairs into the "ocean."

Arriving on the other side of the pool, the actors set up another wedding feast which takes place two centuries later. This banquet again ends with the bride giving birth. Her son travels back to Europe to become a French chef. Returning later to the New World, the chef's offspring becomes the chef of a fashionable French restaurant in New York. Giving his employees a performative lesson in how to cook the perfect fried egg, a lesson in which the actor embodies the "too har-rrd" and "non slimy" egg for the wide-eyed staff, the French chef succumbs to a heart attack and extinguishes the noble lineage.

Plate 3 *Beaches*
This sequence describes the summer travels of a 20th-century Québécois student. She is on a beach somewhere on the French-Atlantic coast, where she discovers—and subsequently seeks to avoid by moving to the opposite corner of the pool—a couple of middle-aged compatriots sunning on inflatable mattresses. The heroine of this sequence is involved with a hero vacationing with his family on the other side of the Atlantic. The story ends with a letter announcing the hero's drowning. The death, imagined in the woman's mind, is physically represented by an actor wading joyously into the pool. He is clutching a beach ball, a ball depicting the globe.

Plate 4 *The Divided Self*
The initial scene takes place in a Mexican village. A Franco-American psychiatrist is earnestly trying to help a troubled man. The man, who sits in stubborn silence on his chair, is plagued by an alien voice. It is the voice of a child embodied by an actress, who, hovering over the actor, speaks in his stead. The psychiatrist, who is also a woman, persuades the patient to leave his chair and travel to an international psychiatric convention in France. Actors depict the anonymous space of the airplane by conducting a ballet based on the regulatory safety rules familiar to transoceanic travelers. The flight terrifies the patient. This terror turns to madness during the convention, where the subject is pinned specimen-like under a projector and made the case study of an abstract discourse on schizophrenia.

Plate 5 *Venice*
The era is the late 1960s. A young art history student from Quebec is touring in Venice. She enters an historic and leaky edifice where an art auction is being held. There she meets a world-renowned pianist who invites her to dinner and then to a Chopin concert he is giving. Flattered, she accepts. They dine at the Venetian McDonald's. This scene takes place in the pool, in the midst of a sea of bobbing yellow, styrofoam plates. The place shifts to the concert hall, where the young woman, overcome by the music or an epiphanic vision, cries out in pain or pleasure and collapses. The scene then changes to a 1990 university classroom. The professor is projecting slides of the famous neo-romantic Canadian painter who committed suicide a decade earlier. The paintings "from

her Venetian period" appear and disappear in rapid succession, to the clicking of the projector and a distant Chopin sonata.

These five plates are self-contained narratives juxtaposed without any apparent continuity. There is no obvious connection between the Icelandic cruisers, Columbus' egg, and the student touring in Venice. Yet, despite the ruptures between the plates, there is a master narrative welded together by the voyages linking Europe to the Americas. All the stories focus on transatlantic voyages performatively situated in the pool.

In subsequent editions of *Plaques/Plates* these narrative shards subdivided, swelled, or disappeared, but all came to center on an individual character telling his or her story. And the pool, once the Atlantic Ocean, would progressively slip into representing the murky waters of the individual psyche. Crossing all the versions, Madeleine, the Québécois archeologist and art student, would synthesize into the painter and future *chef de file* of the "Canadian neo-romantic" movement. Columbus would make one brief cameo appearance—popping up in a spiritualist seance—before disappearing. The Mexican schizophrenic would become a Québécois transvestite played by Robert Lepage, the same actor who played the hero of "Beaches," the hero drawn to the Atlantic Ocean and an unrequited love, drowning while he clutched his beach ball globe to his breast.

By the closing version of the work in progress, the classic structure of a play in three acts with intermissions had replaced the montage of parallel units. The narrative shards would recluster around subjects adrift in a postmodern sea. By the 1990 Montreal version the play's structure was set and would remain the same despite its passage across the Atlantic to the Glasgow workshop and back to North America in 1991. The closing edition of *Tectonic Plates* zeroed in on the individual subject as the site of seismic eruptions.

Subjects of a Venetian Metaphor

"I hate Venice," says one of the drifting characters who is ironically named Constance in the last version of *Plaques/Plates*. "It is such a narcissistic place, with its canals forever mirroring images of the self."

A Venetian plate
A young woman sits on the edge of the pool, her back braced against the legs of a man rowing with a long pole, a figure codified by his blue-striped sweater and red-ribbon straw hat as a Venetian gondolier. Madeleine moves back and forth in synchrony with the gondolier's rowing as he dips his oar into the pool and

calls out the names of historic spots along the Canale Grande.

In the opposite corner of the pool sits the symmetrical figure of a male tourist being rocked to the movement of another gondolier's legs and the sound of the oar dipping in and out of the water. He is a famous European pianist who met the young Québécois art student a little earlier at the "Venice Preservation Society" auction.

The continual swish of the two oars is punctuated by the gondoliers' evocative litany of Venetian sites. "Santa Maria della Salute, Ca'd'Oro, Ponte di Rialto."

At the Rialto Bridge the two gondolas pause. A woman dressed in the white, gossamer skirts of a classic ballerina approaches the edge of the pool and then plunges into the water.

Apparently oblivious to the event, the tourists glide by each other, and the gondoliers—whose faces are neutralized by black stocking masks—continue their rowing and routine listing of Venetian wonders: "Ponte di Rialto, Palazzo Grimani, Ponte dell'Accademia." As the boats glide past each other, the gondoliers suddenly recognize other. "Ehh, Angelo," shouts one. "Ahh, Giuseppe," responds the other. Then both continue their litany of tourist sites.

Over the course of the four-year work in progress, the cultural origin of the pianist shifted according to the actor, mutating from French to Welsh. Madeleine, the Franco-American hippy and future *chef de file* of the "Canadian neo-romantic movement" was played by Marie Gignac throughout all the versions and retained her Québécois origin. The finality of this character's story would, however, fluctuate in its travels. In one version she commits suicide and becomes posthumously a famous artist. In another version Madeleine lives to enjoy the recognition of her work. As for the two masked and uniformed gondoliers, they remain perpetually cloaked in anonymity except for this brief flash of recognition in the private universe of Venetian gondoliers.

By the Montreal version the play had come to center on individual characters whose biographical fragments told a few stories about a few people whose lives intersected. The stories flowed into one another. The only division marked in the program was "Il y aura un entracte" [There will be one intermission]. These characters were thrown together in two primary sites: Venice, the heart of the European romantic movement, and what is today, literally, a sinking city; Manhattan, the location of postmodern transients and proverbial port of entry to the Americas. However the characters drifted through time and space, the diegesis would continually circle back to Venice and New York, improbable anchors of a subject at sea. The five protagonists who surfaced in the Ottawa version of *Plaques/Plates* were:

Madeleine
An art history student from Quebec travels to Venice sometime in the latter 1960s. Touring Europe to discover its art first hand—and to drown her unrequited love for Jacques, her art history professor—her Venetian discovery leads her to become a painter.

Constance
In Venice Madeleine meets Constance, the exotic alter ego of the Québécoise. The Polish girl is an erstwhile ballerina who repeatedly performs the dying swan to an invisible, heroin-induced audience. Although Constance plunges to her death in a Venetian canal, her image persists through other stories. She emerges from her watery grave as a romantic muse in cemeteries or concert halls or paintings. And she seems to direct the narrative of a father who abandoned and abused her as a child.

Stewart
Constance's father is a Scottish sailor, a port to port drifter. Stewart learns of his daughter's death—reported by her boyfriend from the Venetian trip—in a bar on the Scottish coast. Stewart's incestuous encounter with his daughter, a girl he hardly knew, traces the defining thread of his story. His narrative is revealed through images in a psychoanalytical seance where the aphasic and bewildered Stewart relates his history as an abused child and an abusive father.

Jacques/Jennifer McMann
Jacques is the former art history professor of Madeleine's fantasies. After his psychoanalysis, Jacques becomes Jennifer. She is the host of a high-culture talk show, a late-night radio program on literature broadcast from New York by Radio Canada. In New York the marginal Jennifer meets another marginal character, Kevin from Alaska. This encounter leads to her death.

Kevin
He is a radio technician from Juneau, Alaska. He has come to New York as a guest of an Oprah Winfrey show on eligible bachelors. He is attracted to the francophone Jennifer, who appears as an exotic and authoritative figure, key to the great European culture Kevin so admires from afar. Learning that his imagination has played a joke on him and that his "Jennifère" is in fact a "Jack," Kevin strangles the radio announcer.

Antoine
He is an employee of a rare and used books store in Quebec City. He is also mute and his history is never told. But he is connected to the other characters from Quebec. He is Madeleine's *confident* and Jacques' former lover. He is the listener to their stories. He bids good-bye to Madeleine when she first departs for Europe sometime in the latter 1960s. Two decades later he responds to the painter's plea to seek out Jacques in the wilds of Manhattan. Overcoming his terror of airplanes and the New York subway, Antoine travels to the metropolis. It is the mute clerk who discovers Jacques' body.

Two master narratives bind these drifting subjects together. One is the undercurrent narrative of George Sand and Frederick Chopin, Romantic artists forever in search of each other, of self-expression, and of the ineffable sublime. Particularly Sand—whose persona was ostensibly gender-divided and whose life appeared as a series of contradictions between the woman and her art—crystallized into the shattered subject of a neo-romantic Venetian metaphor.[12] The second is the psychoanalytical narrative. Three of these five characters—Jacques, Madeleine, Stewart—are undergoing the talking cure and any one of their biographies could be considered the story line of the final version.

There is no center to the last edition of *Plaques/Plates* other than the western subject drifting in a postmodern sea and staring into a mirroring pool, which only reflects a mute and mutating image. The production went from the expanse of an illusory transatlantic subject to the equally ungraspable landscape of the individual psyche. The only englobing narrative binding the four-year theatrical journey is that of travel itself. Ultimately the subject is the tourist, crossing through and crossed by the multiple sites of the journey. This brings us back to Théâtre Repère's recurrent theme of the Québécois traveler and to the question of identity politics on the international stage.

Notes

1. The casts, as listed in the programs, were the following.
   Toronto: Lorraine Côté, Richard Fréchette, Sylvie Gagnon, Marie Gignac, Robert Lepage, Alexjandro Moran[sic].
   Québec/Montréal: Normand Bissonnette, Céline Bonnier, Lorraine Côté, Richard Fréchette, Sylvie Gagnon, Marie Gignac, Robert Lepage, François Pick.

Ottawa/Glasgow: Michael Benson, Normand Bissonnette, Céline Bonnier, Boyd Clack, John Cobb, Lorraine Côté, Emma Davie, Richard Fréchette, Marie Gignac, Robert Lepage, François Pick, Jim Twaddale.

2. Since 1994 Théâtre Repère has been absorbed into Robert Lepage's Ex Machina, an international multi-media production organization which retains a home base in Quebec City.

3. Diane Pavlovic, Tenir l'univers dans sa main, *Cahiers de Théâtre Jeu 45*, 1987, p. 11.

4. The most illustrious example of a Québécois company achieving international fame is the Montreal-based Cirque du Soleil, which functions entirely with visual imagery. Other examples include Carbone 14—originally founded as a mime troupe in 1979—and Théâtre de la Marmaille. All have exploited visual languages in international coproductions, but outside of Théâtre Repère, none have risked performing in French for non-francophone audiences.

5. Michel Tremblay interviewed by Linda Gaboriau, *Théâtre Québec 8* (newsletter of the Centre d'essai des auteurs dramatiques in Montreal).

6. *The Polygraph,* which treats a police investigation that director and co-author Lepage became involved in, was performed at the 1990 Brooklyn Academy of Music "Next Wave, Next Door" festival. (See my comparative review of Repère's *Polygraph* and Carbone 14's *Dormitory* in *Theatre Journal 23:2*).

7. For a complete list of Lepage's phenomenal production through 1995, including the theatrical saga *The Seven Branches of the Ota River* and the film *The Confessional*, see *Robert Lepage: Quelques zones de liberté* (Charest 1995).

8. Marie Gignac interviewed by Aline Gélinas in *Voir* 1 March 1990, p. 10.

9. Considering Frederick Chopin's distaste for public performance and his virtual terror of the public gaze, this theatricalization of a Chopin concert reinforces the *in absento* quality of the artist. The persona materializing in the actor, the piano, and the immediate act of the performance bear the sign of Chopin's absence.

10. In 1838 Delacroix painted Chopin improvising at the piano while Sand looked on. The painter's sketch of the original shows Sand sitting behind the pianist. Split in two by the first buyers of the painting, the Chopin half and the double sketch are among the holdings of the Louvre in Paris. The Sand portrait is part of the Ordrupgardsammlingen in Copenhagen.

That the Sand painting pops up at a Parisian art dealer's, a Venetian auction, and a New York restaurant throughout *Plate's* journeys is obviously based on the demands of the theatrical metaphor and not on historical accuracy. Even within the fiction, the authenticity of the painting, bartered off with tourist art and useless chairs, is highly doubtful.

11. A popular legend describes Columbus distracting his sailors bent on mutiny by challenging them to stand an egg on its head. The solution is, of course, to crush half the shell.

12. On a poetic level, Sand was the perfect subject of this postmodern Venetian metaphor, drifting between lovers and reflected as a fragmented self. Performatively, the writer was never embodied by an actor, but her image surfaced more and more clearly through the four-year work in progress.
On a more literal, historical level Sand did travel to Venice prior to her liaison with Chopin, in the company of another Romantic artist, Alfred de Musset. Sand, prone to mothering younger and frailer artists, nursed Musset through a bout of typhoid fever before his departure and her liaison with the Italian doctor who had treated him. Sand cherished Venice "as a living being" (Hofstadter 1979:221); the Adriatic city figured in her *Lettres d'un voyageur* and other novels.

164 Tectonic Plates

CONSTANCE (Céline Bonnier): Venice is such a narcissistic place.
Photo: Johnnie Eisen, courtesy Rhombus Media Inc.

Chapter Six
Geopoetics/Geopolitics

Improbable Mediations

During the course of my own work in progress writing about *Plaques/Plates*, I have repeatedly circled back to the Théâtre Repère, to the small group of actors from the peculiar Franco-American community named Québec. Early on in my research, I was struck by how the work—marked by a postmodern intercultural mythos—seemed tied to a culturally specific location, or rather to the cultural politics which define contemporary Quebec. At the same time I have been troubled by the fact that the production managed to slip over both local and global politics. *Plaques/Plates* uses the seismic metaphor in every possible way except to describe a politically divided world.

This is the world which penetrated my space during the writing process through the radio, television, newspapers, public rumor, and communications with friends and relatives in the Americas, Europe, the Middle East, Asia, and Africa. Earthquakes appeared minor compared to the wars on all levels—from large scale military operations to ethnic clashes—which occurred during the four-year work in progress. As I have sought to retrieve my experience as a spectator of the *Plaques/Plates* performances, I have marveled at the discrepancies between the politically agitated world outside the theatre and the essentially harmonious world inside the theatrical space. I retain the impression of drifting through a pleasant dream full of rich and beautiful images, in a cocoon which shuts out political turmoil. I know that if current events are played out on the stage, they automatically become historical fiction negated by the "this is not real" theatrical premise. I certainly know that the Repère work is not a political discourse. The Repère creators do not dramatize events too close to contemporary reality. If *Plaques/Plates* addresses the political, it does so obliquely. Still I wondered at the fact that the production had manipulated the intrinsically violent tectonic metaphor and wound up with a geopoetic rather than a geopolitical picture.

After all, even within the limited Euro-American parameters of the production, the world was coming apart. In Europe—the alternate pole of this bicontinental work in progress—people were still bickering over European unity while the Soviet Union was disintegrating. The Berlin Wall crumbled and was literally picked apart by fêtards celebrating the end of a regime and a long-imagined reunion of Germany. In Canada the fragile confederation was again challenged by the collapse of the Meech Lake agreements.

What is the relation between a theatrical production—spanning two continents and four years, yet remaining a very small arena—and the geopolitical stage? The founding jigsaw puzzle *mappa mundi* inevitably invites such comparisons. The current events on the geopolitical stage offer a parallel subtext to the work in progress. These shadows appear clearly in the evolution of the ballerina persona who commits suicide in Venice. Constance is the disturbed Polish ballerina of the Montreal and Ottawa versions. Originally, in the Quebec City production designed before the events in Eastern Europe, the ballerina was Czech and physically handicapped. She had broken her leg in an automobile accident and could never dance again. This character laments the fragmented history of her country which she compares to her broken body.

Scanning the relation of the four productions to their political contexts, I have come to a bifurcated conclusion. The first prong is obvious: the Repère avoided the political because it would have prohibited a geopoetic mediation of the world through the theatrical ritual. The second prong is more subtle: while denying any political agency—just moving with the drift of current events—the *Plaques/Plates* metaphor allowed the coopting of any political occurrence during the four years. A mere reference in the program announcing the show is enough to bring the political into the production. The 1989 Quebec City version juxtaposes earthquakes in Armenia, Japan, Algeria, and California to political tremors in Eastern Europe, in China, and in Canada. The 1990 Montreal theatre bill refers briefly to the Meech Lake talks and the rebirth of Québécois separatist sentiment.

I gradually came to see *Plaques/Plates* as an extremely sophisticated political strategy. This was brought home to me through an interview with Robert Lepage conducted by Paul Lefevre (*MTL*, March 1990:229). Lepage states that the fact the work would be performed with Scots or Catalans was purely fortuitous, "... due to the hazards of international financing." It is hard to believe that a project whose telos was the coming together of Québécois, Celtic, and Catalan actors was purely coincidental. The marriage is too perfect to be true. All three are subnations which have manifested the separatist cause in relatively non-violent ways, and all work through language to promote their cultural differences.

The major problem in locating the ideological underpinnings of *Plaques/Plates* is that politics, ostensibly dismissed from the production, move under the guise of a nebulous cultural metaphor. When one raises the question of whose culture, the problem of political agency resurfaces. Yet, tautologically, every time the geopolitical rears its ugly head, director Lepage and other commentators on the work retreat into the default category of culture.

Cultural or Political Shock Waves?

In preparation for the Glasgow/London/Ottawa productions, Repère creators gathered with Glasgow actors for a three-week workshop. The workshop opened with the original *ressource sensible*: the jigsaw puzzle map of the world. Lepage asked the actors to choose pieces of the map for improvisations. When the actors compared images, they found that the Scottish and Welsh actors (whom the Repère actors dubbed "the Celts") had made associations which differed radically from those of the Québécois (whom the Glasgow Tramway actors dubbed "the Americans"). The British actors' associations were in the realm of apartheid and genocide, nuclear plants and nuclear war heads, droughts, famine, global pollution, torture and dictatorship. The French-Americans' associations centered on personal anecdotes, such as visits from friends, trips they had taken, postcards they had received from abroad.

In her article "Shock Waves Bring 1990 to Crescendo" (*Sunday Times Scotland*, 25 November 1990), Mary Lockhart was quick to perceive this as "cultural differences between Scots and North Americans" which shocked both. Marie Gignac reported the same story not as shock, but as an amusing incident of little consequence. "On a bien ri," the actress told me. The discrepancy between the two groups of actors reverberated in the reporting of the incident and suggested that the widespread European stereotype of the politically naive "North American" held true. Here geopolitical awareness was perceived as a cultural marker.

But was the difference in the actors' world view due to "national" character (Celtic or American or Québécois)? Or did it reflect a more localized and transient culture, not that of North America or Quebec or even that of the Repère theatre, but that of a specific artistic project entitled *Plaques tectoniques/Tectonic Plates*. Lepage made a perplexing comment on the workshop incident. In another Glasgow article ironically entitled "Celtic Soil Brother," Mark Fisher cites Robert Lepage.

When we had the workshop, we would be talking about relationships, family things, but the Celts would talk about what Australia is doing to its environment or what horrible things are going on in South America. In Canada there are TV shows for that! (*The List,* 23 November 1990)

There are certainly as many television shows in Great Britain for that. And numerous Americans, Canadians, or Québécois would have exactly the same reaction as "the Celts" if invited to make associations with pieces of the world map. The planet is more than an intimate network of personal relationships; discordant visions are not necessarily due to cultural differences.

The problem in locating a cultural subject—this "we" which Lepage refers to in the above quote—is evident in the naming of a small group of actors as representative of Celts, Scots, Welsh, North Americans, or (French) Canadians. Cultural difference is always defined by the agents involved in a communication act. The spokesman of *Tectonic Plates* is North American in the eyes of the Glasgow critic. For Lepage, it is easy to dismiss the Celts' citing the rampant problems of the "global village" as simply cultural dissonance. Culture is one big sponge absorbing personal or political differences in an interpersonal communications act.

The amusing discrepancies which appeared in the Glasgow workshop had less to do with cultural specificity than with the gaps between the seismological metaphor, geo-economic realities, and the artistic project at hand. By the time the work in progress reached Glasgow, the thematics had already centered on the psychoanalytical subject and the artist, which left little room for the geopolitical. In the final Ottawa production this world relayed through the media would symbolically crystallize in the radio tower of the set which periodically sent out electronic beats. The unmanageable world outside condensed into noise, messages which could not be decoded. As Lepage stated, "In Canada there are TV shows for that."

Critics and Cultural Sensitivity

Responding to negative comments on *Plaques/Plates* from Québécois critics, Lepage demonstrates how the cultural can be made to absorb any ideological or aesthetic difference. In a curious inversion, the director is interpreting the tepid reception Montreal critics accorded the first editions of *Plaques tectoniques* to cultural sensitivity. In what might appear to the outsider as home territory, some of the press had panned the production.

...Tectonic Plates was praised sky high in London, nominated for a Lawrence Olivier award, whereas in Montreal the same production was shot down; some criticized us for using visual stuff for its own sake. To hear them you'd think we were just a bunch of gadget artists trying to snow the audience. Everything is quite relative and depends on the sensitivity, on the culture of the people we perform for. (Translated from October 1991 Lepage interview with Jean-Louis Tremblay, *A l'Affiche*)

The criticism Lepage is speaking of was evident in a particularly scathing review (*Le Devoir*, 24 March 1990) by the major representative of the Montreal critical establishment. For Robert Lévesque the production is but the vehicle of "showbizz et le monde des variétés" whose content is of such a naive and superficial nature that it discourages any serious analysis. In what seems to be a personal war, Lévesque directly attacks Lepage, "qui semble en panne" [who seems to be out of ideas], for the collective production's lack of intellectual cohesion. The performance purporting the grandeur of tectonic plates is reduced to a mere rumble, an incoherent prattle.

However, it is not true that *Plaques/Plates* were systematically shot down by the Montreal critical establishment. Many critics declared they were enchanted and lauded Lepage as a visionary. One went so far as to cite the work as announcing the year 2000.[1] However, critical response from Montreal was much more divided than it had been for the *Dragons* epic and much more reserved than the London and Glasgow reviews, as the press file I received from the National Arts Center before the Ottawa performance indicates. This hefty dossier on the work of Lepage and Théâtre Repère contained very few reviews in French of this particular production. Because promotional press files are always selective compilations and because this file did contain an imposing number of articles in French praising previous Repère productions, the gap is significant. But is this a 'cultural gap' as Lepage pretends when speaking of the "culture of the people we perform for." Where is the culture located if not in language and collective memory? Here the director perceives "la sensibilité culturelle" either through the success he has known across the Atlantic—and he has always seen his work as more European than American—or to the immediate chemistry of the performance.

The first three versions of *Plaques/Plates* were, with the exception of one actor from France, the production of Québécois actors. Why would a Québécois production be dismissed by Québécois critics for reasons of cultural sensitivity? And why would a Québécois production in French resonate with a British audience? To be loved in England when one is speaking from a francophone minority nation which has been historically defined as threatened by anglo-hegemony, and to be rejected in the cultural capital of French America is a painfully ironic experience. Why would Lepage, who is from Quebec City and has consistently touted his Québécois roots, interpret this discrepancy as a cultural problem? Certainly this is not due to linguistic codes in multilingual Montreal nor to the correspondence of "visual stuff" and cultural sensitivity.

It is surprising that Montreal critics targeted this production as relying on visual gadgetry. Montreal is after all a cosmopolitan center of music, dance, performance art, and international festivals, all of which amply exploit spatial graphics rather than text. The visual artistry of Repère was already apparent in the *Trilogie des dragons* which had met with almost unanimous praise from the local press. What was the problem with this production?

Undeniably, language and multiculturalism are sensitive issues in Quebec. On the level of minority national politics, I suspect that the criticisms of visual primacy and lack of text relate to the deep-seated fear of disappearing as a linguistic community. If the Québécois verb is the primary marker of the Québécois nation, any interference of other languages may be considered a threat. Although the production is primarily in French, it does employ different languages and speaks of subjects drifting in a postmodern never-never land. Anything which smacks of multiculturalism—which is the currency of federal Canadian discourse—or anything which resembles an undifferentiated, postmodern magma is a threat to minority difference. This is particularly distressing when it comes from a company which was the great national hope for reconciling Québécois specificity and international showcasing.

However, neither language nor cultural specificity appear to be the issue here, but rather the grandiose nature of the geological metaphor as compared with the material production. Nor was the criticism coming solely from home quarters. Bob Wallace, a Toronto critic who has long admired the Repère work, confided the following to me in a personal conversation after the Toronto premiere: "I'm afraid this is just an international festival commodity." The slickness of the 1989 decor designed by Michael Levine or the mercantile context of the du Maurier World Festival at Harbour Front—sponsored by a tobacco company and performed in a 'tasteful' shopping mall—probably contributed to this judgement.

Yet criticism of the work as an empty commodity recurred through multiple versions in multiple venues. One critique which resonated with my concern over the apolitical nature of *Plaques/Plates*—which Lepage might dismiss as a question of incompatible "sensibilités culturelles"—emerged from an unexpected quarter, from a woman who was neither Canadian nor Québécois nor a professional critic, but a West African artist who has adopted Montreal as her home.

A Conversation with Joséphine

Joséphine directs African dance workshops and works odd jobs to make ends meet for herself and her young son. She was delighted I invited her to accompany me to the 1990 Montreal production of *Plaques tectoniques*, because she had seen and loved the *Trilogie des dragons*.

After the performance we went to a café. Joséphine was reluctant to voice what she thought of the show. "C'est beau," she ventured "mais c'est pas ma culture." Why isn't it your culture, I prodded. Gathering steam as she spoke, Joséphine declared that the production portrayed privileged western artists who seemed to be perpetually on vacation, that they were too preoccupied by their "petite personne," and that it was the "same old high-brow stuff" served up in a new plate. "Delacroix, franchement, il faut pas me parler de Delacroix," spit out the West African—with the hint of an acquired Québécois accent—as if the painter represented the whole of the French imperialist colonial world.

I asked why she had enjoyed *Dragons* so much. Joséphine responded that she identified with the two main protagonists, the two girls from the *basse ville* of Québec, who had been forced to emigrate. I pointed out that the problem might lie in the fact that both the French Romantic painter and the little girls from Québec were indeed part of her culture. "Yes," snapped Joséphine, "but you know as well as I do that there's a great difference. You can't talk about culture without talking about class and power and money and all that shit which dictates our lives."

Joséphine pinpointed a problem in *Plaques/Plates* which I had not been able to articulate. Ostensibly the production spoke of a geopoetic universe, fragmented yet glued together in a postmodern magma. The production could not englobe the geopolitical, because this was beyond its scope. Nor could it venture into the postcolonial without seriously compromising its poetic motor. Refusing labels, ideologies, and political agency—drifting among symbolic plates—the Théâtre Repère has little use for the term 'postmodern' and even less for 'postcolonial' which is bound by history and fraught with politics. Throughout the evolution of this four-year work in progress, which was founded in the metaphor of Old and New World divisions and collisions, the colonial enterprise figured in only two brief sequences. And these, I would argue, do represent a specifically Québécois view of the colonial enterprise.

Colonial Banquets

Two brief *plates* referred directly to the 15th through 18th century European occupation of the Americas and other territories across the globe. Both centered around *la table* in its two meanings. The scenes took place around the dining table and both depicted *les plaisirs de la table*. The first appeared in the Toronto premiere version.

This scene dealt with Columbus' transatlantic discovery voyage, sandwiched between two wedding celebrations: a popular fête in Renaissance Europe and a contemporary wedding in America. On one side of the pool, the bride goes into labor and Columbus pops up from under the table cloth with his proverbial egg. The *convives* send off little paper boats to the other side of the pool. There a Texas millionaire is marrying off his daughter to a Mexican groom who gives an elaborate toast in Spanish to which the father of the bride responds in an exaggerated Texan accent, "Well, I don't know what he said, but it sure sounds good to me." The guests at these two banquets—although separated by language, an ocean, and centuries—all seemed to have a wonderful time. The meal and Columbus' voyage appeared a joyous adventure, unmarred by disputed claims to the land or any aboriginal presence. Just where are the Indians in this picture?

The other colonial banquet appeared in the Quebec City version. The first act depicted the six-generation history of a line of French gourmets, the Brillat-Savarins. The production began with the burial of the patriarch and inventor of gastronomy in the Père Lachaise cemetery.

A dinner plate
"The universe and all its living creatures are nourished. Animals feed. Man eats. Man is the only creature who can be nourished solely by the spirit. The destiny of nations depends on the way they eat. The discovery of a new dish contributes more to human happiness than the discovery of a star. The Creator invites man to eat by exciting the appetite and rewards him with the pleasure of the meal."

This over-voice text is set against a funeral scene in which the patriarch—invisible to the mourners sobbing and mumbling liturgical phrases—rises up to cross the pool and join a banquet of his descendants. The last phrases of Brillat-Savarin's treatise are punctuated by the rhythm of knives and forks chiming on porcelain and crystal, of idle chatter and discreet belches. The piano plays a waltz.

As the ancestor settles into the chair of his son, the off-stage voice announces "Tell me what you eat and I will tell you who you are... Second generation: Lucien Savarin." Implements continue to chime during the dinner conversation. The tinkling of voices shaped in French aristocratic accents float about a silent Lucien. "So, dear Lucien, you have returned from the far-away colonies... Lucien used to love to eat, but since he's come back his appetite seems to have waned... A strange affliction, malaria or worse, kept him bed-ridden... He brought back an exotic fruit, long, black and yellow." "Never could I eat such a thing," declares one woman. "Do you think the banana caused his fever?" asks a male guest. "It's one thing to bring back fruits, but quite another this mania of transporting savages over here." "They should simply learn the rules of French grammar and stay in their country." "Believe me, they will never be civilized. Once we've pulled out their gold and diamonds, they will become a burden to France."

As the banquet carries on, a woman creeps toward the table. She wears a ragged tunic and circles around the dinner guests like a hungry animal, stalking and scrounging for crumbs. Eventually she crawls up onto the table where she falls under the knives and forks of the oblivious guests. The waltz of the piano and the resounding silverware becomes frenetic as the savage is carved up.

The diners stand and continue beating the plates with their silverware. As the movement becomes more violent and the waltz shifts to African percussion, the guests slowly pull the tables apart. The white table cloth, weighted down by the woman's body, sinks into the chasm.

The art of gastronomy and the joys of the table, the banter of the guests in the king's French, the masks of civility, and the waltz contrast with the cannibalization of the unexpected guest at the feast. Who is this hungry creature so unmannerly and foolish as to climb up on the sacrificial table? An African, an Amerindian, a woman? There is no psychological particularity to this generic Other nor to any of the diners. It is simply an eloquent picture of colonialism. The only individual who might have a name and a personal history is Lucien, who has recently returned from the distant colonies. But he is as mute as the savage. Not only has he lost his voice, but he has lost his appetite. The idea that "the destiny of nations depends on the way they eat" appears revolting to Lucien. It would seem that the colonial enterprise devours even the colonizer.

How is this, the only scene at all critical of colonialism, to be read in the overall work? Does this sinister picture merely apply to the French colonization of Africa? The tableau was introduced after the incorporation of a French actor, François Pick. Does the setting in France confine this scene to the Africas rather than the Americas? Or are there simply two visions of colonialism at work?

Comparing the 1989 Quebec City banquet to the 1988 Toronto banquet, the discrepancy appears clearly. Both scenes depict the invasion as a moveable feast, but only the second offers a political critique. This might be due to the ambivalent attitude toward colonialism which until recently prevailed in Quebec. Rather than identifying with the colonizer, French-Canadians have long identified with the colonized. The *Conquête* which marks Québécois historical tropes is not the European conquest of America, but the British take-over of the French colony. The political positioning of a former *nègre blanc de l'Amérique* is bound to differ from that of a *Français de France* who has inherited a heavy colonial legacy.

These historical paradigms float in the undercurrents of *Plaques tectoniques*. Yet, if the time occupied in the four-year work in progress determined the importance of the jigsaw puzzle pieces, the 1988 Toronto and 1989 Quebec City version of the colonial banquet would rank among the most minor fragments. Both Columbus' frolic over the globe and the colonial division of the world disappeared in the subsequent versions of *Plaques/Plates*. The Euro-American moveable feast traveled to more localized territory where it would comprise the backdrop of a few world travelers.

Why the original clash between Old and New Worlds—the transatlantic axis between Europe and the Americas at the core of the metaphorical and processual movement of the production—disappeared in the final versions has as much to do with the demands of the project as it does with vague "cultural sensitivities." If there is one single task the work in progress accomplishes, it is to challenge essentialist notions of cultural identity. Why then the recurrent use of the word culture/*culture* to explain away any problem which crops up in *Plaques/Plates*? What is frequently attributed to cultural difference is just as likely related to ideological differences. In fact they are part and parcel of the same paradigm. The apparent obliteration of class divisions or geopolitical strife and Repère's attempt to touch universal "geopoetic" cords constitute a political statement in themselves.

The Local and the Universal

Comparing *Tectonic Plates* to *The Dragon Trilogy*, Lepage stated that the focus in the first case moved from the universal to the local, and in the latter case, from the local to the universal. What might this local or this universal be? Circling back to the original *repères* of the two productions, *Dragons* began with a parking lot in Quebec City which covered an extinct Chinatown; the narrative kernel was the story of two girls from Saint-Roche, who would travel across Canada and the Atlantic. In *Plaques/Plates* the first palpable resource was the jigsaw puzzle map of the world; the narrative—first based on continental drift, on the separations and attractions of Europe and America—would gradually come to focus on a few drifters and their internal divisions.

Yet—in so far as both productions focus on the Euro-American bipolar axis traversing Québécois identity—neither the closure of *Dragons* nor the departure of *Plates* is universal. Great chunks of the mappa mundi are missing and despite the transcultural ambitions of the Repère, the work is bound to the local from the start. As I have pointed out, a Québécois perspective on the colonization of the Americas is inevitably shaped by the particular history of the former French, then British, colony and on Quebec's peculiar subnational status in the postcolonial world. Lepage's reference to the evolution of the work in progress as moving toward the local means, not moving toward Québécois territory, but focusing on the individual subject of the artist. At the same time there is always the hope that the artist's vision touches a universal subject.

In *Prélude*, the 1991 Ottawa program, there is a brief comment—in the two official Canadian languages—from the director. Lepage first introduces the "full and final version" of the work as a challenge involving four years of travel to six cities on two continents "and nearly ten kilometres of paper spewed from various fax machines." The team—composed of actors from France, Quebec, Wales and Scotland—is complete. The desire for closure and the ultimately all-encompassing metaphor is evident in the last paragraph of this preamble.

> It is our hope that these *Les Plaques* will project a profound vision of human relations in your own home, neighborhood, city and country, and, on a much larger scale, in your soul. (*Prélude 13*, National Arts Centre)

Understandably, the director's intentions are to create a harmonious premise to the theatrical ritual and to enclose the work in a holistic ensemble. My project as cultural politics critic is quite the opposite and the contradictions I am seeking out in the relation of the geopolitical or Québécois local political to the poetic abound in the production.

On the level of local identity politics *Plaques tectoniques* not only contains evident references to the bicontinental drift of Québécois identity, but plays with the motors of national anxiety: the fear of losing the language and the concomitant fear of disappearing as a distinct society. The Repère treats these themes with a highly sophisticated sense of irony. Through their use of languages, the actors ultimately propose a new twist to the old problem of bilingualism and Québécois cultural identity, as the following examples from the July 1991 Ottawa production illustrate. Incorporating actors from the Glasgow creation, the last edition of *Plaques/Plates* took place in the Canadian federal capital.

Ottawa may be the capital, but the town has a distinctly provincial flavor when compared to cosmopolitan Montreal or Toronto. The city is situated on the Saint Lawrence; a bridge separates Ottawa, Ontario from the Québécois city of Hull. Just a few weeks before the performance, partisan groups had confronted each other across the bridge.

Although the "great Canadian divide" is never mentioned in the production, the context again seems to be swallowed into the tectonic metaphor. And bilingual, binational dichotomies are projected through the intriguing character of Jacques/Jennifer McMann. As a case study, this split persona opens up numerous interpretations. McMann can be read as a Canadian, as a Québécois, as a Euro-American, as a western subject seeking to bring together the disparate pieces of his/her fragmented identity. Challenging monolithic definitions of the gendered subject, McMann also challenges the notion that language is a stable constituent of identity.

The Strange Case of Jacques/Jennifer McMann

> The title is a poetical metaphor about cultures colliding, dividing and crashing... The work has a lot to do with gender, which is one of the major earthquakes. (*ES Magazine* [London], December 1990)

The story of the man inhabited by a woman's voice crossed all the *Plaques/Plates* productions and gradually evolved into a major articulation of the work. The battle between Jacques and the Celtic goddess announced the transformation of Jacques McMann, a Montreal art history professor, into Jennifer McMann, host of a literary talk-show broadcast from New York by Radio Canada. The sexually/culturally cleaved character has a history within the production itself. (S)he first appeared in the 1988 production, not as a Franco-American intellectual, but as a Mexican villager.

The germ of this character emerged in one of the five *plates* of the Toronto premiere production: "The Divided Self." The actor who created the seminal persona was a Mexican-Québécois who appeared only in this version. In the 1988 sequence Juan is haunted by the voice of a child, a voice which occupies his mind to the point where he can no longer speak. Juan sits, immobile and silent, while two female figures turn around him talking: an ethnopsychiatrist urging him to speak, and an internal ghost who speaks to him in English, a language Juan barely knows. The psychiatrist seems genuinely motivated by her desire to help Juan and takes him to an international symposium. But the voyage is a disaster. The plane trip, where Juan is buckled up and tossed about in turbulent skies, and the symposium where he is seated under bright lights and made a specimen to an international group of experts, prove more traumatizing than his neurosis.

The internal voice, embodied in all of the *Plaques/Plates* productions by the same Repère actress (Lorraine Côté) mutated into the Scottish amazon, Skadi. The psychiatrist gradually shifted from a sincerely concerned ally to a business-like professional who clocks the fantasies she invites her patients to express in office hours. The patient slipped into the slot of Jacques/Jennifer McMann, still internally divided between languages and genders, yet curiously representative of an imminently Québécois subject.

When Robert Lepage took over the role in 1989, this seminal *divided self* became a dominant character and gender division became a pivotal theme. At the start of the Quebec City workshop, when the Repère was looking for connections to pull together the first plates, Lepage decided the piece would revolve around neo-romanticism and that he wished to develop the sexually ambivalent character of George Sand. The novelist, with the shadowy figure of Chopin who had dominated the first version of *Plaques/Plates*, fit perfectly with the overarching themes of the production. Sand—who had lived the tumultuous life of the Romantic artist, had been the lover and protector of a number of male artists, had scandalized and delighted 19th-century art circles by dressing as a man, and had lived by her art in spite of all odds—became the poetic motor of Jacques/Jennifer McMann.

The site of the divided self shifted to fit the new actor/character and the venues for which the production was destined. Lepage thought Manhattan was the most appropriate harbor for the marginal Jennifer McMann. After Jacques (alias Juan) became Jennifer, the persona was transplanted to New York. The character's home shifted from an indeterminate Mexican village to metropolitan Montreal. The character's genealogical origins also shifted into a Québécois/Scottish dichotomy. And when Jacques, the art critic from the University of Montreal, mutates to Jennifer, the hostess of a literary talk-show broadcast from New York, he not only changes gender but language.

As the character became more defined, so did the double occupying the schizophrenic. The nebulous female voice of the first version would become a mythic persona of specific cultural origins, a Scottish goddess who was by the last edition of *Plaques/Plates* to acquire the name of Skadi. Behind the symbolic edifice, there are pragmatic considerations. The Glasgow production was a predefined destination. It is not surprising that McMann bears a Scottish name or that his possessing spirit is a Scottish amazon. After seeing the Montreal version, one of the Glasgow actors said "I see you've heard about Skadi." The Repère actors had not until then, but by the last production, the female warrior had acquired a name and a story of her own. Skadi—whose name is linked by legend to Scotland and Scandinavia—is a fertility goddess. Generous in her proliferation of earthly goods but terrible in her treatment of male subjects, Skadi is an ambivalent goddess who sucks the blood of men to nourish the land. It is this mythic creature doubling as a psychic operator who wields the deadly blow to Jacques and steals into his body. This simultaneous castration/invasion, which takes place during a psychiatric seance, is a key piece to the tectonic jigsaw puzzle. The psychoanalytical narrative is the principle binding the neo-romantic tale of the schizophrenic subject engaged in the impossible search for the unified self.

The character of Jacques/Jennifer McMann is a cluster of Freudian, Jungian, and Lacanian fragments. On one level we can read Jacques/Jennifer McMann, "son of man," as the universal subject of western psychoanalysis or as a postmodern citation of the fragmented self. The subject is not reconstructed through the analysis, but left in pieces which continue to float between identifying poles. Even when (s)he reappears in the following scene as Jennifer, dressed in patent-leather high heels, a blazer, and a pleated tartan skirt, the ghost of Jacques and the body of Skadi accompany her. Having symbolically shed the phallic signifier, but still not a biological woman, (s)he is neither male nor female. Or all of the above.

Other factors which might moor her identity are equally troubling. Jacques/Jennifer appears to have no family nor ethnic origin. Half Québécois and half Scottish—in themselves dubious national origins—the character is a hybrid. She is a radio speaker who discusses world literature on a program broadcast in French from New York. She speaks standard French, a tongue which obliterates regional differences. Yet Jacques/Jennifer *is* from Quebec and her absence of monolithic defining traits may aptly capture, not an essence, but a political nexus which is *typiquement Québécois*. The apparently internationalist McMann leads straight back to the Québécois identity problem.

Rehearsal Implanthéâtre, Quebec City, 1989. In foreground, Jennifer (Robert Lepage). Photo: Claudel Huot, Communication Visuelle, courtesy Ex Machina.

Would the Québécois Subject Please Step Back to Center Stage

In this indecision I can discern... the richest Québécois potential. No more a double negation but a double affirmation... irony, an exquisite Québécois specialty... Quebec, both affirmation and negation of "self."[2] (Larose 1987:177)

There is little doubt Jacques/Jennifer McMann has an identity problem. Jostling between sexual and cultural poles, "bisexual and bicontinental" in the words of the nationalist literary scholar Jean Larose, the character circles back to the Québécois identity question. What could be a more appropriate symbol of the national subject than Jacques/Jennifer, binary and forever circumscribed by quotation and by question marks? And what could be a more appropriate paradigm for identity problems than the psychiatric disorder? Whether named hysteria or schizophrenia, McMann's malady coincides with a national mythos of the lost and divided subject in search of home.[3] Read as a subject-nation, Jacques/Jennifer takes on a particular color. The character's apparent sexual, cultural, and linguistic ambivalence relates to a trajectory in the Québécois political imaginary. If identity is a question of continually playing out one's own contradictions, Jacques/Jennifer is a prototypical motor. Numerous threads connect McMann's problem, so graphically illustrated in the psycho-mythic plate which introduces the character, to the national identity problem and its archaic roots: the subject is cleaved, invaded, and emasculated.

First, the subject is divided. (S)he is of mixed origins, bears two names, and speaks two languages. This is commonplace in Quebec, as in much of the world, and has been for a longer time than nationalist demographers are willing to recognize. But the bilingual and half-breed McMann, who unfortunately bears an anglo name, relates to the threat to the minority *fait français* in North America.

Second, the subject is invaded by the Other lurking within the Self. A feminine spirit, who also happens to be a Celtic deity, occupies Jacques' mind. The enemy within takes over the embattled subject. Jacques becomes Jennifer, and Skadi becomes the manipulator of Jennifer alias Jacques. The enemy penetrates and then attacks from within.

The Trojan horse figure is a long-standing trope of the Québécois identity syndrome. If the collective refuses to overthrow the enemy, then the enemy must be undermining the collective from the inside.[4] This was a convenient explanation of the majority NON vote in the 1980 independence referendum. Why would the people refuse national sovereignty unless the Other—*l'Anglais, le Juif, l'Immigrant*, or *la Femme*—had crept into the collective body and taken over its mind? Third, the subject is castrated. This third phase is the most vertiginous part of the movement and demands breaking down into smaller steps.

Jacques is only symbolically emasculated. He does not undergo what is currently known as "gender reassignment." Although Jacques' symbolic castration does not transform him into a woman, it gives him access to a role he quite willingly assumes. What is the relation between the feminized male and the Québécois identity problematic? The trope of the emasculated male bereft of patriarchal authority is a traditional figure of the colonial paradigm. Quebec is no exception, but the juxtaposition of a contemporary feminist mythos with the colonized male has spun off into divergent metaphorical channels. Skadi simultaneously castrates and empowers.

In his analysis of sexist and homophobic metaphors in relation to the Québécois identity syndrome, Robert Schwartzwald[5] has traced a history of the feminized male trope in its displacements. The remanent image of a conquered and domesticated male, subsequently ruled by matriarchs and Catholic priests (the non-generative father and the "man in skirts"), crosses the Québécois historical fresco. But it has branched off to two other loci. The Frenchman—the original *faux père* who abandoned his children in the wilds of the New World—has been frequently depicted in Quebec as a *fifi* or "girly." During the Parti Québécois era, federalists ran the risk of being labeled *fédérastes* (pederasts/federalists). Homophobic stigma and nationalist sentiment combined in a picture of the false male, traitor to his sex and his country, who refuses to assume the position of an adult, independent—and naturally virile—subject.

These sexual-political metaphors are archaic residues which cling to the kilts of Jacques/Jennifer McMann. The character is a perfect rendition of the *faux féminin*. (S)he is a man in skirts. "Jennifer McMann qui vous parle de New York" is also a *fifi*, who speaks in the neutered accent of Radio Canada broadcasters. For a Québécois audience standard French is associated with passing for something one is not; the *français de France* accent is associated with the stereotype of the effeminate Frenchman as compared to the macho North American pioneer. This feminized image of the language is compounded by the fact that Radio Canada is McMann's employer. (S)he has sold out to the federalists or, perhaps worse, to the internationalists. The character appears lost in an hysterical magma, with which the feminine is symbolically linked, and incapable of directing her/his destiny.

Yet, as will appear obvious in the following sequence, Jacques alias Jennifer embraces the feminine role and perceives feminization as empowering. The persona does not invest in the nationalist tropes of a virile libido—in the *Debout* or "Stand up" slogans—but in a feminist mythos of empowerment. The following *plate* projects an incident in the lives of Jacques/Jennifer from Quebec and Kevin from Alaska. It is a much more whimsical sequence than that of the psychiatric seance which first ushered Jennifer McMann into the world.

Gender Can Be Confusing

A New York plate
A long table dressed with a sparkling-white cloth stands at one side of the pool. An audience of empty chairs surround the table. The voice of Oprah Winfrey is piped over the loudspeakers. The topic of the talk show is "Finding an Eligible Man." For this purpose hostess Winfrey has invited a dozen men from Alaska—the land up above with a proverbial shortage of women—to present themselves before an all-female audience.

"Here they are, ladies. All straight, single, and available... this gold mine is from Alaska where men outnumber women thirty-five to one." The radio audience responds with appropriate yelps and screams. Oprah's voice adds, "I can't believe we're doing this."

On stage the voice of Oprah is assumed by the stony-faced female psychiatrist who stands holding a mike. The voices of the Alaskan males are assumed by one performer, jumping from chair to chair around the table and mouthing the words of the different candidates.

"Hi, my name is George and I'm from Valdez, Alaska, land of the midnight sun. I am looking for a woman who will light up my nights." The actor playing the prototypical eligible male, jumps from chair to chair, and grinning at the audience, says "My name is ___ and I'm from ___, Alaska, and I'm looking for a woman who will ___." Or "My name is Kevin and I hail from Juneau, Alaska. I'm a real, live teddy bear."

When he has played a dozen candidates and circled the table, the character last named Kevin sits alone at one end of the long table. The strident voices of the audience and Oprah fade to silence.

A waiter appears and requests Kevin's order in French. In a faltering French laced with a heavy American accent, Kevin asks for a cup of coffee. The waiter returns with a cup of espresso. "Le café n'est pas compris avec le dîner, ça sera cinq dollars," says the waiter briskly. "For five bucks you could have given me a bigger cup," grumbles Kevin.

Jennifer McMann enters dressed in horn-rimmed glasses, a blond wig, high heels, a blazer, and a pleated plaid skirt. The waiter greets her like an old friend and asks if she wouldn't mind sharing the table with Kevin because it is closing time. This request is ludicrous since Jennifer is seated at the opposite end of the table which stretches, a white and barren desert, between the two clients. McMann orders coffee and cognac.

Kevin tries to strike up a conversation in French. "Quatre fourchettes pour si peu de nourriture" [Four forks for so little food]. "C'est la nouvelle cuisine," responds Jennifer. Where is he from, what does he do, and where did he learn French, questions Jennifer. From Juneau, he is a radio technician, and he learned French in Anchorage, answers Kevin. Responding to Jennifer's quizzical look, Kevin explains that he once won a prize in a state-wide radio contest. The contest was sponsored by Black Cow dairy products and the prize consisted of a year's supply of Black Cow chocolate milk and tapes of Berlitz lessons in French, "so I learned French while sipping Black Cow."

McMann in turn reveals she is originally from Montreal and she is a radio speaker, broadcasting in French from New York.

During the course of the conversation which Kevin is valiantly trying to manage in French, the Alaskan states "Mon plus grand désir est de comprendre la *poetry* française." [My greatest wish is to understand French poetry.] "La potterie?" [Pottery?] responds a bewildered Jennifer, "Ah, vous voulez dire la poésie! You mean poetry."

Kevin nods and goes on apologetically: "Le plus difficile pour nous est le sexe." [For us the most difficult problem is sex.] "Ah, bon?" responds a genuinely interested Jennifer. "Oui, nous les Anglaises, on n'a pas de sexe," [We English (women) have no sex] continues Kevin. "Dommage," interjects Jennifer. "Yeah," says Kevin. "*Le* table or *la* couteau, c'est le même chose." [The table or the chair are the same.] "Ah, vous voulez dire le genre," exclaims a somewhat disappointed Jennifer. "Yes," she agrees, "gender can be confusing."

There is a lull in the conversation. Kevin looks around the restaurant and notices the portrait on the back wall. It is the Delacroix portrait of a melancholic George Sand listening to a forever absent Frederick Chopin.

"Beautiful woman," remarks Kevin. "Yes, that's George Sand by Delacroix," murmurs Jennifer, "although I suspect that's just a copy."

"Oh, no," protests Kevin loudly, startling his companion. "Well... maybe I don't know much about art... but I can tell that's a woman." "True, but she took on the name of a man," replies the literary expert and former professor of art history. "It was the only way for her to be recognized as a writer then. Passing for a man was a way to get a piece of the action." Jennifer pauses and then muses, "Today you have to pass for a woman."

Kevin's gaze lingers over the portrait and then moves back to Jennifer. "Well, not in Juneau, Alaska."

He invites her to a late movie. She declines the invitation because she is on her way to work. Then what about tomorrow? insists Kevin. An embarrassed Jennifer clutches at her patent-leather purse. "Really, I can't." "Then let me walk you to work," says Kevin. "Do you see any problem in that?" "No," replies Jennifer, "There is no problem if you don't *see* any problem. It's just that... I'm rather embarrassed. This has never happened before." "What?" inquires an innocent Kevin. Grasping for an answer Jennifer replies, "I forgot my wallet and I can't pay for my drink."

"Is that all? No problem," says Kevin pulling out his wallet. Seeing Kevin is paying for Jennifer's bill, the waiter totals up eighteen dollars.

The couple moves out into the street and the city of New York, depicted by stacks of books whose white back-bindings describe a miniature skyline illuminated by a blacklight. They walk among the distant skyscrapers. Kevin stops and takes Jennifer in his arms. She resists and moves away. But another body emerges in her place. The actress playing Skadi slips into Kevin's arms and lifts her face to his kiss. It is the Scottish amazon who captures yet another man in her embrace.

Kevin Fraser is the reverse image of Jacques/Jennifer McMann. He is, as Oprah tells the audience, a genuine heterosexual male from the wilds of Alaska. As both the last frontier and United States territory, Kevin's origins would locate him as a *vrai male* in an archetypical Québécois gallery. But, just as the skirt and the Radio Canada accent mark McMann as a counterfeit (fe)male, Kevin is hardly a "real male." His vulnerability and naivete totally undermine the stereotype of the heterosexual hero. Kevin, "the real, live teddy bear" has not been chosen among the candidates for mating. He is left alone in an alien environment. Of the three characters in the restaurant, he is the least master of the situation; although the only U.S. American of the group, he is the foreigner and far from being in control. As for his origins, he is not a pioneer nor even a lumberjack, but a radio technician.

Like Jennifer's, Kevin's image wavers between constructed gender tropes. Unlike Jennifer, Kevin is not self-consciously ambivalent, and he does not expect others to be so. If a person wears women's clothes, as Sand does in the portrait, then she must be a woman. If Jennifer bears the name of a woman, then she must be a woman. At least that's the way it is in Juneau, Alaska. The radio technician expects messages which are loud and clear to correspond to reality.

Kevin is not only a radio technician but a radio junky. An avid listener and contest candidate, he has learned French through the media and come to New York to find a prize mate. It is no wonder that Kevin interprets Jennifer's appearance as the fulfillment of his desire. She is a woman, she is a radio personality, and she is French. At any rate Kevin *takes* her for a French woman. What he holds in his arms at the scene's closure is another body and another illusion: the actress representing the mythical Skadi.

For Jennifer, this is the first time she has been *taken* for a woman. Although the character has done everything to pass both as French and a woman, she has not considered that the "opposite" sex might find her attractive. Groping for an answer to Kevin's invitation, she says there is no problem if you don't *see* a problem. McMann, however, is not fully convinced that clothes make the woman. Contrary to Kevin, (s)he is fully conscious of the art of masking. Passing is the name of McMann's game, and it has more to do with art than with sexuality. In this scene, McMann has assumed the costume of a woman as a political choice. She identifies with George Sand, who wore men's clothes in order to find a voice in a male-dominated literary world.

In a subsequent scene, McMann reiterates the reasons for choosing the feminine mask. When the character's former lover—Antoine, the mute *libraire* from Québec—confronts her in New York, and demands to know, in sign-language fury, why Jacques is dressing as a woman, Jennifer spits out in audible anger: "Women's clothes gave me a voice."

For Jacques/Jennifer the skirt has become an access to public recognition. (S)he is the contemporary incarnation of George Sand, whose effigy looms over the table in the New York restaurant scene. The novelist, bearing a masculine forename and wearing pants to assert herself in a patriarchal world, might be the flip-side of McMann bearing a feminine forename and wearing skirts to assert himself in a matriarchal world, but the correspondence is somewhat skewed. The world is hardly female dominated, at least "not in Juneau, Alaska." The powerful Skadi is a mythic agent and not a social reality.

It is of little importance that the empowering feminine may be purely metaphorical. The entire scene is about symbolics, masks, and misinterpretations. Here gender is a costume or a trick of language. Gender can be confusing both for Jacques/Jennifer, whose multiple levels indicate an androgynous polymorphism just under the surface of the female mask, and for Kevin who takes signs for the real thing. The comparison to linguistic *genres* suggests that sexual identity might be as arbitrary as a masculine knife or a feminine table. As Jennifer points out in her last scene, gender ambiguity is a poetic machine.

In the last McMann plate—Jennifer's murder—the radio host meets Kevin at her apartment and is forced to confess that she is not what she appears. At that moment there is the rumbling of a subway passing. Kevin, the "real male," throws himself on the ground because he thinks an earthquake is coming. After the tremors subside, Kevin says "You must think I'm really stupid, mistaking a subway for an earthquake and mistaking a man for a woman." "That's not stupidity," replies Jennifer, "that's poetry." In a sudden fury, Kevin rushes for her throat and silences the voice of Jacques/Jennifer McMann.

Language/Silence

Since my project is to locate a Québécois voice in the postmodern tectonics of this production, I will pursue the language issue marking Québécois identity politics which this production so skillfully weaves into its overall narrative. The poetry of *Tectonic Plates* hinges on a play between languages and silent semaphores. Language, and the fear of losing the language, are key vectors in the elaboration of the Franco-American difference. The final rendition of *Plaques/Plates* destined for Glasgow, which incorporated British actors and took place in the capital of what is *theoretically* a bilingual Canada, exploited language as a ludic and poetic instrument.

Linguistic play is evident in the New York restaurant scene. Kevin's *nous les anglaises* who have no sex and *la potterie française* are a two-tongued game which is best appreciated if the spectator knows both languages and is aware of the Canadian historical franco/anglo dichotomy. Kevin's "le table or la couteau" are not really "le même chose." If there were no difference between and within languages, there would be no poetry. And if there were no difference between and within Jacques and Jennifer (or actor Lepage and character McMann for that matter), there would be no ironic slant to the character. These *gender* differences slip and slide along apparently binary lines. Literary poetics operate through parallels, intersections, and multi-layered ambiguities. Performative poetics operate through a dissonant network of signs and nonsense where verbal utterances can appear as significant as a piano note, or the clink of a glass, or a spectator's cough. *Plaques/Plates* incorporate both into poetics based on the spoken word, forever shadowed by its silent partner.

The final bilingual Ottawa production speaks eloquently of language, noise and silence. The talk cures and talk shows which run through the last edition of *Plaques/Plates* describe both the subject's refusal to speak and a frenzied multivocality, a noise which ultimately renders silence. The visual symbol of the talk shows is the radio tower which dominates the space in the second part of the production. Scenic representation of an illusory polyphony, piping out multiple voices, the radio tower is silent except for intermittent beeps. The audience cannot decipher the code, but can only suspect that messages are being transmitted across the globe. The radio tower is a tower of Babel. Winfrey and McMann are the hosts of talk shows which theoretically give voice to others. Oprah organizes the chaotic public voice by offering the microphone to her 'live' audience: performers of their own stories and spectators whose collective voice swells to high-pitched squeals and thunderous applause. Jennifer's voice is the discreet medium for dead artists such as Jim Morrison whose *riders of the storm* still travel over the air waves.

The metaphoric medium of the talking cure is the pool, whose surface reflects a mute gaze or whose periodic churning announces what should be a verbal tsunami of the subject in psychoanalysis. But the pool is silent. It serves as a metaphorical screen in two respects: it dissimulates and projects through images. The pool hides the story from the analyst and reveals the story to the audience. McMann and Stewart, who are both engaged in psychoanalysis, uncover their neurosis through images. McMann battles with the mythic Skadi in the middle of the pool. An aphasic Stewart reveals his problem through the terrifyingly beautiful image of his violated daughter, Constance, and the superimposed voices of Stewart, the abused son, and his daughter crying "Please, daddy, no." In this production which centers on the troubled psyche, it is hard to know just whose head we, the audience, are traveling in. "Please, daddy, no," could be Stewart's pleading with an abusive father to play the bear or to stop the game, or Constance pleading with her father not to rape her or not to leave. The image of the violated child in an aqua-marine pool marred by clouds of blood and white sheets could be that of the father-son or the daughter. None say "I" in this talking cure.

In her narcotic delirium Constance also produces images in the pool. These are marked by silent semaphores and verbal injunctions to *please, remain silent*. Before and after her suicidal drowning, the erstwhile ballerina dances two interludes in the pool. In one she performs the dying Swan among sailor figures recalling her father who disappeared long ago. White and navy-blue automates manipulate nautical flags signifying "Danger port side," "Danger starboard," or "Save Our Ship." In the other scene Constance performs in a child's ballet class where the *maîtresse* initiates the group into the codes of classical ballet through her movements, while her voice repeatedly barks "Silence!" to the pupils.

The silent language of international codes and the injunction to keep silent are reiterated in the figure of Antoine, the mute *libraire* from Quebec City. Antoine does not speak, but signs. His language is translated into French through the voices of Jennifer or Madeleine. One incident illustrates the play between voicing and silence. It takes place in the bookstore after Madeleine's return from Europe. She is questioning Antoine as to the whereabouts of Jacques McMann. Antoine goes through signing contortions to say Jacques has gone to the *Big Apple*. "Où ça?" exclaims a frustrated Madeleine. Two readers in the bookstore raise their heads and hiss a loud "Shh-sh" to which Antoine responds by gesturing sternly toward a placard above their heads. The sign reads *SILENCE*.

A la recherche d'une voix québécoise

There are three Québécois characters in the final version of *Plaques/Plates*. One is Jacques/Jennifer McMann, who takes on women's clothes to find a voice, but who is essentially a mediator of other voices in the literary talk show. Another is Antoine whose audible voice can only be mediated through others. The third is Madeleine who abandons the talking cure and becomes a painter, expressing her voice through the visual medium. Her journey through an aborted attempt at psychoanalysis and two decisive trips to Venice englobes the overall narrative of the final edition of *Plaques/Plates*.[6] Rather than a linear narrative, it is perhaps the paintings of the fictional artist which link together the fragments of the production.

Madeleine—played by Marie Gignac throughout the four-year work in progress—is the filament binding the stories of Jacques/Jennifer, Antoine, Constance, Stewart, Kevin, and the anonymous art dealer. She is the hippy-traveler of the 1960s whose voyage connects Quebec City to Paris to Venice to New York and back. Each version of *Plaques/Plates* closed with a retrospective of her paintings, which defined her as a key figure in the transparently fictional "Canadian neo-romantic movement." Rising as a shy but persistent phoenix, Madeleine traveled through the work in progress.

In the final version she is the first speaker, whose voice and body serve as conduits to the voiceless Antoine who perceives tectonic rumblings within

Madeleine's "Death of Ophelia" with gondolier (Richard Fréchette) and ballerina (Lorraine Côté).
Photo: Claudel Huot, Communication Visuelle, courtesy Ex Machina.

her body. The last tableau in the Ottawa version pictures Madeleine frozen at the piano while slides of her paintings flash over the surface of the pool. It is appropriate that the four-year work in progress end with Madeleine, the neo-romantic painter in pursuit of an inexpressible artistic truth and the self-effacing traveler from Quebec who finally finds her voice. This voice is both a "small, personal voice" and that of the artist defined retrospectively as the founder of the "Canadian neo-romantic movement" whose inspiration was born in Venice.

A Venetian encounter in Ottawa
While touring in Venice, Madeleine has wandered into an art auction. The auction takes place in the pool, metaphor of Venice, progressively sinking into the Adriatic Sea. Dressed in jeans and a flower-patterned vest, toting her backpack, Madeleine is a striking contrast to the moneyed clients of the auction who have come to save Venice the Eternal from drifting away. One of these clients is an internationally renowned concert pianist.

When the auction is over, Madeleine lingers to examine the portrait of George Sand, which has been purchased by a Texas millionaire. The pianist also stays and approaches Madeleine with a remark about the painting. She tells him the story of the fragmented portrait and how Sand and Chopin are destined to drift around the world without ever connecting.

The conversation turns to the fate of Venice. The pianist declares that if Venice is doomed, why save it. Dying is after all a natural phenomenon, why would cities or cultures escape this? Madeleine, who appears intimidated by the self-assured pianist, remains silent.

There is a pause. The silence in the theatre is palpable.

"Are you an artist?" he questions. "No, just a student," she replies. He presents himself as William Reese, virtuoso. "Are you French?" asks the pianist in a very upper-class British accent. "Non, Québécoise," she mumbles. "And you, you are English?" questions Madeleine. The pianist hesitates and then says, "Uh, no, Welsh."
Both of these replies draw bursts of laughter from the audience.

This fragment contains oblique references to cultural identity which lead back, by a round-about route, to the Québécois identity problem. If Madeleine/Marie is in search of a voice, it is not a national voice, but individual artistic expression which ultimately fuses the fictional Madeleine and the actor Marie Gignac. Yet this small personal voice reiterated through the four-year work in progress does relate to the problem of finding a Québécois voice on the international stage.

Theatre as an internal forum in the construction of a national subject passed out of fashion sometime in the 1980s.[7] Since then, locating even an illusory representation of cultural monovocality, has become increasingly problematic. With the internationalist opening and the recognition of allophones within its borders, language no longer moors the national subject. The Québécois voice I am seeking here speaks of the problem of language itself, which has traditionally held together the North American francophone minority. It emerges from the nexus of linguistic politics which define contemporary Quebec. In an era when the coincidence between language, culture, and identity appears far from self-evident, the issue is not a simple one. How can Quebec maintain a semblance of cohesiveness if not through the language? How can it sell itself on an international cultural market, dominated by the ever-menacing international, i.e. anglophone, voice? How can the nation recognize the status of other linguistic minorities within its borders, when its own, forever liminal, national status hinges mainly on the verb?

The traditional anchor of the collective subject may be as much the fear of losing the language—thus cultural specificity and sinking like Venice into an anonymous sea—than the linguistic vehicle itself. Jean Larose begins his probing essay on the future of the French language in North America with the question "What is more certain in the history of French Americans than the endangered language?"[8] Larose is taking to task the impoverishment of Québécois French, which he claims is selling out to the American junk-media market and the wooden language of technology and bureaucracy. He argues, as have numerous other Québécois intellectuals, that the language can never be secured by multiplying laws concerning its usage or even through independence. The language is an empty symbolic shell if it is not used actively as an intellectual tool.

The malaise is evident in the complaints many local drama critics had with the emphasis on visual plasticity and lack of textual substance in *Tectonic Plates*. The production does not obliterate the *parlure de chez nous*, but it relegates the verb to a tool among others. Significantly Madeleine, the artist whose voice finally emerges in the intercultural magma, works through the visual medium. In the eyes of many Québécois critics, the character could read as a stand-in for the director, Robert Lepage. Focusing on the pictorial aesthetics of the production, local critics have both praised and attacked Lepage's visual artistry, dismissing him as a "gadget artist" or promoting him to "the greatest visual artist of Quebec." The major critique of the work is that instead of progressing toward a more coherent vision, *Plaques* seemed to fall into the jumble of its underlying metaphor: pieces of culture, signs drifting meaninglessly.

More circumspect in his judgement than newspaper critics, a theatre scholar from the University of Quebec, André Bourassa, told me that he applauded the international recognition of Québécois theatre through the works of companies such as Repère or Carbone 14, but that he deplored the virtual disregard for textual refinement since this threatened the development of a literary dramaturgy.[9] It appears that visual aesthetics risk diluting the verb, long defined as the life-blood of the nation. The fact that this verb was always pluralistic and wavering between the oral and the written media, and that it continues to multiply through a flourishing Québécois dramatic literature does not dispel the fear that the verb might disappear in silence or a postmodern babel.

Much is expected of contemporary theatre in Quebec. It must be literature, plastic art, socio-political commentary, the national voice (all the more valid if internationally recognized), and a communal ritual to boot. If the Repère had not succeeded in fulfilling all these requirements in previous productions, it might not have been subject to the criticism that *Plaques tectoniques* was visual gimmickry and superficial prattle without any content. Although the *Dragons*, which first projected the Repère company on the international stage, was equally visually-oriented and employed different languages, critics did not react with the same malaise to the relative importance of the Québécois verb. Although *Plaques tectoniques/Tectonic Plates* does hinge on a Québécois cultural strategy, its ostensibly interculturalist orientation is disturbing.

What is happening here? The artist—who is ultimately the subject of the diegesis and the performance—is speaking through sounds and images as well as another language, which in this case happens to be English. If the artist as medium of the Québécois voice is sucked into the interlinguistic lava dominated by the modern Anglo-American *conquistador*, the development of the language—indeed the survival of the *fait français* in North America—is threatened. The dominant language in the intercultural "no language land" is indisputably English. Assured of its power to the point where it can allow all traces of difference, because it has efficiently cannibalized the Other through the mass-media, the imperialistic and anonymous voice booms over the small voice of the Franco-American nation.

The old fear of losing the language persists in a new paradigm. Many Québécois intellectuals regard the loss of polarity inherent in multiculturalism and multisubjectivity with a suspicious eye. In this they echo the sentiments of numerous feminist and African-American critics who see the diluting of difference in an indistinguishable cultural magma as simply a ploy of the dominant voice. The postmodern mystic of intercultural bonding and joyous heterogeneity—everything is fine here in the global village where everyone speaks English (or "speaks white" as Michèle Lalonde proclaims[10])—is not appealing to everyone. For a minority culture the affirmation of difference is a question of survival. But, at least in the case of Québécois theatre, insular essentialism and monolingual productions confined to Quebec audiences would not be self-affirming, but self-defeating. The Théâtre Repère has developed a subtle strategy of projecting Québécois difference by performing the problem of language itself.

Linguistic Politics in the Tower of Babel

Apparently comfortable with their contradictions, the Repère creators have both denied and confirmed the political nature of their work. This maddening shifting of positions—in itself a political strategy—sometimes occurs within the same speech. In March 1989, immediately following the demonstrations which erupted around the language issue, Lepage declared in an interview with the journal *MTL* that *Plaques/Plates* would inevitably speak of separatism, but that performing with Scottish, Welsh, and Catalan actors was due purely to the fortuitous financing of the international coproduction. It is not so much the question of ideology which the nationalist/internationalist artist refutes but that of individual political agency. The work does not need to have a conscious ideological orientation for it to take on a political character.

In another statement Lepage recognizes the inevitably political quality of theatre, particularly in Canada or Quebec, where any public statement is potentially divisive according to the language and context of its enunciation.

> I think my work has always had a political character... It's inevitable when you start working in other languages, and show the separations of people due to other languages. (Hunt 1989:117)

The separations the director alludes to are not only present in the theatrical frame, but in the differences between the languages spoken on stage and the spectators in the audience. When, as an anti-Québécois demonstration, an entire audience walked out of a 1989 Manitoba performance of *La Trilogie des dragons,* the production became a political event. When the company performed the six-hour saga for non-francophone audiences, particularly for a primarily monolingual U.S. audience such as the 1987 Stony Brook festival or the 1990 Los Angeles festival, the linguistic boundaries appeared as painful rifts. "Tu ne peux pas savoir combien c'est long les dialogues en français lorsque le public ne comprend rien" [You can't believe how long it is, the parts in French, when the audience doesn't understand a word], Marie Brassard, one of the *Dragons* actors, told me. Performing for an audience which does not understand long portions of the dialogue or playing before an audience hostile to the Québécois cause is a challenge. Performing with actors from different milieus is even more problematic.

Something had always bothered me in the evolution of *Plaques/Plates*. Why—in a production which began as a trilingual exploration of "la colonization des Amériques et l'attraction entre les deux continents" and whose 1992 destination was theoretically Barcelona, and perhaps Seville, site of the Columbus quincentennial—had Spanish disappeared after the first production? Marie Gignac gave me a very straightforward explanation. She said the director of the *Festival grec* sponsoring the Barcelona event had changed and consequently so had the orientation of the festival. Thus *Plaques/Plates* became an anglo-franco production for purely pragmatic reasons. "Suppose you had done the Barcelona workshop... Would it have been in Spanish or Catalan?" I asked. Gignac hesitated, then said "In Catalan I suppose, since the actors would be Catalan." The question of whether the Scots or the Welsh might have spoken Gallic instead of English had apparently not come up. "In any case," she continued, "We'd had enough. It was becoming a *véritable Tour de Babel*."

The metaphor intrigued me. Two languages hardly constitute a Tower of Babel. Incorporating the Glasgow actors had not been an easy process, but this seemed less a question of integrating other languages than forming a cohesive team in a short time with disparate voices. The Repère actors have a long experience working together that has, in a sense, created an internal language and allowed them to inject other languages into their productions. Integrating speaking subjects from other backgrounds and languages is another matter.

Language is a Costume

In a 1988 interview, a Toronto critic asked why Lepage consistently used not only English and French, but at least one other language in his productions. The bilingual director replied: "Speaking with an accent, or not, speaking in another language, or speaking in your own language is like a costume you put on" (Hunt 1989:117). If language is but a costume, then it is not the major constituent of the subject or the nation. In Quebec this statement should have been heresy. Yet the *Trilogie des dragons* was hailed as an *oeuvre québécoise*. Lepage's reference to language as a costume passes in this production, because—despite the use of Chinese, English, and French—the *Dragons* saga is told from a specific site, two girls from the Saint-Roche quarter of Quebec City. Chinese might have been a costume, but the Québécois language as a cultural positioning of the subject was a presupposition of this production: "Les personnages de *la Trilogie* parlent Québécois."[11]

When playing French Canadians speaking in English, the Franco-Québécois actors exaggerated their accents. The impersonation of the Chinese characters, also played by Québécois, was a way of exploring the self by donning the costume of another. "We were talking about ourselves through our vision of China," says Gignac. "We said, we're going to do a show about the Chinatown. But we knew what really concerned us was the people we knew, our families, our intimates," says Lepage (Hunt 1989:116).

The incorporation of the Glasgow actors in the last versions of *Plaques/Plates* presented an entirely different problem. Here language might have been a costume, but its fit depended on who was speaking. Comfortable in both English and French, the Québécois actors of the Ottawa French and English versions of *Plates* could wear either garment. The English-speaking actors had more difficulty in the French versions. Because of this, the seams between the language and the speaking subject became apparent. The Ottawa radio critic who asked why—for the sake of the production's verbal flow— "everybody didn't simply speak in their own language"[12] missed the point entirely. More than performing in different languages, the creators of the Ottawa production were performing the problem of language as a marker of cultural difference. By inviting the Welsh and Scottish performers to speak in French, the Repère was also making a political statement. But this statement is much more sophisticated than a simple anglo versus franco confrontational border. The production does not establish clear-cut dichotomies, but rather reveals the multiple fault lines of cultural difference.

Theatrically, the actors we suspect exist behind the characters add another contradictory level. The same radio critic who had found fault with the Glasgow actors' French "because it disturbed the flow of the dialogue," also complained that the accents and hesitations made the audience aware of the actors as "real people." The fissure between the character and the actor is self-revelatory and enters into the theatrical experience. Although we learn nothing autobiographical of the "real people," the audience observes something more interesting: a glimpse of the subject struggling to appear across the representational gap.

Performing Identity in the Gap

"You're French?" asks the pianist.
"Non, Québécoise," answers the art student. "And you are English?"
"Uh... No, Welsh," answers the pianist.

In this exchange between the established pianist and the young student, cracks appear in what might be hermetic identificatory units. She is young and uncertain; he is older and self-assured. She speaks with a French accent; he speaks with a British accent. But the logical assumptions each makes about the other are disturbed by Madeleine's mumbling she is Québécoise. For a brief moment the world-renowned virtuoso loses his poise. He is forced to position himself according to Madeleine. Switching from British to Welsh, William Reese becomes Rhys. In this initial encounter, the character is faced with choosing between surnames and cultural affiliations. The cultivated, international pianist turns out to be a minority cultural subject.

The Ottawa audience reacts to both answers with a laugh. Only two generations ago "the French" and "les Anglais" were the terms Canadians commonly used to define the Other across the great Canadian divide. Madeleine's correction and Reese's response break down linguistic identity into tribal categories. It is not a holistic entity which appears in this case of mistaken identities, but the disjunction itself. When the characters will have learned more about each other, more discrepancies will appear: I thought you were this, but I see you are that. It is in the moment of the shift—in the what you have been mistaken for—that the subject can be discovered.

The laughter indicates both recognition and surprise. The spectators savor the joke of being caught in the jostling of positions along binary gaps: minority/majority, personal/political, self/other. If positioned as 'Canadian', the spectator should recognize the questioning of a British-based identity and the affirmation of difference in relation to cultural hegemonies. If positioned as 'Québécois', the spectator should recognize the Franco-American voice, obstinately insisting "Non, Québécois." The Québécois have, after all, not only survived through affirming minority difference, but turned it into a political capital. But the individual spectator may cross the citational frames of 'French' or 'Welsh' or 'Canadian' and claim all of the above or analogous identities relating to language, origins, context.

The overriding joke is that of national identity itself: inherently self-contradictory, slipping between linguistic and historical, shifting according to the subject's position vis à vis her interlocutor, and most apparent when one is *outside* of the national environment. Identity emerges momentarily in chance encounters across the traveler's landscape. As Lepage indicates, one is much more likely to discover collective bonds while globe trotting, "while drinking a cappuccino in Venice,"[13] than at home where multiple rifts of gender, class, ideology, and personal history atomize the national subject. *Plaques/Plates* moves in the contradictory gray zones where identity seeks definition. The work invites us as audience to travel in the seismic undercurrents.

More than the politics of Québécois identity, it is the poetics of identity in the postmodern moment which are performed through *Tectonic Plates*. It is a (dis)appearing art, a game of catch me if you can, and a delicious play of irony, "spécialité québécoise." Presented through the eyes of the *Plaques tectoniques* world travelers—both characters and actors—identity moves within a triangular paradox. Because neither an original locus nor the individual subject are stable, the traveler never returns home. Because one cannot discard symbolic baggage so easily, the traveler never leaves home entirely behind. And because the Tower of Babel is manageable only as a metaphor, the traveler is forever in search of moorings in a place, a history, a language. Neither the *communauté imaginaire* nor the individual subject can be located within a single site or a monovocal discourse. Ultimately it is in the gap between positions that Québécois identity seeps through, over the permeable border between "extérieur/outside" and "inside/intérieur."

Notes

1. In "Les plaques tectoniques: merveilleux" (*Le Devoir,* 24 March 1990) Jean Beaunoyer says "C'est la première oeuvre qui annonce des années 2000." This statement is immediately followed by a reference to the political context and a quote from Pierre Elliot Trudeau pronounced the previous day: "Nothing is eternal, not me, not federalism." This is an indication of how the artist from Quebec can not avoid being shuffled in the national card game.

2. "Cette indécision, je l'entrevois... comme la possibilité québécoise la plus riche. Non plus la double négation... mais la double affirmation... l'ironie, une exquise spécialité québécoise... Québec, bi-continental, bisexuel, à la fois affirmation et négation de 'soi'." (Larose 1987:176–7)

3. National schizophrenia has been a common theme of Québécois political analysis and dramaturgy through the 1990s. Psychoanalytical tropes of the cleaved and fragmented (in)dividual self in search of identificatory wholeness have contributed to the construction of a collective neurosis, a self in search of a lost self.

4. The enemy within, the old Trojan horse, is a favored trope among Québécois nationalists, who attributed the loss of the referendum to feminist movements, to anglo-others, or to *faux frères* [false brothers] federalists living inside the national territory.

5. See Schwartzwald's "Fear of Federasty: Québec's Inverted Fictions" in *Comparative American Identities* (Spillers 1991).

6. In the filmed adaptation by Peter Mettler, Madeleine's story, told in the first person, is the principal narrative thread. As a cap to the work in progress, the film zeroes in even more closely on the individual subject.

7. The Montreal theatre critic, Robert Lévesque, has declared: "Quebec is finished with nationalistic, self-affirmation theatre. The battle for a distinct society is over for many Quebeckers... it is a *fait accompli*." (Comment related by Vit Wagner, Theatre Kicks Down All the Boundaries, *The Toronto Star*, 16 June 1990.)

8. "Quoi de plus sûr dans l'histoire des Français d'Amérique, que la langue en péril? Cette crainte nous a tenus, elle nous tient toujours, et nous fait tenir ensemble. Pour tenir, il fallut se durcir; voire, pour certains, se fermer, se murer... nous en sommes venus parfois à nous tenir contre l'autre, et à craindre toutes les différences de race, de culture, de religion, de la sexualité, de l'inconscient, de l'écriture, du génie..." (Larose 1987:119)

9. In his review in *Etc. Montréal* 12 (September 1990:58), André Bourassa attacks the overabundance of *paroles* and the lack of *propos*, the *bavardage* [prattling] of images and words in *Plaques*.

10. The activist poet and playwright Michèle Lalonde has written numerous works including *Terre des hommes* (1967) and *Speak White* (1968) where she opposes a grass-roots international solidarity to cultural and economic imperialism.

11. In *JEU cahiers de théâtre* 45 Lorraine Camerlain cites the language of *la Trilogie des dragons* as specifically québécois (p. 19): not an impoverished French or *joual* or franglais, but a verb impregnated with Québécois culture.

12. Alvina Ruprecht, transcript CBO Morning interview, 25 June 1991 (provided by Canadian National Art Centre).

13. "There's nothing to link a person from Winnipeg with someone from Quebec, unless they're in Venice together, sitting in St. Mark's Square drinking cappuccino." (Lepage quoted from interview with Marianne Ackerman in *Imperial Oil Review* Winter 1990). The venue of the article and the patrician attitude underlying the quote point to economic class discrepancies, geopolitical faultlines in which the diversified global subject might be defined, despite its dismissal in the *Plaques/Plates* production.

EPILOGUE

Neverendum

New World culture always dances between the stationary points in the absolute abeyance of closure...
Hortense Spillers (1991:17)

... no one anywhere can be absolutely sure of where they will be or what state their culture will be in, say, in forty or fifty years. But here in Quebec, we are even less sure of the future and I believe this feeling of uncertainty feeds an appetite for what I call "dancing on the volcano."
René-Daniel Dubois

Coda

Conducted from the border area of the wings, this study of performing identities on the national, local, and international stages of Quebec has focused on internal strategies which challenge essentialist notions while reinforcing collective bonds of what can only be framed in prophylactic quotation marks as "l'identité Québécoise." Each presents the problem of Québécois cultural identity in the postmodern moment from a different enunciating site, yet they share a self-conscious irony. All three problematize the notion of a bounded and stable identity by repeatedly flipping across the binary bar separating inside/outside, self/other. The very borders circumscribing *la nation*, the Québécois family tree, the individual subject crisscross and form paradoxical knots.

The 1990 *fête nationale* in Montreal suggests a nation rooted in the tremulous ground of the imaginary. The parade satirizes archaic tropes of French-Canadian nationalism and invites the participants to invent the country of their dreams. The liminality of the *pays à rêver* merges with the utopia [no place] of the fête. The ambiguity of borders and the fluidity of agency inherent in the fête are akin to the dream state. More than the symbolic representations of Québécois history, the event makes a symbolic capital of its own dreamlike nature. The deferred dream may be of greater power in reinforcing the national subject than the political real.

The Parminou's performance of Québécois roots adopts a different strategy. The self-conscious reification of treasured icons of Québécois history and burlesque inversions of Québécois stereotypes have the double effect of distancing the audience from ethnic—genealogical, historical, linguistic—essence while drawing the spectators into the complicity of an inside joke. The affectionate self-mockery thriving in minority identity projects (which have, as Jewish or Black or Asian or Latino humor, become hallmarks of popular American culture) and which can only be voiced by agents from within the community, creates collective bonds in the performative present.

Through its metaphors and its process, the bilingual work in progress, *Plaques tectoniques/Tectonic Plates*, presents the greatest challenge to the notion of a stable collective identity. Cultures and individual subjects are poetically represented as drifting fragments floating in a postmodern sea. Yet the poetry of the piece operates through the maintaining of differences glimpsed across linguistic, sexual, and cultural frontiers which shift according to the relationship of the protagonists—characters and actors—and the perception of the audience. Rather than circumscribing a global, local, or individual identity, the four-year work attacks the very notion of identity as a monolithic whole. Ultimately, the work suggests that identity is the fact of a performative present, a question flushing through each theatrical event, each ephemeral community of the performance.

This Coda might have concluded our excursion into performing identities on the stages of Quebec, were it not for the fact of the October 1995 Referendum which, although rich in theatricality, also recalls the limits of the stage as metaphor. If events surrounding the Referendum were indeed projected on local stages (in homes and neighborhoods), national stages (on the streets and through Québécois and Canadian media), and international stages (media coverage across the globe), the performance could not be contained in representational frames. Although there might have been a certain confusion of reality and imaging—which is by definition the dilemma of the age of electronic reproduction—the stakes were radically higher than a theatrical event. The question of whether or not to become a state hinges on passions and the imaginary as much as on political reality. It is not, however, a question one can walk away from after the performance. It allows less distance for the self-reflexivity and playful irony seen in the three performances I have described. What a Referendum on Quebec's statehood does accomplish is to create a climate of crisis. It is frequently a time of decreased critical powers, when multivocality turns into cacophony, when the reduction to a question of YES or NO renders multiple positions difficult, when the poverty of options impairs the rich complexity of the nation. Paradoxically, it is also a time in which collective identities are brought to life, put to test, and redefined. It is a question which marks the postcolonial era of ethnic collisions and cross-cultural identities and the decreasing capacity of the nation-state to capture this symbolic power.

Pour en finir - The 1995 Referendum

In a facetious but appropriate reference to the exhausting and costly number of plebiscites undertaken in Canada and the recurrent efforts to resolve the "Quebec problem,"[1] the term *Neverendum* was coined by the Montreal anglophone press during the October 1995 Québécois sovereignty campaign.[2] An ironic comment on the political present of the Référendum, it is also applicable to the infinitely divisible nature of the nation-subject and the quandary of Québécois identity. Whether or not Quebec achieves national autonomy, its irrevocable status as an American francophone minority, its dubious capacity to incorporate other populations—*immigrants* and *aborigènes* who do not want to become a minority within a minority nation—and its obligation to sustain the Québécois subject through slippery symbolics and language describe a never-ending quest.

Within Quebec, numerous arguments for and against independence raged over the media, reported even in U.S. front-page and prime-time news,[3] and in the streets of the province. Beyond the national status of Quebec, this event seemed to be a referendum on the latter-20th century status of nationhood itself. Of all the pro-independence arguments, the most problematic was that separation would solve the problem and create a bright new day. The Bloc Québécois organized the OUI campaign under the slogan "Oui, et ça devient possible." What *ça* might be is open to question, but the idea that independence would create a utopic *tabula rasa*, sweep away the past and the inordinate number of social and economic problems the new state would face in the present, was implicit.

More boldly stated, a major argument in popular parlance was "en finir une fois pour toute" [to finish once and for all]. This "finishing" with the federal government, with the three-century-old ambiguous relationship vis-à-vis *les Anglais*, with the internal vacillating between dependence and independence, between sovereignty or sovereignty/association and so many other split-hair semantics, testifies to the exhaustion of the Québécois electorate. Yet as both pro-separatist Jean Larose (1994) and anti-separatist Jean-Pierre Derrienic (1995) have pointed out, this negative argument is hardly a basis for forging a new state.

The illusion that the historical past and the global political present can be erased with a OUI or a NON drifted through both Québécois and Canadian rhetoric. Although many English-speaking Canadians felt a nostalgic attachment to the idea of a bilingual nation or very personal bonds with Quebec and would regret the separation—an end to "Canada as we know it" and perhaps the signal for other provinces to pull away from the federal system—and although some anti-Québécois echoed the "finishing once and for all" sentiment as wishing the problem away and good riddance, for the Québécois the stakes are much higher. "Finishing once and for all" with federal status would only heighten the internal socio-economic problems confronting the fledgling state, create further tensions with indigenous communities claiming ownership to the territory as well as with portions of the Québécois anglophone and immigrant populations, and further complicate, rather than resolve, the collective identity issue.

Atavistic Tropes

The complete scale of Québécois identity tropes underpinning the three performance clusters of this book circulated through the 1995 Referendum campaign along with 'rational' discourse based on global capitalist reality and internal politics. Economic arguments were invoked on both sides of the question. OUI partisans cited Merril & Lynch reports on the viability of an independent Québécois economy, the reduction of taxes paid to Ottawa and dispensing with the waste of two levels of government, and NAFTA. NON partisans cited the loss of federal subsidies to the province, the relocation of international capital, and NAFTA.[4] Although—theoretically—the voters' bottom-line is their pocketbook, financial issues appeared as murky as the symbolic issues which dominated the campaign. The 1995 Referendum was a battle for souls waged in a postmodern moment and which revived archaic and emotionally-charged icons, terroristic and seductive symbols churning in the popular imaginary. The old French-Canadian nationalism which seemed to lurk in the shadows, the historical mythos of *le peuple* coupled with a contemporary myth of a multicultural subject, and the contradictory poles of desire which pull the subject between love and autonomy, dominated the political stage.

Le bon vieux nationalisme canadien français

Lucien Bouchard, who had left his post as minister in the federal government during the Meech Lake crisis and would become the Prime Minister of Quebec after the Referendum, took over the direction of a flagging OUI campaign from Jacques Parizeau. Under Bouchard's leadership, the predictions for a OUI vote shot up beyond fifty percent. Although the OUI did not win out in the final tallying, the fact that, for the first time, the francophone population voted predominantly for separation was considered a victory largely attributed to Bouchard's popularity.

A paradoxical persona, this politician of working-class stock, who had long served in the federal government and was married to a U.S. citizen, proved a pole which magnetized grass-roots Québécois supporters of the sovereignty project, frequently repulsed independent voters who saw him as an opportunist or a chauvinist, and served as foil to federalists eager to prove that the 1995 Québécois nationalist sentiment was antiquated and xenophobic. A charismatic and impassioned speaker whose popularity had increased since his miraculous recovery from myositis which cost him a leg, Bouchard cut a hierophantic figure. Although the Church was neither an active agent nor an overt symbolic channel in this civil political campaign, a religious aura appropriated by the State hovered around Lucien Bouchard. He was despised and worshiped as an idol of the nationalist cause. Adoring crowds gathered to shake his hand, to touch his sleeve. Reinforcing this aura, Bouchard's enemies portrayed him as the "Prince of Darkness who is trying to tear the country apart" (*Maclean's* October 23, 1995).

Bouchard made an unfortunate remark about the low birth rates of "la race blanche," meaning whites in general or white-wool Québécois. Smacking of the Duplessis era, this remark caused discomfort among his supporters and a momentary fury among Québécois feminists and anti-independence forces. More significant than the remark itself—which appears overly dramatic out of context—was the rapidity and the vehemence of the response. The Canadian Prime Minister Jean Chrétien attacked Bouchard as a proponent of the old French-Canadian nationalism where all citizens are white, francophone, and—implicating archaic Catholic undertones—should be producing babies for the nation. It was as if three decades had been swept away to reveal an atavistic and insular French-Canadian national subject waiting in the wings for his cue.

It was this exclusionary *nous* which Jacques Parizeau ushered to center stage immediately following the vote. Responding to the narrow defeat of the OUI, the provincial Prime Minister declared "nous avons gagné." This is the imperialistic *nous* speaking from however minoritized a stage: the French-speaking, died-in-the-wool Québécois who would have won were it not for "l'argent et les ethnies." That money—the financial forces feared from U.S. capital and multinational backlash or money actually spent by the federal government to disrupt the OUI campaign—influenced the popular vote is undeniable. That the blame for the defeat could be placed on Montreal's ethnic minorities—the Greeks, Italians, Eastern Europeans, Chinese who had lived in the metropolitan center for generations or more recent immigrant communities from the Caribbean, Middle East, India, Maghreb, Africa, South East Asia—proved more problematic. Cosmopolitan Montreal, the harbor of immigrant populations where you can easily hear ten languages spoken on a cross-town bus trip, had presumably allowed a national victory to escape. Even if Parizeau had not already determined to quit politics if the OUI was defeated, this remark cost him his political career. Considered more of a liability than an asset to the younger and more globally capitalist oriented political figures[5] directing the new nationalist movement, Parizeau resigned as Quebec's Prime Minister immediately after the Referendum, thus ceding his position to Bouchard's rising star.

History and genes

Fetishist identity tropes have stigmatized and enhanced the persona of political figures such as Lucien Bouchard and Jacques Parizeau. More intriguing are the historic signifiers which shot through the discourse of younger voters. One twenty-some year old nationalist, seen on a Peter Jennings' news program, stated "We lost the war in 1763. We don't want to lose this one." Beyond much of U.S. media strategy to project Quebec's Referendum as yet another ethnic struggle, the remark begs understanding. What is the relationship of this Generation-X Québécois to the historical mythos of a conquered people rising to affirm its identity? Contrary to the amnesiac Punk in the Parminou parody who rejects history and genealogical roots, this man identifies with history to the point of subjectively fusing the past to the present in an atavistic *nous* that incorporates—through time and space—all Québécois and erases other histories and collective identities.

Arguments based on atavistic apologues were the exception rather than the rule in the complex debate surrounding the Referendum. Yet their allure to the voters—both nationalists convinced of their right to an autonomous state and anti-nationalists who used these arguments as proof of the exclusionary nature of the Québécois independence project—is undeniable. Even discourse which adamantly dismissed national identity as an issue was inevitably dependent on symbolic anchors.

Bernard Landry—Deputy Prime Minister of Quebec, as well as Minister of International Affairs, Immigration, Cultural Communities, and Francophonie—repeatedly declared in the televised debates preceding the Referendum that the sovereignty project was founded not in *la loi du sang* [the law of blood] but in the historical/political claim to the land. "Nobody votes with their grandmother's chromosomes," Landry stated. It is the territory, i.e. the current boundaries of the province, which determines the nation. But seeking legitimacy in boundaries drawn through the aleatory paths of history—and inevitably leading back to the usurpation of the land from native peoples—is as problematic as using a genealogically-based subject to define the nation.

Temps de vous laisser parler d'amour?

If arguments for statehood based in clouded economic or legislative reality were uncertain currency, and arguments based in history, roots, or territory are easily deconstructed, perhaps the even more nebulous factor of LOVE could bring about independence. Love of the national self as sung in Vigneault's quasi-national anthem, of the people whose time has come to be loved, but also of others who have fallen in love with Quebec—or the idea of Quebec—might bind the nation. The volatility of love as a motor of the nation and how this could back-fire as a metaphor were brought out in the pro-federalist demonstrations a few days before the Referendum.

In an effort to woe voters to the NON side of the spectrum, the federal government offered drastically cut-rate telephone calls and plane tickets to Quebec. Supporters of Canadian federalism organized a mass demonstration in Montreal on October 27, 1995. Canadians from the west coast through the plains to the east coast maritime provinces converged on Montreal, carrying Canadian red maple-leaf flags and banners with hearts and slogans proclaiming "Quebec, we love you" or, less frequently, "Québec, je t'aime." Considering that Québécois have often complained that the rest of Canada did not understand and did not like them, we might consider this manifestation as an attempt to overturn the feeling of rejection. On the contrary, the demonstration was seen as a cheap manipulation by federal partisans and, in fact, promoted the pro-independence vote.

If you loved us so much, asked Lucien Bouchard, where were you during the Meech Lake talks and after the Charlottetown agreement? The mixture of love and politics would prove indigestible in the 1995 Referendum campaign. Although *Gens du pays* continued to ring through pro-independence fêtes, the notion that love could constitute the protective shell of the state was seriously shattered. Yet, the daisy—and not the lily of the fleurdelisé flag—was the icon chosen for the OUI campaign of the Bloc Québécois. "Love me, love me not" says the daisy, leaving the choice open to whoever is plucking the flower.

Nous le peuple

Tension between the poetics and the politics of identity drove the Referendum campaign. The most evident example of this tension and the romanticizing of a mythical *nous le peuple* was an official document: the *Préambule de la Déclaration de Souveraineté*. Composed by several pro-independence writers, including the poet Gilles Vigneault and the playwright Marie Laberge, the proposed Preamble to the Declaration of Sovereignty is written in a first-person plural which englobes a Québécois pioneering folk—reborn from the 1970s renaissance which had retrieved them from pre-industrial Quebec—in alleged partnership with a host of other peoples who have marked French-Canadian reality: *Autochtones, Anglophones, Immigrants* who are summarily included in parenthetical phrases. Steeped in agrarian metaphors, the document describes a people united by history and bound to the land.

> Voici venu le temps de la moisson dans les champs de l'histoire. Il est enfin venu le temps de récolter ce que semaient pour nous quatre cents ans de

femmes et d'hommes et de courage, enracinés au sol et dedans retournés. (Projet de loi 1 sur l'avenir du Québec, Assemblée nationale, 1995)

[Now is harvest time in the fields of history. At last it is time to gather what four hundred years of women and men and courage have sown, rooted in the soil and turned over inside.]

The Préambule goes on to describe farmers from Old France who would become a founding people—born of a great civilization "enriched by First Nations"—whose tenacity to survive would not be daunted by the 1760 Conquest nor the 1840 Union Act. The prose then reaches out to grasp "la communauté anglaise... les immigrants" to the bosom of what Régine Robin (in Létourneau & Bernard 1994) calls the "Volkgeist State."

Romantic notions of history and the people constituted an on-going subtext to the political rhetoric of the campaign. Because the 1995 independence project could not offer a concrete social plan which would change the material reality of Quebec, or even guarantee its status as the most socially progressive society in Canada or North America, it was the dream of independence itself which polarized the voters into those who believed that with a OUI anything is possible and those who were hostile to, or hesitant to adhere to, the utopic dream.

Artists and the Dream

Between the 1990 collapse of the Meech Lake agreement and the 1995 preparation of the second Québécois independence campaign, artists played a minor role compared to the 1980 Referendum. Rather than the motor behind the independence cause, they seemed to be simply called on for poetic fuel. Among artists mentioned in this work, several *chansonniers* including Gilles Vigneault and Paul Piché, and several playwrights including Marie Laberge, had maintained a firm connection with the national project. However, many others had shifted their attention to the global arena. Theatre companies such as Carbone 14 or Théâtre Repère continued to explore international horizons they had opened in the 1980s; activist companies such as the Parminou had recentered on immediate social issues[6]. As the 1995 Referendum approached, the lack of artists actively engaged in the nationalist project became more noticeable. Pro-independence politicians and a task force of writers and literary agents urged artists to publicly speak out for the OUI.

Numerous personalities from the theatre world accepted the invitation to actively promote the sovereignty-association campaign. These included the born-in-Quebec, internationally recognized director Robert Lepage, and two immigrant playwrights, Abla Farhoud and Marco Micone. Ironically, both of the latter had first forged their reputations through their plays' exploration of the immigrant subject in the provincial and alienating atmosphere of a 1950–70s Quebec.[7] Micone—sounding every bit like a dyed-in-the-wool Québécois nationalist—attempted to rally the immigrant vote by declaring solemnly on television: "L'Histoire vous jugera." [History will be your judge.] Farhoud campaigned for the OUI in more intimate circles, among relatives and friends of the Lebanese community and in immigrant community centers in Montreal.

The two arguments Farhoud offered me in a personal interview (November 1995) revolved around identity and the dream. The first underlines a craving for subjective boundaries: "Okay, so I'm an immigrant and I'll always be the Other. I at least need to know whose Other!" The second relates to the people as an individual with a right to self-realization and the proverbial dream: "You know what it is to have a dream. These people have a right to see their dream come true."

One prominent theatrical personality who declared the dream of an independent and socially progressive Quebec lost—or at least not the stakes of the Referendum—was the playwright/performer René-Daniel Dubois.[8] Presumed a supporter of Québécois independence, but refusing to jump on the band wagon with a public declaration when summoned to publish a letter in favor of the OUI, Dubois cut an iconoclastic figure. Responding to the indignation which greeted his refusal, he declared on Québécois television a few days before the Referendum that the last role the artist should ever play in a society was that of the yes man, that the responsibility of the artist was to challenge and provoke rather than bow to the will of politicians. For Dubois, the choice of YES or NO to a rhetorical hodgepodge which masked the absence of a veritable social program or even the means to exist as a socially progressive nation under the inexorable onslaught of U.S. directed multinational capitalism was no choice at all. Bristling at being singled out as the only "star of the Quebec stage" who refused to campaign for the OUI, the playwright stated there were many, less vocal, artists who preferred to remain silent. Why? Partially because they were intimidated and partially because they could neither give up the dream born in the 1970s nor adhere to the form it had taken in the 1990s. For Dubois "Leur rêve leur a été arraché. Il s'est retourné contre eux." [Their dream was ripped from them. It turned against them.] When asked point blank if he could actually vote NON, the playwright responded he had no idea what he would do, that it was impossible to think in all the brouhaha at a moment when thinking was most important. "If I knew how to draw, I'd draw two little rabbits fornicating on the ballot." The image of a YES/NO mindlessly copulating is unsettling. It conveys the confusion of the issues at stake and a subject perpetually divided, thrusting to and fro, and inexorably multiplying.

The Tectonic Subject

A record 93% of the voters across the province went to the ballot box. The vote split along somewhat predictable lines: traditionally francophone communities in Quebec City and the townships of the Richelieu River area—bastion of the 19th-century *Patriote* movement—voted massively for the OUI; anglophone pockets in West Montreal and the Eastern townships —bastion of the 18th-century Loyalists—voted even more massively for the NON. A sign that the *indépendance* cause had gained ground in relation to the 1980 vote was the majority of francophone votes for the OUI.

As the results were tallied on the night of October 30, 1995, journalists spoke of a deeply divided country. I would argue that the country was also shallowly divided. I do not mean this in any derogatory sense, but as an indication of how voters' decisions as to whether or not Quebec would become an independent state drifted with the emotional and political currents of the moment. It was not only the country, but communities, families and individual voters who were divided in themselves. Positions oscillated from one day to the next. Recalling Repère's metaphor, the country presented a tectonic figure, not of a land mass splitting into solid pieces, but of floating communities and selves, of a mercurial nation-subject.

As the philosopher Charles Taylor declared in the television pundits' analysis following the results: "The nation which voted tonight is not the same as it was fifteen years ago." The voters were not the same. Since 1980, not only had a million voters died or left, a half-million arrived, and some million and a half Québécois been born, but the voters who had participated in the two referendums were not necessarily voting the same way. And it will not be the same nation when—inevitably—the next referendum is held. Ultimately, the national subject is as temporal and infinitely divisible as the self.

The most colorful and whimsical images of Referendum night were the faces painted with the colors and emblems of the Canadian and Québécois flags, masks appearing in the crowd waiting to hear the results, partying and panning for the camera behind the very straight-faced journalists clutching their microphones. One mask stands out in my mind: a half face painted red with a white maple leaf surrounding the right eye, the other half painted blue with a fleur-de-lis surrounding the left eye. As a backdrop to the flow of statistics and political rhetoric which allowed both sides to claim victory, the mask told a story not only of the divided subject but of the nation as a costume.

One of the most curious aspects of Quebec's identity quest is its metaphorical base in the divided self. Schizophrenia, a favored trope, aptly depicts the subject's cleavage and desperate search for wholeness. More than a division of personality, schizophrenia is a quest for an objectified and stable identity. Driven by the fear of losing the self, the subject seeks an impossible objectification and stillness, thus driving it farther and farther from the perceiving subject.

Historically, the "national schizophrenia" has related primarily to Quebec's relationship to a dominant Anglo-Other. A hegemonic dichotomy is the most limpid of identificatory paradigms. Currently, however, the Québécois identity search must include others who have spun off on their own identity quests: immigrant communities whose projects may or may not coincide with *indépendance* and First Nations whose own national project clashes with Quebec's. Ironically, if Quebec were to become an independent state, this would promote other claims to nationhood. The nation is infinitely divisible; as it seeks to englobe others, it creates fractures in its constitution. Rather than seek out an illusory unity, the Québécois could well create a state enriched by its history as a minority and its current diversity. Rather than perceiving atomization and fluidity as pathological, the nation might consider the tectonic subject as a healthy basis of the state.

What appears clearly is that there can never be a total coinciding of the unstable and often contradictory forces of Self/Identity/Language/Nation outside of dubious totalitarian or fetishist frames. Even if taking on the mantle of statehood, Quebec will not have solved its identity problem. Because there are too many other identities vying for space on its *INSIDE* national stage, because *la langue française* is neither a given nor a monolithic defining factor, and because of its position as the only North American francophone nation on the *EXTERIEUR* stage, Quebec must necessarily continue to play out the question of identity. For the artist it is what René-Daniel Dubois calls "surfing on the volcano."[9] It is a gymnastic exercise repeatedly performed in the present, a sliding on the crest of geopolitical and geopoetic lava, without losing one's tenuous footing in the local.

Notes

1. The October 1995 Referendum was only the second vote on Québécois sovereignty undertaken in the province. However, since the collapse of the Meech Lake agreement and the rise of the Bloc Québécois, the referendum has been at the top of the political agenda and polls have repeatedly been conducted to determine positions for and against separation.
   In addition to these and a Canada-wide referendum held in 1992 to approve or reject the Charlottetown agreement on modifications to the Constitution—another aborted attempt to reintegrate Quebec into the constitutional family—Canadian citizens have incessantly been subject to election campaigns and called to vote in national or provincial elections repeatedly. The ubiquity of electoral campaigns and the apparent inability of political structures to resolve the problems facing society have contributed to the general disenchantment with political leaders. A December 1995 survey conducted by the magazine *L'actualité* entitled "Crise de confiance" claimed that only 4% of the Québécois electorate trusted in their leaders.

2. Unlike the question posed in the 1980 Referendum, the 1995 ballot stated clearly this was a vote for Quebec's becoming an independent state or not. The second clause of the question—"after having made a formal offer to Canada for a new Economic and Political partnership"—was less clear since the terms of this partnership and whether the federal government and the other provinces of Canada would be open to negotiations of this type were quite theoretical.

3. Writing about these performances from Philadelphia, I was dependent on the news I could gather from not only personal contacts in Quebec, who themselves transmitted media bytes as well as their take on the Referendum, but on the international media. These included TV 5 broadcasts in French from Paris and Montreal on the international news channel, news mediated by CNN, NPR, ABC, NBC, and print versions of the events. Used to furrowing out coverage of Quebec, I was startled to see how much attention was given to the Referendum. The *Philadelphia Inquirer* ran a full week of headline and front page articles. I was also struck by the professionalism and serious investigation into the Quebec problem of the National Public Radio and *Inquirer* journalists.

4. The North American Free Trade Agreement was an ambivalent cipher. Pro-independence factions claimed it would allow an independent Quebec to secure markets in North America; anti-independence partisans argued the United States might not accept the fledgling nation into the NAFTA club, an argument backed up by the Clinton administration's caution to Quebec to

remain within the Canadian Federation.

In my efforts to bring this work to publication, I have been repeatedly told that NAFTA is a major issue. Having pursued this track, I have become convinced that NAFTA is a product of the mythical global state founded in a magical world market economy. I have yet to understand any inroads the agreement has made in equating capitalist and democratic ideals or just what difference NAFTA has made in the lives of Mexican, Canadian, or U.S. American citizens.

5. The trio directing the Québécois Block majority in the Canadian Parliament included Parizeau, Bouchard, and Mario Dumont. The latter was a polished, thirty-some figure who skillfully oriented the direction of the OUI campaign to include Québécois business people and create an aura of material security amidst the passions churning through the 1995 Referendum.

6. These issues ranged from relationships with Native Canadians to domestic violence in Quebec. For an update on the Parminou's evolution and a close study of the latter topic, see Martineau and Mac Dougall's essay forthcoming in *Contaminating Theatre: Studies at the Intersections of Theatre, Therapy, and Public Health* (Eds. Mac Dougall and Yoder, Northwestern University Press).

7. See Micone's trilogy on Italian immigrants in Montreal: *Gens du silence* (*Voiceless People*) and *Addolorata* (trans. Maurizia Binda in *Two Plays* published by Guernica, Montreal 1988) and *Déjà l'agonie* (*Beyond the Ruins*, trans. Jill Mac Dougall published by Guernica, Toronto 1995). See Farhoud's *Quand j'étais grande* (*When I was Grown Up*, trans. Mac Dougall in *Women & Performance 9*) and *les Filles du 5-10-15* (*The Girls from the Five and Ten*, trans. Mac Dougall in *Plays by Women: An International Anthology* published by UBU Repertory Theater, New York 1988).

8. Performer/writer Dubois has served as both the darling of the avant-garde and a renegade outcast among Montreal artists. His *Ne blâmez jamais les Bédouins* (*Don't Blame the Bedouins*, trans. Martin Kevan published in *Quebec Voices*, Toronto: Coach House Press 1986) was a one-man sensation before later becoming an opera. Dubois is best known in the U.S. for the filmed production of *Being at Home with Claude* (original title, trans. by Linda Gaboriau for *Canadian Theatre Review 50*).

9. In November 8, 1990 address to Arts Midwest, American tour bookers, published in *Théâtre Québec* (Newsletter of the Centre d'essai des auteurs dramatiques in Montreal).

Bibliography

Aléong, Stanley
    1981   Discours nationalistes et purisme linguistique au Québec. *Culture* 1 (2):31–41.
Anderson, Benedict
    1991   *Imagined Communities*. London: Verso.
Andrès, Bernard et al.
    1985   Théâtre québécois: tendances actuelles. *Etudes littéraires* 18(3).
Assiniwi, Bernard
    1973   *Lexique des noms indiens en Amérique*. Ottawa: Leméac.
Atwood, Margaret
    1972   *Survival*. Toronto: Anansi.
Aubry, Suzanne
    1983   *Le théâtre au Québec*. Montreal: Centre Québécois de l'Institut International du Théâtre.
Axtell, James
    1992   *Beyond 1492: Encounters in Colonial North America*. New York: Oxford University Press.
Barth, Frank
    1969   *Ethnic Groups and Boundaries*. Boston: Little, Brown.
Beauchamp, Hélène
    1981   History and Current Situation of the Theater of the Birth and Early Existence of Quebec. *Revue de l'Institut de Sociologie* 4:851–69.
Belair, Michel
    1973   *Le nouveau théâtre québécois*. Montreal: Leméac.
Benjamin, Walter
    1969   *Illuminations*. Translated by Harry Zohn. New York: Schocken.
Bhabha, Homi K.
    1990   DissemiNation: time, narrative, and the margins of the modern nation. In *Nation and Narration*, ed. H.K. Bhabha. London: Routledge.

Bibeau, Gilles
   1995   Tropismes québécois: Je me souviens dans l'oubli. *Anthropologie et Sociétés* 19(3):151–98.

Bissoondath, Neil
   1994   *Selling Illusions: The Cult of Multiculturalism in Canada.* New York: Penguin Books.

Blau, Herbert
   1990   *The Audience.* Baltimore: Johns Hopkins University Press.

Bonar, James de Gaspé
   1985   Art and Politics: The Theology of Culture in Contemporary Quebec. *The Arts, Women and Politics* (Arts Research Seminar 2). Ottawa: The Canada Council, Feb. 1985: 65–72.

Bonhomme, Jean-Pierre et al.
   1989   *Le syndrome postréférendaire.* Montreal: Stanké.

Bourgault, Pierre
   1989   *Moi, je m'en souviens.* Montreal: Stanké.

Bouthillier, Guy and Jean Meynaud, eds.
   1972   *Le choc des langues au Québec, 1760–1970.* Montreal: Presses Universitaires du Québec.

Brenneis, Donald, ed.
   1992   Imagining Identities: Nation, Culture, and the Past. *American Ethnologist* 19:4, (November).

Brotz, Howard
   1980   Multiculturalism in Canada: A Muddle. *Canadian Public Policy* 6:41–46.

Brunet, Michel
   1969   *Québec Canada anglais, deux itinéraires, un affrontement.* Montreal: Editions HMH.

Butler, Judith
   1990   *Gender Trouble: Feminism and the Subversion of Identity.* New York: Routledge.

Cartier, Jacques
   1986   *Relations* (Critical edition of Cartier's 1534–42 *Relations de voyage*, edited by Michel Bideaux). Montreal: Presses de l'Université de Montréal.

Charbonneau, André et al.
   1981   *Québec, ville fortifiée, 1600–1900.* Ottawa: Parks Canada.

Charbonneau, Hubert et al.
    1993 *The First French Canadians: Pioneers in the St. Lawrence Valley*. Translated by Paola Colozzo. Newark: Universiy of Delaware Press.

Charest, Rémy
    1995 *Robert Lepage, quelques zones de liberté*. Quebec: L'Instant même, Ex Machina.

Chicoine, Marie, L. de Grosbois, E. Foy, and F. Poirier
    1982 *Lâchés lousses: les fêtes populaires au Québec, en Acadie et en Louisiane*. Montreal: VLB.

Clifford, James
    1988 *The Predicament of Culture*. Cambridge: Harvard University Press.

Clifford, James, and George Marcus, eds.
    1986 *Writing Culture: The Poetics and Politics of Ethnography*. Berkeley: University of California Press.

Clift, Dominique
    1982 *Quebec Nationalism in Crisis*. Montreal: McGill Queen's University Press.
    1989 *The Secret Kingdom: Interpretations of the Canadian Character*. Toronto: McClelland & Stewart.

Colbert, François
    1982 *Le marché québécois du théâtre*. Quebec: Institut de recherche sur la culture.

Coleman, William D.
    1984 *The Independence Movement in Quebec, 1945–1980*. Toronto: University of Toronto Press.

Collectif Clio
    1992 *L'histoire des femmes au Québec*. Montreal: Le Jour.

Conjonctures
    1983 Minorités au Québec 4.
    1988 Le Québec et l'autre 10 & 11.
    1989 Cultures en exil 12.

Cook, Ramsay, ed. and trans.
    1969 *French-Canadian Nationalism: an Anthology*. Toronto: Macmillan.

Cotnam, Jacques
    1976 *Le théâtre québécois, instrument de contestation sociale et politique*. Montreal: Fides.

1977 Du sentiment national dans le théâtre québécois. Festschrift article in AN 77–2–105:341–68.
Coulombe, Pierre A.
  1995 *Language Rights in French Canada*. New York: Peter Lang.
Dagenais, Angèle
  1981 *Crise de croissance: le théâtre au Québec*. Quebec: Institut québécois de recherche sur la culture.
Davis, Susan G.
  1988 *Parades and Power*. Berkeley: University of California Press.
Derrienic, Jean-Pierre
  1995 *Nationalisme et démocratie: réflexion sur les illusions des indépendantistes québécois*. Montreal: Boréal.
Dion, Léon
  1987 *Québec 1945–2000*. Quebec: Presses de l'Université Laval.
Duchacek, Ivo, D. Latouche, and G. Stevenson, eds.
  1988 *Perforated Sovereignties and International Relations*. New York: Greenwood Press.
Dumont, Fernand
  1993 *Genèse de la société québécoise*. Montreal: Boréal.
  1995 *Raisons communes*. Montreal: Boréal.
Dumont, Fernand, ed.
  1991 *La société québécoise après 30 ans de changements*. Quebec: Institut québécois de recherche sur la culture.
Duvignaud, Jean
  1977 *Le don du rien: essai d'anthropologie de la fête*. Paris: Stock.
  1980 *Le jeu du jeu*. Paris: A. Balland.
Elbaz, Mikhael et al.
  1996 *Les frontières de l'identité: modernité et postmodernisme au Québec*. Paris: l'Harmattan.
Falardeau, Pierre
  1995 *La liberté n'est pas une marque de yogourt*. Montreal: Stanké
Feldman, Elliot J., ed.
  1980 *The Quebec Referendum: What Happened and What Next?* Cambridge: Center for International Affairs, Harvard University.
Fenwick, Rudy
  1981 Social Change and Ethnic Nationalism: An Historical Analysis of the Separatist Movement in Quebec. *Comparative Studies in Society and History* 23:196–216.

Féral, Josette
   1989 *La culture contre les arts: essai d'économie politique du théâtre.* Sillery: Presses Universitaires du Québec.
   1992 Pouvoirs publics et politiques culturelles: enjeux nationaux. *Cahiers de théâtre JEU* 63:95–101.

Foster, Hal, ed.
   1983 *The Anti-Aesthetic, Essays on Postmodern Culture.* Seattle: Bay Press.

Gagnon, Lysiane
   1985 *Chroniques politiques.* Montreal: Boréal.

Garreau, Joel
   1982 *The Nine Nations of North America.* New York: Avon Books.

Gauvin, Lise and Gaston Miron, eds.
   1989 *Ecrivains contemporains du Québec.* Paris: Seghers.

Geertz, Clifford
   1973 *The Interpretation of Cultures.* New York: Basic Books.

Gennep, Arnold van
   [1937] 1977 *Manuel de folklore français contemporain* Vols. 2–3. Paris: Picard.

Gill, Robert
   1980 Quebec and the Politics of Language: Implications for Canadian Unity. In *Encounters with Canada*, ed. W. Reilly. Durham: Duke University Press.

Glazer, Nathan and Daniel Moynihan, eds.
   1975 *Ethnicity.* Cambridge: Harvard University Press.

Godin, Jean-Cleo and Laurent Mailhot
   1980 *Théâtre québécois.* Montreal: HMH.

Griffen, Anne
   1984 *Quebec: The Challenge of Independence.* Rutherford, N.J.: Fairleigh Dickinson University Press.

Groulx, Lionel
   1934 *La découverte du Canada: Jacques Cartier.* Montreal: Granger Frères.

Gruslin, Adrien
   1981 *Le théâtre et l'état au Québec.* Montreal: VLB.
   1983 Dix ans de création collective (entretien avec le Parminou). *JEU Cahiers de théâtre* 28.

Guédon, Marie-Françoise
   1983 A Case of Mistaken Identity. In *Consciousness and Inquiry: Ethnology and Canadian Realities*, ed. F. Manning. Ottawa: Canadian Ethnology Service.

Guindon, Hubert
   1988 *Quebec Society: Tradition, Modernity, and Nationhood.* Toronto: University of Toronto Press.

Hall, Stuart
   1981 Notes on Deconstructing the 'Popular'. In *People's History and Socialist Theory*, ed. R. Samuel. London: RKP.
   1989 Cultural identity and cinematic representation. *Framework* 36:68–81.

Hamblet, Edwin
   1971 Quebec's Theater of Liberation. *Comparative Drama* 5:70–88.

Hamelin, Jean
   1964 *Le théâtre du Canada français.* Quebec: Ministère des Affaires Culturelles.
   1976 *Histoire du Québec.* Toulouse: Edouard Privat.

Hamelin, Jean and Jean Provencher
   1983 *Brève histoire du Québec.* Montreal: Boréal.

Handler, Richard
   1984 On Sociocultural Discontinuity: Nationalism and Cultural Objectification in Quebec. *Current Anthropology* 25:55–71.
   1988 *Nationalism and the Politics of Culture in Quebec.* Madison: University of Wisconsin Press.

Hayne, David
   1978 National Identity in Quebec Literature and Theatre. *Proceedings & Transactions, Royal Society of Canada* 16:79–91.

Henripin, Jacques and Yves Martin, eds.
   1991 *La population du Québec d'hier à demain.* Montreal: Presses de l'Université de Montréal.

Hobsbawm, Eric
   1990 *Nations and Nationalism since 1789: Programme, Myth, Reality.* Cambridge: Cambridge University Press.

Hobsbawm, Eric and Terence Ranger, eds.
   1983 *The Invention of Tradition.* New York: Cambridge University Press.

Hunt, Nigel
   1989 The Global Voyage of Robert Lepage. *TDR* 33(2):104–18.

Hutcheon, Linda
　1985　*A Theory of Parody: The Teachings of Twentieth-Century Art Forms.* New York: Methuen.
　1989　*The Politics of Postmodernism.* London: Routledge.
Jacques, Daniel
　1991　*Les humanités passagères: considérations philosophiques sur la culture politique québécoise.* Montreal: Boréal.
JEU Cahiers de théâtre
　1976–1990
　　　Le Théâtre Parminou 1.
　　　1980–1985: l'ex-jeune théâtre dans de nouvelles voies 36.
　　　Festivals en question 38.
　　　Vinci (entretien avec Robert Lepage) 42.
　　　La Trilogie des dragons: Théâtre Repère 45.
　　　Le théâtre dans la cité 50.
　　　Le théâtre expérimental 52.
　　　Théâtre et homosexualité 54.
Kongas-Maranda, Elli
　1979　Ethnologie, folklore et l'indépendance des majorités minorisées. In *Emerging Ethnic Boundaries*, ed. D. Juteau. Ottawa: University of Ottawa Press.
Kristeva, Julia
　1977　Le sujet en procès: le langage poétique. In *L'identité* (dir. by C. Lévi-Strauss). Paris: Quadridge/PUF.
Kruger, Barbara and Phil Mariani, eds.
　1989　*Remaking History.* Seattle: Bay Press.
Kruger, Loren
　1992　*The National Stage: Theatre and Cultural Legitimation in England, France, and America.* Chicago: University of Chicago Press.
Lalonde, Michèle and D. Monière
　1981　*Cause commune: manifeste pour une internationale des petites cultures.* Montreal: Hexagone.
Langlais, Jacques and David Rome
　1991　*Jews & French Quebecers, Two Hundred Years of Shared History.* Translated by Barbara Young. Waterloo, Ont.: Wilfred Laurier University Press.
Laplante, Laurent
　1989　Maudite langue! *Nuit blanche* 36 (Summer):32–39.

Larose, Jean
  1987 *La petite noirceur*. Montreal: Boréal.
  1994 *La souveraineté rampante*. Montreal: Boréal.
Latouche, Daniel
  1979 *Une société de l'ambiguité: libération et récuperation dans le Québec actuel*. Montreal: Boréal Express.
  1990 *Le bazar: des anciens Canadiens aux nouveaux Québécois*. Montreal: Boréal.
Leblanc, Alonzo
  1985 L'évolution du théâtre québécois. In *Littérature québécoise: voix d'un peuple, voies d'une autonomie*, ed.s. G. Dorion and M. Voisin. Brussels: Université de Bruxelles.
Legris, Renée, J.M. Larrue, A.G. Bourassa, and G. David
  1988 *Le théâtre au Québec: 1825–1980*. Montreal: VLB.
Létourneau, Jocelyn
  1989 The Unthinkable History of Quebec. *Oral History Review* 17(1): 89–115.
  1991 Le saga du Québec moderne en images. *Genèses: Sciences sociales et histoire* 4:44-71.
Létourneau, Jocelyn and Roger Bernard, eds.
  1994 *La question identitaire au Canada francophone*. Sainte-Foy: Presses de l'Université Laval.
Lévesque, René
  1986 *Attendez que je me rappelle*. Montreal: Québec-Amérique.
Liberté 203
  1992 *Le Québec des écrivains: un sondage exclusif sur l'indépendance* 34(5).
Linteau, Paul-André et al.
  1986 *Histoire du Québec contemporain*. Montreal: Boréal.
MacAloon, John J., ed.
  1984 *Rite, Drama, Festival, Spectacle: Rehearsals Toward a Theory of Cultural Performance*. Philadelphia: ISHI.
Mac Dougall, Jill
  1988 Festival des Amériques: Montreal 1987. *TDR* 32(1):9–19.
  1990 Growing, growing, growing, grown. *Women & Performance: Feminist Ethnography* 5(1):144–55.
Mandel, Eli and D. Taras, eds.
  1987 *A Passion for Identity: An Introduction to Canadian Studies*. Toronto: Methuen.

Manning, Frank, ed.
   1983   *The Celebration of Society*. Bowling Green: Bowling Green University Popular Press.

McRoberts, Kenneth and Dale Postgate
   1980   *Quebec: Social Change and Political Crisis*. Toronto: McClelland & Stewart.

Monière, Denis
   1977   *Le développement des idéologies au Québec*. Montreal: Québec/Amérique.

Morison, Samuel E.
   1971   *The European Discovery of America*. New York: Oxford University Press.

Morrissonneau, Christian
   1983   Le peuple dit ingouvernable du pays sans bornes: mobilité et identité quebecoise. In *Du continent perdu à l'archipel retrouvé: le Québec et l'Amérique française*, eds. D.R. Louder and E. Waddell. Quebec: Presses de l'Université Laval.

Moss, Jane
   1986   Corps spectaculaire: Quebec Womens Theatre. *Modern Language Studies* 16(4):54–60.

Nardocchio, Elaine F.
   1982   Espace scénique et société québécoise. *Incidences* 6(1–2):39–46.
   1984   The Individual and the Community in Quebec Theatre of the 1970s. In *Regionalism and National Identity: Multidisciplinary essays in Canada, Australia and New Zealand*, 1984 proceedings.
   1986   *Theater and Politics in Quebec*. Edmonton: University of Alberta Press.

Newman, Peter
   1987   *Caesars of the Wilderness*. Toronto: Viking.

Parker, Andrew, ed.
   1992   *Nationalisms and Sexualities*. New York: Routledge.

Prideaux, Tom
   1966   *The World of Delacroix 1798–1863*. New York: Time-Life Books.

Québec Match
   1989   1959–1989, Les années passion.
   1990   Les années défi: portrait du Québec à la veille du XXIe siècle.

Rawkins, Philip
    1984   Minority Nationalism and its Limits: A Weberian Perspective on Cultural Change. *Canadian Review of Studies in Nationalism/Revue canadienne des études sur le nationalisme* 11(1):87–101.

Richler, Mordecai
    1984   *Home Sweet Home*. New York: Knopf.
    1992   *Oh Canada! Oh Quebec! Requiem for a Divided Country*. New York: Knopf.

Rioux, Marcel
    1969   *La question du Québec*. Paris: Seghers.

Robert, Jean-Claude
    1975   *Du Canada français au Québec libre*. Paris: Flammarion.

Rogel, Jean-Pierre
    1989   *Le défi de l'immigration*. Québec: Institut québécois de recherche sur la culture.

Ruddel, David
    1987   *Québec City 1765–1832*. Ottawa: National Museums of Canada.

Rumilly, Robert
    1975   *Histoire de la Société Saint-Jean-Baptiste de Montréal*. Montreal: Aurore.

Said, Edward
    1983   *The World, the Text, and the Critic*. Cambridge: Harvard University Press.

Salone, Emile
    1970   *La colonisation de la Nouvelle-France*. Paris: Guilmoto.

Sand, George
    1979   *My Life*. Translated and adapted from *L'histoire de ma vie* (1854–55) by Dan Hofstadter. New York: Harper & Row.

Sarrazin, Jean, C. Glayman and M. Jerome, eds.
    1979   *Dossier Québec*. Paris: Stock.

Schechner, Richard
    1988   *Performance Theory*. New York: Routledge.

Schlesinger, Philip
    1991   *Media, State and Nation: Political Violence and Collective Identities*. London: Sage.

See, Katherine
    1978   *Towards a Theory of Ethnic Nationalism: Northern Ireland and Quebec Compared*. Toronto: International Sociological Association, Canada.

Silverman, Kaja
   1983   *The Subject of Semiotics*. New York: Oxford University Press.

Simon, Sherry
   1994   *Le trafic des langues*. Montreal: Boréal.

Simon, Sherry, P. L'Hérault, R. Schwartzwald, and A. Nouss
   1991   *Fictions de l'identitaire au Québec*. Montreal: XYZ.

Smith, A.D.
   1990   Towards a Global Culture? *Theory, Culture & Society*, 7(2–3): 171–91.

Snyder, Emile and Albert Valdman, eds.
   1976   *Identité culturelle et francophonie dans les Amériques*. Québec: Les Presses de l'Université Laval.

Spillers, Hortense, ed.
   1991   *Comparative American Identities*. New York: Routledge.

Spivak, Gayatri Chakravorty
   1987   *In Other Worlds: Essays in Cultural Politics*. New York: Methuen.
   1990   *The Post-colonial Critic: Interviews, Strategies, Dialogues*. Ed. Sarah Harasym. New York: Routledge.

Taussig, Michael
   1993   *Mimesis and Alterity*. New York: Routledge.
   1996   *The Magic of the State*. New York: Routledge.

Thwaites, Reuben G., ed.
   1896   *The Jesuit Relations and Allied Documents*. Cleveland: Burrows Brothers Company.

Vallières, Pierre
   1968   *Nègres blancs d'Amérique*. Montreal: Parti pris. (Translated as *White Niggers of America* by Joan Pinkham, London: Monthly Review Press, 1971.)

Venuti, Lawrence, ed.
   1992   *Rethinking Translation: Discourse, Subjectivity, Ideology*. London: Routledge.

Waddell, Eric
   1981   Post-Referendum Quebec: A Geographer's Reflections. In *Aspects of the Constitutional Debate*, eds. J. Clarke and S.F. Wise. Ottawa: Carleton University, Institute of Canadian Studies.

Wallace, Robert
   1990   *Producing Marginality*. Saskatoon: Fifth House Publishers.

Weaver, R. Kent, ed.
  1992 *The Collapse of Canada?* Washington, D.C.: Brookings Institution.
Weinmann, Heinz
  1987 *Du Canada au Québec: généalogie d'une histoire.* Montreal: Hexagone.
  1990 *Cinéma de l'imaginaire québécois.* Montreal: Hexagone.
Whisnant, David
  1983 *All That Is Native and Fine.* Chapel Hill: University of North Carolina Press.
Williams, Dorothy
  1989 *Blacks in Montreal: 1628–1926, An Urban Demography.* Cowansville, Qué: Ed. Y. Blais.
Wilshire, Bruce
  1991 *Role Playing and Identity: The Limits of Theatre as Metaphor.* Bloomington: Indiana University Press.
Winks, Robin
  1971 *The Blacks in Canada, a History.* New Haven: Yale University Press.
Winsor, Chris
  1987 A Certain Number of Choices: Nationalism and Theatre in Quebec. *Canadian Theatre Review* 61 (Winter):30–34.
York, Geoffrey
  1990 *The Dispossessed: Life and Death in Native Canada.* London: Vintage.
Young, Brian and John Dickinson
  1988 *A Short History of Quebec, A Socio-Economic Perspective.* Toronto: Copp Clark Pitman Ltd.

Index

Acadia, 41n.14, 79, 99. *See also* Canadian provinces: New Brunswick
African, 78, 92, 94n.13, 171, 173
Allophone, 3, 8n.2, 66, 93n.6
Anderson, Benedict, 73
Anglophones: in 19th century, 16, 20, 23; as minority in Quebec, 3, 48, 50, 66, 93n.6, 191, 204, 208
Anthem, national: *Gens du pays*, 11, 36, 44, 63, 65, 66, 207, 208; *O Canada*, 16, 21, 28
Anti-semitism, 29, 30, 41n.18
Artists and nationalism, 11, 32, 33, 65, 66, 76, 143, 193, 208–210. See also *Chansonniers*
Asselin, Olivar, 24, 41n.13
Atwood, Margaret, 132n.3

Bas-Canada. *See* Lower Canada
Bédard, Réjean, 125, 133n.6
Bhaba, Homi K., 2
Bill 101, 2, 8n.3, 44
Bill 178, 3
Birth rate, 60, 70n.6, 124–6, 206
Bissoondath, Neil, 70n.4
Blackburn, Richard, 13, 14, 33, 39n.1
Bloc Québécois, 204, 208, 214n.5
Borduas, Paul-Emile, 32, 33
Bouchard, Lucien, 46, 65, 205–208, 214n.5
Bourassa, Henri, 27, 41n.13
Bourassa, Robert, 34, 47–49, 80, 83
Bourgault, Pierre, 68
Brassard, Marie, 143, 194
British North America Act, 16, 25

Cabot, John, 39n.2
Canada Arts Council (CAC), 33, 93n.2
Canadian constitution, 3, 44, 45, 69n.1, 213n.1
Canadian National Arts Centre (CNAC), 136, 140, 144
Canadian provinces (other than Quebec): Alberta, 41n.15; British Columbia, 26; Manitoba, 26, 46; New Brunswick 16, 25, 41n.14; Newfoundland, 39n.2, 41n.15, 46, 99; Nova Scotia, 16, 25, 41n.14; Ontario, 16, 25, 176; Prince Edward Island, 26; Saskatchewan, 41n.15
Carbone 14 company, 162n.4, 192, 209
Carignan regiment, 104, 105, 116, 117
Cartier, Georges-Etienne, 21
Cartier, Jacques, 15, 16, 28, 39n.2, 40n.12
Catalan, 139, 166, 193–4
Catholic Church: influence in New France, 18–19 (*see also* Jesuit); opposition to 19th-century rebellions, 19, 21, 22–26; relation to French-Canadian nationalism 6, 16, 29, 33; after Quiet Revolution 17, 34–36, 54, 60, 205, 206
Celt, 154, 166–8, 176
Champlain, Samuel, 16, 28, 40n.12
Chansonniers, 11, 36, 50, 66, 209. *See also* Leclerc, Félix; Piché, Paul; Vigneault, Gilles
Chinese, 142, 146, 175, 195
Chopin, Frederick, 142, 150, 151,

154–8, 161, 162 nn. 9, 10, 163n.12, 177, 183, 190
Chrétien, Jean, 49, 206
Clift, Dominique, 60
Columbus, Christopher, 39n.2, 139, 140, 156, 158, 163n.11, 172, 174, 194
Conquête (Conquest), 3, 19, 22, 73, 174, 209
Coureur des bois, 109, 111, 113, 116, 117, 129, 130

de Gaulle, Charles, 34
Delacroix, Eugène, 142, 149, 154, 155, 162n.10, 171, 183
Derrienic, Jean-Pierre, 204
de Verchère, Madeleine, 78
Disappearance, fear of, 49, 80–83, 88, 94n.7, 170, 192
Distinct society, 13, 45, 47, 48, 176
Drolet, Jacques, 81, 94n.8
Dubois, René-Daniel, 201, 210, 212
Duceppes, Jean, 65, 66
Duplessis era: Union Nationale government, 29–33, 40n.9, 41n.18; as historical referant, 44, 58, 60, 61, 81, 206
Durham report, 23
Duvernay, Ludger, 20, 22, 23, 28

Education reform, 33, 34, 61
Ex Machina, 162nn.2, 7

Fait français, 2, 36, 180, 192
Farhoud, Abla, 47, 67, 210, 214n.7
Festivals: Barcelona, 139, 194; Brooklyn Academy of Music, 1626; Festival du théâtre des Amériques, 140, 144; Quebec City, 79; Toronto, 139, 140; Victoriaville, 76
Fête Saint Jean: origins religious holiday, 18–20; origins national holiday, 20–22, 36
Filles du roi, 99, 100, 108, 109, 111, 113, 115, 127, 129
First Nations: Cree, 80; Huron, 19, 40; Iroquois, 15, 19, 28, 78; Micmac, 16; Mohawk, 70n.3. *See also* Indians
Fleurdelisé, 32, 50, 51, 66, 86, 208, 212
Fréchette, Richard, 136, 137
Front de Libération du Québec (FLQ), 34–35

Gender play, 88, 98–102, 176, 177, 181–6
Gignac, Marie, 136, 137, 140, 146, 159, 167, 188, 194
Global refusal. See *Refus global*
Godbout, Adélard, 31
Grande noirceur, 29–31, 44. *See also* Duplessis era
Great Darkness. See *Grande noirceur*
Groulx, Lionel, 28, 30

Habitant, 19, 39n.6, 41n.17, 108, 109, 111, 113, 119, 124
Handler, Richard, 4, 8n.4, 94n.9
Harper, Elijah, 46
Hébert, Louis, 28, 41n.17, 98, 132n.1
Hochelaga, 15, 16
Houde, Camille, 30, 32
Hydro-Québec, 31, 34, 62, 80, 121, 122, 133n.5

Immigrants: as New World French colonists, 18, 104, 106, 109, 111, 116, 122; in Canada and Quebec, 46, 47, 49, 50, 74, 77, 84, 92, 94n.13; as invading Other, 94n.7, 180; relation to Québécois nationhood, 2, 4, 8n.3, 66, 67, 203, 204, 206,

208, 209
Independence movement. *See*
Artists and nationalism;
Parti Québécois; Referendum
1980 *and* 1995
Indian: origin names Canada and
Quebec, 15, 16; relation to New
French colonists, 18, 19, 39;
relation Québécois national
politics, 46, 48, 70, 208, 209;
theatrical representations of,
110, 111, 116, 117, 121–4,
130, 172, 173. *See also* First
Nations; Métis
Irish, 20, 21, 31, 84, 92

Jean-Baptiste: as popular name and
as patron saint, 22, 40n.8; as
child, 24, 40n.12, 53, 54
Jesuit, 18, 19, 28, 112

Laberge, Marie, 8n.5, 208
Lac Meech. *See* Meech Lake
agreement
Lalonde, Michèle, 193, 198n.10
Landry, Bernard, 207
Language legislation. *See* Union
Act; British North America
Act; Bill 101 *and* 178
Larose, Jean, 2, 44, 69n.2, 180,
191, 197n.2, 198n.8, 204
Latouche, Daniel, 72–74, 82, 104,
131
Laurier, Wilfred, 25, 26
Leclerc, Félix, 11, 36
Lepage, Robert: career of, 143–5,
162n.7; on culture and
language, 167–71, 176, 194–5
Lesage, Jean, 33
Lessard, Jacques, 141, 145
Létourneau, Jocelyn, 33
Lévesque, René, 17, 34–36, 43, 44,
51

Liberal Party of Quebec:
democratic reform, 29–31, 33,
35, 60, 61; under Robert
Bourassa, 3, 45, 49, 58
Louis XIV, 84, 98, 99, 114–5
Lower Canada, 15, 16, 19, 20–23,
40n.11

Maple leaf, 16, 24, 39n.3, 208, 211
Martineau, Maureen, 75–77, 93n.3,
214n.6
Marxist, 33, 39n.4, 77
Mc Donnell, John, 20
Meech Lake agreement, 6, 13,
45–48, 51, 66, 205
Mercier, Honoré, 26
Métis, 26, 117
Mexican, 140, 157, 158, 172, 176,
177, 214n.4
Micone, Marco, 210, 214n.7
Ministère des Affaires Culturelles
(MAC), 75, 77, 81, 84, 88
Minority: francophone in
the Americas, 5, 12, 16, 24, 25,
27, 180, 191, 203; populations
within Quebec, 3, 50, 53, 61,
77, 204; Quebec as minority
nation, 3, 5, 12, 17, 25, 47, 69,
73, 170, 212; role in collective
identity, 6, 17, 24, 70n.4, 170,
191, 202
Monpetit, Edouard, 32
Mulroney, Brian, 48, 49
Multiculturalism, 48, 70n.4, 131,
138, 170, 193, 205

Nelson, Robert, 22, 40n.11
New France. *See* Nouvelle-France
North American Free Trade
Agreement (NAFTA), 45, 61,
73, 205, 213–4 n.4
Nouvelle-France, 12, 15, 16, 18,
19, 28, 39n.6, 41n.17, 73, 84,
91

October crisis, 35–36
Old Quebec City, 5, 6, 74, 75, 78, 79, 80, 83, 85, 88, 93n.5

Papineau, Louis-Joseph, 20–22, 28, 41n.13
Parizeau, Jacques, 49, 205, 206, 214n.5
Parti Libéral du Québec (PLQ). *See* Liberal Party of Quebec
Parti Québécois (PQ): rise to power, 11, 13, 17, 34–36, 77; legislation and 1980 Referendum, 2, 36, 43–44, 79. *See also* Bloc Québécois; Bouchard, Lucien; Lévesque, René; Parizeau, Jacques
Patrimoine, 75, 81, 83, 88
Patriot movement, 16, 20, 22, 25, 35, 40n.11, 51, 211
Plaques tectoniques/Tectonic Plates: concept and evolution of, 139–41; performers of, 161–2n.1 (*see also* Fréchette, Richard; Gignac, Marie; Lepage, Robert)
Piché, Paul, 66, 209
Psyche, "national", 14, 68–69, 73, 79, 82, 93n.6, 180–181, 198n.3 212

Quebec Day. See *Fête Saint Jean*
Quiet Revolution. See *Révolution tranquille*
Québécois Party. *See* Parti Québécois

Race, 21, 27, 28, 48, 60, 206. *See also* Anti-semitism
Referendum of 1980 on Québécois independence, 4, 34, 43–44, 50, 51, 79, 83, 93n.6, 209, 213n.2
Referendum of 1995 on Québécois independence, 6, 70n.7, 203–214
Refus global, 32–33
Révolution tranquille, 14, 17, 33–34
Richler, Mordecai, 8n.3
Riel, Louis, 26
Robin, Régine, 209
Romanticism, 142, 149, 154–61, 163n.12
Rumilly, Robert (as SSJB historian), 14, 20–32, 40n.9

Sacres, 87, 89, 94n.12, 105, 127
Saint Joseph Day, 18, 40n.8
Salut vielle branche!: concept and style of, 80–82, 103; performers of, 93n.1 (*see also* Bédard, Réjean; Drolet, Jacques; Martineau, Maureen)
Sand, George 154, 155, 161, 163n.12,177, 183, 185, 190
Sauvé, Paul, 33
Schwartzwald, Robert, 181, 198n.5
Scottish, 5, 21, 148, 149, 151, 160, 166–8, 175, 177, 178, 184, 193–5
Seigneurs, 18, 19, 40n.6
Self-mockery, 74, 92–93, 102, 103, 110–111, 130–132, 202
Simon, Sherry, 138
Société Saint-Jean-Baptiste (SSJB): origins of, 20–24; after Quiet Revolution, 36; role in 1990 fête, 49, 66. *See also* Rumilly, Robert
Spanish, 29, 104, 106, 140, 172, 194
Spillers, Hortense, 201

Talon, Jean, 19
Taylor, Charles, 211
Théâtre Parminou, history and method of, 75–77, 214n.6
Théâtre Repère, history and method

of, 141–6. *See also* Ex Machina
Tourist perspectives: author's, 50, 78, 80; in Old Quebec and S*alut* production, 2, 78, 79, 84–86, 89–92, 99, 106, 131; in *Plaques/Plates* production, 161, 171–4, 188, 197, 199n.13
Tower of Babel, 6, 187, 193–194, 197
Treaty of Paris, 16
Tremblay, Michel, 93n.4, 143, 162n.5
Trilogie des Dragons/Dragon Trilogy, 142, 143, 146, 156, 169–71, 175, 192–5, 198n.11
Trojan horse syndrome, 52–57, 180, 198n.4

Trudeau, Pierre Elliot, 34, 35, 197n.1

Union Act, 16, 23, 209
Union Nationale. *See* Duplessis era

Vallières, Pierre, 39n.4
Vieux Québec. *See* Old Quebec
Viger, Jacques, 20, 21
Vigneault, Gilles, 10–12, 36, 44, 50, 63, 66, 69n.2, 207–209

Welsh, 159, 167, 168, 175, 190, 193–6
Women's rights, 30, 31, 57–60
Weinmann, Heinz, 22, 69, 94n.12

Francophone Cultures & Literatures

General Editors: Michael G. Paulson & Tamara Alvarez-Detrell

This series will include studies about the literature, culture, and civilization of all French-speaking countries except France, i.e. studies on the Francophone areas in Africa, the French-speaking islands in the Caribbean, as well as studies that deal with the French aspects in Canada. Cross-cultural studies between these geographic areas are also encouraged. The book-length manuscripts may be written in either English or French.

Authors wishing to have works considered for this series should send a one page synopsis to:

> Dr. Michael G. Paulson
> Department of Foreign Languages
> Kutztown University
> Kutztown, PA 19530